"I keep telling myself that she j
every book she amazes and s

Praise for the futuristic fantasy of
Robin D. Owens,

**Winner of the 2002 RITA Award for Best Paranormal Romance
by the Romance Writers of America**

"Another terrific tale from the brilliant mind of Robin D. Owens. Don't
miss it."   —*Romance Reviews Today*

"A taut mixture of suspense and action . . . that leaves you stunned."
—Smexy Books

"Sexy, emotionally intense, and laced with humor."   —*Library Journal*

"Each story is as fresh and new as the first one was."   —Fresh Fiction

"[A] wonderfully imaginative series."   —Romance Junkies

"The romance is passionate, the characters engaging, and the society
and setting exquisitely crafted."   —*Booklist*

"Maintaining the 'world building' for science fiction and character-driven
plot for romance is near impossible. Owens does it brilliantly."
—*TRRC Reading*

"[Owens] provides a wonderful, gripping mix of passion, exotic futuristic settings, and edgy suspense. If you've been waiting for someone to do
futuristic romance right, you're in luck, Robin D. Owens is the author
for you."   —Jayne Castle

"Engaging characters, effortless world building, and a sizzling romance
make this a novel that's almost impossible to put down."
—*The Romance Reader*

"Owens paints a world filled with characters who sweep readers into an
unforgettable adventure with every delicious word, every breath, every
beat of their hearts. Brava!"   —Deb Stover, award-winning author

Titles by Robin D. Owens

HEARTMATE

HEART THIEF

HEART DUEL

HEART CHOICE

HEART QUEST

HEART DANCE

HEART FATE

HEART CHANGE

HEART JOURNEY

HEART SEARCH

HEART SECRET

HEART FORTUNE

HEART FIRE

HEART LEGACY

HEART SIGHT

GHOST SEER

GHOST LAYER

GHOST KILLER

GHOST TALKER

GHOST MAKER

Anthologies

WHAT DREAMS MAY COME
(with Sherrilyn Kenyon and Rebecca York)
HEARTS AND SWORDS

Heart Sight

Robin D. Owens

Berkley Sensation
New York

BERKLEY SENSATION
Published by Berkley
An imprint of Penguin Random House LLC
375 Hudson Street, New York, New York 10014

Library of Congress Cataloging-in-Publication Data

Names: Owens, Robin D., author.
Title: Heart sight / Robin D. Owens.
Description: First edition. | New York : Berkley Sensation, 2017. | Series: A Celta novel ; 14
Identifiers: LCCN 2017029533 (print) | LCCN 2017032826 (ebook) |
ISBN 9780451488183 (ebook) | ISBN 9780451488176 (softcover)
Subjects: LCSH: Man-woman relationships—Fiction. | Life on other planets—Fiction. |
Paranormal romance stories. | BISAC: FICTION / Romance / Paranormal. |
FICTION / Romance / Fantasy. | GSAFD: Fantasy fiction. | Science fiction. | Love stories.
Classification: LCC PS3615.W478 (ebook) | LCC PS3615.W478 H477 2017 (print) |
DDC 813/.6—dc23
LC record available at https://lccn.loc.gov/2017029533

First Edition: December 2017

Printed in the United States of America
1   3   5   7   9   10   8   6   4   2

Cover art by Tony Mauro
Cover design by Katie Anderson
Book design by Kristin del Rosario

To Kay (Cassie Miles),
can't do this without you.

Acknowledgments

Many, many thanks to C. J. Rite for brainstorming ideas for chapter one, Charie Craig for the name of the shop that makes ice cream, and Betty Monych Shoenbaechler for help with a series blip I ran across . . . as well as Sandy Heaberlin for her fantastic character list of the Celta series. Sandy as well as Tine MacKay, Sarah Mallon, and Deb Swenson for information regarding the Hawthorn colors . . . Fred Riley, Sandy Kaye, and Michelle Kaye for being my beta readers.

Characters

The Hazels:

Avellana Hazel: second daughter of D'Hazel and T'Hazel (heroine!)

Rhyz: Avellana's Familiar Companion FamCat

GreatLady Coll D'Hazel: Avellana's mother

GreatLord Chess T'Hazel: Avellana's father

Coll HazelHeir: Avellana's sister

The Vines:

GreatLord Muin (Vinni) T'Vine: FirstFamily GreatLord, the Prophet of Celta (hero!)

Flora: Vinni's Familiar Companion housefluff

Arcto Vine: tutor

Bifrona Vine: housekeeper, matriarch of the Vines

Vine Guards:

Duan Dewberry Vine (Chief of Guards)

Armen

Fera

Plicat

Southern Vines:

Bicknell Vine

Perna Vine

Baby Vine

And sundry cousins, including several cooks . . .

Investigators:

Garrett Primross: Private Investigator, liaison between the First-Families and the Druida City Guards (hero of *Heart Secret*)

Ilex Winterberry: Captain of the Druida City Guards (hero of *Heart Quest*)

Other Important Characters:

GreatLord T'Ash: blacksmith, jeweler (hero of *HeartMate*)

Gwydion Ash: second son of T'Ash and D'Ash

Antenn Blackthorn-Moss: architect and friend of Vinni and Avellana (hero of *Heart Fire*)

Tiana Mugwort Blackthorn-Moss: Priestess and friend of Vinni and Avellana (heroine of *Heart Fire*)

Cal Marigold: a boy who is the reincarnation of Tab Holly

GreatLord Saille T'Willow: matchmaker (hero of *Heart Dance*)

GrandLord (FirstFamilies) Draeg T'Yew: fighter, consort of Loridana (hero of *Heart Legacy*)

GrandLady (FirstFamilies) Loridana D'Yew: personal armor crafter (heroine of *Heart Legacy*)

And cameo appearances by various others!

One

❦

DRUIDA CITY,
424 years after colonization,
summer

*H*e *never saw visions of his own future, not* Vinni *T'Vine,* <u>the</u>
Prophet of Celta. No, he only experienced occasional tightening of
the muscles at the back of his neck and dread slithering down his
spine. Usually those symptoms indicated a threat to his HeartMate,
Avellana Hazel.

Tonight the feeling morphed into the regular nightmare and he
suffered through the horrific dream in his own ancestral bed. The
vision where he held a pale Avellana, her gaze fixed on his, her last
breath coming out with an *I love you, Muin,* then her eyes losing the
lifespark and fogging with death. From the plague.

But even dreaming he knew the plague had finally been beaten
back, this particular deadly one mastered and not to return to deci-
mate the colonists of Celta. Healers now knew how to treat that
sickness, to triumph over it.

Then his lover faded from his arms to stand waving at him from
a balcony, and the balcony broke and she plummeted down onto
unforgiving flagstones. He wrenched his mind from the sight, only to
see her motionless and dead pale on the grass of a Druida City park,
a poisoned candy in her hand.

More recent dangers giving rise to new visions.

WAKE UP! His heart gave a huge and heavy thump. He felt the warmth as if it had pounded outside his chest, groggily lifted his hand, and touched the soft fur of his Familiar Companion, a housefluff—a rabbitlike creature. With every stroke his breathing steadied along with the pulse surging in his blood, the twanging of his nerves.

Long soft ears brushed his face as Flora lowered her head. He felt the slightest damp touch of her smooth tongue on his cheek.

The rest of him was damp, too. He lay in his own sweat, the coverlet unable to draw away the amount of perspiration he'd emitted.

Only a few seconds had passed since he'd held a limp Avellana—no, opened his eyes so he'd see Flora, the embroidered canopy above him, rather than—

Yes, his Fam touched noses with him. He *reached* with all his senses for Avellana, felt their bond as open as usual. He'd instinctively hidden his fear from her. From her pulsed creativity and art and . . . a hint of spirituality . . .

Nevertheless, he needed to go to her.

He looked around him and blinked at the soft golden light—dawn? Hadn't he had an appointment at T'Elder's at dawn? Maybe that was yesterday?

Not dawn, Flora said mentally. *Sunset. Dinner soon.*

And the memories of the day wheeled in his head.

"I fell asleep?" he rasped, still confused by everything except that his HeartMate lived. He glanced at the viz panel that had stopped floating above the bed where he'd been watching a comedy, then turned his head to see that it had folded itself and lay on the cabinet next to the bed.

Yes, you napped, Flora said.

"I don't nap," he said stiffly. "Sometimes I rest. And it's been a long day after a long night." He sighed. "As *the* official birth Oracle, I attended the birth of the Honey twins last night. I also kept my consultation appointments today."

The babies were beautiful.

"Yes, but the night stretched. GraceLady Mignontette Honey complimented you on your fur and thanked you for your help."

Flora sniffed. *She has useless FamCat.*

"Who will be fine with the babies."

He removed Flora from his chest but felt the burden of a vision unreleased, unresolved, untold. Even though he'd sensed Avellana was fine, he needed to see her. Make sure she lived and glowed with health and stayed safe. Defend her if any threat appeared.

Currently she lived on Mona Island, where he'd convinced her to go three months ago, the last time he'd felt danger to her in Druida City.

"Residence." He spoke to the intelligent house itself, T'Vine Residence. "In fifteen minutes, inform the Family I will not be joining them for dinner." He'd be gone by then, teleported away.

Again? Flora didn't have much facial expression, but she scrunched her nose, lifting her upper muzzle from two big front teeth. Her ears twitched, then angled. *You skip dinner more than one this waxing twinmoons, more than two. They will talk and talk and talk, and yammer and yammer and yammer, and argue and—*

"I hear you, Flora." He sat up and swung his legs over the side of the bed. Like the cover, his clothes should have wicked away the sweat, but he figured those daily spells had worn away after the long and stressful consultations he'd had today. He rubbed the back of his neck, drying it, flaking away old sweat.

"I need to see Avellana, to teleport to her."

Again? A grass-scented huff came from his Fam. *I will go, too. Avoid the talk and yammer. Though you will argue. Better you argue with FamWoman because you want her to stay away from the city with many scaries and she supposed to come home tomorrow.*

True. Any time he'd sensed danger to his HeartMate since she'd been five, he'd persuaded her Family and Avellana to leave Druida City.

His whole body tensed, his nostrils widened, and he caught the odor of his own distress, the general smell of his suite—sunshine and an herbal mix he liked—and Flora. He *should* clean up. He couldn't take the time. Yes, his whole spine stiffened, his muscles taut with warning. "Boots on," he ordered rustily, not thinking he could handle that physically. They formed around his feet and calves.

He needed Avellana, his love, his HeartMate . . . though they had not HeartBonded yet. They'd promised their Families they'd wed first. Because they belonged to two of the highest-status Families, such an alliance demanded long negotiations of the marriage contracts, planning, and formal rituals. Two years' worth of delays.

He'd only shared a few instances of intimacy, sexual teasing, and petting with Avellana. Only three real sessions of lovemaking. Just thinking about that hurt. Physical aching need for her, emotional loneliness that she continued to live apart from him and he couldn't walk into the GreatMistrys Suite and see her. His own fault, that, though it didn't mitigate the hurt . . .

The artist colony on Mona Island was easily within his teleportation range. He scanned for her location, found the nearest empty teleportation pad. "'Porting in three. One and holo, two and—" Flora hopped into his arms and he left.

Dusk had reached the low-lying island sooner than his hilltop castle. Or maybe he'd lingered too long in his bedroom. As soon as they landed in the outside garden, Flora jumped into leafy bushes. He heard munching.

He sensed Avellana in the Circle Temple.

Straining all his Flair, he tried to evaluate each droplet of the atmosphere for threat to her. He felt nothing but didn't trust . . . anything, not even his senses.

He leapt off the teleportation pad and flicked the signal to show that it was available, ran down the path in the direction of the Circle Temple. As he sucked in air, he smelled the heady aroma of flowers, blooms that didn't flourish in T'Vine gardens. Summer scents that spoke of sunshine and heat and the humidity of an island instead of a plateau above an ocean. Around him lush trees and bushes grew in wild abandon, not carefully trained so they wouldn't be a detriment to the security of a FirstFamily castle.

And he couldn't see through those bushes to know if villains lurked.

Like everything else on Mona Island, artists had conceived and built Circle Temple. The stone appeared creamy and mellow in the fading light. As he surged toward the northern door, he found it ajar. His gut clenched. Without thought he teleported to the threshold, shoved the door wide open.

Stopped in surprise when he saw Avellana sitting on the floor, forehead furrowed in concentration as she moved curved fingers in the three-dimensional holo painting she worked on. A comprehensive scan showed him no one else in the one-room building.

Safe! He held his breath so as not to alert her to his panting, his running. He wanted her to stay here longer instead of return to Druida City. The setting where he'd just dreamed of danger. Again.

The small artist colony on an equally small island had kept her safe for three months. But to prevail upon her to stay, he must finesse the situation.

So he stood and watched her and calmed. A sweet jolt had gone through him at the sight of her, as usual, even though those big blue eyes hadn't been aimed his way. He appreciated how the light touched a streak of white in her medium-brown hair, a lock at her left temple that had appeared after her last Passage to free her Flair.

Her old and comfortable clothes didn't display her curves well, but he knew the feel of her breasts in his palms, the curve of her hips.

Brow furrowed, her hand gestured in a wavy motion. A line of textured color deepened the bark of the Ash tree in the center of the Great Labyrinth. He sucked in his breaths gently, let them out quietly, knowing better than to disturb her focus when in the midst of creative expression.

The fact she'd created a holo for the temple piqued his curiosity. She'd left the dominant faith of Celta two years before, the one that worshiped the Divine Couple, the Lord and the Lady. Avellana had become an adherent of the Intersection of Hope religion. That creed had developed on the starships during the centuries-long trip from Earth to Celta.

When she'd learned of the precepts of the Hopefuls, they'd made more sense to her than the doctrine she'd grown up with. So Vinni found it surprising that she sat in the middle of Circle Temple. But on the other hand, she'd only been here on the island for a few months. Not enough time to design an Intersection of Hope chapel and have it built, even if she found other devotees.

She stared at her work, finally nodded and added the deep purple curlicue of her signature, then glanced at him. Of course she'd sensed when he'd arrived on the island and stood in the doorway, even if he'd masked his emotions.

"One moment, Muin, while I finish my project, please," she said coolly.

He did visit her at least once a week when she resided outside Druida City, but she wouldn't have expected him tonight since she'd be back at D'Hazel Residence the next morning.

With a glance at him, her fingers snapped and all the three-dimensional holographic paintings and murals in the temple activated. He missed a couple of steps toward her as he staggered through one of the Lady and Lord planting a garden. He swore he could smell the rich herbs, the equally fertile dark-brown earth.

A joyful dancing tune began and echoed through the huge temple chamber. Avellana stared at him with watchful eyes, so he wrenched his gaze from her to study the art . . . all the art, including the parquet patterns of the wooden floor around the rose-streaked brown marble center stone.

Circles of holograms projected at regular intervals from the middle of the temple to the walls. Marking the size of various ritual circles depending on the number of people. On the walls hung old-fashioned paintings and tapestries.

He stared at the two-meter, exquisite mural that only Avellana could have done. "I'm surprised you're working on a piece in a temple for a religion you no longer believe in."

"That is not quite true, Muin," she said, standing.

Another pulse of attraction as she said his name. Only his beloved Avellana called him by his given name.

With a Word she removed dust from her clothes. She wore a simple tunic-and-trous set, roomy enough to move around in, of a dull brown . . . and very soft and thin from many cleansings. Her comfort clothes. "I believe the predominant religion is right for those who believe in it, and, of course, it pervades our society so there is no escaping it, so one must acknowledge that. I am also a product of my training and my Family's beliefs; they suffuse and influence me."

She gestured for him to join her, and he did so. As soon as he caught her fragrance, his shaft went hard. With a thought he loosened the front of his trous so they wouldn't bind, and wouldn't show at a glance that he fought for slippery control over his libido. The desire that just standing next to his HeartMate and breathing her scent caused.

Another flick of her fingers and all the paintings and murals vanished except for hers. Unlike most of them, her holo was a perfect lower half sphere reflecting the actual bowl of the Great Labyrinth to the north of Druida City. Studying it, she brought her hands from shoulder width together, and the painting collapsed upward on itself until it appeared like a two-dimensional rendition, hanging vertically. She stepped back a couple of paces and he matched her strides.

Then she angled the painting to horizontal and pushed it down until it touched the floor and the center round stone and matched the keystone in size. Muttering encouraging words to herself under her breath that Vinni couldn't quite catch, she sank her painting *into* the stone, so the top of the stone showed her work. Long minutes passed and sweat beaded her forehead.

With the lightest brush of his fingers, Vinni touched her temple and whisked the excess moisture away. She chanted a couplet, fast and loud, that rang in his ears, shouted, "Engrave and Set in Stone!" and clapped her hands. Flair surged through the room, knocking Vinni back a step, sending shudders rippling through his body. Secondary creative psi power or not, Avellana matched him in the potency of her Flair.

She moved to the middle of the temple and crouched, scrutinizing the circular center stone that now showed her painting. It looked perfect to Vinni. She turned and grinned at him, nearly danced to him, the satisfaction of fulfilled creativity limning her face. His less-spiritual self yearned for a different kind of fulfillment with her as he recalled her face during climax. *Do* not *think of that. Shut it down and up and behind a solidly locked door.*

After taking his hand, she quickly dropped it, stepped aside, and focused her gaze on her painting. She inhaled and exhaled, then raised her arms and said, "Activate the holo mural titled 'Great Labyrinth.'"

Around them the Great Labyrinth formed, filling the room. The rim of the crater matched the top of the walls before they gave way to the dome of the temple. In the three-dimensional mural, Vinni stood at the exit from the center onto the meditation path that wound up the bowl.

"It's a fabulous work." He turned in place. "I would guess this holo mural is an exact miniature replica of the Great Labyrinth." Automatically, his gaze went to his own shrine the Family had established—saw the trellis supporting blackberry vines around a wooden-and-glass enclosure, the marble-topped no-time food storage unit stocked with wine and cheese. If he strained his ears, he could imagine he heard the tinkle of the tubular wind chimes he'd made of glisten metal and glass.

"Of course it is an exact replica." She sounded offended.

"Of course."

He watched as her own gaze went to the tiny depiction of the Hazel Family shrine, close to the bottom of the crater. The Hazels had dowsed for water decades ago and chosen a parcel where they could free a spring for a pond. A hazel tree stood beside the water. Unlike ancient legend, the spring didn't house any Earthan salmon. Those fish hadn't done well in the waters of Celta, though the starship *Nuada's Sword* had some swimming around in its great greensward garden pools.

Slowly, Avellana turned in place, studying her work as if checking for errors. As far as Vinni could see, there were none. Truly time to feel her out about staying on Mona Island. "Will you be sad to leave here tomorrow, Avellana?"

She met his eyes with a serious gaze of her own. "No. I am weary of not being home. I left matters undone, such as my murals for *my* faith." She hesitated, dropped her eyes; their bond blocked a little spurt of *something*. Avellana had a secret project she kept from him? That's how it felt. And from the size of the block, an undertaking important to her that she didn't wish to share with him. Intriguing.

But their relationship was never static, always in flux. One of the reasons he loved her.

Avellana gestured to the illusion of the Great Labyrinth rising around them. "I have paid for my food and lodging, my use of a free workshop, and all the lessons I received, with this piece of work."

"No one could say you didn't give full value," he murmured, sending his huge pride in her through their bond.

Dipping her head, she said, "Thank you. I thought I would see you tomorrow when I returned to Druida City."

Carefully, keeping his face set in serene lines and his tone bland, he said, "I would prefer you remain here."

Her entire body snapped into straight rigidity. "Absolutely not!"

Two

Her eyes darkened from summer blue to stormy ocean sapphire, and she accused, "You have *seen* more danger for me, haven't you?"

He reached out to clasp her fingers, but she whisked away from him, stuck her hands in her opposite sleeves.

"Yes, I've felt more menace aimed at you."

Her jaw tightened, then released as she asked, "What is this danger?"

"I don't know."

"Is it localized to Druida City?" she said, persisting.

He couldn't answer.

"So it could even be here." She pulled her right hand from her sleeve and swept a gesture around the chamber, including the open door he'd come through and foolishly hadn't shut and locked behind him.

He said, "I don't sense any threat to you here."

"Now, tonight." She stamped her foot as if in emphasis to the place and time.

"Now, tonight," he agreed. "But peril stalks the streets of Druida City."

Her brows went up and down. "More populated areas will always include a higher percentage of accidents—"

"Not accidents. Deliberate threat directed toward you as its target."

Eyes remaining angry, she said, "So you believe that whatever danger I might have been in three months ago in Druida City continues."

"Yes."

"And when did you determine this?"

He rubbed the back of his neck. "Just tonight."

She sighed and he *felt* her quashing her irritation. Stepping forward, she put her hand on his forearm and he caught her fingers and linked their hands. Thank the Lady and Lord, he touched her and she touched him, skin to skin, finally.

When she spoke again, her words were too even and proceeded in a rhythm that warned him she'd given the topic much deliberation. "You sent me away from you and my home and Druida City when the plague came six years ago, and when it resurged eighteen months after that." She squeezed his hand. "Thinking back, could you, ah, give me an actual percentage of how much danger I was in from the sickness?"

"No."

"No?"

His nape continued to tingle but he wouldn't rub it again.

Her gaze sharpened and she said too quietly, "At that time could you gauge the amount of danger I was in, Muin? During those plague years?"

He wanted to lie, but never would to her, not to mention she'd know truth from lies through their bond. "No."

She paused, still considering him. Then she jerked a hand toward a wall bench that ran around one-quarter of the temple, barely able to be seen through the illusion of the labyrinth.

"I have been thinking, you see," Avellana stated.

As he'd figured. She'd been thinking. Unfortunately.

Withdrawing her fingers from his grasp and tucking her hands in her opposite sleeves, she moved with stately grace as if in a formal dance across the floor to the bench. And he understood that they now danced—dueled—with words.

When she sat, he did, too, and she angled a bit toward him and he could only touch her knee with his thigh.

"You never told us, told *me*, how much threat you sensed to me, ever. Not when you spoke to my parents or us as a Family. I know that during your professional consultations, you understand how likely the future or futures you see are to come to pass. I know you are very capable at using words to . . . finesse . . . your clients into taking the path you believe is right for them."

He stiffened. "Manipulate, you mean."

"I deliberately did not use that word, Muin." Her chin jutted. "But the fact is that you are accustomed to using your primary Flair of prophecy to *see* what will happen, then you have lifelong experience in analyzing those visions and choosing what you think is best."

"You've said that twice. That I determine people's futures."

She hesitated. "You guide them. As any counselor or mind Healer would." She looked away, then back at him and met his eyes. "I know you ache when your clients do not take your advice or when you . . . misjudged . . ."

He flinched but said nothing. She'd been around him a time or two when he'd read his visions wrong and someone had suffered.

She gave him a straight look. "To return to my previous point, I know that you do not experience visions of your own future, and I have thought long and hard on our various discussions—"

"That must have been depressing."

She lifted her brows at his interruption that meant to deflect. "—discussions when I have been persuaded to leave. Yes, they and the memories of them have been trying, particularly in contrast with the nights where we make love in our dreams."

He stilled, swallowed, didn't look at her, because this nicely pillowed stone bench would make a fine place to have sex.

"As I was saying. You do not receive visions about yourself, and it has occurred to me that you do not receive visions with enough detail about me, either. I do not think that you are able to distinguish how . . . deadly . . . a threat to me might be." She waved a hand but he felt the intensity of her focus upon him. "For instance, whether it was, say, a ten percent likelihood or ninety percent probability that I would succumb to the plague when it swept through Druida City six years ago."

She gave him a quick, oblique glance, then stared upward.

He followed her gaze to a huge three-dimensional holo mural curved around the dome of the ceiling showing the Lord and Lady embracing, looking at each other with complete love and trust in their eyes.

While he felt the trust between himself and Avellana slipping away from his grasp.

"Can you tell me such a percentage?"

"No."

"Not then, nor now?"

"No."

"So," she said with her standard exact deliberation. "You felt danger to me from . . . something . . . three months ago." Without turning her head, she looked at him from the corner of her eyes. Her lips had pressed together.

He didn't reply.

"You intimated to me, to my parents, that I might be caught in the accidents happening to youngsters—the balcony giving way under Aurea Holly, the terrible introduction of poisonous celtaroons where they could bite the children of Walker Clover in the GuildHall."

"That's right. I'd felt a threat to you at that time and that's what I believed." He needed to watch her expressions, so he angled toward her and now only their knees touched.

"Exactly how much of a threat, Muin? Twenty percent that I might be harmed? Forty? Eighty?"

He stayed silent.

She turned to gaze at him with darkening eyes. "You cannot gauge the danger to me, can you?" Then she bit off her words. "All this time, when you felt danger and convinced my parents or me to leave, you couldn't tell whether I was in slight danger or truly doomed to perish."

"Any threat should be taken seriously."

"Not quite an answer, Muin. Could you *ever* weigh the accuracy of your premonitions about any danger to me?"

He clenched his jaw, then replied. "Not since your psi power began fluctuating when you neared First Passage."

"All this time," she whispered with a voice foggy with tears, her head averted.

Scooting over, he curved his hand over the soft pliancy of her cheek. His woman. His. "The dreams and feelings are always intense." He paused. "I can't take chances with you."

Her jaw flexed before she answered. "I will consider why that is so, and we will discuss that point later. What concerns me this moment is the result of this overprotectiveness, Muin."

"I can't take chances with you," he repeated. "I *did* sense danger in Druida City for you during that time when the fanatics of the Traditionalist Stance political movement targeted people to kill." His own jaw clenched.

Inclining her head, she said, "You felt the danger to me, and as usual, in that time of fear and anger by the FirstFamilies, you convinced my parents and me that I would be, as usual, better off outside Druida City."

"I was right, the fanatics did nothing outside Druida City."

"That is true, but I was—am—unlike the other prospective victims. First, I am an adult, and those other assaults were on children."

"You are fragile."

She hissed in a breath between her teeth and snapped. "I am *not* as fragile as you and my Family believe." Another of her deep breaths raised her breasts beneath her work tunic. Fleetingly he recalled how those breasts felt in his hands, and the thought distracted him when he couldn't afford for his mind to be derailed.

"I am an adult and *not* fragile. Second, unlike those others, one of my parents was *not* a Commoner. I am the child of two Nobles of the FirstFamilies. I would not have been considered a proper victim by those terrible fanatical killers."

Her hands remained in her opposite sleeves. He reached out and touched the wrist of her close hand, drew it from her sleeve. He enfolded her hand, his palm warming her cold one. Then he linked fingers, made sure their bond was large and steady. "Yes, dear one, you would have been a target."

She gasped, then he saw her swallow and finally she moved close enough that they touched all along their thighs. He wished she'd allow him to take her on his lap.

"You believe that," she said.

"The Traditionalist Stance aimed their hatred at those who were different—children of FirstFamily Lords and Commoner women. Offspring of a new nobleman who rose to become the most powerful man on the planet, the Captain of All Councils of Celta." He paused. "People recall that a member of my Family tried to kill you because he didn't deem you acceptable to be my wife and GreatLady D'Vine. Despite the fact that your Family and mine and the Ashes have kept your powerful Flair secret, others know there *is* a secret. A deadly secret involving you. The secret that made someone of my Family think you so different and unusual that you don't belong with me."

"That I deserve to be killed before I beget children who might also be so very different," she said flatly, extending the line of reasoning to its final point.

"That's right." He kissed her fingers.

"The Traditionalist Stance movement is discredited and destroyed."

"But I don't believe all the culprits were caught."

Tilting her head, she said, "No?"

"No." He paused, kept his voice steady and heavy with solemnity. "I, and some of my friends—"

"The other FirstFamily Lords of your generation." Avellana nodded. "Your social group. And allies."

"And allies," he confirmed. "We believe one of the ringleaders escaped, a lover of Folia Yew, male or female, a person who is a member of one of the FirstFamilies."

She stilled. Her head pivoted slowly toward him. "And that is the danger you think you sense for me now?"

"Yes," he replied simply.

"And this evil person might want to hurt me. Because I am different, my Flair makes—made"—she corrected—"me different."

"Yes."

She stared back at the mural, her eyes moving as if she studied the technique.

Then she snapped, "What are the percentages, Muin?"

"I don't know!"

"Then no one does. And I will no longer put my life in Druida City on hold for you. My life *with* you."

"Avellana—"

"*No.* I will not stay here." She jutted her chin. "You must accept my decision and deal with it, Muin."

Before he could find words to finesse the situation, to persuade her, a cat yowl split the air. Rhyz, Avellana's tom FamCat, zoomed through the door, then screeched, *What is this? WHAT IS THIS? We are NOT in the labyrinth. I don't LIKE this.*

"You know it is a mural, Rhyz," Avellana said, her voice terse . . . as she rarely was, especially with those she loved.

Make it go away! The cat cast about as if looking for Avellana and him.

"Ask me nicely."

A cat sniff. *Puh-lease make the labyrinth go away.*

"Very well." Avellana flicked her fingers and the mural shrank, flattened, and settled back into the center stone of the temple.

Rhyz swaggered up and stood, hair slightly raised, staring at Vinni. The Fam lifted his upper muzzle to show his fangs. *You, again, coming to argue with my FamWoman.* His tail flicked. *Only coming when you want to take, not to give.*

"That is not true," Avellana said.

The cat slid his eyes toward her, then back toward Vinni to glare at him. *We are tired of you keeping Us out of Our Residence and with strangers.*

"That is enough," Avellana scolded, but a surge of truth came through her bond with Vinni at her Fam's mental words.

The going-away party for you has started. We must attend.
Avellana jerked upright. "I am late. I am off schedule."
Yes, he, with all his quarreling, made you late.
"I must go, Muin." Her lips pursed and she stood. "As it is, I will
have to do a wretched Whirlwind Spell to cleanse and change for the
party."

She hadn't said anything about his sweat-odor, Vinni noted. His
words must have spurted through their bond with his emotions, because she caught his thought, as they occasionally did with each other.

You do not smell bad to me, only like my hardworking Muin,
Avellana sent him telepathically.

A nice sentiment, but his muscles didn't relax under the emotional
stroking.

"No one will care if they see you in your work clothes," Vinni
pointed out.

"*I* care. I want to wear appropriate clothes for the party, to honor
my friends."

There is excellent food at the party that we are missing! Rhyz
lifted his nose.

"That is right. They have several gourmet chefs here on Mona
Island."

You are not invited, Vinni, said Rhyz. He turned his back and
sauntered away from them, stopped at the western door, and waited
for Avellana to open it for him, as if he couldn't open it himself with
his Flair or teleport out.

Vinni hadn't risen, so Avellana bent and pressed her lips to his. A
tender gesture, though he could feel her anger at him decrease, then
spike, then even out, then rise . . . and his love didn't like unruly emotions.

"I love you, Muin, but I remain angry with you." She kept her
face near his. "The fact is that you lied to me all these years."

"I didn't—"

"You misdirected. Both me and my Family. That is the current
issue bothering me, though there are others."

"Others?"

"Yes, your belief that I am fragile, the imbalance of our relationship, your lack of trust in me—"

"Avellana—"

She raised a hand, palm out. "No. We will talk of these concerns later. Currently I am late for an event my friends are giving in honor of me." Stress laced her voice. Walking to the west door, she opened it for Rhyz. He looked out, up at her, then back at Vinni.

You go, the cat sent mentally.

"Yes, I am late." She angled toward Vinni. "If you leave now, you can catch the next ferry back to Druida City. It will give you time to think, as opposed to teleporting back to your home"—she glanced at her wrist timer—"where they will be serving dinner and will expect you to be clean and dress formally." She walked out the door and didn't look back.

Rhyz sauntered up to him, tilting his head to meet Vinni's eyes. *We have been many places over the years when you sent us away. North when the plague raged in Druida City. South to Gael City and also to the Cherry Resort in the time of more sickness. We stayed with D'Marigold and T'Marigold in their Residence at the edge of Druida City during my FamWoman's Passages. But Avellana does not like travel as much as I. She wants to go home and stay there. I think once she is there she will not be budged again, because you have sent her off so many times already. You have lost that ability now, and some of her goodwill and trust. You think on that, Vinni T'Vine.*

He answered the FamCat mentally, *And you guard your Fam-Woman.*

Rhyz turned and sashayed back to the door, tail waving. *I always have. I always will. Better than you, 'cuz I stay WITH her.*

As soon as his last paw cleared the threshold, the door slammed shut.

Vinni sat in the cool temple, all his muscles tight. He'd finally reached his limit with Avellana, and why hadn't he understood he was coming up on that? He laughed shortly. She'd spoken of inequalities of their relationship, and now he knew she'd just taken charge of that relationship.

He hoped she would be more generous with him than he had been with her.

*A*vellana *fell asleep and found herself walking in the Marigolds' gar-*den at dawn—the Residence where she had spent all three of her Passages to free her Flair. Her Family and Vinni had believed that without the help of Signet D'Marigold, a catalyst, Avellana would die. Looking back from adulthood, she concurred. She remained close to Signet, especially since the woman patronized artists and had been the first to emotionally support Avellana in her holo painting. She considered Cratag Maytree T'Marigold like an older brother.

So she enjoyed the familiar gardens and took the path through the groomed beds to the grove at the juncture of the river on the south and the Great Platte Ocean on the west. D'Marigold Residence stood at the far southwestern corner of Noble Country that held most of the FirstFamily estates.

Avellana loved this piece of land and made sure to visit it and give extra care to the trees if she spent any time with the Marigolds. She moved to the point where she could watch the summer-sleepy river join the ocean, a little less crashing here than up the coast. Water sounded in a myriad of rhythms, and she smiled and let the ebb and flow of the surf wash away the irritation of the day. The sun speared light on the river, turning it a jeweled emerald, and colored the white-tipped waves coral.

But she jolted when Muin's long fingers closed over her left shoulder. She said nothing but should have anticipated that he would join her tonight for dream sex . . . or simply to be together outside reality.

Three

At various times in their lives since she had reached adulthood at seventeen, she or Muin had pushed for marriage and the HeartBond, but the other had hesitated.

When she was twenty-two, she and Muin had finally gotten properly engaged. Naturally their Families preferred a long engagement to negotiate the contracts and alliances. But that had taken, so far, two years. *Far* too long.

Now in the interior of the dream, she said nothing, and he did not speak, either. But he dropped his hand and moved close behind her, wrapped his arms around her, and pulled her close to his body. His shaft was erect, and that caused her pulse to jump, her core to heat and clench as need filtered into the dream—his and hers—and her own sex to dampen in readiness for him.

"A beautiful place," he rumbled, and she could have sworn his breath stirred the tendrils of hair at the top of her ear. "But I prefer our own place." He dropped his arms and urged her to turn around and face him. As she did, her head naturally tilted up.

Though his lips curved slightly, his blue-gray eyes showed sadness. She had watched that sorrow creep into his gaze more and more as he practiced his craft. She believed that for every positive, cheerful, and wonderful future he saw, dark and dreadful visions also threatened. She did not know what to do to bring him to a more lighthearted identity again. She thought if they wed and HeartBonded she could ease that melancholy in him, though of their original personalities, she had always been the more serious.

He put his hands on her shoulders and the setting dissolved from the land overlooking the river and the ocean to a garden outside T'Vine Residence. At her request many years ago, Muin had claimed this particular strip of garden because the fewest windows overlooked it, and only Family members with telescopes could see. The first spell she and Muin had done together had been erecting a privacy dome over the area.

That did not matter in a dream, of course, nor did the fact that their clothes had vanished. His erection lay against her stomach, long and hard and hot, and she felt the heat of her own desire flag her cheeks pink. Her nipples tightened.

"Avellana," he whispered.

"Yes," she replied. It would always be "yes" to loving with Muin, no matter how difficult the reality outside the dreams.

He stepped back and drew his hands down her arms, and that touch primed her for the linking of their hands, all the sensitive nerves in their palms meeting in intimate touch. She lifted her eyes and their gazes met, too, and their bond had swelled to a huge throbbing cable of a rich yellow hue.

She had heard that the HeartBond glowed golden, but that connection could not be made with dream sex. Physical mating must occur and she yearned for that, so much that wetness dampened her cheeks.

He framed her face, wiped away the tears with his thumbs. "Let me love you, Avellana. I need you so much tonight."

Unlike most of the times when they met in dreams she did not answer, "Always." Tonight she said, "Yes."

His eyes tinted from bluish to gray, the more sorrowful hue, and she lifted up the few centimeters to meet his soft mouth with her own and closed her eyes.

Of all the moments of their lives, she liked best when his lips touched her.

He opened his mouth and pressed his tongue against her lips and she let him in to stroke her tongue and their hips arched together, rubbing, teasing until the nerves on her skin tingled with fire that swept throughout her body. Then they lay on soft cropped grass with that smell mixing with Muin's sex fragrance and the tall wildflowers bowed over them. The stalky blooms covered them more and he slipped into her and muttered something she could not hear, but she *felt* was "home."

She opened her lashes and found his gaze soft and blue. Such changeable eyes he had, her lover, her only lover and only love, her HeartMate. He filled her, long and thick and rigid, and he did not move because he knew she liked this moment, too, where they lay linked, bodies and hands and gazes, totally connected. Before they moved and she got locked in her head with the selfish pleasure of rushing toward orgasm.

His expression turned from tender to strained, and her lips curved in a complacent smile. She liked when he lost control; he did not do that very often in their dreams and never during those three times of in-person bonding.

"Av'ln'a." He slurred her name, even as his eyes lost focus on her and turned inward. She angled her hips a centimeter and he groaned and became pure man, only physical with none of his huge intelligence, his great Flair. Primal man and her mate.

Then the sensations he gave her and the spiraling desire flowing between them stopped all thought, and she could only move as primal woman and his HeartMate. She raised her legs and clamped them around his narrow hips, moved her hands to his wide and muscular back and held on. Vaguely she understood that as her nails dug into his dream-flesh he groaned and sped up the slick plunging until he yelled and held still and hard over her. She reached for the shattering he always delivered. She hit the peak and broke apart and saw the structure of life and death and the colorful spinning dandelion florets of her very own Flair, and then she sank back into her body and mind.

If they had been corporeal, she would have bloodied his back, but her hands fell limply from him and into the grass. Her panting sounded loud in her ears, and she had to blink to see the beads of perspiration on Muin's face.

Then he rolled and she lay atop him and heard his heart beat, matching the rhythm of her own. Or her pulse ran with his. She had never been aware enough to feel whose matched with the other's. Perhaps they fell into the exact cadence at the same time.

She propped herself on her arms against his chest and stared at her love. Now his eyes had closed. His shoulder-length blond-brown hair showed strands dark with perspiration.

Passion faded from him slower than from her, and she could take these minutes to scrutinize him, how he had changed. All life's alterations reflected here. The lines by his eyes and mouth had been etched deeper; a few more strands of silver in his hair waved over his temples. He was a young man, but his Flair had aged him.

And perhaps worry for his HeartMate, her.

She ran her fingers through his long hair. "Muin." Then she sighed and laid her head on his chest. "HeartMate."

He responded, "Yes." His hand lifted and stroked her hair.

"I do not know how I could bear our outside life if I did not have these loving interludes."

"Me, either." His slate-blue eyes opened and centered on her, and her spirits sank as she understood she had introduced reality into the conversation and there would be no after-sex affectionate cuddling.

And then Muin made a gesture and they stood, fully clothed in their nightwear. She wore a short silkeen tunic with tabs on the shoulders, he loose trous that did not reach his knees, of a deep color that she could not see in the twilight but was probably dark green—and the time of the dream had changed from dawn to twilight. Muin preferred evening and night for sex for some reason, while she liked greeting a new day full of potential with loving.

Now they walked through the wildly artful garden of Mona Island, and she provided the dreamscape with true features. He took her hand and near-danced her to the white gazebo constructed of thin wood rods and slats in an airy fantasy of posts and dome. As usual, he instinctively felt what she liked best about each place she had stayed.

Vinni whirled his lover up the steps of the gazebo, around the small space, then stopped them in the middle, surprising a smile from her. He'd seen that smile after they'd made love, but it had faded when he'd moved them vertical. Once in the center, cool mosaic tile under their feet, he said, "If you stay here on Mona Island, I will come and be with you." He moved close and kissed her mouth gently, tenderly, lingering when it curved down.

Her brows slanted down, too. "And we will love in the flesh instead of dream? I am very tired of dreams, Muin."

"I think your sister added a new condition to our marriage contract regarding the loyalty ceremony from the Vines just yesterday."

Her breath escaped in a huff. "I will speak to my sister and parents. I will *not* let this betrothal drag on much longer."

He had to kiss her again. Her lips firmed under his and he touched his tongue to them so she'd open her mouth, but she didn't. More, she even drew back to stare him in the eyes. Her gaze scrutinized him, and the link between them pulsed with her intense focus, but he didn't know what she sought, what she wanted.

"I will not wait more than two and a half more months, Muin. If you wish me to tell those negotiating for your Family that, I will do so. Tomorrow is the first of the month of Holly, then comes Hazel, my Family's month, then *yours*, Vine. Let us set the date for Vine new twinmoons at the beginning of the month."

He stared at her, beautiful in the evening light, and thought on her words. He had made a shot at changing her mind but realized he hadn't expected to do so, though he would have carried through on any promise he'd made.

As for marrying her in two and a half months . . . his heart bumped at the thought, the yearning. But he wasn't quite sure whether he'd be able to find and neutralize the threat to her in two and a half months . . . According to his nightmares, their enemy's intention to harm her seemed to wax and wane, perhaps had been put aside for different goals, like the attacks on children of Noble and Commoner marriages earlier in the year.

He *thought* he understood the motive of their enemy. He or she considered Avellana a mutant, a freak, her primary Flair too extreme for her to be allowed to be a powerful FirstFamily GreatLady.

Because she'd nearly killed the whole Ash household—people, Familiar animal companions, even Fams in the adoption rooms—when she'd been a child. To resurrect a newly dead Fam.

That was the secret that everyone who knew of it kept hidden. Avellana could bring back the dead, but at a massive cost.

Nor could Vinni gauge the future path revealed by such a motive. He couldn't even find the wake a terrible chain of events should show. It was like trying to grab a quick and slippery water snake by the tip of its tail. Unlike most of the FirstFamilies Council, he didn't believe they'd caught all the Traditionalist Stance fanatics. He thought one or two more might lurk hidden within the Residences of the highest Nobles.

Avellana trailed fingers down his cheek, and just that touch had him hard and ready for her again. "You went away in your head, Muin."

"I don't want to talk about this now."

Again she frowned. "You rarely want to talk about our marriage."

"It's boring."

She raised her brows and he conceded, "The ritual itself might be all right, and the result is highly anticipated and desired."

"The *rituals*—we will be blessed by my spiritual advisers, too."

"Yes, and that slowed down the pace of our joining considerably." Just the notion depressed his lust.

"Muin," she warned.

"I accept that we will spend days of ritual on the wedding."

"And after each of the formal ceremonies, we will have a big party," she pointed out in a satisfied tone. "With food and dancing and cheerful conversation and blessings. The blessings of many people who love us and wish us happy."

"That *is* a plus." His gaze wandered down, but she wore an opaque nightshirt and he couldn't see her breasts or the rosy nipples he liked so much.

"You agree?" she pressed.

"Huh?"

"Our handfasting and wedding, within two and a half months."

Now he concentrated on her mouth, watched the movement of her lips, barely heard her words. His body satiated, his mind began to drift into sleep, and he sensed her thoughts slowing, too.

Though the bond between them stayed throbbing and solid and profound, her dream self began to thin as she slipped into sleep, her eyes blinking slowly at him.

"One . . . last . . . question, Muin."

"Yes, dear heart?"

As always the affectionate term made her smile.

"Are you trying to control me by sex? So I will stay here on Mona Island? And you'll come and we'll make love and HeartBond and all?"

The questions sharpened his brain. He hadn't made all those promises, had he? "Could I control you with sex?"

"No." Her eyes narrowed. "I should be angry with you, but I am too tired. I will be later."

"I know," he murmured, and watched her vanish, and didn't know if she'd heard him or not.

Four

❤

Thirty-five minutes after the dream loving with Muin, Avellana had awakened. The more she thought of the past, the more irritated she became, the anger she had suppressed for so long beginning to break free. She loved him, but he hurt her. Time and again.

She examined every situation she could remember. Vaguely she recalled the first time her Family packed up and left due to Muin's fear for her—when she had been five years old. That threat had come from the Black Magic Cult. Her parents had not listened to Muin, but to the guardsman in charge.

Since that guardsman also had a prophetic Flair, she believed that threat had been solid and predictable, and extremely dangerous to her.

She recalled the series of accidents during the time of her first Passage, those dreamquests to free her psychic power, her Flair. *Those* incidents must be the basis of Muin's fear. He had not told her, at that time, that danger threatened, and she had escaped death by the slimmest of margins . . . twice.

Perhaps every time he had experienced a vision since, it had come with the same intensity, so he could not truly differentiate between what might be minor or major. It all felt the same to him.

So now every time he felt a twinge of peril for her, he overreacted and overprotected? That could be a viable theory.

She rose and began to pace. Her FamCat gave her a dirty look, then abandoned her to hunt . . . or at least sleep in beds of flowers that did not grow in Druida City.

All night she thought and paced. She considered her relationship with her HeartMate and how she and Muin would work through all the problems that seemed to multiply in her mind. He had not agreed to marry within the two and a half months she wanted. Perhaps she should have doubts about that, also, and rebalancing their relationship so she *felt* like an equal to him.

The next morning, still confused about her future with Muin, Avellana kept a pleasant expression on her face as she said farewells to her friends before leaving for the ferry from Mona Island to Druida City.

A few meters away from the town and tromping down the road to the ferry, wanting so much to be *home*, Avellana freed the rein she had kept on her resurging emotions.

She had never been so angry at Muin. Irritated, yes, there were bound to be clashes when you grew up with a loved one. And in *every one* of those clashes that regarded her safety, she had given in. Because she *believed* he had seen danger to her and helped her avoid it. She had been so very grateful.

Now she constricted the bond between them to as narrow as—as narrow as one of Flora's whiskers. She didn't want to share her anger with him, or want him to be able to gauge her emotions and find some way to talk her around to his view of matters.

He had not taken her "no" for an answer in the temple, had come to her in her dreams not only for a loving connection but to try to make her reconsider her decision.

Nor did she want to feel his fear or anger.

Flora, Vinni's Fam, says he dreams of your lifeless body often, her FamCat, Rhyz, said mentally as he walked before her, waving his tail. *That is not enjoyable for him or her. You know this because you feel it, too, his sense of the danger to you.* The ginger tabby stopped and looked back at her. *We FEEL this, too, his nightmares and his danger.* Rhyz's muzzle had scrunched. *Don't we?*

Shifting her shoulders and releasing some irritation, she replied telepathically, *Yes, we do. But he took all those nightmares as TRUE, fact, when he did not KNOW whether the harm to me might be a hurt cuticle or death by the plague. Every single instance he treated as if he KNEW I would perish when he could not ascertain how great the danger to me might be.*

Rhyz sat in the middle of the path and rumbled. *It is a bad thing, thinking you will lose a companion.*

"Oh, Rhyz!" She stuck her satchel over her shoulder with a spell and picked up the heavy cat. He purred and licked the underside of her chin. She did not forget that he had been FamCat to Gib Ginger. Whom the Black Magic Cult had drained and murdered. They had drained Rhyz, too.

Avellana buried her face in his fur, smelled the thyme he had slept in the night before.

I do not want to lose another Fam! her cat shouted in her mind. He rubbed his head against her face. *I have put much effort in keeping you safe,* he scolded. *I was there all three times you suffered Passage to free your Flair. I experienced some of the dreamquests with you.* He huffed and his whiskers tickled her.

"I know you did," she said, her voice muffled against him.

I do fear for you, also, he said in a matter-of-fact voice. *FamMan Vinni fears for you, too.*

He fears too much and knows too little and guesses too wrong.

Does he? We are awake this morning before him and he is in that nightmare again, is he not?

Oh, yes, now that she opened her link with Muin, choking fear poured through their bond. Fear for her.

We cannot live like this, Avellana said. *Muin and Flora and you and me. We must control and mitigate this fear.*

I spoke to him harsh and true last night. Like I talk to you now. But he is the Prophet of Celta, how wrong can he be? asked Rhyz. He hopped from her arms and ran down the trail to the dock and onto the ferry. There he paused and sniffed at the people who had already boarded.

She should have known everyone on that ferry, as she knew everyone in the town on Mona Island and had even met those artists who preferred a hermit's life away from the village. But a stranger stood near the rail, with his head turned toward the road. She and Rhyz had split off from that road and taken the closer footpath. Now she faded back into the deep shadows of the trees and waited and watched.

The unknown man grinned down at Rhyz, stooped and petted him, but continued to stare up the road to the ferry, as if scanning for . . . her? Then his gaze shifted to the less well-defined path and he peered in her direction. Her heart had picked up pace—due to Muin's fear as he thrashed in a dream, due to Rhyz's anxiety. She touched the lock of her hair that had gone white during her Passage. That marked her as different. Easy to see.

She had wanted to take the ferry to Druida City, as most people did. She liked feeling normal and tried to put herself in as many experiences as she could to do that. And she enjoyed sailing, being on the ocean.

Traveling by ferry no longer seemed wise. No one in her Family, nor Muin, knew her teleportation range. Even she did not. She did not like taking risks and had not experimented to see how far she might teleport. But she knew she could reach D'Hazel Residence in Druida City, carrying Rhyz. Or even Muin's castle outside the city.

Her Fam teleported into her arms. *I don't like that man. He smells bad! And he snuck on the ferry in Druida City and came here this morning. I smelled it on him. Druida City bar and liquor. Let's go home!*

She thought she heard an angry shout, and the man ran off the ferry. So she teleported away, landing on the pad in the bottom of the square tower of T'Vine Residence that held Muin's suite. Avellana stood there, considering the situation, heart pounding hard from the whiff of fear Rhyz had transmuted to her and the exertion of teleporting so far so quickly, without the preparation of recalling the light of the chamber and the new furniture arrangement and counting down . . .

Before she stepped off the pad, the private door to Muin's apartments upstairs opened with a near-explosive rush and he strode to her, his face forbidding. "What happened?"

Yowl! That came from Rhyz, starting at a low rumble and rising to a high shriek that no doubt sounded beyond human hearing. Her FamCat leapt from her arms, raced around the room. *We are home. We are home.* He stopped in front of Muin and jumped to his shoulder, licked his ear. *I smelled a bad man on the ferry, so we came right here!*

"A bad man," Muin said in a too-even tone.

Curving her fingers around the strap of her satchel, she said, "He did seem to show an interest in me."

"Can you describe this person?" His voice remained still too uninflected.

With a sniff, Avellana flicked her fingers and created a three-dimensional mural that hung in the dim light.

I saw him closer, Rhyz said, then formed a picture in his mind and sent it to them both. With a few alterations, Avellana modified the holo and muttered a word to finalize and save the image. "I have set the call Word of the hologram to *Suspect,*" she stated stiffly. "The mural itself is attached to where your fingers are on the door frame this moment."

With narrowed eyes, Muin studied the holo. "It appears this person has some sort of enhancement spell on his features. In fact, he looks like the recently deceased Arvense Equisetum."

"The Equisetums belonged to the Traditionalist Stance movement."

"Most of them, yes." Muin seemed to be speaking through clenched teeth. "So this guy might know them well enough to copy their features."

"Oh." She practiced her breathing. "The man's frame would be the same, though."

"Not much to go on."

The bad man came from here, Druida City, on the first ferry to dock at Mona Island, Rhyz informed Muin.

His gaze flashed to hers, smoldering. "Mona Island is small and everyone knows everyone else, and the artists are of a more progressive bent and less likely to harbor secret Traditionalist Stance fanatics."

"I am sure you had every single person on Mona Island investigated before you sent me there," Avellana shot back.

All GreatLord manner, Muin inclined his head.

"I will *not* go away again." She hissed out a breath, felt her expression solidify to stony. "If they, whoever my enemies—"

"*Our* enemies."

"—our enemies are, they apparently had no difficulty finding me at Mona Island."

"But they waited to strike on the ferry. They didn't try to infiltrate the small island artistic community. You could be safe there. I could hire a bodyguard—"

"*You are not listening to me. I will not* be told 'go there, come here' anymore." She gained more height as each vertebra of her spine snapped into place, stiff with anger. "I want my *home*. You have never lived anywhere other than your home, have you? You do not know how it is to learn a new area, put yourself out for new people and understand their differences, sleep on a different bedsponge. You do not know what it is to *ache* for your own rooms in the house you were born in, to wish to see your Family every day." She sent him a furious glance. "To wish to see your HeartMate every day."

"You're wrong in that. The ache for my HeartMate is in my blood and bone. I long to see her every day."

The heat of his yearning, at this moment, shocked her, but she set it aside, leaned forward as if she could impress her words on him as she locked gazes with him. She expanded the link, mental, emotional to the fullest and sent him all her emotions: the anger, the feeling of betrayal, the hint of despair that she would have to fight him, pitting her wish to organize her own life against his fear for her.

"There is no Hopeful chapel on Mona Island, no spiritual community of like minds. I answered thousands of curious questions from the creatives there, but not one person expressed an interest in joining the Intersection of Hope. I want to be here, in Druida City, where there is a goodly congregation of Hopefuls. Where there is a gorgeous Cathedral of my faith just outside the city. I want to work on and finish my holo murals for *my* faith that I left unfinished. The most important work of my life and I left it. I am *done* listening to you, Muin."

She took a big breath and said something she had never imagined she would. "I do not wish to see you for a while, Muin. Not until I am less angry with you."

Their bond roiled with wildness, with the wish from them both to act rashly, accuse each other, say nasty things. She must leave before either of them did or said something that would send cracks through their relationship and make it harder to mend.

Meeting his gaze, she said, "Do not contact me for a week, so that we might cool down from our rage with each other, Muin. And absolutely *do not* tell my Family of this latest *feeling* of yours."

"Don't mock my feelings, Avellana."

She bit her lip. "I am not. I do not wish you to speak to my parents *ever again* about any danger you sense to me."

"Or?" He stayed stiff and still. "Are you issuing an ultimatum, Avellana? What will you do?"

Her head jerked aside but she knew he had noted the tears in her eyes. "You," she replied. "You are the one who does the ultimatums, makes the hard lines in our relationship that I have not been able to gainsay or cross."

She waved her arms, understood she would shortly lose control and shriek at her beloved. Not acceptable behavior.

"Rhyz?" she asked in a choked voice.

With a growl and his own irritated emotions pummeling her, the cat leapt to her shoulder and the spell-shelf there to hold him. In another instant, she teleported home.

And sank into her favorite chair that smelled of *her* and no one else, saw the deliberately calm tinted pale-blue walls of her sitting room, all the small treasures she had collected over the years and could not take with her.

The tears she had held back for long minutes trickled down her face. Rhyz hopped to the fat curved top of the plump chair and rumbled a loud purr. *We are HOME!*

Avellana sniffed, picked up a tapestry pillow her sister had made her last year since she had lost the original on her travels, and squeezed it. Lavender scent wafted around her.

"Welcome home, SecondDaughter Avellana," D'Hazel Residence said in his deep male voice.

"Thank you, Residence," she sniffled.

"We have been notified that a suspicious person might have been awaiting you on the ferry, and we have the holo of him, which we forwarded to the guardsmen of Druida City, along with the fact that the facial features were modeled after the late Arvense Equisetum."

Muin. She had asked him not to tell her Family, and when had he ever put her wants over her safety? Wait, no, she had not requested that he ignore the man on the ferry. She had asked that he would not inform her Family of his premonitions. His *unknown percentages* feelings.

Rhyz dropped his paw from the top of the chair to her shoulder, extending his claws so they went straight through the material to prick her skin.

She understood his gesture. Yes, Muin might be right that they had enemies who targeted her.

Because she was different and some people considered her a freak.

Because of her powerful Flair that had led to the huge secret.

Because of her religion, which the Traditionalist Stance did not like, simply because the founder of that movement had coveted what a Hopeful member had. Had sent a mob after the Family of that member.

Now through sheer stupidity, all who continued to stand with the discredited members of the Traditionalist Stance felt that people who did not believe like they did were evil.

She would always be different.

Would she be killed because she was?

Five

She was gone, and had left so angry at him that it ripped a hole in Vinni. Numb and stiff-legged, he stalked to the wall scry panel and took care of the business of protecting Avellana.

Then he just stared at the gloomy, wide space of the ground-level tower chamber. When he'd come of age at seventeen, he'd had all the furniture in this room left over from his predecessor removed to storage. He'd planned to keep this place bare because he wanted no one except him—him and Avellana—to feel at home here.

But he wasn't the only Vine who refused to take "no" for an answer. The housekeeper had moved in furniture a year ago, and since then he'd met here with the innermost circle of his Family now and then.

Last month the room had been refurbished with new, and a little more, furniture. He thought he—and this room—had gotten caught in some internal competition that no one would speak to him about.

But if he raised his voice in an outraged shout, it would still echo through the dim chamber.

Much shouting and yelling and yammering and arguing, Flora said as she hopped down the last step from the bottom landing she'd 'ported to. *Oh, FamMan, you feel . . . very angry.* She trembled so her fur rippled.

He snapped shut his bond with her, and with Avellana, whose emotions raged wildly. Walking slowly so he wouldn't scare his Fam-Fluff, he said in his mildest telepathic voice, hoping the love he sent enveloped her, *We will work this out.* He bent and petted her, then picked her up.

Because we all love each other. Me and you and Avellana and the cat Rhyz.

That's right. But her recitation of their names had sparked an idea.

He wanted his HeartMate guarded, wanted every single greatly Flaired person watching out for her since she stayed here in Druida City.

Time to call his allies together.

*H*e called his most powerful allies—each and every one of the twenty-five FirstFamilies—to meet that morning.

Although he'd set the gathering in GreatCircle Temple, the meeting ended in disaster. Vinni watched as the web of alliances his Family had put into place and kept for nearly a century unraveled. He kept his face impassive, but that damn well hurt.

Two Families refused to protect Avellana, obviously believing whispered rumors of her strangeness. That she was a mutant. Infuriating him.

Those two repudiated their ties with Vinni and Avellana's Family, the Hazels. And Vinni wondered if the two Families included people who belonged to the violent fanatics, the Traditionalist Stance movement. He didn't know where all his enemies lurked.

Now he wouldn't be able to ask those Lords and Ladies to find them.

And the FirstFamilies Council broke into two major camps. That made him wary of the future . . . though no terrible prophecies poured through him as it had happened, thank the Lady and Lord.

Because the FirstFamilies Council *must* work together—or not.

Clash and nothing would get done. Bring the ill will into great magical rituals over the year and the quality of life for the general society of Celta would decline.

What a wretched mess.

After everyone else left, Vinni remained to speak with Avellana's parents, GreatLady D'Hazel and her consort Chess Rowan T'Hazel.

They had wanted to know if he'd seen danger for their daughter again. As he looked at their strained expressions—surely he and Avellana had put some lines in those faces—he answered with the truth for the first time in years. "I do feel some, but I can't judge the amount of threat to her."

That seemed to reassure them, and he felt a twinge of guilt that he'd misled them all these years. So he added, "My most pressing concern is with regard to the Families who cut ties with us both—" He shook his head. "They're frightened."

At that D'Hazel let out a sigh. "Yes, they are frightened because the world moves too quickly for them now. They see more Commoners becoming Flaired and powerful, and those two FirstFamilies believe that erodes their power."

Her HeartMate snorted. "They don't consider that *their* power and their Flair are increasing, too."

"They're worried about Avellana," Vinni said.

D'Hazel slumped. "We're all worried about Avellana and have been since she tried to fly and fell and nearly died at the age of three."

"Hmm," T'Hazel said. "Perhaps we could have folks spread the rumor that whatever oddness our little girl has in her Flair is because of the fall, not inborn."

"It could even be true," Vinni said.

T'Hazel looked at him sharply. "Could it?"

"It could be true."

"Mincing words and shading meanings," D'Hazel said. "But reassuring frightened people so they calm down and have a chance to *think* is a good policy. Let's go home." She linked arms with her husband, then glanced at Vinni and away. "Avellana is angry with you."

"There's irritation on both sides," he affirmed.

"Relationships are like that," T'Hazel said.

"—so we are not inviting you to dinner any time soon, Vinni," D'Hazel ended.

He let his face fall into a pained expression. He usually ate with the Hazels at least once an eightday. "Condemning me to my own Family dinners."

"That's how relationships are," T'Hazel repeated, tilting his hand back and forth. "Ups and downs."

"Not so merrily met, Vinni," Avellana's mother said, altering the usual farewell phrases, "but at least we know whom to watch."

Vinni bowed to them. "Merry part."

"And merry meet again," they all said in unison, and the Hazels teleported away.

Sending his pent-up annoyance into the floor to give the temple more energy to cleanse the area—physically and of the emotional distress he and his allies had stirred up—Vinni also transferred the meeting fee to the temple's coffers. Then he teleported to his private den in his tower.

The fundamental issue for Vinni was whether the Birches or the WhitePoplars had fanatics in their Families who would harm Avellana. He'd have to scrutinize every note, every bit of information he had on them.

But first he contacted his lesser Noble allies—the Marigolds and the Clovers and others—also requesting they increase their awareness of Avellana and any threats to her.

Since these were people he'd personally allied with, and not a part of some generational deal, he talked to them more easily because he considered them all friends. Cratag Maytree T'Marigold offered to guard Avellana, but she'd hate that, so Vinni reluctantly turned the man down, unless it became absolutely necessary in the future. And Vinni prayed that he'd get some very intense advance warning if that happened.

He'd put up with bloody nightmares if he could save Avellana.

* * *

*A*vellana, *I sense that you did not sleep much last night,"* D'Hazel Residence said in the masculine lilting tones of a long past T'Hazel. "Why don't you take a lovely bath in your tub and have a nap?"

Avellana frowned. "You are not monitoring my physical data, are you, Residence? No one gave you such orders?"

The floor under her chair creaked in a snifflike punctuation. "I know your energy is low from the way you landed. Also, you *did* move through my shieldspells when you teleported, so I sensed your vitality."

"You did not answer my questions, Residence." Avellana had learned to be specific and persistent in her requests for information.

A longer creak like a sigh. "No, SecondDaughter Avellana Hazel, I am not monitoring your health. You requested that I stop doing that when you became an adult, and your Family agreed."

Oh, yes, Avellana remembered that fight. Rather like something that might come up next when she announced her own new plans—after *she* had obtained some data.

"Thank you, Residence, for giving me the privacy you do your other inhabitants." She paused and repeated a heartfelt phrase that she said often, but neither her Family nor the Residence believed. "It was not your fault that I tried to fly from the second-story window and fell when I was three years old."

"Of course not," the Residence said. But she knew that tone. He yet felt guilty. They all did. A burden she wished none of them, including her, continued to carry.

A spritz of lilac swirled through the room. She had missed the spring in Druida City, and Mona Island's more tropical location did not support well-blooming lilac bushes.

"Thank you for the scent."

"You are welcome."

"I missed it." She swallowed hard.

"I am glad you returned. You should stay here."

Closing her eyes, she replied, "I have missed Druida City and my Family." She gave herself a few minutes to relax and as the soft blanket edge of sleep moved closer to envelop her, she drew in a big breath and her mind slipped to the next scheduled item of the day. She sat up straight in her chair. "I must go up to the Cathedral."

She needed to see the progress of the decoration inside by the wood and stone carvers, the latest additions and embellishments. More, her fingertips *itched* to trigger her own unfinished art, four huge holo paintings. After this time away, she must consider them with regard to newly learned techniques. She had to decide which mural she wished to work on next.

"A bath? A nap?" the Residence prodded.

She would receive more solace from being in a building that resonated with her deepest-held beliefs, but she did not tell that to the Residence. This was home, yes, but she was only one of many generations of children to be born and raised here, and her destiny would be to leave D'Hazel Residence upon the event of her marriage to Muin, when she became GreatLady D'Vine.

The Intersection of Hope Cathedral had been raised no more than two years ago, and *her* contributions to that place could be a great and long-lasting legacy. She had no doubt the holographic murals she created would be valued until the end of the Cathedral itself, far, far, *far* in the future.

"Thank you for offering your suggestions, but not right now." She paused but could not stop from adding, "A bath and nap are not on my schedule and they would put me behind on the goals that I wish to accomplish today." She summoned her own calendar sphere to view the daily agenda for the Cathedral that the ministers published for the congregation.

Frowning, she noted the weekly "Meeting of the Chief Ministers on Hopeful Business," set for today along with the list of the ministers—the same ministers who had commissioned the building of the Cathedral.

At that time, the idea of a spiritual path based on a journey had resonated with her. More than the religion she had grown up in. So she had studied and been accepted as a member of the Hopeful sect. Since then she had been agitating for an equal number of female and male Chief Ministers. She felt deeply that two of the four Chief Ministers representing the four spirits of her faith should be female. Probably because the dominant culture around her—the Celtic culture—emphasized the equality of the Divine Couple.

But it seemed no progress in *that* had occurred while she had been away.

She must speak to the Chief Ministers about this concern. A sufficient amount of time had passed so that two Chief Ministers could transition out and two new *female* Chief Ministers could hold the highest office of the Intersection of Hope religion.

Avellana rose and moved to her bedroom to disrobe, then to the waterfall room for a quick shower. She did not care which of the four spirit representatives became female—the childlike self, adult vitality, wise maturity, or the guardian—but she did consider her religion would be better when both women and men stood as Chief Ministers in the sacred intersection. Time to remind the Chief Ministers of that.

She scrubbed away the film of Mona Island and luxuriated under the herbed waterfall at the exact temperature she liked.

Confronting the Chief Ministers meant more conflict. She gritted her teeth in a smile. Last night and this morning with Muin, later this week or next with her Family, and now with the Chief Ministers.

She was becoming downright fierce.

Six

♥

Four evenings later, Vinni paused his glider at the foot of the Vines' hill before the switchbacks upward to T'Vine Residence. Like many First-Family colonists, the first Vine had gone overboard when constructing a home. So grand he didn't want to live inside the city. He'd claimed the hill and spent his gilt in paying for help raising the gigantic castle.

Or maybe Family legend was correct. Only one of the originally psi-gifted Family that became Vine made it out of the walled ghettos of Earth, and he never wanted to be caught like that again. Thus the hill outside the walled Druida City, the winding road, the three gate-houses, and his own wall around the castle with many towers.

Vinni's forebears also recorded that the initial T'Vine had a smidgen of the psi power of foresight, but mostly a great gift for earth-moving and translocation of objects. He should have gone into the construction business, but he tormented himself for not seeing the future and the deaths of his clan.

So he concentrated on—and married for—the Flair of prophecy.

As with the other pioneers who'd funded the starships and landed here, the first T'Vine had believed that his descendants and the general population of Celta would burgeon as humans had on Earth. He'd built a home to house the huge Family he planned to beget.

Now Vinni and his Family of thirty-five lived in a massive castle modeled after one on old Earth. A place that would house the couple hundred of the Clover Family easily.

A beautiful and intelligent Residence that had always supported him, been more parent than his mostly female relatives and the Vine guards who'd raised him after his predecessor had died. He'd never known his parents, who'd passed on to the Wheel of Stars soon after he'd been born.

Now Vinni supposedly ruled the household. He certainly held the title, but he didn't order his older relatives around—much. But he stood firm when necessary.

Like when he was thirteen and after Avellana's First Passage to free her Flair, when someone in the Family had tried to kill her. He'd demanded another Loyalty Ceremony. Some of his relatives had abandoned the Family rather than take an oath to him.

No, he led his Family. Which didn't mean they couldn't manipulate him as he did others.

"Glider, return home, minimum speed."

"Yes, T'Vine," it replied. Unlike the Residence, the vehicle wasn't intelligent—yet. Vinni had just spent another session with the oldest Alders of the FirstFamilies. They designed and created gliders, and none wanted the title.

Being responsible for the whole Family burdened each individual, and Vinni could relate to that—but at least, even at six, he'd known that he'd be the next prophet. In fact, he could recall his great-MotherDam very well.

Because somehow she'd figured out her own death. He still didn't know how she'd done that, though she'd had over a century to learn how to sift the details of others' futures and understand how they might impact her own.

Vinni shuddered. Her death had not been kind.

And there remained recordspheres she'd coded against him opening until—or if—certain things happened. Apparently she could see *his* future well enough, at least some of the later years. He didn't have memory spheres addressed to him before he'd turned adult.

One would be when he reached his thirty-fifth birthday.

One after he HeartBonded with his HeartMate.

Now and again he'd stare at that glass sphere and ponder what advice might be in it.

He both anticipated and dreaded watching it.

As he reached the first front gate, the shieldspells dropped as the glider sailed through. The arms on the front of the vehicle and the side of the car resonated with the spells, and, of course, the Residence sensed him. With the extension of the walls all around the castle, the sapience of the Residence had expanded to the outermost stone.

Vinni's schedule had continued to be heavy, and he'd managed to skip more than one dinner. He'd also avoided any questions from his Family regarding Avellana and why she hadn't come around after she'd returned from Mona Island. He had, of course, briefed the inner circle of his relatives—those who held the most responsible jobs in the Residence and for the Family—on the defection of their allies and the golden favor tokens he'd collected from the Birches and the WhitePoplars for breaking their agreements.

He sensed something in the atmosphere that warned him that his more proper relatives weren't happy with his long hours . . . and his dodging of the rest of the Family.

He was right. His G'Aunt Bifrona awaited him in the garage. The portly and elegantly dressed woman who carried herself with grace addressed him the minute he emerged from the glider.

"Greetyou, Vinni, my dear. It is too bad of you to make me await you like this in the garage just so I can have a few minutes of your time to discuss a simple matter."

Stifling a sigh and not bowing, he said, "Good evening, G'Aunt Bifrona."

Bifrona held the position of the female Head of the Household, having won that honor among her age-equals in subtle, sophisticated warfare decades ago. He wasn't supposed to have been aware of skirmishes, then or now, but he'd watched and learned. And even at nine, he'd managed to clean up some of the resulting mess and found other estates or mates for the vanquished.

She held out an imperious hand. "Let's speak about this in the bottom of your tower."

Trouble with his Family. Great. "Speak about what?"

Her brows rose at his curt tone, but he decided to be unmannerly to his eldest female relative and jerked his head toward the hallway linking the garage to the large ground-level chamber of his tower. He sensed she wanted a business discussion, so a more businesslike setting she would get.

With a sniff, she swept ahead of him along the corridor to the door—the only inner door to the chamber that she had a key for and would open to her, and that gave Vinni some satisfaction.

He caught up with her to see the room dazzling bright with the circling of three sunlike lightspells. The near-white wood of the new furniture gleamed along with the nap of emerald velvet cushions.

He hesitated as he passed a new teleportation pad. Which hadn't been in the chamber when he'd left that morning. He gritted his teeth, felt the pressure, loosened his jaw, and pasted on a false smile. He glanced at the cabinet timer. Couldn't talk too much or they'd be late for dinner.

Bifrona hadn't seated herself but stood rigid-spined. Continuing to smile, not even baring his teeth like he wanted, he moved closer than she liked because she had to look up at him significantly.

"I—we, the Family, have a request."

"Oh?"

He understood that the weight of Family expectations always burdened the Head of a FirstFamily household if they had more than a few members of that Family. The greatest example of that had been the implosion of the Yew Family three months before.

She wet her lips. More nervous than she pretended to be. "We wish for you and Avellana to lead a First Quarter Twinmoons Ritual four nights from now."

He froze, raised one of his own brows. "You do not give me much time."

"There are many, many"—and doubling her words up like that also betrayed her anxiety—"First Quarter Twinmoons Rituals that

a member of a FirstFamily knows by the time they are thirty like you
or twenty-four like Avellana."

"I see." Yes, his Family tried to constrain him, but more, wished
to put Avellana in a nice, safe box where she'd be stuck being the
GreatLady *they* wanted her to be. Anger surged. The hell with that.
He'd—they'd, Avellana and he would—beat them at this particular
game, as with any other requests that would limit them. "Very well.
Is that all?"

A long pause, then Bifrona replied in a starchy tone, "Yes."

He got the idea she'd just started but wouldn't reveal other requests or suggestions or whatever yet.

He flicked a hand at her, which she didn't like. "Then I'd best
start such arrangements, shouldn't I?" He paused, met her eyes.
"Since it is *my and Avellana's* ritual, you will await instructions as
to the candles, songs, and food we will require."

Bifrona hissed out a breath, but he just stared at her.

"Yes, T'Vine," she grated out, then whisked to the door and opened
it without another word.

As she left the chamber, Arcto, Vinni's former tutor, entered. Bifrona sniffed and inclined her head in the exact amount of courtesy
due him.

Though Bifrona had ruled the house and staff, Arcto had guided
Vinni in his interactions with the other FirstFamilies . . . unless Vinni
escaped him. In those early years, he'd been watched constantly by
Arcto and his guards.

But in those early years there had also been hope that one of his
female relatives would achieve an acceptable Flair during her Passage
to be his heir. Hadn't happened.

A tall, thin, elegant man with hair and eyes the same color as
Vinni's own, Arcto closed and locked the door behind him and
slanted a look at the new furniture in the room. His upper lip lifted
in disdain. "I heard that Bifrona redecorated this area for you." His
turn to sniff. "Furnishings from Clover Fine Furniture."

He'd always been a snob.

"They've always been a good, solid value," Vinni replied. "And since Walker Clover became the first GrandLord thirteen years ago, the company established a new, top-of-the-pyramid-quality line."

Arcto's turn to sniff. "Walker Clover only became a GrandLord due to his Flair—"

"Of course—"

"And the fact that his mother is *not* part of the middle-class Clover clan, but a Heliotrope."

"Ah." Vinni shrugged. He'd been an honorary Clover for a long time, though now that he recalled, Arcto hadn't accompanied him to many of those boisterous get-togethers. "Well, Walker married into the FirstFamilies, and Trif Clover's husband is now Captain of the Guards of all Druida City. Children from both of those HeartMate unions are showing great Flair."

Arcto speared his fingers through his hair and gave Vinni a lopsided smile. "You're right, of course. We progress, as a people and a culture. Since I taught you, and continue to teach our Vine children, I tend to emphasize history and the past."

"You prepared me well for the future." Vinni clapped him on the shoulder. "What can I do for you?"

"I have heard that Avellana finally returned to Druida City, and I want to remind you that I am on the Family list for one of her murals in my suite."

"She's busy right now, but I'll remind the Residence—"

"And Bifrona, who is also on the list, but *after* me," Arcto added with a sharp smile.

"—everyone, of the list, including Avellana."

"Thank you, Vinni."

"You're quite welcome."

With a nod, Arcto vanished.

Well, the second request had been easy, at least. As for the first . . . Vinni let out his own breath on a slow sigh but found his lips curling. A perfect reason for him to see Avellana.

He extended his senses and found her already seated at dinner with her Family, happy and pleased. He considered going to her after his own dinner . . . but that would end late and he'd only have a few minutes with her before her schedule had her retiring to bed.

She had blocked him when he'd begun to walk in her dreams last night, wanting her.

These nights without her wore on him.

*H*e *didn't sleep well and woke the next morning grouchy.* The time Vinni had spent without Avellana had passed too slowly for him. Occasionally he had tried to be in her presence—with others, to see if his allies *did* watch out for her, and they did—but Avellana avoided him and did not speak to him if they happened to meet.

He'd gotten tired of that—all right, he wouldn't lie to *himself*, even if he did finesse the truth in his career—he craved her company. Always had, probably always would. And as long as he faced very unpalatable truths today, he'd acknowledge that he always feared for her, not only because of his love, but because he'd be lost without her. Truth, he could not envision—ha!—a life without Avellana.

So, since it had been a good five days since he'd seen her, and he now had the excuse he needed to speak with her, he went to where she spent most of her time nowadays, the Cathedral of the Intersection of Hope.

He paused before the northeastern door of the Cathedral. This particular wing of the equal-armed cross was dedicated to the spirit of wise maturity, the eldest reaching the end of his journey. Vinni murmured a prayer to his own deities, the Lady and Lord, that he and Avellana would survive to become such elders.

Opening the door, a rush of cool air mitigated the summer heat enveloping him, and the fragrance of sweetgrass, myrrh, and cedar incense wafted out. He trod down the corridor, widening his inner bond with Avellana—one that had snapped into place a year after she'd been born and he'd been seven. His current hypothesis about that unusual bond and other unique facts of his life was that they had occurred due to the nature of his Flair—it had been fully powerful since his birth. He'd had no dreamquest Passages.

He'd reached the center of the cross and circled outside the most holy ground of the altar, then headed toward the meeting room of the four Chief Ministers, where he sensed his HeartMate to be. A few paces from the room, the polished paneled door opened and Chief Minister Younger shot out, emanating joy, nearly skipping. The twenty-year-old man grinned, stopped, and said, "Hey, Vinni!"

Vinni inclined his torso, a bow due to a FirstFamily Lord or Lady, the High Priest or Priestess of his own religion. "Excellency. Greetyou, Chief Minister Younger."

The youngster laughed, his head tipping back. "Nope, I'm not a Chief Minister anymore, thanks to Avellana. It took her three meetings with us, but I'm free. *Free of that responsibility!*" He shot a look over his shoulder. "Or I will be soon. But no more meetings, at least. Later." He trotted away, leaving Vinni blinking and wondering what name he'd call the young man if they met again. He didn't know.

The other three ministers exited the room more slowly, looking more than a little shell-shocked . . . each man staggered. Behind them, Avellana, lovely in bright blue, walked with a spring in her step, appearing self-satisfied with an underlayer of determination.

She'd been very determined of late to order her life and anything that bothered her. Apparently she'd tackled what she considered the gender problem of the Chief Ministers.

What she'd do next, Vinni didn't know, but a hunch had invaded his bones that his plans to keep her discreetly observed and safe headed toward hers on a collision course.

He didn't know who'd win the battle of wills.

Rather exciting when he wasn't apprehensive about her. And their relationship. The whole damn mess.

Avellana's expression smoothed into impassivity when she saw him.

He nodded to his love, then moved toward Chief Minister Foreman—representing adult vitality—who supported the elbow of Chief Minister Elderstone. Vinni took Elderstone's other arm.

"I am fine," the old man said in a crotchety voice.

"You'll be better after we have refreshments," soothed the slightly-older-than-middle-aged Chief Minister Custos, the symbol of the guardian spirit.

Elderstone stopped and drew himself to his full height, taller than the other two, as tall as Vinni. His piercing blue eyes fixed on Vinni. "Is there anything we can do for you, GreatLord T'Vine?" he snapped.

Vinni stepped away, bowed. "Greetyou, Your Excellency. I am here to offer Avellana a glider ride home."

Snorting, Elderstone said, "Good luck with that one." Then he made a short bow to Vinni and took off in the direction of his own office at a more sprightly pace.

The other two ministers nodded at Vinni, then followed.

Avellana raised her voice and called out, "Go in peace; may you journey to the center and find your joyful self."

Vinni had heard that ending blessing before. He watched.

Three backs stiffened. Three men pivoted, irritation showing on their faces, at themselves rather than her, he figured.

As one they bowed, Chief Minister to a member of their congregation, and they said in unison, "Go in peace; may you journey in the light."

Avellana curtseyed to them. Vinni bowed and said, "The light is great. It's a beautiful summer's day."

Without any more speech, they turned back, walking with less stiffness, reminded of their faith and the solace it could give in trying times.

Vinni pivoted toward Avellana. He'd intended to bow deeply over her hand and kiss it—he ached to touch her—but she'd tucked her arms in the opposite sleeves of her long tunic.

"Why are you here?" she asked.

He smiled. "I couldn't stay away from you."

She tilted her head as if listening past the amusement in his tone to winnow the truth. He thought she had heard his veracity because she frowned. She continued to walk around the altar and toward the tiny volunteer rooms, and he kept pace.

"It has recently occurred to me that you use your voice very well."

She glanced at him. His turn to be expressionless. "Sometimes you wrap the truth in what sounds like a lie . . . And I have heard you shade the knowledge of what you have seen to guide someone in the direction you think they should go."

"You're a very perspicacious lady."

"I just know you," she replied simply. A wash of love, tenderness, affection flowed through him.

He wouldn't be unmanly enough to clear his throat, so he spoke through the husk. "I'd like to see the progress you've made on your holo murals here. And take you home." He wanted to savor this time with her before he brought up the ritual thing, which would be problematic.

Maybe she wouldn't agree to do that with him, or would dislike the option he'd thought of on the way here.

Avellana sniffed and said darkly, "I told you last week that I am not leaving *again* at your request. This *fourth* suggestion." She paused. "Because, you know, you very often *did not* request."

So much for not being confrontational.

He replied, "Very true. I convinced your parents that you had to leave the city for your own good."

Her back stiffened. "Do you know how much I loathe those words?"

"Have an idea, yes. Especially since our little discussion about you staying on Mona Island."

She still didn't turn around so he could talk to her face-to-face, look into her eyes. Her gliding steps became more of a march.

"As I said before, I will never 'go there, come here' at your bidding again. *Never.*"

Before he could analyze that deeply, she continued, matching the staccato sound of her steps with her words.

"I am not five years old anymore. I am not threatened by the Black Magic Cult."

The sentences hung in the air, seemed to bounce back from the stone to hit his ears. "Please don't send negative energy into this lovely place." He dropped his hand. "I do want to see how you've progressed on the Cathedral holo murals."

She sent him an inscrutable glance over her shoulder. "Do you?"

"Yes." He stopped, to see how far she'd walk from him, how annoyed she might be. After three meters she halted, swung on her heel, facing him with a scowl.

"I remain irritated with you, Muin."

He strode to her and this time he caught her hand in his own, kissed the back of it, and she let him. They stood there in silence in the cool Cathedral, with light spearing through the high windows, aching for each other.

"Oh, Muin." She sighed out the words. "What am I going to do with you?"

"Anything you want," he murmured.

Seven

His beloved raised her brows at his extravagant answer but withdrew her hand and went back to his lesser declaration. "You want to see my three-dimensional holographic murals?"

"Absolutely."

She passed him, walking back to the intersection of the cross with her usual graceful stride.

The door closest to the walls of Druida City opened and the scent of summer grass wafted in, along with a grouping of footsteps and a guide's voice. "Thank you for allowing me to show you the new Intersection of Hope Cathedral . . ."

They both looked back the way they'd come, but Avellana didn't stop, and that told Vinni that his viewing her work was important to her. As important as it was to him to see it.

When she reached the center of the Cathedral, the junction that the Intersection of Hope cherished, she gestured to the opening of the southeastern arm. "This is the mural I have been working on the most." Above their heads, a three-dimensional holographic image of a near-translucent being appeared.

"We continue to discuss the representation of the guardian spirit," she said in that colorless voice he loathed. Better she rail at him than use the emotionless voice that meant she'd fought and lost too many battles. "Currently it is androgynous and without wings."

"What would you prefer?" he asked, figuring out that arguments with the Chief Ministers had put that note in her voice, not him. Good. Anyone but him.

"I like that the guardian spirit figure in the mural can be seen as a male or female. I prefer androgynous to hermaphroditic, a person with sexual characteristics of both genders. Some of the Chief Ministers want an image of a hermaphrodite."

"Huh," Vinni said. Though he could claim an acquaintance with each one of the men because they were important to Avellana, he didn't know any of them well. Certainly not well enough for him to guess who favored a hermaphrodite.

Avellana sighed. "I will be adding breasts and a penis to the image soon." He knew that tone, too. She'd delay as long as humanly possible.

"But it appears like we might add wings. *White feathered* wings." She gave him a satisfied smile.

"White feathered," he repeated.

"Like depictions of ancient angels. *Not* bat-type wings."

"Oh."

"I like the idea of angels. It is very comforting to think of evolved spirits, even if it is not part of my religion. But the guardian spirit is equally comforting, of course."

"Of course."

Mingled, undefined talk rose into the heights of the Cathedral, diffused into the atmosphere.

"This is my mural of the guardian spirit." She projected her voice so the newcomers would hear.

Vinni smiled; she deserved all the accolades and compliments that anyone could give her, especially since she couldn't practice her deadly primary Flair, and she'd made this secondary artistic Flair her main outlet.

He stepped up to her and put an arm around her waist, let out a quiet breath that she allowed this, and allowed the connection between them to stay at the usual strong width and depth. "Gorgeous piece of work," he said, in equally loud tones. The quick patter of footsteps came as visitors hurried up to them.

He thought he knew most of the members of the Druida City Intersection of Hope, and recognized the guide. The rest of the group appeared to be lower-Noble-class tourists. In the two years since the Cathedral had been built of equal-sized rectangles and different from the Celtic round temples, visitors had flocked to see it. Vinni thought much of the gilt collected by this location of the religion came from tours of the Cathedral, though he wasn't rude enough to voice that particular insight.

Avellana kept the first holo showing, then triggered the other three, one for each arm of the cross, each showing the soul on the Journey that resonated so much with her as a belief system. Deep, intense colors, a fascinating mythological depiction of each of the stages of the journey, tore oohs from the visitors.

People studied each phase in turn. The child toddled from the center of the Great Labyrinth north of Druida City. Above the chubby figure clothed in a loincloth spread the huge Ash tree. Though the real labyrinth had a strongly defined path as a spiritual and meditation aid, in front of the toddler lay smooth grass in all directions, unlimited potential, any pathway he or she could take to the rim.

Again Avellana had depicted the crater and the rising levels of greenery, rich and verdant, promising food and shelter on the soul's journey. The bright star of Bel, their sun, shone high in the deep blue sky, a spring sky.

Most of the tour pivoted to see the next mural, that of a man and woman in the prime of life, crafting an altar halfway up the bowl of the Great Labyrinth, with a trellis behind and to the sides of them, and on that trellis, exact copies of the holos everyone viewed now. More oohs.

Vinni couldn't prevent himself from looking down at Avellana and grinning. She radiated anxiety as she waited for reactions to her work. He pulled her close and her body had stiffened so that she toppled more than bent.

Then everyone looked at the last mural. An old person with white hair, face so wrinkled with age and living that the individual's gender could not be deduced. A long robe like the ones the ministers wore fell in folds; a thin gold band circled the elder's brow. She or he faced them at the top of the rim of the crater holding the Great Labyrinth. This time the path—surely the path the person had carved—showed the deep brown of rich earth against autumn colors of leaves and berries. One foot stepped onto that path, taking the trail back down into the bowl to the Ash tree. One hand rose palm outward in greeting or farewell or both, and the sun shone right above the oldster's head.

Silence pervaded the Cathedral, with only the whispers of the wind against the windows, the breathing of the gathered people. No one even shifted. Then someone sighed, "Zow," and that broke the moment and the visitors shuffled, murmured, talked a little louder. A plump middle-aged woman stepped up to Avellana, met her eyes, and bowed. "Thank you for showing us your art. You have a great talent."

"Thank you for appreciating it," Avellana said, curtseying.

"Now, GentleLadies and GentleSirs," the Hopeful tour guide, a man in his late twenties, said, "let me show you some of the excellent sculpture we've decorated our stone with . . ." He led them away down the arm dedicated to the innocent childlike self.

Avellana relaxed against Vinni and he cherished the feel of her against his side and kept his mouth shut.

After a minute, she drew away, glanced up at him with a mischievous look, and said, "I want some ice cream, you with whom I can do anything I wish."

He raised his brows but returned her smile. "I'll be pleased to provide you with ice cream. At The Merry Treat, Merry Tart shop?"

"Oooh, big spender."

Reluctantly he dropped his arm from her waist and found her fingers and clasped her hand.

When he moved, she didn't, and he stopped.

Her eyes had narrowed, and she spoke in a low tone. "You did not come just to give me a ride home, did you? There is something serious we must discuss."

Vinni sighed. "Yes, I've come to speak with you regarding a serious matter. But I don't want to talk about that here in the Cathedral."

Her lips tightened, then she said, "This is a sacred space, Muin."

"It is also a building where sound carries well, and we have a group of people unknown to us touring." He kept his voice quiet. "None of them seemed to recognize you or me, but I don't want to talk of Family matters where others can hear."

"Very well." She tucked her hand in the corner of his elbow, just like always, and he breathed easier. The crisis point had passed with her. He'd need to step warily, though, with this latest challenge.

Changing the topic, he said, "Chief Minister Younger seemed cheerful when he left."

"He ran out of the Cathedral," she corrected.

"Yes. Why?"

"When something that was joyful to begin with becomes a burden, it is time to lay it down, is it not?" she replied. "He is no longer Younger." Her lips took on a smug cast. "We have chosen a girl of fifteen for that title. She will be marvelous."

But Vinni discounted the latter sentences. Yes, he knew how to shade his voice with truth and . . . lesser truth . . . to subtly guide a person who consulted him for visions of his or her life on the best path, and he'd learned that from listening and studying behavior. Right now, Avellana didn't only speak of Younger. So Vinni would be direct. Keeping his voice a murmur, he said, "Are we also speaking of my prophetic Flair? Because it's always been a burden." He'd meant that to come out lighter, but his lips had twisted and bitterness had laced his tone.

She studied him. "But you used to find some joy in your Flair! I know that."

His chuckle didn't sound entirely mordant. "I did, but others didn't seem to appreciate me telling them of their future."

He'd been brash as a child and a new GreatLord, offering advice instead of waiting to be asked. And then he began to understand that no one really liked meeting him, and even with members of his Family there remained a tiny distance between him and everyone else because of his great Flair.

But Avellana had saved him from an early age, when he'd understood she was his HeartMate. He was never alone because of her. The only thing that scared him in his life was being without her.

He wrenched his mind back to the topic—that the man he'd known as Younger had given up that title and responsibility. And had been glad to do so.

An idea struck him to the heart. Was Avellana . . . could she be . . . speaking of their relationship as something that had been wonderful but had become a hardship?

His entire focus fixed upon her, he saw, heard, sensed nothing else in the world. With a snarl he couldn't suppress, he moved his grip to around her biceps and lifted her, eye-to-eye. "You aren't talking about us. Saying that our relationship was joyful and now it isn't. I *won't* give you up."

And he kissed her. Right there in the Hopefuls' holy Cathedral.

He closed his eyes as held her, gentled his grasp and slid her down his body, let the groan that wanted to tear from him resonate through their bond, internal instead of external. She trembled against him and emotions rushed from her: love and tenderness, a touch of physical desperation—wonderful!—but all tinged with a twining thread of deep red anger. That hurt his heart, and he'd have to work on that . . . when he could think again, because all thought dribbled away.

Lady and Lord, her body against his felt so incredibly wonderful! All he ever wanted to do was to hold her. Keep her close. Keep her safe. She felt *right* as always, her against him. Matching in this as in so much other.

And matching in need. She touched her tongue to his lips and he parted them, craving the taste of her. So long. Five whole days without touching.

Her arms clamped around him and they explored mouths with

tongues. His hands drifted down to above her derriere. Stopped. *Can't go farther. Don't know why but not now. Bad idea.*

She pressed against him and he had to break the kiss into little ones, as he breathed in pants. Her arms went around his neck and she toyed with his hair. And he sizzled hot, hotter, hottest.

Needed to cool down. Ice cream. Yes, let that coat his mouth instead of Avellana's taste . . . though he thought there might be a flavor of ice cream that reminded him of her. When he'd sent her away from Druida City during the plague years, he'd haunted shops that had drinks and pastries and ice cream that approximated her taste.

Sweet and salty at once.

Salty, he thought, because she'd cried sometimes when he'd kissed her good-bye.

"Never again," she murmured, placing her hand on the side of his face, and he understood that she'd sensed what he'd been thinking . . . or feeling. Those farewells wrenched him as fully as her.

A cough. Avellana stepped away from him, and he had a couple of instants to mutter a spell dissipating his passion.

He found Chief Minister Custos, who represented the guardian spirit, staring at them indulgently, or, rather, looking at the flushed faces of them both. The older man gestured. "There's a privacy chamber down the arm of mature vitality that can be used for this sort of thing."

Vinni thought he might look shocked and wild-eyed. But he understood the reasons. The Cathedral continued to need all the energy and emotions people could pour into it, including sexual energy. And . . . he thought GreatCircle Temple might also have such rooms, though he'd never considered that notion before.

With a couple of Words Avellana smoothed her appearance. "Thank you, Chief Minister, but we *are* leaving." She gave the man a little curtsey. She sounded completely in control of herself and the situation.

"May the rest of your day's journey be sweet," the man said.

Avellana's face lit and she laughed delightedly. "It will, we are going for ice cream at The Merry Treat, Merry Tart."

"Blessings to you," Vinni said, yet feeling disconcerted. So he covered that by bowing again, this time with many hand flourishes.

Custos nodded to them and retreated to the center and down the arm where the tour group guide lectured.

Vinni snagged Avellana's hand and walked with her to the northeast portal.

Once outside in the bright light of the small white sun in the deep blue sky he took her arm, though the area around the Cathedral had been smoothed from the original rocky space.

If she hadn't truly forgiven him, she still allowed him to touch her. Five days had been four and two-thirds days too many without her.

Since there continued to be few gliders in Druida City, he and Avellana had to walk a little ways to the packed dirt area where Vinni had parked, the only glider around, though he kept gathering information from his senses so he'd soon be able to teleport.

Now he stood on Varga Plateau, where they could see the smudge of the buildings of Druida City in the distance and the more prominent landmark of the starship *Nuada's Sword*. He relaxed, feeling more like himself, GreatLord Muin T'Vine who celebrated the Celtic religion of the Lady and Lord.

Avellana sighed. "To answer your earlier question, no, Muin, I wasn't referring to our relationship as having lost joy. Though we haven't formally HeartBonded, I don't think either of us would survive the loss of the other," she said matter-of-factly. Then added, "Though I think we could live apart, as we have always done, successfully enough."

Irritation spurted through him, turning his vision red. Easy, easy.

Now he *did* clear his throat. "Since you refuse to be guided by my—"

"Fears?" she asked quietly.

He stopped, simply stood frozen, no words coming.

"Aren't you tired of being fearful, Muin?"

Eight

Vinni's mouth opened, but he remained speechless and closed it.

Her steady blue eyes met his. "I am tired of being fearful, and of your worry."

"Our relationship is a burden for you."

"No!" she replied swiftly. "Of course our relationship is not a burden." She paused and didn't look at him. "At least not to me."

"I just proved I don't consider our relationship a burden." He moved in front of her and sank down until she couldn't avoid seeing him, and waited until she looked at him. "Our relationship is a joy. The best and truest thing in my life."

She caught her breath. Held out her hands and he took them, straightened.

Her lips trembled a little and the emotional bond between them that had constricted now expanded, flowing wide and deep with exchanged feelings. From her, he felt complete acceptance of . . . fate. And determination. He barely heard her exhale but scented the sweetness of her breath.

Her pupils dilated and they stared at each other. "I will say again, we are close enough despite not accepting the HeartBond, that we might not survive the death of each other."

"No," he said. "You would live if I perished."

She hissed and shook her head. "Why do you persist in thinking I am different than I am? We must discuss *that* in depth also—but later." Reaching up, she placed her palm against his cheek. "I would not like to live if you were gone from the world, Muin. I would slough off my body, and my spirit would continue on its journey until I found you again."

And his soul would circle on the Wheel of Stars until she caught up with him.

With a grimace she stepped from him and touched the door of the glider so it rose. "You need to practice acceptance of that fact, Muin, stop denying that we are already tied too closely to survive without one another. Stop *thinking* and *feeling* and *believing* that you can protect me from everything." Her gaze drilled into him. "I have accepted that."

They stared at each other, until he cut his gaze away.

"So. Let us get into the glider and you can tell me what situation has come up that we should discuss."

You could NOT have forgotten ME. Avellana's ginger tabby FamCat swaggered from the bushes, burped, sat, and tended his bloody whiskers.

Vinni considered him overly plump and groomed. As far as he knew, Avellana combed and brushed him every day. Rhyz stared at Vinni and smirked, sent him a private telepathic message. *My Fam-Woman loves Me. I am with her EVERY DAY. She does not like you right now.* One side of the cat's muzzle lifted to show a fang.

The cat had struck well. Vinni's jaw clenched. Under her words and her surface feelings, he felt the low ripple of her continuing annoyance at him.

Do not say so, Rhyz! Vinni heard his love's telepathic projection to her Fam, her mindspeech laced with steel. She sniffed. *You stir up trouble when we have temporarily smoothed the rough waters between us.* She paused before continuing. *And we are going to confront another problem soon enough.*

The cat's ears perked up. Troublemaker. He trotted over to the glider.

Vinni's new glider. He'd recently purchased a new one—a vehicle in colors and fabrics pleasing to Avellana and that would only seat the two of them—but he liked being alone in a small space with her. So often he and she met when Family watched.

And now he had to put up with the FamCat, too. He reached out with his mind to check on his own Fam. Flora snoozed on her pillow in her basket in Vinni's sitting room.

With a wave of the hand, he kept the glider door open on Avellana's side, then thinned the top of the vehicle to an in-built weather-shield that revealed the scenery. No reason to hurry back to the city.

He hadn't noticed the cat slipping into the glider until Rhyz lay on the back Fam perch and sneezed. *Too much smell of HOUSE-FLUFF.*

"Too bad," Vinni said, entering the glider. He set the thing to self-navigate and pushed the steering bar into the dashboard.

Avellana settled in and fastened the safety web, smiling. "This is a beautiful vehicle."

"It's good for the two of us," he replied. He hit the ignition button; the landing gear folded into the body of the glider and it proceeded smoothly, more slowly than if he'd taken the controls. He wanted every moment he could get with his love.

Her smile fading, Avellana angled toward him. "Tell me what is wrong, Muin."

So he laid out Bifrona's request, ending with, "I'm not sure why they asked us to lead the circle. Whether they want you to conform to their standards . . . or for some even less acceptable reason."

Avellana exhaled a sibilant breath, then turned to stare at him. "Is this why you wanted me to stay away from Druida City? You think someone in your household is working against us? That this request is a way to discredit me?"

"Discredit us," he corrected in a stern tone.

"Discredit us," she repeated.

Bad peoples, Rhyz grumbled.

"We have a conundrum, Muin," she said as the glider carried them across the plateau toward the tall, strong city walls of Druida. Not looking at him, she said, "I don't mind acting Lady to your Lord . . ."

And his lust stirred at that, yes, it did.

". . . but I will not compromise my own faith. I will not be a Celtic God and Goddess Worshipper and a Hopeful. That is wrong. And, besides, I told my Chief Ministers that I would not do so."

"Then we will commission a whole raft of rituals from Priestess Tiana Blackthorn-Moss that will include both our beliefs. I can be more flexible. Can't we both agree that the Lady and Lord reveal different aspects of themselves throughout the year? That could be seen as a journey, no? An eternal journey. And we could call the Lady-as-Maiden also the inner childlike self. We can use concepts such as that, which we both agree on, as basis for our Family rituals."

Avellana turned back to him with wonder in her eyes, staring at him as if he were a hero. "There are many aspects of the Lord and Lady." Avellana whispered a tenet of the Celtan faith.

"Yes, and that would include, for each, the four spirits and avatars you cherish in your own religion."

"This might work for us," Avellana whispered.

"Yes."

"I've spoken to the High Priest and High Priestess about this, of course," Vinni said.

"Naturally." She tilted her head. "What did they say?"

"That I am a FirstFamily GreatLord and one of the rulers of the planet and I, and my household, must survive, and to do that, we all must remain flexible." He drew in a breath. "And that our Celtic religion is inclusive, our Lady and Lord are not jealous deities. In fact, they stated that you, as a Hopeful, will have a more difficult time of finding rituals matching ours; the Intersection of Hope is not so inclusive and has particular procedures that must be included."

"Oh." Then she remained silent for a while. "The Vines wish us to lead First Quarter Twinmoons," Avellana murmured. "Three nights from now, including tonight." She pursed her lips. "We will have to work hard on this." But her tone streamed determination with the lilt of challenge.

Vinni touched the nav console. "We can go directly to the Turquoise House, where Tiana lives, and request she begins work on our ritual."

"Oh. You have thought on this."

"Yes." He began to relax, let a side of his mouth quirk up. "We should actually keep Tiana on retainer."

That surprised a chuckle out of Avellana, and that he had done so warmed his blood clear through.

"Thank you, Muin."

He took her hand and raised it to his lips. "You are always welcome, my own."

Avellana sighed. "So, duty, as always, before pleasure. We will have ice cream *after* our meeting with the priestess."

"I promise."

I LOVE ice cream. Rhyz licked his chops.

"Glider, change nav to the Turquoise House."

I love the Turquoise House, too! Rhyz said mentally, adding a rolling purr.

"Because you like to fight Ratkiller," Avellana replied. "It is a tomcat territorial issue."

A standard male issue, Vinni thought, but didn't say so.

Avellana shifted in her seat. "We should not simply drop in on the priestess. That is not courteous."

Ratkiller won't care, Rhyz added.

"The priestess could be at GreatCircle Temple."

"I believe she is home." Vinni had confirmed the woman's schedule with the Turquoise House itself before he'd entered the Cathedral to see Avellana.

"Please scry her, Muin."

He did so with the new in-glider scry screen. Tiana Blackthorn-Moss looked out at him from her scry panel, the background behind her the leafy sunroom she considered her office.

"Greetyou, Vinni."

"Greetyou, Tiana." He got right to the point. "I—we, Avellana and I—wish to hire you. Or we wish to put you on a retainer."

She nodded. "I can guess why."

"The ritual you and your mother wrote during the building of the Intersection of Hope's Cathedral sparked Avellana's personal epiphany, but I remain a devotee of the Lady and Lord. We need ceremonies that are acceptable to us both."

"I rather thought so," Tiana replied.

"My Family thinks to pressure us into leading a ritual circle for First Quarter Twinmoons in a couple of days."

"Three nights from now, including tonight," Avellana corrected.

A light gleamed in Tiana's eyes. "I can help you with that."

Another woman who liked a challenge.

"We're on our way."

They pulled through the greeniron gates and into the front courtyard of the Turquoise House a few minutes later. The ride between them had been silent, but tender, their bond wide open on both sides.

FirstLevel Priestess Tiana Blackthorn-Moss met them at the door and gestured them in. "Welcome."

"Welcome, T'Vine and GreatMistrys Hazel," said the House itself.

"Greetyou," Avellana replied. "I am glad to finally make your acquaintance, Mugwort-Moss Residence. You are very pretty." She called the sentient House by its official name instead of its old nickname, the Turquoise House or TQ. "I particularly like your tinting and your glow."

"Thank you!" The House sounded thrilled.

"Good to be here again, TQ," Vinni said, then stepped forward and embraced his friend's wife. "And it's great to see you again, Tiana. Thank you for making time for us."

She waved a hand. "Easily done. I'm pleased you came." She cleared her throat. "As a priestess of the Lady and Lord, I would like to speak to Vinni alone first, Avellana."

"All right," Avellana said.

Where's Ratkiller? Rhyz offered the priestess a grin.

Tiana Blackthorn-Moss sighed. "In the back grassyard, I believe."

The tom trotted to the cross-corridor and took a right. Which let Vinni know Rhyz often visited this place.

"I will remind Rhyz to behave himself," Avellana said, and followed after her cat.

Vinni wondered why she thought her Fam would listen to her.

"I'll do the same," Tiana said, and Vinni felt a ripple in the atmosphere that the priestess spoke privately and telepathically to her own Fam—Felonerb Ratkiller, even less likely to listen to his FamWoman when it came to fighting.

Avellana called, "Please let me know when you wish me to join you."

He got the idea that she wanted to spend more time outside on this beautiful day.

Of course, Tiana said mentally to both him and Avellana, then led Vinni to a small four-person seating area in her office. Vinni welcomed the sound of the burbling fountain. Soothing.

He sat first, on a twoseat where Avellana could join him, and the priestess took an opposite club chair.

"I can give you a simple ritual celebrating First Quarter Twinmoons that will please both you and Avellana, and be easy for your Family to follow, before you leave." She smiled. "I have one that my own Family has often used and my mother approved."

"Thank you. I want nothing my Family can argue about, but we also *must* have ceremonies that do not violate any Hopeful principles. Avellana is a new convert and I don't want to cause her grief with those who are her spiritual guides in her religion."

"I understand." She looked at him, and her tone became contemplative. "You might consider that the Chief Ministers of the Intersection of Hope are realistic enough to bend some of their rules for you, a FirstFamily GreatLord and your HeartMate."

Vinni blinked. "What?"

"Which is why I wanted to speak with you alone and not you and Avellana."

Nine

*A*n *interesting notion, Tiana," Vinni said. His mind began to zoom* with options and alternatives.

"Yes, thus this meeting with you. I will also need to meet with her privately, so I can discover her understanding of her faith and ensure the rituals I create for you are comfortable for her. However, for this first instance, the ritual I did for my Family will work."

"Thank you." He paused. "So the ministers might not be as strict with her and us as I'd thought."

Tiana raised her eyebrows. "You're a very wealthy GreatLord with a great deal of power. More than that, you have a significant amount of a vital Flair. They will not want to alienate you."

He grunted. "They'll want to keep on my good side."

She inclined her head. "As any person with sense would like to keep on the good side of any FirstFamily Lord or Lady."

"I can see that, now."

"So we have more flexibility with the Chief Ministers, and I'm thinking that Avellana will accept some . . . alternatives that are not as strict as what the founding Hopeful members intended. Their religion has, after all, been on this planet for over four centuries, with members living side by side with those who worship our Divine Couple."

He should have figured this all out before.

"And," Tiana pointed out, "Avellana didn't grow up in the Hopeful religion. She probably doesn't *feel* all the minor nuances of their belief system. She's attended our rituals all of her life. Been the focus of them, too, I believe."

"Yes."

"So a bending of ours and a slight divergence from the ceremonies of hers should feel acceptable to her, not disrespectful, and"—Tiana grinned—"as a part of my service to you, I will submit my rituals to the Chief Ministers for approval, and I will defend any minor deviation. That way you and Avellana can be seen as being above any conflict."

"Excellent!" Vinni smiled back at her. "We'll both compromise," he said. "Which is what HighPriest T'Sandalwood and HighPriestess D'Sandalwood told me when we deliberated about this." His smile faded. "But my Family is going to be more rigid. I believe that is now my—and Avellana's—major consideration."

Tiana nodded. "Ensuring your Family accepts the rituals is a consideration of all of us: me, the HighPriest and Priestess, the Chief Ministers. We don't want to put any pressure on this situation that will cause a Family to fragment."

"No." He studied the priestess. She appeared *whole*, completely at peace with herself and able to project that serenity to others. He could only envy her that inner acceptance. Not only that, but she seemed also completely unafraid of what he might see in her future, and being around such people was a relief. No flinching, false smiles, and fleeing him.

"I'm glad you understand the parameters of our problem and can take charge of it."

She nodded. "But if either you or Avellana has an issue with my work, you must let me know so we can all adjust."

"Yes."

"Shall I call her back in?" Tiana asked. "Though our Fams have remained courteous to each other under her supervision, I'm sure a 'friendly' testing of who-is-best will happen within a couple of minutes after she leaves."

"Ah." He sent a telepathic broadcast. *I will remind you, Rhyz, that when we leave TQ we will go to obtain ice cream . . . unless you need an animal Healer. Then ice cream will have to wait.*

After a quick laugh, Tiana chimed in. *Ice cream sounds good to me, too, and I would share some with you, Felonerb.*

Not need ice cream, Felonerb shot back, but Vinni caught the tinge of a lie in the Fam's words.

Then Vinni commented aloud, "I do want you to understand that Avellana is my priority. If there is an item in a ritual that would be comfortable for Avellana but not my Family, we will ensure that Avellana is pleased."

"I understand." Tiana paused, appearing thoughtful. "I believe I can create three rituals that should be acceptable to all parties in the next week. As for now"—she translocated a piece of papyrus that held a short ritual—"'The Childlike Self as Embodied by the Divine Masculine and Divine Feminine Sung to the First Quarter Moons.'"

He scanned it, simple words everyone knew in a pattern everyone knew, songs his Family knew. His solo spoke of love for the Lady and Lord; Avellana sang to "free her childlike self" and referred to herself as that. Maybe some of his Family might have a problem with that, but it would be seen as being extremely picky by most. He let out a breath. "This is good."

"Thank you," Tiana said.

And he felt grateful that of her birth Family, the Mugworts, Tiana's father had been the Celtic believer and her mother the adherent to the Hopeful religion. It matched Vinni's and Avellana's situation and made this demand from his Family simpler to fulfill.

Avellana walked in, holding a dusty and leaf-bedewed Rhyz. He lay in her arms stomach up and purring outrageously. One look told Vinni the cat had succumbed to good catnip.

Rhyz opened one eye. *Greetyou, Vinni, greetyou, Priestess.* He yawned. *Do not put me anywhere near the fountain—*

"Where even one drop of water might fall on him," Vinni ended for the now-sleeping cat.

"This particular batch of catnip made him drowsy instead of hyperactive," Avellana stated, frowning a little as she placed him on the twoseat beside Vinni. Not an optimal spot for the Fam, in Vinni's opinion, but he said nothing.

"Felonerb must have shared." Tiana smiled.

The Turquoise House spoke. "I directed the Fams to a new feed chute and gave them some special catnip."

TQ had drugged the Fams into insensibility.

"How's Felonerb?" Vinni asked.

Tiana laughed and tapped her temple. "Sleeping the sleep of a happy cat. Thank you, Residence. A warrior denied his battle. Good thing Hazel Residence is too far away for him to want to go tonight."

"I do not think that Felonerb knows how to teleport to D'Hazel Residence." Avellana rubbed her Fam's belly, and he snuffled and rolled to his side. "And Rhyz and I have not been back so long that he is bored with the hunting on the Hazel estate and would wish to return here and test his mettle against Felonerb."

Vinni held out the sheet of papyrus. "Here's an already-written ritual for First Quarter Twinmoons. Check it out."

"I think it should be acceptable for you, Avellana," Tiana said smoothly. "But I do need to learn the style and wording that you prefer, so you might want to meet with me privately."

Avellana nodded. "All right, but I loved the ritual you made that we all took part in when we raised the shieldspells for the Intersection of Hope Cathedral." Her gaze went to the window that looked out the side of the house. "I must admit that of the few rituals I've attended at the Cathedral, some appealed to me more than others." She sent Vinni a glance and he felt her irritation at him upsurge. He'd cut her off from the Cathedral outside Druida City and its ceremonies. While he regretted it, and knew his time of keeping her safe outside the city was over, he didn't think he would have changed his behavior in the past.

"I like the rituals that Chief Minister Custos makes the best, and in such order I prefer Younger, Elderstone, and Chief Minister Fore-

man. That is to say, I like Chief Minister Foreman's rituals the least."
She paused. "But Chief Minister Younger is no longer Younger as of
today."

Tiana perked up. "No?"

"No, the Chief Ministers have appointed Tena Basil to the role of
the Younger, who represents the childlike self. She passed all the tests
and trials and has shown herself to be a superior person, perhaps a
prodigy." A note of satisfaction infused Avellana's voice.

"Fascinating."

"Since it is official, I can tell you of the appointment. The next
ritual at the Cathedral will be her investiture."

"Ah." Tiana made a wiping gesture. "Setting the gossip of the
spiritual community of Druida City aside, please peruse the ritual,
and see how it suits. As I told Vinni, I can craft three larger rituals
fairly quickly before you and I meet, which will make the process go
smoother. If necessary, we can modify them. As we work together,
I'll learn what resonates the most with you."

Avellana's face lit. "That sounds wonderful." She reached over
Rhyz and took Vinni's hand, and he thanked the Lady and Lord for
that natural gesture. Avellana said, "And you already know the es-
sential Celtic Divine Couple concepts that your HighPriest and High-
Priestess will allow, and will make allowances for the Vine Family.
My future Family."

"I will try to make the change in your rituals as painless as possible for the Vine Family. Start putting in a new prayer or song, let
them become accustomed to it, then add in another feature."

"Very good!"

"I can also take turns with the rituals that have little sexual content between the Lady and Lord, in asking one of my elder female
relatives in turn to participate as Lady to my Lord," Vinni added.

"Perhaps," Tiana said, then added in her diplomatic priestess
voice, "We will consider that. And, depending on how hidebound
and traditional your Family is, some may like the variation of rituals." A smile ghosted around her mouth. "And the Hopefuls have a
holiday near Yule that includes gift giving, so the children of the

Family will be pleased, since we do our big gift giving about a month and a half before, at Samhain New Year's."

"That is correct!" Avellana blinked. "The children will have two gift-giving holidays!"

Vinni snorted. "Not sure about that."

"I think it's a wonderful idea."

"The Hazels are a smaller Family than the Vines."

"Yes." Avellana frowned. "This seems to be a preliminary testing of my—our—ability to lead the Vine Family in a spiritual manner, but it will not be the last. Eleven nights from now, including tonight, is Holly Twinmoons." The bond between them reflected her concentration. "I don't know that I want to emphasize Holly moons, warrior moons. But moonslight . . . journeying and growing by moonslight . . . that might be something. We could consider."

"A journey. Hmm. Maybe we can take the Family to the Great Labyrinth, and we could all walk . . ." He shook his head. "No, we'd be better off staying in the Family grove and celebrating in a ritual circle there. The Family will be watching us."

"Of course." But she slanted Tiana a glance. "We will need to modify the circle to a square in some rituals."

"Yes, but not, perhaps, the four great seasonal ones."

"No." But Avellana's tone was hesitant.

He touched her chin. "We need to be absolutely in agreement and present a united front to our—the Vine Family."

Her lips pressed together, and she sent him a quick mental thought. *We must wed soon!*

He replied telepathically, *We will discuss that again later!*

Within two and a half months! she shot back.

Vinni squeezed Avellana's hand and changed the subject. "Tiana, as I mentioned before, we can consider keeping you on a retainer to create all our rituals in the future."

A grin lit up Tiana's face, and her brows went up and down. "That is very flattering and gratifying, that I will have a good income from you."

"I think so," Vinni murmured. "I thought about a sliding scale."

He flicked the papyrus Avellana read with a finger. "For something already done, and a minor ritual such as First Quarter Twinmoons, the fee should be smaller than a ritual you create especially for us. Perhaps a flat fee." He named a figure and Tiana blinked.

"Agreed."

"I will pay, too. This should not come only from Vinni and his personal gilt. I have my NobleGilt given to me for my holo painting by the Councils, gilt I inherited from my FatherDam, and my own gilt and personal investments."

"Investments?" Vinni asked.

She sniffed and didn't look at him. What investments? He got the distinct idea that she hadn't listened to her mother or her sister, who handled the Hazel Family investments. Had she gone to Laev T'Hawthorn, the financial wizard? Vinni knew she hadn't consulted *him*. He found his shoulders stiffening and relaxed them.

The priestess waved a hand. "You decide that between you."

"But that you show your work to the Chief Ministers and let them vet it is a great boon for us," Avellana said.

"Yes, the base figure I had in mind should be significantly higher than I originally planned." He named a figure. "Or we can do a monthly stipend."

"I like the monthly income." And Tiana quoted a different amount of gilt.

He eyed her, wondering if he should haggle.

We can afford to be generous, Avellana sent him.

Vinni thought that whatever gilt problems Tiana Mugwort Blackthorn-Moss might have had before, her best friend was Heart-Mate to Laev T'Hawthorn and he'd have helped Tiana and her husband, Antenn Blackthorn-Moss, with investment advice.

Avellana's comment continued to niggle at him.

And, no, Vinni would not negotiate with Tiana. Chuckling in response, he said, "Then we're agreed."

"When would be good for us to meet privately, Priestess?" Avellana asked.

The priestess handed Avellana a small crate of vizes. "Why don't you review these and tell me which rituals you like the best, and which part of each ceremony you prefer."

An analytical task for Avellana, one she'd focus on, excel at, and that would smooth her ruffled feelings about bending her will to his Family's desires. She nodded, glanced at Vinni, and handed the viz crate to him, picking up a still-pretty-limp Rhyz. "Thank you, Priestess Mugwort Blackthorn-Moss."

And Vinni hadn't heard Tiana called by all her surnames in . . . ever, not since the formal announcement in their wedding ceremony.

Tiana stood and inclined her head. "You're very welcome, Great-Mistrys Hazel, and please call me Tiana. I hope we can be friends." She smiled warmly at Avellana.

Avellana considered that, then nodded. "I would like to have you as a friend, Tiana. Please call me Avellana. I do not have many friends. I only had a few before I began spending so much time outside Druida City, and now I am unsure how many yet remain my friends."

The atmosphere around him wavered and Vinni got a little jolt as he understood that Avellana spoke to Tiana mentally. His curiosity itched, but he couldn't press right now; neither of the women would tell him what they spoke about. Something female and friendly.

It was rude to speak telepathically to another in a group, but he and Avellana had just done so, too. Ha. He'd led Avellana astray into bad habits.

When she went away, she tended to be more formal. Now he had her back, he could loosen her up more. Maybe.

"And now, ice cream," he said lightly, offering his elbow to Avellana.

Ice cream, murmured Rhyz, opening one eye. *I will sleep until we reach the treat place. Ice cream is good, but catnip is BETTER, and I had very good catnip.*

Avellana whispered a short anti-grav spell on her Fam. He lay easily in the circle of her left arm, and she linked her right arm with Vinni.

Good.

"Thank you for your welcome, Tiana. Thank you for your accommodation, Mugwort-Moss Residence."

"I am pleased to have hosted you," the Residence said.

At that moment Felonerb swaggered in, a very scruffy and scarred gray and brown brindled cat. *Ice cream for US, too!*

Tiana laughed. "Vinni, please show yourself and Avellana out. Merry meet." She gave Vinni the beginning words of Noble farewell.

"And merry part," Vinni and Avellana said together.

"And merry meet again," Tiana ended, then turned to a no-time that must contain ice cream.

Vinni led Avellana out of TQ and back to his glider. "I have a little no-time in this vehicle; perhaps I should stock it with ice cream."

Avellana gasped as she lifted the door. "Truly, a no-time?"

"Yes."

"How wonderful!" Her pretty smile and warm gaze made him feel like the best man in the world. She tucked a sleeping Rhyz onto the Fam shelf, pulled the safety webbing he'd earlier disdained over him, and took her own seat. Staring out the front window and not at Vinni, she said, "You do not have to treat me to an ice cream."

"Yes, I do. You've been very nice to me today."

"I have."

And to torture himself, he wanted to see Avellana lick an ice cream cone.

Ten

Vinni parked the glider a few spaces down from the cheerfully colorful front of The Merry Treat, Merry Tart shop.

Avellana loosened her webbing and turned to wiggle her fingers at Rhyz. He floated toward her as Vinni left the glider, circled around, and lifted her door open.

She sent her Fam out first on an invisible shelf of an anti-grav spell. Then she exited, looked furtively at the mostly empty sidewalk, and adjusted her clothing so each seam lay straight and her clothes looked perfect.

After that, she took Rhyz in her arms.

Both arms, which meant Vinni didn't get to hold her hand.

The café greeter, a plump woman with curly brown hair, looked askance at Avellana holding Rhyz. "I'm sorry," she said stiffly. "We do not allow Fams here."

"Oh," Avellana said blankly. She stepped aside and, as soon as Vinni was in, headed back out to the sidewalk and to his glider.

Meanwhile the woman bowed deeply to Vinni. "GreatLord T'Vine, it is very good to see you again!"

He nodded to her, then turned. "Thank you, but I can't stay; my HeartMate, GreatMistrys Hazel, and her Fam—"

The woman winced. "My deepest apologies, but we do not have anti-hair, anti-bacteria, and anti-allergy spells on our shop, so we cannot legally accept unbespelled Fams."

"Ah, of course." An idea had come to him and he wanted Avellana and Rhyz in here more than ever. So he said, "I assure you that both Avellana and I can spell such shields on the FamCat so no ill can come from him."

The woman flushed. "We have a . . . device given to us by the authorities to test such spells."

"That will be fine." He smiled; he'd come to crave the café's salty caramel ice cream. He'd heard this place served the best mint cocoa chip that Avellana loved. "We'll be right back."

"Thank you." The hostess-server sighed in relief.

Vinni strode back to his glider, where Rhyz now stood and shook himself out muttering about missing his ice cream treat.

"Merry Treat, Merry Tart doesn't have a spell to keep Fam-stuff to themselves, and allowing an unshieldspelled Fam in an eating establishment is against the law," he told a frowning Avellana.

"Oh. That is a concern." Her forehead wrinkled a little more. "It is not good if people become uncomfortable because of Rhyz. And not acceptable to break the law." She looked down the street with yearning, wet her lips. "You said they have the best mint with cocoa chips ice cream."

"I don't recall that."

"It was a year ago when you visited me in Toono Town." Glancing down at Rhyz, she said, "We can bring out some salty caramel ice cream for you."

Vinni stared at the cat. He'd had no idea Rhyz liked the same kind of ice cream as he did. Didn't want much of any similarity with the Fam.

Rhyz plopped down on his ass, lifted his nose, and twitched his whiskers. *I want to go into the pretty store.* He looked sly. *It is a more modern ice cream store and shop than we have been in since the last time we came to Druida City.*

"I know," Avellana said wistfully. "All right. I will put a shield-spell on you."

"And I," Vinni said.

Avellana pokered up. "I am capable."

Rhyz licked his paw. *She IS. She spells Me so all the time.* He paused. *Has Flora been in that fun place?*

"Flora doesn't like ice cream."

At this point a couple of lower Nobles advanced, appearing amused at the trio of them, until they recognized Vinni, then they scuttled by, heads down. They didn't want to meet his eyes, see if *he* saw any flash of their futures.

When he turned his attention back to Rhyz, every hair of the cat sparkled, coated with anti-everything. But the Fam had obstructed Vinni, so it was his turn to torment the cat. With a negligent wave of his hand, he sent a full-covering shieldspell over the Fam, suppressing a smile at Rhyz's squeak as the Flair lifted him from his paws and coated them, too.

"There, that's done." He held out his hand to Avellana and she put her fingers in it.

Too many spells itch! Rhyz grouched.

Vinni smiled, knowing what Avellana would say next.

"Better too many than not enough." She walked with him toward the ice cream shop, leaving Rhyz behind.

The cat sped through Vinni's legs, trying to trip him, but he merely hesitated one step.

After they entered the shop and the hostess had checked Rhyz's shieldspell, Vinni led Avellana to a table in the far corner, slightly away from others and only able to seat two. Rhyz tucked himself under the table, still grumbling at the itchiness of the spell.

While Vinni and Rhyz waited for their dishes, and Avellana her cone, Vinni said, "You protect Rhyz."

"Yes, of course."

"You wouldn't come into here where you thought they discriminated against him and might hurt his feelings."

"That is right. He is my companion and is with me. I do not leave him behind."

Not quite the point Vinni wanted to make.

"But if the woman had been mean to Rhyz, you would have defended him."

"Yes."

"And if she tried to hurt him, perhaps poison him with a sweet like the criminal did with Marin Holly, you'd have protected him."

Avellana's eyes narrowed. "Yes."

I can defend and protect myself! Rhyz growled.

"As can I." Vinni took Avellana's hands across the table, cradling them in his fingers. "But it is good to know I can count on you to protect and defend."

Her brows rose and she tilted her head. "You would let me fight for you."

Again, not the concept he wanted, but he'd work with it. "Yes. You love me."

"I do."

"And you'd fight for me, defend and protect me."

Her chin set, and then she said, "No, Muin, I am never going away again. Give up on that concept."

At that moment the server delivered the ice cream, bending down to slide a fancy scalloped pink bowl under the table to Rhyz.

Avellana sent her a brilliant smile as she accepted a large cone of thin, crispy sweet crepe wrapped around mint cocoa chip ice cream. "Thank you! Everyone says your ice cream is the best." She glanced around. "And your shop and café are so pretty."

"Thank *you*."

The women beamed at each other, and then the server left. Avellana murmured a spell to keep her ice cream from dripping on hands and clothes, then dove in. She concentrated on her ice cream, and Vinni concentrated on Avellana—and ignored the slurping and grunting noises coming from under the table.

Yes, he enjoyed watching Avellana swirl her tongue around an ice cream cone. Naturally his mind had gone to sex, and when they could have it again.

Through their bond, he felt a persistent underlying annoyance at him. Despite the morning they'd spent together, she would not welcome him in sex dreams this night.

So, maybe, he'd have to plan another in-person loving. Perhaps better now when her annoyance at him continued to seethe like a bottom layer of lava; she wouldn't be tempted to HeartBond with him. He could trust her to not do that. Despite the fact that she loved him and wanted to wed with him.

Yes, he needed to make love with her, telepathically or physically. And he yet hoped that their bond was such that she'd survive if he died—and that was deceiving himself according to her.

He wondered if he exasperated her enough, she would leave the city.

No.

And he persisted in thinking how to manipulate her, protect her from the shadowy dangers he yet sensed.

He was in a bad way.

*A*vellana *had eaten three-quarters of her ice cream and wonderful* crispy cone—and thank the four spirits she'd *finally* returned to the city that *had* treat shops and mint cocoa chip ice cream—when her perscry, personal scry pebble, squawked. She had a call. Another loud cry of a tropical bird that screeched through the shop.

Muin appeared startled.

With her free hand she reached into her sleeve pocket and touched the top of the glass teardrop to silence the squawk, staring hungrily at her cone. She *would* savor that minty, sweet crunch to the end.

Hurry. One nice, big bite. Perhaps unmannerly, but she did not care at this very moment. She wanted the flavors coating her tongue before she launched into more talking and talking. Another confrontation that arrived a little sooner than anticipated.

"Avellana?" her lover asked, curiosity in his eyes. Always curious, that one. A reason, she thought, his Flair suited him. He would be interested to see what came in the future, calculate how he could angle the wheel of fortune and turn the fate to the best outcome for his client.

But he no longer prized his Flair. She thought that dangerous. So she would help him with it.

Then a series of musical notes came from her pocket.

"My mother," she said, as if he would not recognize the wispy chimes of the ancient tune for the Head of GreatHouse Hazel. She munched another large bite and gazed down at the portion left. Of course she would like to tilt her head and bite off the tip of the cone and slurp it, but that would be vulgar in public. Yet she wanted every droplet. Another cone, even.

Especially when her perscry lilted the waltz her father loved. She met Muin's eyes. "My father."

She murmured an anti-grav spell to hold the cone in the air, then tapped a finger to keep the ice cream from melting and the cone from going soggy and, worse, dripping on her favorite, royal-blue damask tunic and trous. Muin had given the garments to her, but she did not think he recalled.

Never too many protection spells.

That idea teased at her mind. She had heard that the new D'Yew specialized in protection spells. Perhaps Avellana could purchase one and ease Muin's mind. Though currently she had allocated most of her gilt into one primary investment—thus the scrys.

And Father's tune rippled once more.

Reaching into her pocket, she retrieved the pebble, tapping it so it showed herself and Muin and that they ate. "We will be right there," she stated, then offered the glass drop to Muin. He and her parents usually thought the same way.

Muin put his spoon down and took the small scrystone. His smile as he watched her gobble her ice cream faded into his serious expression. He inclined his head. "We should be there within a half sept-hour."

"Good!" The loud word came from Avellana's older sister, Coll, not on the screen.

"We will await you and Avellana in the ResidenceDen," her father said, and signed off.

"Avellana?" Muin asked, rolling her pebble between his fingers.

During the short interchange between her Family and Muin, she had finished off her ice cream, simply eating, *not* savoring, a shame.

"You do not have to attend the discussion, Muin," she said, letting him drop her pebble into her hand.

His face hardened further, but when he spoke, it was in a mild tone. "Another altercation, Avellana?"

"Probably," she said. The previous percentage of ninety had now reached ninety-nine point ninety-nine percent.

"So you've had, ah, rocky discussions with me, the Chief Ministers, and now your Family."

She narrowed her eyes; he sounded nearly amused.

"I sense that you anticipated this meeting, too."

She had known her Family would learn of her activities and would disapprove and there would be yet another dispute and argument in her life. "I am making my life the way I want it to be."

A flash of sadness came into his eyes, reflected in the feelings flowing through their bond. No doubt he could also sense her lingering irritation at him and his past high-handed ways . . . just as, now that she understood his motivation better, she could sense his nightmarish fear for her and his bedrock need to protect her.

"Naturally, you can come with me to the meeting with my Family." Her own voice sounded colorless.

He put his hand over hers. "You think I always side with your Family. And it's true when I feel danger for you and want you out of the city."

"Like now, but I am not leaving, Muin."

"I can see that, since I have watched you set about making changes in areas that bother you." He squeezed her hand and his fingers felt warm on hers. Perhaps she had made the cone too cold.

Or perhaps being nervous chilled her hands.

"But other than agreeing with your Family about protecting you from danger, I'm on your side."

She studied him. He believed what he said. "We shall see," she replied.

He played with her fingers. He had not often done so, but she found she liked such contact.

"So, your sister called you first?" he asked.

"Yes, Coll, HazelHeir."

His mouth quirked. "You use squawking as her scry tone?"

Avellana dabbed her mouth with her softleaf, folded it, and placed it on the table, ignoring the two women who passed her with lovely ice cream cones. She had learned not to regret treats she couldn't have. "Coll is an excellent nag. She sounds like that, sometimes. I think she got it from a bird in one of the Botanical Garden conservatories. She loves me, but she wants me to be . . . a normal person, I suppose. I am not a normal person." She had never been normal, not after she had tried to fly when so young, and then when she had exercised her main Flair, which shocked everyone and made them afraid.

"No, you aren't normal. You're extraordinary and beautiful."

"She is handling many of the finances of the Hazels now. She likes doing that task more than Mother does."

His fingers stilled on hers. "What have you done?"

"What I believed I needed to do. I have my own gilt, you know, Muin. Not as much as you or the rest of my Family, but it is mine to do with as I please." She rolled her Fam, who had fallen asleep, from her feet to the floor, then she rose.

We're going now? asked Rhyz telepathically, waking up.

Yes, Muin answered mentally.

The cat nosed out the pink bowl and Avellana translocated it to the table, licked clean. She tapped it, setting a noisy cleansing spell on the dish, including sanitation. So all could see that she took care of her Fam and the public.

With a swagger and a purr, Rhyz came out from under the table, then leapt onto the invisible shelf-spell she had attached to her shoulder.

He sniffed at Muin. *She loves Me the most because I have stayed with her ALWAYS.*

Muin flinched, but Avellana did not contradict her Fam.

Throwing his softleaf on the table, Muin stood. "What have you done with your gilt?"

Yes, she had known she could catch his interest with that statement, but she yet lifted her chin to match his gaze. "What I wanted to. What I believe in." Letting a breath sift from her lips, she said, "You should go on to your Family, give them the new ritual we will use for First Quarter Twinmoons, three nights hence. I can handle this situation with my Family."

"I'm sure you can. However, I'll accompany you."

"All right." She put her hands in her opposite sleeves and concentrated on a pretty gliding walk to the door, aware people watched them, and these customers recognized Muin, and now knew her identity.

Muin nodded to the proprietors, a female couple, authorizing payment or putting the bill on his account. Which indicated they knew him well here, odd since she was the one who preferred sweets. She inclined her head toward them and sent a mental *Thank you.* They returned smiles to her.

He opened the door for her, and she moved through it and up the walk to his glider. Rhyz shot ahead.

Muin took her hand in his warm, strong, and callused-from-fighter-training one. "Remember, we're in this together."

She said mildly, "That would be a change."

And she knew she'd hurt him, but she continued to deal with the deep hurt he had inflicted on her, too. She wondered if he would follow through on his words with actions, or if he would side with her Family, as usual.

She had hated those years without Muin. Worse was when she got to come back to Druida City only to be banished again after a month or two. She set her chin. Never again. She would live or die with him.

Eleven

At home, a reenergized Rhyz hopped from the glider and left her. He wanted to patrol his territory and continue to check out the new scents he had found since they had returned, and prove to all the other cats he was alpha.

Muin walked beside her, shortening his stride slightly to match hers.

Once inside the small, chunky castle that did not reflect the Hazels' innate and delicate Flair of intuition, but did show a slight rigidity of the scientific mind—also a gift of their Flair—Avellana's steps slowed.

She began a breathing pattern a Hopeful minister had taught her, a rhythm that, like the religion, suited her better than what she had learned as a child.

Muin stopped at the elegantly carved large door of the Residence-Den, where they both sensed her Family lay in wait for her. He bowed and opened the door and she sailed through with chin high and a gliding gait. It was more important than ever that she demonstrate her status and adulthood.

The three who made up her inner Family circle sat there, her sister narrowed-eyed and stiff, upright in a wing chair . . . perhaps a little too aware of her new position as head of the Druida City Botanical Gardens.

Her parents sat together on a plush green-and-brown-patterned twoseat, holding hands. They watched her with gentle fondness. Her mother held the title D'Hazel, and her father, a marine biologist studying tide pools, had married into the Family. They were, as they had always been, a unit. The lines on their faces made them look older than their true ages, and Celtans experienced extremely long lives. Avellana thought that she and her situation had etched many of those lines.

Their intimate Family relationship did not match what she had seen and heard reported about other Families. Not even First-Families.

When Coll noticed Avellana studying her, she smoothed her expression from a scowl. "Avellana, we are concerned."

Of course they were. They always were.

Muin touched the small of her back and she moved toward the chair he indicated, an equally fat-cushioned, but low-backed, one in deep green. When she sat, he surprised her by staying beside her instead of walking over to lean against the fireplace surround, his usual spot. He curved his fingers around her shoulder. And not as if he kept her down in her chair.

No, in support. She *felt* the bedrock of love from him. But then he thought this conversation would be about finances and gilt, and not veer off into her safety.

All conversations derailed into her safety, and she already knew at what point that would occur. So she had prepared.

Still, she loved the tenderness flowing in their bond . . . and glanced up. He, too, had more lines in his face in comparison to his friends the same age. But not all because of her, many due to his own unique nature and Flair.

Coll coughed gently. "Thank you for coming to speak to us as we requested."

"Of course," Avellana said. She could not avoid her Family after all, not even in a small castle. The Hazels had never been prolific.

At one time there had been three children per couple, but that had not happened in a few generations despite the fact that her parents, the first in four generations, had found and wed their HeartMates.

Everyone said that marrying HeartMates *could* bring more blessings to the Family than simply love between the couple—it would increase the happiness of the Family, perhaps bring more children, definitely increase psi power, Flair.

She wondered if anyone had done a realistic study on that.

Her sister coughed again. "Avellana," she said in a too-gentle voice that ruffled Avellana's nerves.

"Please don't patronize me, Coll," Avellana replied.

The stiffness came back to Coll's spine, and her parents' smiles faded. Muin squeezed Avellana's shoulder.

She parted her lips to let out a small sigh that only Muin could hear. "My apologies. I suppose you wish to discuss finances."

Coll coughed. "I think you should review your decision-making for a certain investment."

"It is too late. I have already invested in that project," Avellana pointed out. She had depleted her trust account by three-quarters.

A sweet smile from Coll. "I'm sure that when we speak to the principal, he will refund your gilt."

While Avellana struggled with her irritation, her father murmured, "Yes, finances first."

Which meant she would have to talk about her spiritual conversion again. In the fog of suppressed feelings that flowed to her through the usual filtered bonds with her Family, she sensed they continued to worry about her religion.

She sat up straight. "I know that all of you think you have indulged me." Oh, yes, she saw reaction to those words, had to *think* to keep her fingers from pleating her silkeen tunic. "That you believe that my change from the major religion our ancestors followed, and which you celebrate, is a minor phase. Perhaps you feel that I changed my belief system since I knew that providing the Cathedral with art from my Flair, my psi power, would fulfill me."

Clearing her throat, she gave a small nod. "That is true. The three-dimensional holographic murals demand much from me in the way of creativity, and I know my art will last centuries. Working in the Cathedral also provides me with social interaction with other artists who embellish the Cathedral, and the Hopeful Chief Ministers who direct my work, which I prize." She wondered whether to point out that many people along her journey did not treat her as lesser, then decided not to bring up that issue.

Instead, she met the eyes of her parents, then her sister. She sent a little pulse of affection to Muin as he squeezed her shoulder in complete and solid support. "But I will not return to the religion of our forebears. I belong to the Intersection of Hope now. I am a Hopeful." She tried out a smile and thought it appeared strained.

She counted seconds as she drew in her breath. "And I am tired of your attitude that you are indulging me like a child." Once more she stared at her Family, each in turn; only her sister dropped her eyes when Avellana held their glances. Avellana did not envy Coll being the heir, shouldering the whole responsibility of the Family, though when Avellana wed Muin she would be a FirstFamily GreatLady, too. But she would share that with Muin and *he* was the holder of the Vine title. She would be consort to Muin and nearly equal to her sister.

If she took a stand now.

"I am done with your overprotectiveness." Their *smothering* of her. "I *will* be considered an adult, an equal member of this Family." She looked up to meet Muin's hazel eyes and noted the expression he believed to be impassive but sensed an edge of worry. "I *will* be an equal partner." She pushed words from a dry throat, across a dry tongue, and through dry lips. "Or I will walk away from all of you, stop the marriage negotiations."

Her parents and sister appeared stunned and confused.

Muin's eyes took on color, and she felt his swirling emotions. Perhaps he fought off a vision, perhaps he allowed one, perhaps he simply let his emotions sweep through him and rule. She had never quite dented that last innermost private shield of his. And she had never thought she knew all of him. Unlike him with her.

Angling her chin, she said, "And that statement both winds me back to the topic of gilt and gives me a basis for the . . . comment"—she would not call it an ultimatum—"I just made. Speaking of partners, I am a partner with Antenn Blackthorn-Moss in the new village of Multiplicity, to be built outside the walls of Druida City over the next couple of weeks. I will have my own home there, already designed specifically for me. I will establish my own life there until Muin and I marry within the two and a half months in which I asked all of you to finish the negotiations and ritual wedding planning. And if that does not occur, I will continue to live in Multiplicity until it does."

Her sister squawked, and that almost made Avellana smile.

"That is . . . that is . . . a very *odd* notion of community." Coll waved her hands. "That a new place should be built when there are plenty of buildings . . . houses . . . that our forefathers made here in Druida City that stand empty!"

"I am odd," Avellana replied coolly. "I like the idea of a variety of people." She smiled at her fixed-stare parents. "Rather like the original starships themselves. A mixture of artisans and Flair-tech scientists and—"

"Different social classes in one neighborhood!" The words exploded from D'Hazel.

"I will not be the only member of a FirstFamily living there. Vensis Betony-Blackthorn will also be moving to the community."

Her parents shared a look but said nothing. Vensis Betony-Blackthorn had not been born into a FirstFamily but was a distant cuz adopted by FirstFamily GrandLord Straif T'Blackthorn. As if blood mattered more than love! As far as Avellana was concerned, it did not, and she did not think most people of Celta thought that. The planet her ancestors had claimed as their own remained tough for their descendants to thrive on. Celtans had founded only a few towns. And now she would help establish another.

Only the FirstFamilies, descendants of those who had funded the starships and had passed the long voyage in cryonics tubes, believed a true bloodline mattered much.

"Antenn Blackthorn-Moss didn't tell me you'd bought a home in

the community," Muin said, his tone grating. Muin considered Antenn a good friend.

Avellana's jaw clenched, then she loosened it to speak. She also set
her feet flat on the floor so she could send heated annoyance into the
rug and the stone beneath. She had known this confrontation would
not be easy. She must persevere. "I did not just buy a house. I am his
silent partner in this endeavor." Now Muin appeared startled. "Silent
partner means he does not reveal that I am a principal in this venture
to others." She gave a little sniff. "And I think I will make an acceptable return on the gilt I invested."

Again she scanned the faces of her most beloved people in the
world. "Perhaps not as much as any of you would do, but this is a
dear project to me."

Her sister, taller than Avellana and more voluptuous, but with the
same brown hair and blue eyes, frowned. A very take-charge woman,
Avellana's sister. She had been successful in her botanical Flair and
had created a variation of a weathershield spell for crops that had
added to the Family fortune. She was an equally fortunate investor.
That contributed to her consequence and her self confidence.

Looking pained, Avellana's father glanced around the room.
"Leaving here, your childhood home, just after you returned."

"Just after I have returned against Muin's wishes. He would
rather I remain on Mona Island," she pointed out. She had told her
Family days ago of her conflict with Muin and why they had argued,
and informed her parents and sister that they could not budge her
from Druida City, either.

"Unlike the rest of you," she added quietly, "I have learned to live
outside the Residence, alone with only my FamCat in an apartment
or cottage. I am accustomed to that, and I have spent much time
thinking of a home of my own, and when I heard of Multiplicity, I
contacted Antenn Blackthorn-Moss." She smiled as she recalled the
meetings. "I liked the idea of the village, and he drew up a house for
me *right then* and it felt like it would suit."

A cool wash of hurt came from Muin. She steeled her heart.
Too bad.

"What of the security?" he asked.

"There will be layered security shieldspells, some provided by Lahsin Holly herself." That had been an upgrade with the gilt she had provided.

"I haven't been to the area." Muin's voice remained gritty, and his fingers lay gentle on her shoulder . . . because he wanted to tighten them, she got from their bond. Then he removed his hand and crossed to the wall near the windows and leaned there with negligent grace. His eyes had cooled back to his regular light blue-gray. He had become proficient in suppressing his emotions, his Flair gift, that showed in his changing eye color, once everyone in their social circles understood what such a fluctuation meant. Then people would escape his presence as soon as possible.

"But there isn't a wall around the village, is there?"

"The shieldspells will be the best."

A muscle flexed in his jaw, then he said, "I like the idea of physical barriers, too."

"I understand, Muin, since you wished me to remain on an island. But I assure you, the community is small. We will soon know all those who live there."

He grunted. "Before then there will be a lot of people milling around." He flicked fingers in a wave. "Construction people, those having their homes built like you, visitors with too much time on their hands around to gawk at another Antenn Blackthorn-Moss project." Muin's expression turned dark, his features set.

"Prospective investors, people who will want Antenn to design houses for them and who will buy plots and shares in the community." She smiled and rubbed her hands. "We will make a lot of gilt."

And Muin's shoulders relaxed. His eyes warmed and lips curved. With her pleasure, she had teased him from his current concern.

Her sister returned to the first topic. "When I reviewed our accounts, I found that you withdrew three-quarters of your inheritance." She leaned forward, nearly thrumming with tension. With a huffed breath, she smoothed her scowl away, but the scolding words hung in the air.

"Yes," Avellana said.

"I—we don't approve. And why would you do that!" Coll demanded.

"It is my gilt." Avellana kept her own tones even. She had prepared. "And I have told you why." She wet her lips. "I have become accustomed to new experiences and now I want to live with like-minded people."

"Antenn isn't living there, in Multiplicity. He wouldn't leave Druida City or the Turquoise House," Muin stated.

Avellana raised her brows. "Of course not, these homes will be brand-new and not intelligent."

Her parents shared a look, then said, "We love having you here at home."

They stared at Coll and she rubbed her eyes, slumped a little in her chair.

Watching them, Avellana did what she had wanted for a long time, had decided she would never suppress again. She drew in a huge breath, then simply blasted all her love for her Family to them. Her parents and Coll rocked back in their seats, her mother gasping, then bursting into tears.

Muin pushed away from the wall and came to her, his expression tender. He paused by the arm of her chair as if he would seat himself there, then went behind her and laid his hands on her shoulders.

Pride and wonder and approval washed from him to her.

Her father hugged her mother tight, and then they both turned damp gazes to her. "We love you very much, too. Must you leave?" begged her mother.

"I believe it is for the best. I wish to popularize Multiplicity to others." She smiled. "And I know those who have already purchased plots and had homes designed. I will fit in with them." None of them would ever think her *lesser*. "My house is scheduled to be built in two days, on the day of First Quarter Twinmoons." She looked up at Muin with a smile. "But I assure you I will be fine to officiate that ceremony with you for the Vines in the evening."

After a considering gaze, her mother said, "No, Avellana."

She raised her chin. "About moving? I am an adult." Avellana straightened her spine. "Here in Druida City, in our circles, everyone knows my background and believes I am fragile." Again she sent a glance around at each of the others. "At other places where I have lived, that is not so, like on Mona Island. I like being taken as I am; I have become used to that, and I do not wish to be treated like the child everyone hovered around."

Coll raised her brows and allowed herself a tongue-click. "We are all defined by our past, and what people who've watched us grow up believe of us."

D'Hazel smiled with approval at her older daughter. "That's right."

Coll continued, "So you don't intend to mingle in our social circles? That will be hard on Vinni, and the Vines."

Avellana clenched her lips together at the denigrating comment, then loosened her jaw and gave a little laugh. "I have irritated my sister, Coll, and she snapped at me."

Everyone stared.

"Instead of Coll treating me like a baby." Avellana nodded. "This is a very good first step. Thank you all."

Her parents seemed to blink in unison. Coll laughed, too, and flung up her hand in a swordfighter's gesture of touché that made Avellana eye her narrowly. Coll had a HeartMate, a lower Noble, who fenced well. She and he would wed after all the FirstFamily negotiations with the Vines finished and Muin and Avellana had married.

"We love you, too, Avellana. It is just that we have always feared losing you," her mother said.

She could only repeat her stance. "I want to be a real part of this Family, an equal, not a delicate person who must be shielded."

"By leaving us?" Coll whispered with a rasp. Her eyes appeared a little watery.

"I think it might be best if I visited often, but lived elsewhere."

A long silence fell on the group, despite the stares aimed at her, the fluctuating emotions of her Family throbbing through all their links. Closing her eyes with the effort, Avellana met the wariness and worry with love and smoothed out the Familial bonds. Linked with her, Muin helped.

"Oh, very well," her mother said.

Nearly overtalking that agreement, Coll spoke abruptly. "You will take some special stones from D'Hazel Residence for your house, so it can become intelligent in the future." A rush of feelings came from Coll that Avellana had no time to sort through, except that she sensed her sister had made some sort of basic internal adjustment with regard to herself. To accept her as an adult.

Triumph! But she kept her expression mild.

"Yes, I would like to take a HeartStone from D'Hazel's store if it can be spared," Avellana said. She waited, but the Residence did not comment, either aloud or telepathically to her individually or them as a Family.

"You should also take any furniture you might want from our storage rooms," her mother said reluctantly.

Her father shot Muin a look.

"Since I haven't seen the project, and I am concerned with your—" Muin stopped and coughed. "Let's go inspect the area. You can show me your plot." Muin patted her shoulders.

Avellana slanted him a look. "Do you not have other appointments?"

He shrugged. "They can wait."

At that moment, his calendar sphere appeared, flashing, pinging, and stating, "Saille T'Willow wishes to have an immediate and short appointment for you as Oracle for his daughter. The last waves of her First Passage are subsiding and the Willows understand this is an optimum time for prophecy."

"You *must* go, Muin," Avellana urged. "This is time sensitive."

His jaw flexed, and then he dipped his head. "Yes, I must go." He swept the room with a glance and bowed to her Family. "Please excuse me."

"Of course," everyone echoed.

"I'm 'porting to Saille's. Do you want me to leave my glider for your convenience if you wish to visit your land tract?"

"No, thank you. I told Antenn I would wait until tomorrow to view it again, since he is currently handling the preliminary tasks before the construction."

"Right, I'll order it back home." He brushed a kiss on her lips, so fast she could barely taste him. She *did* experience a spiraling excitement from him at the thought of the Willows. "Muin?"

But he just lifted his hand in farewell and vanished.

Twelve

❤

Vinni arrived at the teleportation pad in Saille T'Willow's Residence-Den and found the man pacing the room. "Thank the Lady and Lord you're here. The swells of Alba's Passage are fading, and you insisted—"

"I know," Vinni said. "Show me."

Saille snorted, grabbed Vinni, and the next thing he knew he landed in the gloom of a darkened chamber filled with the herbal incense to aid Passage. A girl, small for her age of seven, whimpered on her bedsponge, her hand held by her mother, Dufleur Thyme D'Willow.

Dufleur sighed, then smiled. "Is it true?" she asked.

The boldly colored vision surrounded Vinni, flickered through several images of the girl as girl, young woman, wife of a young man, then faded. He wiped a hand across his eyes until they cleared to normal and nodded. "Yes. She will be my son's HeartMate."

If he and Avellana weathered the next few months, but he masked all his concerns.

"And her Flair?"

Vinni scrutinized the child on the bedsponge before him and narrowed his eyes. This time he shook his head. "I don't know. Still in flux perhaps, though definitely strong enough to be FirstFamily Flair."

Alba opened her eyes. "Maybe I can fly."

A shudder ran through all three of them as they remembered Avellana.

"People don't fly. We teleport from one space to another," Dufleur told her.

Alba's mouth turned mulish.

Her mother continued, "We are descended from spacefarers who used dimensional portals. And *we* use dimensional portals to teleport. It's easier for us than moving our mass, takes less energy and strength."

"Perhaps you should take her to be Tested for Flair," Vinni said.

Dufleur, mistress of time, shrank a little in her chair, coughed, and said, "I don't think she'll follow in my footsteps, with my power."

Saille let out a breath, clapped Vinni on the shoulder. "Good, that's good." Saille's gaze cut away from meeting Vinni's eyes, and a false smile brightened his face. "You and, ah, Avellana, don't need any more, ah, strong and peculiar Flair, like shaping timestreams."

And Vinni wondered what Saille knew of Avellana's secret.

"Peculiar!" Dufleur protested.

Saille crossed to her and kissed her temple. "You must admit that manipulating time is not the same as . . . uh . . . smothering fire or raising stones to construct buildings or moving earth . . ."

Dufleur sniffed. "My Flair for time is an interdimensional Flair. More like yours—"

"My matchmaking Flair is a very *human* Flair, human relations," Saille interjected.

"—or Vinni's," Dufleur continued, "or Avellana's."

"Avellana's Flair is for three-dimensional holo painting," Vinni emphasized.

"Of course," Saille said.

"Of course," Dufleur repeated.

But Saille seemed to take on an uneasy air as if he went along with the lie about Avellana's primary Flair. He moved defensively to block his HeartMate and daughter from view.

"I'll be going now," Vinni said quietly.

"I'll pay—"

"Not necessary. This was my personal request of you and I am glad for any help I can provide." Vinni summoned a natural smile. He flicked a hand. "Our children will marry, after all, and we will be in-laws. Later."

"Later," Saille and Dufleur replied.

Once again Vinni 'ported quickly away from a scene, this time arriving in the corner of his bedroom . . . shuddering with reaction to the powerful but brief vision and teleporting twice within a septhour. He staggered to his favorite chair and sank into it.

His head pounded, an unusual occurrence, but he understood that his blood rushed through his body as a reaction to simple fear. Or not-so-simple terror.

He and the Hazels had tried so hard to keep Avellana's secret from getting out, but Saille and Dufleur knew.

Probably all the FirstFamily Lords and Ladies knew.

No wonder his premonitions of danger to Avellana had been so prevalent. Hard for two people to keep a secret, let alone, Lady and Lord, at least twenty five, not counting those members of his own Family who knew what happened seventeen years ago.

If every FirstFamily Lord and Lady knew, then that knowledge might be—most probably was—communicated to the remaining hidden fanatics of the Traditionalist Stance movement.

Extremists who had no compunction in killing *children* whom they believed "too different" than themselves.

He hunched over and put his head in his hands.

Soft patterings came to his ears as Flora left her basket and hopped over to him, onto his chair, and squeezed under his arms to comfort him. His loved Fam.

The Fam who had died.

And whom Avellana had brought back to life.

That was her primary Flair. Bringing the dead back to life. And Flora had been very newly dead, her spirit still accessible to Avellana. *And* bringing one small young housefluff back to life had drained every member—animal, Fam, and person—in a FirstFamily Residence, including affecting the intelligent house.

No, no one wanted Avellana to practice her primary Flair.

But every person who lost a beloved would want Avellana to bring back their newly dead.

Avellana's psi power stood against the true beliefs of their basic religion—that each soul cycled on the Wheel of Stars between lives. That people had more than one life. Reincarnation.

Vinni recalled that the man who'd attempted to murder Avellana had called her an abomination due to her Flair.

He had absolutely no doubt that other fanatics out there believed the same and wanted to kill his HeartMate.

She'd been threatened most of her life, and he'd shielded her, sent her away as much as he could, hurting himself and their relationship, and now had forged a woman who wanted to live on her own in a new community.

What he had done had succeeded in the short term but failed in the long term and complicated his life.

His mind flailed around, trying to find options, solutions, how to protect her here in the city where the fanatics were based.

I will help. Flora snuggled close.

And you are not alone in this, Muin. Why do you never ask ME to help? Avellana chimed in telepathically. *I can feel your distress.*

He straightened to lean back in his seat as he marshaled his thoughts but held Flora.

A sigh whispered from Avellana along their link. *You do not trust me.* Her mental note took on an all-too-familiar irritated note. *You do not trust me to recognize danger, to avoid it, to defend myself.* Now a sucked breath Vinni could *nearly* hear instead of the sigh.

I find the fact that you do not trust me in those matters highly offensive.

Oh, Vinni replied telepathically.

You must learn this, Muin, to trust me. She sent the sound of her own heart pulsing, slowly, along with an ache. *It hurts that you do not trust me and have never trusted me to take care of myself.*

He stopped the words that he didn't think she could take care of herself, she was fragile, to be protected.

But that standard emotion of his must have pulsed through their bond, because her stormy emotions slapped at him. *I am STRONG, Muin.* A pause, and he sensed her controlling her ire. When the red of anger faded, she continued. *A WOMAN who has been through what I have, my injury as a child, my Passages, the deadly threats, is STRONG. A woman who never practices any aspect of her primary Flair, and evolves her secondary Flair to take the place of that Flair, who keeps huge secrets, is strong. And being sent away again and again means I had to deal with new people and new places on a regular basis, develop my own resources, does it not?* Now she sounded bitter.

Avellana, he soothed.

A mental sniff. *Are you saying you trust me? Do not lie to me with words, Muin. Do. Not.*

I am sorry I sent you away, that I damaged you and US.

That is surprising, she returned mildly, as if he'd finally chilled her annoyance.

What? he questioned.

That you admit guilt in this matter. You hardly ever do. I have noticed that men do not like saying such things and rarely apologize. He felt a pulse of pure curiosity from her.

I don't like being at odds with you, arguing with you, and it's time I admit my faults so we can put this behind us.

Now a hint of suspicion laced her feelings, as if she thought he might be manipulating her.

No, Avellana, I am sincere in my apologies. You said we should be partners in this—

In this as in all other areas, dear Muin.

He let his own sigh out. Between the two of them, Flora and Avellana . . . well, and with his own brain tired and emotions wrung, he'd come to accept that their old style of relationship had vanished. The one where he'd been in control.

Now they must move on as partners, whatever shape that might take.

We are in this together. Promise me, Muin.

Yes. Together.

A wave of sweet tenderness and relief poured from her to him.

It has only taken you a few days, Avellana said admiringly. *You are such a very satisfactory HeartMate, Muin.*

Thank you, Avellana. He kept his tone humble.

You will no doubt continue to try to manipulate me, she said.

And you will continue to be direct, he replied.

That seems to work the best for us. But we ARE partners, Muin. A hesitation. *Like the Lady and Lord.*

Yes, he agreed.

And you will walk my journey with me from now on? she asked.

Yes, absolutely.

I have been lonely.

Me, too.

I will walk with you and Vinni, too! The astringently smug cat tones of Rhyz jumped into the tender moment.

And I will hop along on all our journey together, said Flora, wiggling in approval.

Hmmm, came a considering purr from Avellana's FamCat. *Perhaps I will saunter as I accompany you on your journey. Or traipse. I like traipsing. Sometimes I might prowl. Or zoom—*

Skitter, Vinni said drily. *I have known you to skitter.*

I do NOT, Rhyz insisted.

Perhaps it is because he spent so much time with the FamFoxes when we lived in Gael City, Avellana stated. *He moves somewhat like a fox at times.*

Not true.

Yes, it is, she replied.

And Vinni's insides tightened with aching hurt at the byplay between the three of them, and the memories that Avellana and Rhyz shared that he was not part of. Images flashed between those two that he barely caught. Years of time together. Without him.

He had protected his love, but he finally realized the extremely high cost.

He spent some time in the afternoon speaking with various members of his Family about the First Quarter Twinmoons ritual that he and Avellana would officiate as Lady and Lord. Several appeared surprised that she had agreed. He blandly handed out the ceremony he'd received from Tiana Blackthorn-Moss, informing his relatives that since Avellana would be taking part in their rituals permanently, as with the addition of any spouse, songs and prayers would be updated and changed.

Though he kept his smile to himself, he enjoyed the fact that he had stymied the ill-wishers in his Family who'd tried to confound him, and had done his own smooth manipulation. Yes, he'd ensure that his relatives supported him and Avellana, or the ones who didn't would be gently encouraged to live on one of the other Vine estates.

So he believed that he and Avellana had handled the first bout thrown at them as the leading couple of the Family. Her status would soon be cemented when they performed the ritual.

Another error on his part, not including her in the Family gatherings during the last few years.

In the couple of septhours before dinner, Vinni approved his portion of the marriage and alliance contracts with the Hazels—and hoped Avellana never learned that he had been one of the people stalling the agreements.

He took a turn in the top-story sunroom of one of the secondary towers attached to his personal square tower—opening the petals of the glass dome to the air, leaving only the shieldspell against any bugs that would make it up three stories.

From here he could easily see the walls of Druida City a half kilometer away, and, to the southeast, the spires of the Intersection of Hope Cathedral. He walked the circumference of the room, checking on the plants and small two-person pool in one quadrant, and then, still restless, he took the stairs to his workroom below his bedroom suite.

There he crossed to his workbench and studied the three wind chimes projects he'd laid out on the long counter—one of glass, one of large metal tubes in the ancient gamelan tonal scale, and the final one of small solid rods of polished precious metals—gold, silver, copper, and glisten that he'd gotten from T'Ash. Vinni eyed the various sizes of the cylinders and wondered if they would work at all for sound.

And, of course, all three projects were for Avellana—mostly ideas for her suite here in his tower.

He spent nearly an hour on the tube chimes, hanging them in the proper order he wished. Knowing the winds that flowed around his castle well, he set the size of the disk so they would sound as often as she preferred. He knew her tastes well, too.

All too soon he had to dress for dinner.

*V*inni, dear," said *G'Aunt Bifrona at the dinner table, and a frisson of* warning slithered down his spine.

Now she wanted something *else* from him and brought it up so those of the Family at dinner would know and pester him about it. Her smile showed her opening volley, and he gritted his teeth for missing the signs of upcoming battle. Biding her damn time.

"We're worried for you," Bifrona stated, unconsciously echoing what the Hazels had said to Avellana.

That was Family for you. Always worried. And who was *we*? A different *we* than those he'd spoken with that afternoon, whom he'd thought he'd had in line?

He lowered his lashes to scan the people—mostly women—at his table, made notes of those who appeared uncomfortable. So Bifrona had known how to catch him off guard and when to bring up whatever other matter concerned her. But he knew his Family equally well and could see whom she'd already convinced of her plan. Three-quarters of the table.

The head chef, a massive man, actually came out into the dining room and placed a large platter of cheeses and fruit on the table. He paused beside Bifrona and set a large hand on her shoulder in support, glowered at Vinni, then without another word marched back into the kitchen. Vinni drank some wine, then set the crystal glass deliberately on the linen tablecloth. As he glanced down at his nearly bare plate, he understood that he should have known this wouldn't be a standard dinner; he'd savored all his favorite foods, and the springreen wine appeared only on special occasions.

Family. Always meddling.

His stomach had always been touchy, so he murmured a couplet under his breath to settle it. Then he met Bifrona's gaze with a bland smile. "I'm sorry you and others are worried on my behalf. What bothers you that we did not discuss this afternoon?" He sent a glance around the table, chided softly, "I would have thought you would have brought up such a matter when we talked earlier?"

She gave a tiny cough. "It is not only *my* concern."

Vinni shrugged, waved his hand for her to continue, irritating her enough that a line formed between her brows.

Then he picked up the wineglass to use as a prop, focusing his gaze on that and concentrating more on the familial link between himself and others rather than being distracted by any expressions. He sensed that some relatives not at the table knew of Bifrona's plans, such as several of the guards.

No one had bothered to warn him, and that caused an inner ripple of wariness. He needed allies in the Family, particularly now.

"We believe that you should consult with GreatLord Saille T'Willow, the matchmaker, to confirm your, ah, longtime feeling that GreatMistrys Avellana Hazel is truly your HeartMate after all."

The words blindsided him. He flinched as anger jolted through him. He could feel his eyes changing as the words triggered a prophetic vision. Looking down the table, he saw ripples of colorful

auras outlining his relatives. Many shrank back in their chairs as if
trying to hide. For most of them he saw symbols instead of faces. Cuz
Nava would be taking that job at the excavation site of the starship
Lugh's Spear. Several others showed marks of marriage or Heart-
Bonding. He'd been wrong earlier, half and half split between "his"
camp and Bifrona's. He smiled.

People gasped.

Blinking, he looked at Bifrona, flinched again when he saw a silver wheel—the Wheel of Stars, that place where a soul went after
death. This time he narrowed his eyes to focus on how strong a probability this was, if he had any chance of diverting death. Ninety percent that she would perish before the end of the year. Nothing he
could do to save her without commandeering massive resources of
the Family. He sent a telepathic command to the Residence. *Schedule
an appointment with a FirstLevel Healer for Bifrona as soon as possible.*

Yes, T'Vine, the Residence responded.

"Muin Vine, how dare you practice your Flair at this table with
your relatives," Bifrona snapped.

He grabbed the wine and gulped it down. He'd promised them all
as a boy that he'd do his best to block any prophetic vision for a Family member. He'd let this foretelling just roll over him. Granted, stopping an impromptu revelation cost him. From the strength of this
one, if he'd choked it off, he'd have blacked out.

Eighty percent of the time, he could control his Flair, and always
during a paid session in his specially designed office.

He breathed deeply and held up a hand to one of the relatives who
liked serving dinner—a cuz who enjoyed eating first in the less stuffy
environment of the kitchen—and the woman filled his glass to nearly
the rim. Waves of surprise and sympathy for him emanated from her.

After another sip, Vinni forced his Flair-vision away and answered more gently than he might have. He loved his Family, and
Bifrona, and would cherish her while he could.

"My deepest apologies that I could not control my Flair." He inclined his head toward her. "Your surprising words triggered my psi

power before I could stop it." He paused, made sure he met no one's eyes. He thought of what else came through on the fringes of his Flair. Someone had used Bifrona for his or her purposes? A secondary scheme to remove Avellana from the Family? Or had the First Quarter Twinmoons Ritual plot been a distraction?

Lady and Lord knew he and Avellana had concentrated on that today.

"I agree to see Saille T'Willow," he said into the throbbing silence. "I will be glad to make an appointment so he can evaluate my relationship with Avellana. As you may or may not know, I saw him today, as an Oracle for his daughter's First Passage." He paused. "It would have been better had you previously told me of this matter." Again he reached for the wine and smiled when his fingers showed no trembling. "In fact, I'd like to schedule several consultations with members of this Family and Saille T'Willow." He met another cuz's gaze. "Lacinia, you're seriously interested in one of the Clovers, yes? We'll set up a meeting with your gallant and you and T'Willow."

"Oh, yes, Vinni!" Lacinia gushed. Her wavering allegiance shifted firmly to him.

He raised his voice so it would echo throughout the huge castle and courtyards and gardens his ancestors had built. "Anyone else who wants a session with Saille T'Willow, please let Bifrona know." He tilted his head at her, keeping his expression mild. "Have you already made an appointment for me?"

She flushed red, nodded.

"And have you discussed this with the Hazels?"

Her lips thinned before she answered stiffly, "Yes, with Great-Lady D'Hazel herself."

"Odd that she didn't mention that to me when I saw her earlier. And I'm sure she has said nothing to Avellana, either." He stared at Bifrona until she dropped her gaze. "All right." His glance skimmed the twelve people at the table; many of this particular group believed as Bifrona did—but that didn't include the one who'd put her up to this. "I will speak to Avellana to ensure she'll accept the consultation." He'd tell her it would be quick and easy and, most of all, interesting. Like him, she enjoyed Saille as a friend. Vinni twitched his lips up in an unamused smile at Bifrona. "Avellana doesn't care for people making decisions for her. I trust you and D'Hazel examined Avellana's schedule and placed the appointment in an acceptable time slot?"

"Yes, of course," Bifrona said. She lied.

Breaking with tradition to let the lady of the household end dinner, Vinni stood and caught up his glass. No reason not to remind them all that he held the title and the most Flair in the Family. "I'll contact Saille for the details, why don't I?" Also good to remind everyone that Saille T'Willow had signed an alliance with Vinni, and Vinni only, no generational alliance.

"Good evening, my Family." Vinni bowed to them all, left the room, and immediately teleported to his suite.

"Residence?"

"I am here, T'Vine," replied a cheerful female voice patterned on a long-ago ancestress. "A FirstLevel Healer will examine Bifrona tomorrow during her midmorning break."

All right, so he'd just done the same to his G'Aunt as she had to him. Good enough. "My calendar sphere did not inform me of an upcoming consultation with Saille T'Willow regarding my Heart-Mate, Avellana Hazel."

"No, T'Vine, that appointment was just confirmed this morning."

"From now on I want all pending appointments made by anyone else in the Family and including me to be immediately forwarded to me, as I believed was standard procedure."

"Ah," the Residence replied. "GreatMistrys Bifrona changed the reporting process two eightdays ago."

"That is not acceptable. My schedule, especially concerning my business appointments, must be strictly under my control and only under my control. We charge a great deal for my time and my Flair, and I continually deal with extremely nervous clients. I must know my calendar exactly so I can prepare for each event."

"I hear you, T'Vine. It will be done."

"Thank you, Residence." He walked from his sitting room to his bedroom. "Clothes off and to cleanser," he ordered. By the time he reached the huge generational bed, he was naked. He plucked his favorite robe from a clothes stand and donned it, flopped down on the bed with his perscry in his hand. Flora hopped from her blanket at the foot of the bed onto his chest.

Greetyou, FamMan.

He answered aloud, "Greetyou, Flora."

I love you, FamMan.

"I love you, too, Flora."

Always.

"Yes, always." He stroked her ears with one hand, soothing for both of them, and contemplated his perscry. He felt a need not only to speak to Avellana but to reveal even more of himself.

He'd been careful with her at the Hazels', had temporarily forgotten that she'd said she wanted to learn him better. "No watching your words with me all the time. No hiding things from me." He could at least give this a shot.

Thirteen

*S*taring at the underside of the cream-colored canopy embroidered with a mandala supposed to rest his mind and Flair, he reviewed his HeartMate's schedule. Avellana should be "reposing and digesting" dinner now, probably sitting in the herb garden behind D'Hazel Residence.

"Scry Avellana." He flicked the glass perscry pebble with his thumb.

Her face formed in a life-sized holographic image projected from the personal scry marble, looking down at him. And he got a quick kick in his heart, as usual.

"I am here, Muin."

"Greetyou, Avellana."

"Greetyou." She paused. "What is wrong?"

"I was ambushed at dinner."

Her eyes widened. "By your Family?"

"That's right."

"Again?"

"Yes."

"That is not good, Muin." Her lips pursed and she gave him a straight look. "I should have returned sooner so they would know me better and we would not be having these problems."

"They would always have caused us problems."

"Is that also why you sent me away?" Her eyes narrowed. "You needed to concentrate on your career and have an easier time with your Family?"

He ran his fingers through his hair. "I don't know, Avellana, and I'm weary of discussing that."

"But we do have an issue with the Vines."

"Yes."

"I accept that. Now what?"

"They want us to meet with Saille T'Willow."

Her forehead crinkled. "Why?"

"To make sure we're still HeartMates," he said bluntly, and heard his own voice get rougher and deeper with annoyance that he'd thought he'd gotten over.

"We have always been HeartMates. All of our lives. This does not make sense." They stared at each other. "You think those of your Family who oppose our marriage instigated this," she finally said.

"Yes, I do. And, in fact, they have made the appointment for us. I don't know when it is."

"You are angry."

"Yes."

Her chin jutted. "I do not like this, either."

"They told me that they'd placed it on your schedule."

She hissed, then ordered, "Calendar sphere!" at the same time he called up his own holographic silver ball.

"Show me the appointment with Saille T'Willow." Again they spoke in unison.

Avellana's sphere projected the written date and time; Vinni's showed the rectangle of the day and the blocked time.

She gasped. "It is a two-septhour consultation on Mor morning, the first day of the week! When everyone is at their first meetings, and our standard weekly special time together with no one else around! How dare they!"

Vinni chuckled, and her blazing gaze fixed on him.

"I'm thinking that Saille knows that and finessed the consultation for that time."

Her scowl turned to a considering frown. "You do?"

"Yes."

"It says my mother will accompany me. No. Calendar sphere, remove D'Hazel from the meeting with GreatLord Saille T'Willow, confirm with T'Willow and GreatLord Muin T'Vine, and forward my refusal to D'Hazel's calendar sphere."

Avellana's sphere blinked.

"Confirmed that D'Hazel will not attend," said Vinni. He smiled at his HeartMate. "Your mother will be unhappy."

"It is our life and our love."

"Yes."

She grumbled under her breath.

"What?" asked Vinni.

"It will cost a lot of gilt. And your time and Saille's time and my time will be wasted."

"No," he said softly. "Not wasted. We'll see how HeartMate consulting works. That will be good to know in the future."

"You think so?"

"Yes." He smiled sharply. "As for the gilt payment—Residence, take the payment for Saille T'Willow's consultation out of the general Household fund."

Avellana stilled. "That is the account your G'Aunt Bifrona handles. Such a disbursement will deplete the fund."

"She *will* have to watch her budget closely for the next month. Something she has not had to do for years."

"Bifrona has been courteous to me."

"She's a courteous woman. She's also the person who requested we be Lord and Lady at the Holly First Quarter Twinmoons Ritual the night after next *and* requested that we see Saille T'Willow professionally. Let her understand that there will be consequences of her decisions to meddle in our affairs."

"Are they her decisions?" Avellana asked softly.

He smiled approvingly at his love. "I think she is being prodded by someone else—or maneuvered, something I wouldn't have expected of a lady of her experience, so perhaps she has a blind spot with regard to one of my relatives. Or perhaps she hasn't realized how she is being used. Making the cost of her decisions or this blind spot very evident may have her rethinking her position in the Family, and doubting whoever might be dropping poisonous ideas in her ear."

Avellana nodded. "A very good strategy, Muin."

"Thank you." He paused.

Her calendar sphere pinged back into existence, and a soft female voice he'd never heard said, *Time to practice your craft.*

Pure joy shone on Avellana's face, and she stood and brushed off her tunic.

"Avellana?"

"I am spending the night in the Hazel HouseHeart! Alone! And doing a mural there for my Family!"

"Wonderful," he said, but the vague notion that he'd be able to invade her dreams and make telepathic love with her faded. "You deserve this time with D'Hazel HouseHeart."

She nodded. "Yes, I do. And everyone in the Family has contributed a piece of art to the HouseHeart except me." She twirled. "Now that will change. I have thought a great deal about this piece." Her smile turned sly and she dipped her head. She wouldn't reveal Family secrets, even to him. "Good night, Muin."

It wouldn't be as good a night as he'd hoped. "Good night, beloved."

Her face softened further, her eyes showing tenderness and yearning. Then she ended the call.

Vinni said aloud, "Residence, have three guards, including the Chief, meet me in the sparring salon in the guard tower." That way others could watch his form—and he'd had the best fighter training gilt could buy and could usually take down ninety percent of his own force.

After changing into his sparring robe and trous, Vinni teleported to the wide square chamber that took up a whole floor of the guards' tower in the third gatehouse to the castle.

He noted that all but those on duty lounged around the room on the rolled-up mats against the stone walls. Frowning, he realized that his guards had slipped again into a gender ratio of seventy percent male, thirty percent female. He preferred a more balanced force.

At least one of the females wore the blackberry leaves of a Lieutenancy, one step down from the Chief. She stood intimately close to Vinni's old tutor, Arcto, and they flirted.

The Chief of Vine Guards, Duon, a big man and relative newcomer to the Family, shambled up to Vinni. He came from a cadet branch of the Vines who'd moved south to Gael City, the last of that line. His features seemed doughy, and he had a skewed nose, but appearances were deceiving. Vinni knew him to be a clever and rough fighter.

Occasionally Vinni could beat him.

For an instant, seeing the Family colors and uniform he wore, Vinni mourned the man who had betrayed him years ago. But that visceral reaction was washed away by continuing anger that someone he'd trusted had tried to kill Avellana. No, he couldn't forgive that, and now and then he checked on the guy who continued to slowly drink himself to death in the tough seaports along the Plano Strait.

After the incidents, Vinni had insisted on another Loyalty Ceremony, one slightly modified to include language that each Family member pledge loyalty to his HeartMate, before and after he and his lady HeartBonded.

And those vows had been a compromise—one he'd had to fight for. He hadn't been allowed to include Avellana's name. An unnamed HeartMate had satisfied some people doubtful of his thirteen-year-old feelings.

But Avellana remained his HeartMate from the first time he'd sensed her soon after her birth to now. Members of his household might still be wary of her, but soon she would be D'Vine.

And everyone in Druida City had recently seen what happened to people who broke their Loyalty Vows and Vows of Honor—a threefold punishment fell upon them in reaction. They suffered physically, mentally, and spiritually.

Duon stood before Vinni, jerked his head in a respectful nod. Then the Chief gestured to his two Lieutenants and said in a heavy and slow tone, "Like I said in my papyrus report earlier this week, T'Vine, I have replaced my previous First Lieut, Plicat, with Armen here."

Duon hadn't gone into the reason for that substitution in his terse report; he'd said if Vinni had wanted to talk to him about Plicat's demotion, Vinni should request Duon come to his office.

Vinni had decided to leave the decision unquestioned. He'd gotten the impression from the feelings he'd experienced from Duon a couple of days earlier that Plicat's behavior hadn't come up to the Chief's standards. Vinni thought the man might be too strict, but he would review the situation after it had settled. He certainly wouldn't say anything negative to Duon right now, in front of his people.

He looked around for Plicat.

"Guard duty, walking the east wall," Duon stated.

"Good to know," Vinni said mildly before turning to Armen. "Congratulations on becoming First Lieutenant."

"Thank you, T'Vine."

With a bow to the woman, Vinni said, "Glad to see you've been promoted, Fera." He glanced at the three of them, then widened his gaze to the rest of the guards. "Keep up the good work." He smiled and gave the trio a fighter's bow. "Let's spar!"

A few minutes later his Healer diminished his bruises in the Infirmary. On the whole, he'd been pleased with his own performance, and the exercise had certainly banished the edgy lust from his system. In his match with Fera, he'd worked up a sweat but had defeated her with no more than medium effort. He'd felt her determination to get better.

Armen had tried his hardest to take Vinni down, but he thought that was from pure fighter pride.

Duon had let Vinni bring their match to a draw, a politic thing to do.

Yet an odd feeling lodged between his shoulder blades, buzzed at the back of his mind. Someone—perhaps more than one person—

had watched him with repressed anger. Strong enough emotion that he'd felt it since he was the Head of the Household, and probably because he had the greatest Flair. He also thought that the person or persons did not realize he could sense their concealed ire. More than frustration or the need for more status in the Family that seemed to push Bifrona, edging on ill will.

Something to be aware of.

And as he thought of Bifrona, the chime sounded for the last meeting of the day with his relatives and "good nights" before they retired. He sighed. Formal, as always. That wouldn't change when Avellana came, either, since she preferred more formal manners than he. Because she understood people better when they acted in the social norms.

It would take him some time to loosen her up, and, with her, make the Family more casual, as the Lords and Ladies of his age group had done.

Fourteen

*A*vellana had finished her mural of a circle of ancestral Hazels hold-ing hands just after TransitionBell in the wee hours of the morning.

She had been wide awake then and very pleased with the holo-graphic painting since the HouseHeart had observed her creativity and gushed about the work.

Each GreatLord or GreatLady represented, as best as she knew, a personality of the Residence. Though the current Residence identity was male, as was the HouseHeart, other individuals were available if the GreatLord or GreatLady, or the Residence itself, felt the need for a change.

The Residence had been thrilled, too, and the odd back-and-forth talking between the HouseHeart and the Residence had given Avellana uncomfortable tingles in her head, so she had excused herself. She walked in the night-blooming flower garden for a while, and Rhyz joined her for some silent contemplation before she went up to her bed.

Happy with her contribution to her Residence and Family, she fell asleep quickly and sweetly.

A tinkling tune from her old-fashioned scry bowl chimed insis-tently, drawing her from a deep sleep. "Here," she mumbled auto-matically.

"This is Blackthorn-Moss; meet me at Lookout Ridge promontory above our village, transnow, for the dawn."

"Antenn?" she asked sleepily. Her business partner had insisted she call him that, and after three months of working with him, she had agreed. Naturally, she had offered her own given name to him at the same time.

"Want you to see the town layout 'afore we start work this morning and also to double-check your parcel."

"Oh." She sat up, rubbing her eyes. She did not know her new land well, and teleporting to an unknown area held great danger. "I do not think—"

"Come *on*, Avellana!" he growled.

She considered a few seconds, looked for Rhyz. Like always, he enjoyed being outside near dawn and dusk, prime hunting time for him.

Rhyz, she sent him. *Could you and I teleport to the rocky ledge overlooking our land? I know you have been there more often than I.*

Of course! She got the idea of a twitching tail. *Fun! Will we watch the construction today? Many building mages and much Flair!*

Her contribution had doubled the size of the community to fourteen unsold houses she and Antenn would construct, and her name had brought in ten other people to buy plots and build their own homes in various styles.

"Avellana!" the man called from her bowl. She glanced over but saw no holo projection. "I am going transnow." The turquoise light faded.

She hopped from bed, glancing out at the bands of sunrise brightening the window. No time for dressing in a nice formal robe, and she would not do a Whirlwind Spell when she might need all her Flair today for teleportation spells. So she slid into pantlettes, breastband, a loose knit tunic and trous, and old boots for this meeting. She would dress more formally later.

Here I am! Appearing at the end of her bed with a wide grin and twitching whiskers, Rhyz waited until she scooped him up.

He settled, then said, *I* can take you there! *I* know the ridge fine!

She shared her memories of the times that she had been on the ridge overlooking the landscape, not one of those instances at night or in the dawn. Then she went to the window to look out, saw a clear sky and the twinmoons one day from first quarter. Fixed the phase of them in her memory, merged it with Rhyz's vision.

On three, commanded Rhyz. One FamCat, two new house, THREE!

A couple of instants of white-gray-black images from Rhyz, then they alit, Avellana stumbling—thankfully away from the drop-off—and Rhyz jumping to her feet. He paced back and forth as they looked down below at the smooth land in a crescent of hills with a wide stream running through it. Her parcel bordered that stream, the Tarryall.

Behind her, she could hear the ocean no more than two kilometers distant. They would lay out a path from the town square to the beach. That would be done next week, after all the houses went up. Excitement pulsed through her.

She caught a whiff of an odd smell—not sea or land or greenery—thought she saw a blur from the corner of her eye, dark against the rose dawn sky. She frowned, turned. An arm rose, came down. Her head exploded with pain.

Muin! she cried out, heard Rhyz hiss, felt him launch himself against her body even as it fell onto unforgiving ground and she rolled toward the edge of the drop-off. Despair smothered her along with darkness.

Muin! Vinni woke to a shriek of fear and danger.

"Avellana!" he thundered. He searched for her, knew she lay unconscious somewhere.

Flinging himself from the bed, he stood, shaking. No prophetic dream last night. He'd thought she was safe in D'Hazel HouseHeart.

His windows showed as light rectangles. Dawn. He *would* teleport to her. Follow their link and hope. No time to waste.

He drew in a deep breath.

Wait! Flora cried. *Rhyz fights bad man! Talks to me. We link.* She shoved dark images into his brain. He caught the link, merged it with his own with the FamCat.

Fligger! Where the *hell* were they?

Ridge near new house, Flora said. *Pick me up. I have GOOD link with FamWoman. Our lives are twined together. Go on three. I will GUIDE!*

Sucking in his breath, he could only pray, and hope, and . . . use Rhyz's open mouth to push human words out, warn the assailant. Maybe. "I come to save my HeartMate."

And Flora 'ported them away and he sent her power and energy, and they landed hard and he danced away from the edge of a fliggering *cliff* and caught his foot on a bundle—Avellana—and he *yelled!* "I'll get you, fliggering—"

Rhyz screamed aloud, then mentally gloated, *I have man flesh under my claws.*

A black shadow against the brightening sky flung Rhyz, and Vinni jumped to catch the cat, fell, cushioned their landing with Flair, thankfully missing Avellana.

He rolled to his feet, arms still full of cat.

Flora had teleported to Avellana, whuffled a soothing patter, and stayed close against her.

Blood showed on Avellana's scalp, ran down her face, but Vinni *felt* the pump of her heart, the push of her lungs. Other good life signs. Not slipping into death. Not.

I am a hero! I saved FamWoman! Rhyz screeched mentally, then went limp in Vinni's hands. Fligger.

Moving fast, Vinni translocated his Fam to his shoulder, stuck Flora there with a spell. He crouched and began to slip his hands under Avellana's twisted body. Stopped. He did a full turn, memorizing the sky, the top of the ridge, the close bushes, the distant landscape.

With a jerk of his arm and a snapped couplet, he leveled a spot on the ground and put that in his mind's eye, soaking up all tactile sensations to project, particularly the quality of light.

An exercise that all who teleported learned and practiced. He took two paces away, then called telepathically, *FirstLevel Lark Holly, please teleport here at once!*

Vinni placed a Fam translocation amulet on Rhyz and activated it. He'd arrive in D'Ash's Animal Healing Office and trigger an alarm.

Two minutes later, not only Lark Holly but two SecondLevel Healers straightened Avellana out on the ground. Lark had already done a skull scan and mended a slight concussion. Lady and Lord knew, the Healers of Celta knew Avellana's head and skull and brain all too well.

Vinni stood still, draining nervous energy into the ground instead of pacing.

Looking up at him, Lark said in professionally soothing tones, "We will teleport her to Primary HealingHall, Noble Room One, on three."

They did so.

Before he could follow, Flora nipped his ear. *Do not want to go to FamMan Heal place.* She trembled. *Do not want!*

After her resurrection Flora had never wanted to go to any HealingHall, or even the Fam Healers. He always had those come to his Residence if she had a problem. Nor did she ever set paw in the Residence where she'd briefly died.

"Can you teleport home by yourself? It's nearly fifty kilometers home," he asked.

You have too much worry-energy. Give me. I will go to my basket and bed.

Pulling her from his shoulder, he looked into her sweet face. *Thank you,* he said, mentally, more intimately. *Thank you for helping me teleport here and save my Lady.*

She rubbed her head against his hand. *She my FamWoman, too. Fam animals 'port better than humans.*

"Yes." Fams had different teleportation capabilities than people; they could usually find and teleport to their people and not worry about landing inside a person or object.

And the pretty wheel is nice but she and you not ready. And bad mans got her!

Vinni shuddered. "All those things are true." Though he'd never asked Flora about when she'd died. Apparently she'd seen the Wheel of Stars that he and those of the Divine Couple believed in.

You must find bad mans.

"You think more than one attacked Avellana?" He itched to go to Avellana but must discover what Flora had sensed that he hadn't.

Rhyz will know better. He smells better. I hear better and heard one. But they are always more than one.

"I'm afraid so."

I go now.

So Vinni gave her the energy for her to teleport herself—he smiled that he had recognized his fragile Fam needed to do things for herself but it had taken recent lessons for him to accept that with Avellana—and teleported himself to the main pad of the HealingHall.

Striding into the chamber, he found Avellana dressed in a gown and the three working over her.

"Setting a continual mending spell into her skull," Lark said. She glanced at Vinni. "I've taken care of the minor injury to her brain, nothing to worry about there."

His breath whooshed out. "Thank the Lady and Lord."

"Yes." Lark stepped away from the bedsponge and a Healer took her place, Avellana's bruising fading under her hands.

Joining Vinni, Lark pulled him away to a small sitting area off to one side of the large room, matched his serious gaze. "Vinni, Avellana was attacked."

"I know."

"I have already contacted the guards. You'll have to speak with them."

"I don't know much. Heard her cry my name telepathically. Our Fams helped me 'port there."

"I have not notified her Family. I'm letting you do that," Lark said.

"Thank you." He rather dreaded telling the Hazels. He rubbed the back of his neck. This whole thing echoed back to the assaults on Avellana when they were children.

Looking at the timer on the wall, he let a breath flow out. The Hazels did not rise near dawn, and they, like him, would have thought Avellana safe in D'Hazel HouseHeart. With luck, she would be Healed and well and home in time for breakfast, and he and Avellana could present this as a past event.

Finally the Healers stepped away from Avellana's bedsponge, murmuring cleansing spells that whisked around the room and sanitized Vinni as well as everything else.

"She needs to rest, and should awaken in a few minutes," Lark Holly said.

"Naturally, I'll wait." He went to the comfortchair that would conform to his body, sat, and took Avellana's warm hand. Their bond widened until he knew she felt safe and loved and some of his own tension faded.

"Naturally, you'll wait." Lark's lips compressed, and Vinni knew that she'd be telling her HeartMate, the heir to another FirstFamily Noble title, of the attack on Avellana. So both news and rumors would run through the FirstFamilies before breakfast.

He and Avellana must plan to counter those.

With a nod at him, Lark left the room. The other two Healers bobbed curtsies to him, and followed her.

The guardsman I scried is consulting with the Captain of the Guards of Druida City, Lark sent to him telepathically, and Vinni let out a relieved breath. He wanted to get all the facts he could from Avellana first. And whenever the FirstFamilies were involved, a liaison from the highest level of the guards came to interact with them.

Always the best service for the FirstFamilies, just like being here in Noble Room One. Vinni acknowledged the privilege but remained thankful for it. Thankful, too, that his class had been reminded not too long ago that no one was above the law, not even members of the

FirstFamilies who believed their Flair and wealth and status entitled them to anything.

Or fanatics of the Noble class who thought that society should remain the same.

He glanced at Avellana, so beautiful. Not as fragile as he thought, but remaining a target for those zealots who considered her religion bad, thought her innate psi power made her defective or a freak or whatever other word they used because she was so different than anyone else.

Each generation, particularly among those who had great Flair and married to produce children with even more, gained in the strength of their psi power. Vinni had the recordsphere of his predecessor's oracular reading at his birth. She'd called him stronger in Flair than herself—the previous GreatLady D'Vine—by approximately four times, and was proud of that fact.

Furthermore, highly Flaired children—such as he and Avellana—had begun to develop standard skills earlier, such as teleporting. Avellana had been able to teleport at age seven.

Of course each generation seemed to evolve new abilities, such as Avellana's Flair for bringing back the dead.

Or the new GrandLady D'Yew's facility for personal shieldspell armor.

Personal armor.

A knot in his gut loosened.

Experimental and expensive, but he'd haul Avellana to D'Yew—

"Muin?" Avellana's fingers twitched in his, and her head turned toward him. "You are thinking very hard."

He dropped his head an instant as he lifted her fingers to his lips, to arrange his expression, but kissed her fingers fervently.

"Tell me what happened." His tone sounded only a little rough.

Avellana blinked. "I got a scry from Antenn to meet him at the ridge before the project started this morning." Her lips pressed together.

Antenn, get to Primary HealingHall Noble Room One NOW! Vinni roared to his friend.

Fifteen

Brows down, Avellana fretted the edge of her blanket with the hand Vinni didn't hold. "No." She paused. "I do not think so."

"What?" Vinni asked.

"What!" Antenn demanded as he flung open the door.

He stopped on the threshold, sucked in a breath, and stared at Avellana with goggling eyes. "Avellana." He surged forward. Vinni stepped in front of him and pushed him away.

"No." Avellana's voice came thin. "I do not think Antenn scried me." Her gaze went to Antenn. "I do not think he requested I meet him on Lookout Ridge above our prospective community."

Taking a step sideways so he could see Avellana, Antenn said, "No. I didn't. We'd agreed that the final walkthrough would be me and my subcontractors this morning at WorkBell. No investors, including you—especially you as we are keeping your partnership secret from the public. Some secondary roads will be constructed, nothing much to watch." He flicked a glance at Vinni. "WorkBell is well after dawn at this time of year. And the raising of the homes won't start until tomorrow morning. *Then* you can come, along with other homeowners."

"Yes." Avellana nodded. Her lips pursed. "I think I was the victim of a repetition spell. He did not call me 'Avellana.' He did not respond to my questions, he merely demanded I meet him on the ridge. Impatiently."

Anger licked through Vinni. "You tend to obey demands." He—and her Family—had taught her that.

"Yes. It will be different in the future." Avellana lifted her chin. "I determine more of my own actions now."

"I didn't scry her," Antenn snarled. He appeared fully dressed in professional architect clothes. Actually too nice for a raw site visit, Vinni thought, but Antenn knew all about the image he wanted to project, paid more attention to that than Vinni did. Something she and Antenn must have found they had in common.

"Hey, Vinni." Antenn held out his arm to grasp.

Vinni did. "Greetyou, Antenn."

"Why don't you give me details on what happened?" Antenn's gaze went back to Avellana. Stepping lightly, he moved to the other side of Avellana's bed.

With a spellword, she raised the bedsponge until she sat. "I received a scry that I thought came from you." She frowned. "The scrybowl water showed Turquoise, the color of your Residence."

Antenn touched her on her shoulder and, when she looked at him, said, "I will only call you on a perscry from now on." His smile showed strain. "I can't afford to lose my partner."

A shade in his tone made Vinni believe he spoke the truth. "If you need gilt—" He stopped, but knew the damage had been done.

Antenn's face hardened as he turned to Vinni. "No." Antenn drew himself to his full height, some centimeters less than Vinni, his shoulders straightened with pride. "If you could think for even an instant that I would harm Avellana—"

"Of course not." Vinni let his mouth twist. "I was frightened for Avellana. I do not act well when someone threatens Avellana." He met her eyes. "Not for years."

Antenn let out a gusty breath, one side of his mouth kicked up. "Yeah, I'm like that with Tiana."

His calendar sphere appeared and pinged. "I need to head out to my first meeting for a walk around on the community land, double-check the roads before we lay them today, do a final survey before we construct tomorrow."

"Can *you* teleport there?" Vinni asked.

"Yeah, I can. I've had my eye on that property since I finished the Cathedral, and been there nearly every day for the last two years."

"Can anyone else teleport there?" Vinni asked.

"I don't know. Maybe some of the surveyors, some folk from my office. More likely the assailant came by glider or stridebeast. I put in the main gliderway from the road from Druida City to Gael City right away, as soon as I decided on the plan and bought the land." He patted Avellana's shoulder again. "When I sent the rumor out about founding a new town and asked for investors or people interested in buying plots, this lady was the first one to get back to me—about a year ago. We really didn't get rolling with the plans of each lot and selling the parcels and designing the houses until four months ago."

Vinni said slowly, "It's someone who knows Avellana is a silent partner in this venture." He glanced at his love.

She frowned. "I do not think I told anyone. Rhyz knew, of course, but I did not tell my Family or you."

"I know that," Vinni said with awful politeness.

"The artists on Mona Island are all very happy with their own well-established community, so I did not speak of Multiplicity. I am sure my banker, T'Reed, knew—"

Antenn snorted. "Uptight guy, wouldn't unpress his thin lips to spill a word."

"No, he wouldn't," Vinni agreed. He stared at Antenn.

"Ah. Hmm. Well," Antenn said, "most everybody in my office knew, an open secret. I don't know who my people would have told." He shrugged. "Maybe some of the contractors knew, particularly since we discussed Avellana's home most because it is slated to go up first thing tomorrow afternoon."

Avellana said, "Antenn referred a couple of people to me regarding buying into the community, Tica Daisy and Arbusca Willow Paris, and we met." She glanced at Vinni and away. "My former nanny and best friend, Aralia Clover, fronted for me, but . . ."

"An open secret, with those involved in the design and construction areas," Vinni repeated.

"Yeah," Antenn confirmed.

Vinni nodded. "That is yet one aspect to keep in mind, and also it's unlikely that someone who owns land in Multiplicity teleported ahead of her and ambushed Avellana."

Antenn grunted. "I'd call that scenario unlikely. In fact, I'd say it would be risky for anyone except me to 'port there. I haven't seen anyone at the site except me without land transportation."

"We should ask Rhyz whether he saw or heard a glider or stridebeasts, or even the rare horse," Avellana said.

"Yes," Vinni said.

Avellana cleared her throat, and they looked at her.

"Thinking back, I am not sure whether the voice on the scry was Antenn's. It was low and rough and sounded impatient. I concentrated on the content." She lifted and dropped her shoulders.

"So not someone who recorded me secretly and used my words in a repetition spell." Antenn sounded relieved. "I didn't miss observing that. Good."

"But a man," Avellana said.

"Or a woman who used a spell to alter her voice," Vinni pointed out. "Still, good info to know."

"Yes," Avellana and Antenn said in unison.

Avellana hesitated, frowning. "I am quite sure a male attacked me, and he seemed to be the size and shape of the man on the dock."

"What man on what dock?" Antenn asked.

"Later," Vinni said.

"All right." Antenn's calendar sphere alarmed again. He glanced at Avellana. "Do you intend to show up and watch the construction tomorrow?"

"Of course. It will be exciting!"

"Good. I'm glad. Not sure how much crowd we'll have, but at

least one owner of every house that's going up will be there. Maybe not both of a couple, but one."

"My neighbors!" Avellana beamed. "I have not met all of them yet."

"Right," Antenn said. "We *will* have an observation tent." He shared a quick smile with them both. "Including good food and drink throughout the day. *Not* on Lookout Ridge, but on a gentle hill across the valley."

"Sounds great," Vinni said.

Antenn waved a hand at them. "Later." He vanished.

Vinni made a circuit of the room, pacing and thinking.

After a minute, he heard a telepathic stream in his mind from Rhyz.

I am Healed. Danith D'Ash is WONDERFUL. *I am* ALL GOOD NOW.

Avellana answered telepathically on the channel between all four of them, Vinni and his Fam, her and Rhyz, *I am very glad. I love you, Rhyz.*

I love you, too. I come to you soon. I get food here before I 'port.

I am at the HealingHall, Avellana projected.

I know, the cat said, and Vinni got echoes of slurps. He checked on Flora, who slept through this interchange.

When he turned back toward Avellana, she plucked at the covers again and wouldn't meet his eyes. He came over to sit next to her, took one of her hands, and sent her reassurance through their bond. "What's wrong, love?"

She met his gaze, then glanced away. Her cheeks pinkened. "I am mortified. I told you I could protect myself, but I did not. I did not even question the scry."

"It came to your home scry bowl, which meant someone has your bowl locale, but perhaps not your perscry image and tune."

"Yes."

"Now we know that, you can change your bowl locale, forward scrys that come to your personal scry bowl to the general scry at D'Hazel Residence and to one of my bowls."

"I can do that." Her fingers twisting under his, she admitted, "Before he struck me, I did not see the man. Did not even sense him."

"You've told me more than once that you have learned to live in other places, with other people due to our separation."

She cast him a look from under lowered brows.

"During the times I sent you away," he admitted. He rolled his shoulders at the tingle of warning that had lodged along his spine. "I have learned to be more . . . wary. To sense danger better."

"Sense danger." She said the words as if testing them. Her gaze met his. "A physical sense? Not linked to your prophetic Flair?"

"More like developed as I lived here. Druida City has been a dangerous place to some lately."

"Not to you!"

He shrugged. "Who knows? Some people will always resent the FirstFamilies, those who remain at the top of the society—with centuries of wealth and Flair."

"You said a physical sense," she repeated.

"Also developed as I continued with my fighter training."

"Oh. It may be a male thing. I believe Rhyz has such very good senses."

Vinni didn't think gender mattered, but training and attitude. The females closest to him *hadn't* developed that acute warning system—Avellana and Flora. His female relatives were more attuned to the politics within the Family than outside T'Vine Residence. At least, he thought so, except for the guards.

The room brightened as sunlight hit the lowest edge of the window. Avellana looked at the timer. "Breakfast in three-quarters of a septhour at home." She glanced at Vinni. "We should be there."

"Yes."

"You'll come, too."

"We're a unit, Avellana. Best show everyone that." He'd be damn sure that everyone in the whole city knew the consequences of any threat to Avellana.

She slid back her bedcovers and Vinni averted his glance from her womanly body barely covered by the thin HealingHall robe. From the corner of his eyes he watched her stand with no trembling. Good.

"Where are your clothes?"

"I bled on them. I cannot dress in clothes I bled in!" Her voice rose.

"Of course not," he soothed. The Healers would have sent her clothes to professional cleansers, then they would be donated to the temple charity. "Just translocate some clothes."

"Yes." She frowned as if considering her outfit. Glancing at the timer, she said, "Clothes for breakfast with my Family, then working at the Cathedral on my murals."

He cleared his throat. "I want to get this decision out of the way. When you go to Multiplicity tomorrow morning—"

"I am leaving one septhour before WorkBell so I can observe the construction from the first to the last." She paused. "Until we must leave to prepare for leading the First Quarter Twinmoons Ritual." She lifted her brows. "Will that be late afternoon or evening?"

"We decided on EveningBell, though I wish it had been Last Quarter Moons and midnight." He smiled sharply. "I know being up at night bothers you no more than it does me."

She nodded solemnly. "You will always be called out during odd hours because of your profession. I must become accustomed to that to be a good HeartMate since we will share a bed."

He really wished she hadn't said that, and that she wasn't standing so close to a bedsponge in a thin covering. He could bespell the suite for privacy . . .

But her lips curved with a small smile and she dipped her head in agreement. "I like the night."

More words that had his body reacting. Reluctantly, he cooled his blood.

"So if the erection of the homes tomorrow lasts until sundown, we can observe it all." *Why* had he said *erection*?

"Yes. That is good. I am very involved in the undertaking."

"Back to my point. I will pick you up tomorrow morning in my glider and we'll go to the site together."

"All right."

"Promise me you won't teleport anywhere you don't know in the future." That came out more rough and demanding than he'd intended, but he didn't care.

She looked at him. "I promise."

"After breakfast today, I will take you to the Cathedral."

"All right."

"And we'll be relying on Rhyz's instincts for danger." Until Vinni could figure out something—several options—to protect his love. Definitely an amulet that would translocate her here to the Healing-Hall if she was hurt. Personal armor, Rhyz's instincts. How to stimulate Avellana's instincts?

Avellana raised her arms. "Clothes to me, now!" Underwear and a very nice tunic and trous appeared on the bed—the blue of Avellana's eyes, trimmed in a Celtic knot pattern in metallic thread of Hazel green-brown and a pale green shade the Vines used as one of their tints-of-green colors. That she wore his color touched him.

He turned his back as she donned pantlettes and breastband—of emerald, another Vine shade—that he'd told her looked particularly good against her skin. To focus on something else, he said, "A good choice of clothes. Very traditional cut."

"I like the style of my childhood better than current fashion. I prefer a tunic below my knees and cut up the sides and really full trous gathered at the ankle. I think it is more elegant than short tunics and narrow legs." She paused. "I plan on wearing a tunic-and-trous set like this tomorrow, also. You think it will make an appropriate statement for a person who is having her own house built in Multiplicity?"

"The person of the highest status?" he asked.

After sighing, she said, "Yes."

He turned. She'd put her hair up in a simple coronet, not overly fancy braids. "I think you look great."

Her mouth softened. "You always do." Her brows came down. "*You* are not dressed for breakfast or any appointments you might have this morning. What is your schedule?"

His mind went blank. He had to look down at his clothes to see what he wore. Hadn't he slept nude as usual? He couldn't recall. But standard, good, walk-around-the-Residence trous and tunic clothed him, *not* night stuff, thank the Lady and Lord. Had he clothed himself during teleportation? He shouldn't have been able to do that . . . but it had happened once or twice in the past when he'd feared for Avellana. A secret he'd told no one.

Lifting his foot, he stared at a sturdy, well-worn work boot that didn't match the rest of his garb. Wiggling his toes, he found he even had knit liners under the boots.

"Will you do a Whirlwind Spell to cleanse and dress yourself?" she asked.

"I hate those."

"Everyone does."

With a sigh, he visualized clothes of elegant cut and material, obviously heavily spelled. He would open the top of his new two-seater glider and they would travel through the main part of town. He definitely wished to indicate to all who saw them today, and all who watched the building of Multiplicity tomorrow, that he, Great-Lord Vinni T'Vine, supported his HeartMate. Cross him at your peril.

"Whirlwind Spell!" he ordered, and suffered through the scouring of himself, including his sensitive bits, and found himself dressed as he'd imagined in under a minute.

"Very nice." Avellana came up and took his arm.

The door to the chamber opened and Rhyz swaggered in. *Vine glider is here. We will get home in time for breakfast.* He licked his whiskers. *When I tell everyone what a hero I am, I will get EXTRA GOOD food.* He aimed a glance at Avellana. *I want furrabeast cubes, not shredded furrabeast.*

"Oh, all right," she said. They moved to the door, following the FamCat. "We'll be relying on your instincts for danger."

I know. I FELT that when you talked through our bond. He put an extra flick in his tail. *I sense danger good. I have learned that.* Then a darkness flooded his thoughts, terrible images that Vinni couldn't see clearly.

Avellana dropped her hand from Vinni's and picked up her heavy tom, cradled him against her breasts, and said telepathically, *I love you, Rhyz.*

I failed my first FamMan.

Vinni sent love to the cat down their bond. *You didn't know danger threatened him.*

And you were very young. You did not know how to help him, Avellana pointed out.

"Everyone failed," Vinni said aloud as they walked down the empty hallway to the side entrance where his glider waited. He reached over and rubbed the cat's head, then continued. "You have kept Avellana safe all these years. You will not fail her. None of us will."

"Including me. I will be watchful," Avellana said.

*S*hock rolled through the Hazels as they heard the tale—which Vinni and Avellana had kept until after breakfast.

"We had hoped that you would never be in a HealingHall bed again," D'Hazel said in a stifled voice as she rose from the table and came around to hug Avellana.

Putting his softleaf down carefully, T'Hazel met Vinni's gaze, and he felt the anger radiating from the older man.

"Life has been quiet since Avellana returned to us. We didn't anticipate this," he stated, each word precise.

"Avellana has kept close to home and to the Cathedral," Vinni said in smooth tones. "Yesterday we had ice cream in public."

"I see."

Her sister rose and stormed around the room. "I don't like this at all."

"No one does, dear," D'Hazel said.

"Today I will be commissioning a protective amulet to teleport Avellana to a HealingHall if injured," Vinni assured them. He held out a hand to her. "Can I have the pendant you're wearing to send to T'Ash so he can incorporate it into a new piece?" He refrained from reaching over and pulling the fine gold chain he saw her wearing out from under her tunic.

Blushing slightly, Avellana drew the necklace up from under her clothes, and he saw that the chain held three items: a stacked ring of four thin bands that resonated of the Hazels: her mother, father, and sister individually, and the Hazel Family and Residence as a whole, in different metals featuring various gemstones.

The other two items Vinni had given her. One was a tiny ring, a betrothal ring, that fit her finger as a child, woven of silver and gold strands in eternal Celtic knotwork. Now that he thought about it, she'd worn it on a chain the few times they'd made love. Seeing it had touched him then, as it did now.

Lastly, the current engagement ring he'd given her a couple of years ago—which they'd decided she wouldn't wear—more fool he.

Snagging the chain from her fingers, he unclasped it and slid the skycrystal set in gold on the ring finger of her left hand. When they wed, they'd wear marriage bands on both wrists. He'd already had one for her and one for him made. She'd requested that she, too, order a pair—one for him and one for her.

"Zow." Coll breathed the word. "That is a huge ring, Vinni."

He grinned, took Avellana's hand in his own, and angled it back and forth so the blue facets caught the light and flashed. "It suits us." He kissed her fingers, released her hand, but palmed the small ring, feeling the fizz of his Avellana in the energy. "I'll send the smaller ring to T'Ash."

Avellana appeared hesitant.

"He'll do something fabulous with it," Avellana's mother said matter-of-factly, but with a twinkle in her eyes.

"Yes." Avellana sighed the word. "I can trust him with it. And one of the Alders will place the retrieval spell on it. I can trust the Alders, too."

"Yes," Vinni agreed. "And I'll set up an appointment with D'Yew for a personal armor spell for Avellana." Since he sat next to her, he touched her hand.

Coll gasped and stared. "They say the price on those . . ."

Vinni waved it away. "I can afford it."

"Yes, of course. But it is our expense," stated D'Hazel.

"No," Vinni said. "According to the engagement and marriage contracts that should have been delivered from my Family to yours today, all expenses regarding Avellana's safety now fall to me."

Avellana's mouth fell open. "But *why*?"

"We are equally wealthy." D'Hazel's tones were stiff.

Vinni took Avellana's hand. "I want everyone to know that Avellana is a member of my Family, including Avellana." He drew in a breath, aiming his gaze at Coll. "And I have more contacts among my generation than you."

He heard her grumble from across the table, but she said nothing further, just lifting her cup of caff and sipping.

Carefully, D'Hazel stated, "My Family knows of the contretemps at the, ah, council ally meeting."

"What contretemps?" Avellana asked.

"Alliances have shifted according to personal beliefs regarding conservative entrenchment or progress," Vinni said.

She frowned at him, pressed her lips together, then eyed him. "Later you will explain exactly what that means."

He rolled a shoulder. Then, smiling a nice, sharp-toothed smile, Vinni glanced at his wrist timer and said, "I have a full consultation this morning with FirstFamily GrandMistrys WhitePoplar, the Daughter'sDaughter of FirstFamily GrandLord Eadha WhitePoplar. Charged him the max amount."

D'Hazel's mouth hardened. "Good. He's one of those who broke our alliance."

"Yes."

"Did this council contretemps concern me?" Avellana persisted.

"It concerns all of us," Vinni replied.

"I—" Avellana began, but five calendar spheres appeared, their tones oddly melding into an unusual rhythmic tune. Everyone at the table had upcoming appointments.

In a concerted rush that seemed a habit of long standing, the

Hazels hugged and kissed Avellana and left, waving to Vinni on the way out, leaving the more deliberately moving Avellana standing. Then she seemed to gather herself together and angled herself toward where he stood, less than a pace away.

"I saw your calendar sphere for tomorrow. You have a full day of important appointments. Rhyz and I will go to Multiplicity in one of the Hazel gliders."

"Why are we arguing about this now?" Vinni grumbled.

"Because I will want to meditate on the way to the Cathedral and I think you should, also, both there and back, and then you will be busy all day and avoid me to *not* speak of this."

He set his balance. "Tomorrow we can drive to Multiplicity in the Vine glider; I'll leave you at the site"—and with people, but for sure eyeball the whole situation before his workday began tomorrow so he could be sure that Avellana would be safe—"and come back when my first appointment is finished."

"I do not—"

He pulled her to him and kissed her. He meant it to be a mere brush of lips, but her partly open mouth tempted him and he had to tangle his tongue with hers and suck for not only the taste of her creamy caff but her own self. When his brain began to fuzz, he stepped away.

"I want to spend more time with you in public. And I know this enterprise is special to you and I want to share the excitement with you."

"Oh." Her slow smile kept him rooted to the spot instead of hauling her off with him as soon as she agreed. "Oh, yes, Muin, that would be lovely."

"Good." He took both her hands and kissed each back, dropped one, and set the fingers of her other hand formally on his arm. "Let's go." He started walking to the front entrance to the castle and the glider.

"But your calendar sphere alarm . . ."

"Was set to include time for a waterfall and dressing appropriately, a formal breakfast with my Family, and some meditation time. As you said, I'll meditate on the way to and from the Cathedral." He said good-bye to the Residence as he opened the front door.

"Our meditation will prime our creativity for our work. It will be a short, quiet trip," Avellana said as he handed her into his glider.

"You can be very restful." He kissed her hand, then went around to his door and entered the vehicle. After he closed and locked the doors and set the safety webbing, he set the glider to navigate itself. "I have the Cathedral coordinates, but I'll need those of Multiplicity for tomorrow and most particularly for your house."

And yes, just saying that irritated him. Acknowledge the annoyance and vanquish any negative feelings, since the situation excited Avellana.

Yes, he'd chosen to keep her safe at the expense of enriching their relationship, and now he reaped the consequences of that decision.

She smiled and took his hand that rested on the steering bar and linked fingers with him, then he *felt* her easily descend into a meditative trance and he followed.

Sixteen

❦

$\mathcal{A}$t the Cathedral, Vinni kissed Avellana more chastely than he wanted, but figured people watched, so all to the good. And though he wished to stay with her—in fact, it became more difficult by the minute to *not* be with her—he set the glider to return home automatically and teleported to T'Vine Residence.

He prepared quickly but well for his consultation with Tosa WhitePoplar. He'd give her MotherSire, FirstFamily GrandLord Eadha WhitePoplar, no cause to believe that Vinni would shirk his duties because the man had broken their alliance.

Tosa arrived on time, and their appointment went fairly well. A pleasant enough woman of twenty-seven, she remained rigid throughout his reading. Not because of any council politics or the disagreement between himself and her MotherSire, but because she disliked that he could see her future and feared what it might bring.

The usual reason everyone avoided him, even when he walked down a city street. Of course he'd been known to have visions meeting someone as he walked down a city street . . .

Tosa loosened up when he advised that she consult a matchmaker and that Vinni anticipated that she'd be wed and in a good marriage by this time next year. And at the very end of their session, she tentatively asked about prospective children. When he told her that he saw three, she left T'Vine Residence full of glowing confidence.

And he felt quietly satisfied that he'd helped her and done his duty by GrandLord WhitePoplar.

Nor should that man have any problem with the results of the consultation. He would be pleased to hear that his Daughter'sDaughter would meet a good husband and give the WhitePoplars a strong lineage.

Vinni *had* sensed indirectly through his visions for Tosa that the breaking of GrandLord WhitePoplar's alliances with several of the FirstFamily Lords and Ladies would wear on him. But Vinni had no obligation to tell either Tosa or Eadha that, since that did not affect Tosa so much as to alter her future.

Vinni'd been as professional, charming, and easy in manner as he could manage. Perhaps he'd even given Tosa a good impression of him. She had weight in her Family, though she would never take the title. He'd told her that, too, and she'd been much relieved.

He'd no sooner finished a waterfall and changed into more comfortable clothes than a Druida City Guard showed up for Vinni's report on the attack on Avellana. Since several septhours had passed, he could keep his temper when he thought of the assault. He condensed all the information he and Avellana and Antenn and Rhyz had deduced. The guard stated that he'd want to talk to each of them individually and put Vinni through a too-long examination of all the details he could remember.

At the end of that meeting, Vinni scried T'Ash and commissioned a protection and retrieval amulet from the GreatLord—who'd been expecting his call. Vinni translocated the small ring and saw T'Ash rolling it in his fingers, eyes narrowed in thought before Vinni cut the scry.

Then he attended the second-shift lunch at his own Residence, where he announced that he'd be spending the next day watching the construction of Multiplicity.

None of the older people at the table appeared interested, but some of the youngsters under the adult age of seventeen asked if they could accompany him, and Vinni agreed to run a Family bus there and back.

Casually, Vinni observed his Family, large for a FirstFamily. He hoped that he didn't house any traitors, but his gut had tightened and he simply didn't know.

The rest of his day progressed in another deep consultation and meeting with various Family members. He realized that some of them still treated him with the respect he'd earned as a child, but not quite the same as if he'd come into his title as a mature adult. With that irritation, he understood how Avellana felt.

And by the end of the day and after the tiresomeness of attending another formal dinner, he *ached* for his lover.

She was right on so many levels, as he'd learned the past few days. Another reason why he couldn't wait another six months or year until he finished whoever threatened her before claiming her as his own, HeartBonding with her, even if they didn't formally wed.

Since she insisted on staying in Druida City—or Multiplicity—and working in the Cathedral, he couldn't control his urge to be with her.

He picked up Flora, who snuffled in his grip and wiped her damp nose on his hands, then made a little grumbling noise that he took as acceptance of being placed on his lap and petted as he sat in his favorite chair in his sitting room.

And scried Avellana.

"Here, Muin," Avellana said. She looked fabulous, sweet-faced and sitting on a bench in her favorite garden behind D'Hazel Residence.

He let a sigh sift from his lungs. "Good to see you, Avellana." And though he'd often kept touch with her through scry and telepathy and sex dreams, just *knowing* she was in the same city eased him at an innate level.

"Yes, Muin." She smiled. "I always enjoy seeing you."

After clearing his throat, he said, "And I'd like to see you in person, and as I said before, spend more time with you. There's an advanced training general melee at The Green Knight Fencing and

Fighting Salon in a septhour and a half. Saille T'Willow might be there and we can speak with him about our matchmaking appointment on Mor. Will you meet me at The Green Knight?"

Her shoulders squared. "I am not ranked high enough as a fighter to be allowed to take part in that melee."

"Forgot," Vinni said, petting Flora.

"I am not a good fighter," Avellana stated. She grimaced. "Even if I had not been surprised this morning, I would probably not have been able to grapple with my assailant and win." Her lips pursed before she continued. "I spoke with the guard investigating the incident for a full septhour and a half."

"I spoke to him for a long time, too," Vinni replied. "And T'Ash is designing a protective-retrieval amulet for you."

"Thank you."

"And you might not be a great physical fighter, but you can defend yourself well enough."

"That is true."

"But you could observe the bout at The Green Knight," he offered. "You're always welcome there."

Avellana glanced away. "We are limiting our sexual congress because we don't want to HeartBond."

Just hearing her prim words stirred him. Physically. He cleared his throat. "Yes."

Without looking at him, Avellana said, "I think my lust for you would overtake me if I saw you in such circumstances."

He wanted to know more: What circumstances? Hot and sweaty? Physically active? Competing? "Oh," he said.

"Tonight there is also a service at the Cathedral. I think I will attend and do a prayer journey."

"Blessings, then," he said, managing not to grumble. But maybe they should stick to being with each other during the day and in public.

"Blessings to you, too." She paused and met his eyes, a small, intimate smile on her face. "And thank you for telling me of this event and situation and your concerns." Her smile widened. "We can do this."

"Of course we can."

"Merry meet." She began the usual Noble good-bye.

"And merry part," he replied.

"And merry meet again. I will see you later, Muin."

"Until later."

Her image vanished and now he had nerves to work off. Wouldn't hurt to practice his moves. He'd head to The Green Knight anyway.

*A*vellana contemplated all the <u>discussions</u> she had had with her Family, and, most especially, Muin.

The scent of the herb gardens wafted around her, the true smell of home to her. She had taken a mixture of these very herbs in sachets wherever she had traveled, though the fragrance faded after two weeks. Tonight she had come to study the gardens and decide on the proper proportions for her own flower and herb beds in Multiplicity.

Instead she had turned over each word people had spoken and matched it with the *feelings* she had sensed attached to the utterances.

She believed she had finally made the points she had wanted to for years. At age twenty-four, her love and her relatives finally considered her an adult.

Perhaps they thought that during the Passages to free her psi power, her brain had mended. And if they believed that, they would project the idea to everyone else around her.

Eventually she might not be considered damaged and fragile by some of the other FirstFamilies.

And her Passages *had* worked on her brain, rebuilding synapses, carving new pathways, Healing most of the damage she had incurred when she had flung herself out of the castle window at three years old, thinking she could fly.

What she had told no one, not even Muin, and what she did not think he knew, was that she could still feel a bit of damage—a little skip in her thoughts, a little kink at times. Something she did not believe others experienced.

Throughout her life, she and her Family had visited the best mind-counselor of the planet, naturally a FirstFamily GrandLady. Their last session had been when she had come home for a brief visit to celebrate her mother's Nameday three months ago.

At that time she had asked her Family and their mind Healer counselor about such a *sense*, they had all stared at her, so she knew the oddity lived in her brain.

But she firmly believed that, too, would eventually Heal. Or that it did not affect her in any way. She was *not* any of those words that had been whispered through her links with others from unknown persons . . . defective, unnatural, *freak*.

She felt just as human as anyone around her, any woman of her age, any other artist she had met or worked with in Toono Town or on Mona Island.

Do not think of all the negative slurs. Do not accept negative energy in her life. Muin and her Family acted on that; she *would not*.

She stood, being mindful of all the positive aspects of her life: She was home with her Family and Muin, she was having a *new* and *personally designed home* built for her tomorrow, and, best of all, Muin and she would be wed within two and a half months.

Keeping the delight of these thoughts flowing, she walked with deliberate pace down the gray flagstones toward the Residence.

When she entered the intelligent house, she opened all her senses to soak in the atmosphere.

Her mother and father conversed in the sitting room of his suite, minds gently busy with surface thoughts and the deeper feelings of the HeartBonded. Avellana bit her lip. She wanted that togetherness and life-and-death link *so much* with Muin.

Be positive. In two and a half months they would hold wedding rituals, and perhaps HeartBond in loving before that.

Her sister and her HeartMate walked through the newly refurbished suites they would move into after their marriage in the autumn. *Their* plans proceeded well.

Not one small buzzing tendril of a mind focused on her or worried about her. Not even the Residence itself.

Nearly dancing up one staircase after another, she reached the storage rooms at the very top of the small castle.

She opened the door to the chamber the Family currently used, and one of her first holographic murals showed as a faded outline on the wall. She had installed it here herself, and wondered about leaving the holo painting in that particular place, where it could be the first thing people could see if it activated.

Stepping over to the mural, she touched the side of the outline. The seaside holographic painting swirled on, heavy surf breaking against a jagged line of rocks a couple of meters away from a short, sandy beach. It looked like high tide. She had programmed the painting to reflect the tides at that slice of coast thirty kilometers away.

Her mind flickered with disjointed thoughts—how she could revise the holo now and make it better. How it would remain here in the storage area. She would not move this painting to her new home.

Most of all, how she looked forward to her very own place—an abode made especially for her by a person who had consulted her, like nothing else in her entire life.

Even her Fam, Rhyz, had not been hers alone.

A house, hers alone. One that she would place HouseStones for. Eventually those HouseStones would gather enough energy from the earth and the atmosphere and the Flaired people living within it, and would become an intelligent Residence. That usually occurred within two centuries.

But the length of the current amount of time for a sentient house to develop might change, shorten. HeartStones continued to gather Flair and evolve and mutate just as people did.

No. Not mutate—*develop*, or, perhaps, *evolve*. She did not like the word *mutate* because *mutant* had been applied to her.

Avellana? the Residence itself whispered to her mind.

She stopped her winding progress to the door to the older storeroom and answered aloud, because the House liked that. "Yes, Residence?"

Have I failed you? It continued the telepathic conversation, though she knew it had a virtual voice and speakers.

"Of course not, dear Residence."

But you leave me.

She considered, then said, "I am sorry if I hurt your feelings, Residence, but it is not you who has been . . . problematic for me. The other members of my Family have either too few or too many expectations of me. They do not let me *be* myself, walk my own path. I believe—believed—that I had to prove to Mother and Father and Coll that I am an adult—"

We celebrated your adulthood after your Third Passage, the Residence said.

"Yes, but that has not stopped any of my Family—my human Family members—from instructing me in how I should live."

A pause, and dust rose and whirled as air moved in a change of atmosphere. *What you say is true.*

"So I wished to invest my gilt in a good project, and I heard of Multiplicity, and the idea of a planned multi-status-level community appealed to me."

Druida City is a planned multi-status community, pointed out the Residence.

"That is true, but it is not new. I—" *Do not say* wanted *or* yearned for. "—liked the idea Antenn Blackthorn-Moss had for an individual and personal dwelling for me."

Now the door she headed toward rattled. *That is a very strange notion. A house holding only ONE person.*

"And my Fam," Avellana said. "And I will not be there long," she soothed. "I will be moving into T'Vine Residence within two and a half months. I am telling you this in confidence, and only you."

I am a very trustworthy Residence. I have known, and now know and hold many secrets.

That almost distracted her. She cleared her throat. "I intend to wed Muin within two and a half months."

The atmosphere seemed to hum around her. *You will have the wedding ceremony here in the Great Hall?*

"Muin delivered his final negotiations today, I believe. I do not know the contents of that document or what my parents and Coll wish in this matter."

I deserve to have the wedding and the ritual! This is your home and I am YOUR Residence. T'Vine Residence will have you for the rest of your life, and so I will tell it.

"Ah, yes. In any event, I will convert my home in Multiplicity into a studio for when I wish to . . . create in a totally peaceful atmosphere that reflects only my style."

T'Vine Residence has many more people residing within than I do. People who could bother you. I commend your foresight.

All right, a definite rivalry here that Avellana had known nothing about. She said, "But I do want to see this interesting house in Multiplicity built, and place HeartStones in it so that it can become an intelligent House—"

I can give you a pebble or two from my own stones to use!

Avellana infused her voice with sincerity. "I am deeply grateful for that. I hesitated asking you for them last night."

Can I see the aspect and plans of this new house?

She let a relieved breath whisk quietly from her. It appeared she and the Residence had gone beyond hurt feelings. "Yes, absolutely." With a Word, she translocated a roll of papyrus plans to land within the curve of her fingers.

A light-spell flickered on, illuminating an old, scarred table set in the middle of the room.

When she reached the table, she cleared off a large area, then unrolled the plans, accepting the fact that the Residence could perceive the drawings, though she did not know exactly how.

Creaking came from a multitude of places in the room, a wall joint, the floor, even the door she had been walking to . . . the lock clicked and it opened.

That is a small house. D'Hazel Residence sounded pleased.

"Yes, the space cannot compare to you."

And of an unusual shape, octagonal.

"That is right." The Celtan culture preferred circles, but Avellana found straight lines cleaner and wanted something unique.

With too many windows. Now the Residence sounded disapproving.

Avellana loved that each wall consisted of mostly glass.

Not good enough security. A small snifflike crack. *Too much light.*
She had always thought D'Hazel Residence too dim. She kept her
mouth shut as she turned over the page for an artistic rendering.

Another house-sniff and comment. *Two-dimensional. Did you
not do a three-dimensional holo?*

Surprise spurted through her that D'Hazel Residence had guessed
a secret only Antenn Blackthorn-Moss knew . . . She had done all the
three-dimensional renderings of the model houses and client homes
that Antenn had provided to his other clients and the newssheets.

"Yes," she squeaked. "Here is the holo of my house." With a finger flick she activated the mural embedded in the two-dimensional
drawing, and the three-story octagonal house sprang into being. As
the Residence had commented, her new home consisted of mostly
windowed walls on the first story, then a smaller second story stacked
atop the first and a third cupola space. She smiled just looking at it.

Acceptable for an art studio, D'Hazel Residence said.

"Yes."

*And for living for a limited time period. Not at all good for a
Family,* he ended dismissively.

Avellana shuddered once as memories she had inadvertently received from Antenn Blackthorn-Moss's mind rippled through her
brain—he had grown up in the defunct slum Downwind in a small
shanty made of thin metal and wood materials, and that had housed
his mother, himself, and his lost mad older brother. She understood
that many Earthan Families would have been pleased to live in her
home that would be built tomorrow.

Avellana? prompted the Residence, as if needing reassurance.

"No," she murmured. "I would not raise children in that house.
It will be enough for me and Rhyz." She paused, then said, "D'Hazel
Residence?"

"Yes?" This time he replied aloud.

"As you know, the humans are having trouble negotiating our
wedding and I am getting impatient."

"It has been no long amount of time," he stated.

"That is true for you. But I think the human members of the Hazels and the Vines are simply fussing over unimportant details. I am sure if you and T'Vine Residence consulted together, you could, ah, guide Muin's and my Families better."

"That is a thought," D'Hazel Residence said. "Neither your parents nor Coll looked at the new proposal that T'Vine delivered today."

Avellana found her teeth clenched. Obviously her wedding was not a priority for her Family; the notion had probably been around so long, it was taken for granted. She loosened her jaw and replied, "Thank you for telling me, Residence."

"You're welcome, Avellana. I have been unable to view the documents myself." Some rustling around. "I will wait and watch . . ." His words faded out, but general sounds continued as if the Residence murmured to himself.

With a smile Avellana closed the holo painting of her house and rerolled the papyrus sheets, once again glad she had invested in Multiplicity. She had surprised her Family and Muin with her actions, the financing of the new community, the design and purchase of her house, and the news she would live away from D'Hazel Residence.

Though she thought that each of her Family members would definitely check out her home and the town of Multiplicity.

Glancing around the chamber, she saw a few items she wanted for her home . . . and it occurred to her that neither the Residence nor her Family cared what furnishings she might take from storage. As a member of the Family she could have what she wanted. She vaguely recalled ornate and garish furniture gilded with gold leaf, too expensive to dispose of, and knew if she wanted she could have a houseful of that, doubling the value of her home.

No. Instead, she moved to a corner that held very light summerlike furniture of rattan and bamboo formed into fanciful shapes. This would do well for a house of many windows.

At first, she had considered filling her new home with many plants but had decided that she could not trust so much in the future in which she would be able to care for them. Even now, she believed that Muin might whisk her away to some other town.

But better for Muin and her to confront all their problems, whether with their Families or the fanatics of the Traditionalist Stance movement, or whatever issues the FirstFamilies had with her, than to leave again.

She would stick.

As the sun slanted lower into the room, she let her own pleasure sift into the motes of light, and thought of Muin, and how very serious he had become.

How long had it been since she had heard a big laugh from him? She could not recall.

Perhaps the continual bad dreams of threat to her, and his own nature, had dimmed what she had believed to be an innately positive nature.

But she thought, as she considered the furnishings around her, that Muin's responsibilities weighed heavily upon him. His duties to his Family, to his lineage and his ancestors.

The need for the people of Celta itself to have a good prophet to guide them.

Sitting in a lightweight fan-back chair made of heavily woven plant stalks that would look good in her new home, Avellana considered the times she knew of when Muin had steered someone into a better personal future. He had helped those individuals take a path that had led to a better result for their Family, for the city itself, and more.

Not only she, but their society itself was blessed to have him. She wondered if he knew that. She did not think many people gave him positive comments; certainly not as many enthused about his work as her own. Easier to love a holo painter. She smiled.

But did Muin realize he got little emotional support and positive reinforcement from his peers? Did others? What of his Family?

Though the last few days had been full of contention between them, she did not doubt that he loved her deeply. As she loved him.

Not being together had been a mistake. One she should have corrected years ago.

Now that she remained in Druida City, she *would* encourage Muin to embrace a more positive nature.

And she would make sure he received his due from others, too.

That decided, she understood she wanted to be with Muin. Right now. Her lips curved as she considered the vitality of the energy of The Green Knight Fencing and Fighting Salon, so different than the serenity of a loving Family home—where three of the four main inhabitants were female.

Running down to her own suite, she took a quick waterfall and dressed in expensively casual clothes. After all, The Green Knight Fencing and Fighting Salon catered to those of the highest status of society.

One last minute of checking her clothes and hair—and appreciating her own sparkle of eyes and big smile at the thought of seeing Muin again—and she teleported away.

Seventeen

Vinni stood close to the line separating the fighting area from the rest of the room, enjoying the ambience of a place where he knew his exact status and people gave him the respect due to his training. In fifteen minutes the bell would ring for the general melee of advanced fighters. A couple of times a month, he attended Open Melee for his class—the best fighters in the world.

His thoughts circled back to Avellana. She rarely came here, nor did she participate when her class—intermediate—held Open Melee.

She'd trained under the best but had never reached higher than intermediate. She didn't think well on her feet and, more, didn't consider fighting a priority in her life.

Of course in the villages where she'd lived there hadn't been an excellent fighting salon. He didn't know if there had been local clubs or not. He'd concentrated on getting her away from the city and into places where her artistic ability would be supported.

And, of course, when they'd spoken, it was rarely about training to fight.

Still, he wished she'd come to be with him.

And with that thought, he felt her presence nearby. He turned away midconversation with Tinne Holly, a FirstFamily second son, the owner of the place and one of the premier fighters of Celta.

Staring at the doors to the lobby, Vinni waited for Avellana to appear.

*S*he had been right. *Even before she took the steps up to the main door* of The Green Knight Fencing and Fighting Salon, she saw people— dressed as expensively as she was—lingering outside the building. Most of the noblemen carried swords on one hip and blazers on the other—elegant and costly lethal weapons studded with jewels.

She had not even thought to strap on her long dagger or small blazer, though other women wore such deadly accessories.

Avellana hurried up the steps and opened the door to the lobby. Even the best herbs could not totally mask the scent of sweat.

Here, too, people stood in clumps of conversation, though most of them wore fighting robes with colored belts indicating their status. Some of the robes showed hard wear and tattered hems, but all of them held the hum of costly bespelled cloth and appeared tailored for the individual. Not only those of the highest Nobles, but also their guards, who sported the colors of their houses—Holly, of course, Ash, Ivy, even a couple of Muin's Vine guards.

Glancing around, she saw that the walls had been retinted in a light golden-yellow color and the teleportation areas fitted with new pads since she had been here last.

A good thing that she had teleported to Antenn Blackthorn-Moss's business's back courtyard a few blocks away, because she knew that light. She had not been in The Green Knight for three years.

To her right, writing above the double door stated, "Shooting Range." An area she had never visited.

Before she took more than a step inside, the older man behind the appointment lectern said, "The little Hazel girl, isn't it? Avellana?" and she froze. Her gaze had skimmed over him, just noting that someone stood there, but now she realized she had made a mistake.

Immediately she sank into a curtsey for FirstFamily GreatLord

T'Holly as he came forward, his big, toned body moving with athletic ease.

The whole room had gone silent and people stared at her. She fought a flush down with sheer will and a tiny spell.

"Greetyou, T'Holly."

"Yes, it's Avellana." T'Holly nodded. Had her FatherSire or MotherSire lived, they would have been a little older than the man. His white-blond hair showed no gray.

"You aren't dressed for fighting, though I am sure you had classes here."

No use for it; despite the minor spell, her cheeks felt the heat of blushing. Meeting his light-gray eyes, she said, "Yes, I took instruction under your uncle, Tab. I believe tonight is the night of Open Melee for the advanced fighters; I only reached intermediate."

His expression went blank for an instant, and when he spoke again, he measured his words. "I think you should consider rejoining this establishment."

So he had heard of the attack on her in the dawn. No doubt it had spread from the FirstFamilies down throughout all the layers of nobility by now. She could feel the gazes of everyone else in the room focused on her. People who only knew *of* her and had not seen even a shade of her for years.

She dipped another little curtsey, though she sensed the man would have preferred her to give a fighting bow. "Muin is here tonight. I am here to support my HeartMate," she said pleasantly, reminding everyone of that particular status.

Yes, she was the younger daughter of D'Hazel, perhaps considered fragile or odd or . . . who-knows-what in each person's mind . . .

Looking up at T'Holly, she gave him her best, most carefree smile. "You do not think I am fragile."

He grunted and heavy-lidded eyes lowered. "My uncle Tab didn't consider you fragile. He welcomed you here and taught you."

She nodded, then swept a glance around at those who observed this interchange. "He invited me to attend training here at the age of six." Truth, though she did not actually start classes until she reached eight.

"We don't coddle any of our trainees. You aren't fragile." T'Holly's gruff voice had her straightening her spine.

She looked around again, this time meeting those who returned her gaze. "I am not fragile. And I am here to stay in Druida City." Turning back to the GreatLord, she stated, "I will renew my membership here in The Green Knight Fencing and Fighting Salon."

A gleam came to T'Holly's eyes. With a snap of his fingers a large book-construct materialized between them. "General Intermediate training takes place every Twinmoonsday at EveningBell." He scrutinized her. "But I think you should have personal one-on-one instruction with my cuz Nitida Holly."

Avellana lifted her chin. "No."

T'Holly appeared taken aback. Not many people said "no" to him.

She let him see her eyes slide left and right at the still-avid watchers. "I would prefer a small class of three or four."

T'Holly nodded. "I understand." The book flipped transparent pages, then stopped and solidified enough that the man could tap a finger on a page. "We'll put you in a small class after the beginners test to advance to intermediate. New classes will begin two weeks from today at AfternoonBell."

"That sounds acceptable." She raised a hand, palm vertical. "Do not charge D'Hazel. I have an account with T'Reed's bank. Forward any statement and notifications to my new home in Multiplicity the day after tomorrow—Avellana Hazel's house. It is being raised tomorrow."

Frowning, T'Holly said, "Multiplicity?"

"The new community going up to the south of Druida City." She raised her voice so she would catch the ears of those who had stopped listening to her conversation with the GreatLord. Time to take advantage of all those interested in her and do a little promotion. "Roads and gliderways have already been made. The wonderful architect Antenn Blackthorn-Moss and his crew will be building my house and several others tomorrow, along with a few model homes."

With a sardonic smile, T'Holly said, "Avellana Hazel's house in Multiplicity."

She returned a sweet curve of her lips to him. The Green Knight Fencing and Fighting Salon would make a great deal of gilt from her membership, so the Hollys should be gracious enough to let her speak of her own business.

Then her brows dipped in concentration. "You should have known about Multiplicity; Antenn Blackthorn-Moss is your nephew, as is Vensis Betony-Blackthorn, who will also have a house raised in Multiplicity."

T'Holly waved a hand. "Youngsters. Didn't pay a lot of attention. Hard enough to keep my own grandchildren straight. Confusing."

And she did not believe that for a moment.

"Seven minutes before Open Melee," came an announcement.

The book-construct vanished into thin air and T'Holly stepped close and formally offered his arm. "Allow me to escort you, Great-Mistrys Hazel."

"Of course." She let out a quiet breath. He had helped her a great deal by treating her like any other FirstFamily daughter. And though her status within these environs as an intermediate fighter was low, outside these walls she should be recognized as a woman born into a FirstFamily, one who would be the wife of a FirstFamily GreatLord.

Whatever gossip said of her, whatever people thought of her, she *did* belong to the highest level of nobility on Celta. And she had equally powerful Flair, even though she would never use her primary gift.

She walked with T'Holly to the double swinging doors inset with small glass windows. To their left, a young man, also a Holly with pale hair and gray eyes, stepped up to the appointment lectern.

The doors opened and she caught a glimpse of other Hollys—Tinne Holly, who owned The Green Knight, and his older brother Holm, the heir to the man beside her.

With a quick glance, she determined that her Muin and T'Ash were the only other FirstFamily title holders here.

T'Holly walked her over to the fat rolled mats that served as seats for observers and bowed himself away, joining the other fighters at the line. A groan went up. Avellana had heard that now and then he could beat his sons and be *the* fighter of Celta once more. The results of his broken Vow of Honor had lingered longer than anyone would have anticipated.

She wiggled her butt until she felt solid and comfortable, and met Muin's gaze, smiling. He stood at the line on the far side of the room.

*I*rritation sizzled through Vinni.

As soon as some of his friends and allies saw Avellana walk in on T'Holly's arm, they moved from their previous positions around the room to crowd next to him to be in her line of sight.

Oh, yeah, he knew what would happen now. They'd try to take him down before his HeartMate, make him look worse than he was. A sharp elbow got him in the ribs as Barton Clover pushed next to him and gave him a wide and toothy smile. Vinni gritted his teeth.

Yeah, there were guys he knew he couldn't beat, including Barton—the three Holly men, the older GreatLord T'Ash . . . at least T'Marigold and T'Blackthorn were out of town. He wouldn't make the top five, but he'd be in the top nine.

The bell dinged and the melee began.

Fresh and humming with energy, Vinni spurted away from those who wanted to take him down immediately, headed for targets of his own that he knew he could beat.

Tried to move away from thought to that place where only physical action mattered and his body ruled. Engaged in combat.

Yeah, winning, winning. Defeated both of his own guards, and, no, they didn't let him win.

This one, tough fight, too long grappling, but won!

Behind you! Avellana alerted.

He dropped to the floor and, when a torso lunged over him, pulled the guy down and pinned him.

And after that, his and Avellana's vision seemed to snap together, an event that didn't often happen. He'd rarely heard of it occurring between HeartMates. He saw through his own eyes but also had some sort of split vision, and felt, equally oddly, that his balance was *better*. Because he was anchored with his HeartMate.

Spin kick left! she yelled mentally. He did, and Barton Clover hit the floor. Zowie. Score!

Barton Clover out, Vinni eyed those standing. With a gulp of air, he went after T'Ash. If Barton could beat the man now and again, Vinni could, too, with Avellana's help.

But at the last minute, too many came at him at once and he took the fall—but ranked in the top five! Eye stinging from a last-minute glancing blow, many of his bruises aching, he accepted the hand of Holm Holly to rise and settled into his balance, gauging his pain levels and letting the tight bond between Avellana and him snap under the burden of thought. And, yeah, that caused him a few dizzy instants.

Slowly, Vinni stepped toward Avellana, his body feeling slightly different. When he blinked, he saw Barton Clover sitting next to her, being charming—just to rile Vinni, he was sure, because every time Vinni saw Barton with his wife, they looked deeply in love. Also sitting on the mats were a couple of guards in the light blue of Ivy, Vinni's former tutor, Arcto Vine, who must be waiting for Fera Vine, and WhitePoplar guards who watched him with disapproving stares.

But he concentrated on the glint in Avellana's eyes. That gleam of attraction with an edgy lust that he saw too rarely.

He should invite her to bouts here more often.

Someone snorted beside him, and he became aware that Holm Holly walked with him. The man swung a towel around his neck, then touched his swollen bottom lip and winced as the Healing spell reduced it to normal. With a narrowed gaze and balanced to attack should Vinni do something foolish, Holm studied Vinni. "You've never reached the level you did tonight in Open Melee."

Vinni smiled blandly. Holm's chin jutted as if he listened to the onlookers' conversations, including Avellana's, behind him. Then he shook his head. "I've never seen anything like the bond between you two, so close she can help with instantaneous fighting." He punched Vinni on the shoulder. "Good job." Then he turned and bowed to Avellana. "Good job, GreatMistrys Hazel."

Her expression held only innocence.

Holm laughed and slung his arm around his brother's and T'Ash's shoulders and they walked off the floor, T'Ash grumbling a bit.

Vinni offered both his hands to his love, and she put hers in them, and the connection that sizzled between them made him glad he wore a groin guard so his instant hardening couldn't be noticed by everyone. Through their connection, he realized she'd forgotten everyone in the room but him, and he grinned. He held her hands, matching tender gazes with her until he sensed Barton had moved away and he and she now stood within a circle of space.

Finally, he said, "I'm glad you changed your mind and came."

Her hands trembled in his and she drew a breath before withdrawing from him and smoothing her face into a polite expression. Tucking her hands into her opposite sleeves, she replied, "I am always pleased to be with you, Muin."

"Let me grab a waterfall and we'll walk a while." He frowned. "Did you take a glider here?"

"No. I teleported behind Blackthorn-Moss Architecture and walked."

Vinni grimaced. She obviously knew the pad behind that business, but not here. No, he wouldn't comment. With a nod, he said, "I'd like to walk with you." He paused. "In public."

Color came to her face. "Yes. I would like that, too."

"Wait right here." He drew his brows down. "Don't flirt with other men."

She chuckled and he felt pleased he'd drawn that from her. Except for his physical soreness, he felt good all around and headed to the men's locker room with a spring in his step.

* * *

*A*vellana *watched* Muin *stride across the room, and realized the* chamber had mostly emptied out while she had been staring at her HeartMate.

Muin never moved so well in his life as when he fought—well, except in bed, during those real-life times when they'd made love.

Because when he fought and made love, he relied on his muscles and got out of his head. Her Muin was usually thinking. But throughout the melee he had moved with easy masculine grace—deadly grace if he didn't pull his punches like everyone else.

She understood that they had linked in an unusual manner and with unusual closeness, and a shiver went through her. Though, it seemed, Holm Holly knew of such a link that encompassed the augmentation of *physical* efforts. So, in that, she—they—weren't unique. She had learned to dread the term *unique*. Many times it meant *too different to be trusted*, or, simply, *freak*.

Before she could drop into brooding, Muin exited the short hallway from the locker rooms and walked across the mostly empty main sparring area to her.

His hair showed dampness and she understood he hadn't done a complete drying spell.

He offered his arm to her. "It's a warm evening; let's stroll along the street outside."

One of the main business avenues of Druida City, so they *would* be public. "I would love to." She took a breath in of sweat and hormones—male and female—and wrinkled her nose.

Muin laughed. "We're leaving now."

As they walked through the salon, she *felt* like a couple, a power couple, and the few people in their path stepped aside. Soon they had left the building and Muin turned right, toward downtown and opposite the direction from which she had come. The Druida-scented humid summer night air lay softly against her skin like a benediction, home. She tilted her head back to see the darkening sky, the bright galaxies of stars blinking into view.

"I love it here."

"But you're leaving Druida City for Multiplicity."

"You should be happy I will not reside in the big city, but a small area where everyone will know everyone else."

"Plenty of isolation there, too, for villains to attack."

"Like this morning. I do not want to argue with you, Muin."

He slipped his arm from the elbow link and put it around her shoulders for a brief squeeze. "I know. My fault, I brought it up, when I should just be glad to see and walk with you."

"Perhaps the adrenaline and other natural chemicals in your blood are not fully absorbed."

Chuckling, he took her fingers and twined them in his, and the standard rush of emotion flooded her. Affection, passion, love.

"About Multiplicity   " he began again, and she sensed he had taken her hand to check the truthfulness of her answer, rather amusing since she thought he could read her expressions like no other and would not need the physical connection.

"Yes?" She had no secrets regarding Multiplicity to hide from him.

Muin clasped her hand, enveloping her fingers. Without looking at her, he said, "Do you need gilt?" He cleared his throat. "In the time before we're wed?"

She chuckled and squeezed his fingers. "No, Muin."

"For, ah, furnishings for your new home?"

"I am taking items from the D'Hazel Residence storage rooms. Like most FirstFamilies we keep objects instead of throwing them out when our tastes change. I am very pleased with my selections."

He made a grumbling noise.

"Muin?" she asked.

"G'Aunt Bifrona added more stuff to the bottom chamber of my tower."

"Oh."

"I wanted that tower for you and me, only."

"No one can teleport into the floors above, or the secondary towers, or the roof, or take the staircases or omnivator. We can let your Family have that room."

"It's the principle of the thing. They have the whole rest of the castle. My personal tower should be *private.*"

"It does not matter."

"And we've strayed from my original topic."

She shook her head. "I do not need gilt."

"I got the impression that you made a significant investment in Multiplicity."

"I did, most of my personal inheritance. That which is not allocated for my children." She grinned up at him. "And I will make a lot of gilt. *We*, Antenn and I, will make a lot of gilt from Multiplicity." She shrugged. "I live frugally and have few expenses." Waving to a shop window exhibiting the latest fashions, she said, "I have all the clothes I need and do not need more. And, soon, when I am not donating my work to the Cathedral and I am doing more commercial holo paintings, I will also make much gilt from that."

"And you can get an annual NobleGilt from the council for contributing to society."

She nodded. "I am not well known, so I will be doing quite a lot of free holo paintings to accept that gilt. But I am at the beginning of my career, so it can only grow."

Pausing and not looking at him, she added, quietly, "I believe Antenn may be a little strained financially. He would not accept gilt from his parents, the Blackthorns, nor from the Clovers on his mother's side—"

Muin grunted, frowning. "I don't recall him asking his peers about this. Those of us who trained with him in his class at The Green Knight. We're still pretty close."

"Networking in action," Avellana murmured.

"That's right."

With a shrug, Avellana said, "I do not think he would speak with T'Hawthorn about this."

"No. Laev, T'Hawthorn, is the best financier ever, but he likes to meddle, and I don't see him keeping his mouth shut or his fingers to himself if he had a piece of Multiplicity."

Avellana actually giggled. "All the FirstFamilies Lords and Ladies meddle. Every single one of them."

Muin stiffened beside her. "I do *not*."

"You did nothing but meddle in my life." She laughed aloud, glad she could do that with this topic.

"That's different. You're my HeartMate. I don't meddle in my friends' lives."

"I am your only . . . meddlee?" She hooted. "You have been showing up to meddle in people's lives since you were nine years old."

He opened his mouth, must have realized he could not finesse the well-known truth, and shut it, paused a moment, then turned down the street that led to the theater district. "I'll talk to Antenn about a partnership, strictly hands-off."

"In his *next* project. Neither Antenn nor I will let you in on Multiplicity."

"Hmm." Muin sighed and bent toward her ear. "One night," he whispered. "This one night where we don't disagree or argue."

"We have been doing very well already tonight, Muin."

That sounded a little too exasperated to him, so he pulled her close and kissed her soundly—no tongues, except a swipe of his over her lips. She relaxed in his arms and he cherished the feeling of her soft body against his. Then he let her go and she stepped back, looked up at him with the tenderness he'd seen earlier—that had been all too absent lately. She rubbed the front of his tunic, put her right hand over his thumping heart.

An ache for her, for them to be truly at peace together, suffused him, nearly unbearable. So he kissed her on her forehead.

In silence they turned . . . and nearly ran into a boy of seven and a young woman in her early twenties—the boy was Cal Marigold, the son of Vinni's and Avellana's good friends who had helped them with Avellana's Passages to free her Flair . . . who had saved Avellana's life and sanity.

Vinni recognized the woman as one of Cal Marigold's teachers—voice, Vinni thought.

"Greetyou, Cal and GentleLady Diguetti," Avellana said cheerfully.

"Merrily met, Avellana and Vinni! It's good to see you," Cal enthused.

But Vinni stood stock-still as the the tingle of his Flair started at the base of his spine, zipped up to his brain, then spread along his nervous system. He knew with reluctant fatality why his nerves had been on edge and why he'd taken this road.

Because he was supposed to meet these two.

The air around him increased in pressure and he could *feel* his eyes changing color as his prophetic magic kicked in. He'd have thought Avellana hadn't sensed the change in him except she linked arms with him.

He heard a high and gurgling gasp, no doubt from Foo Diguetti. "Cal, come along," she ordered.

"I'm sorry, Foo." Cal sounded sad. "I think it's too late. The vision is upon him."

And Vinni *saw*.

Both the voice coach and Cal had gone pale.

"I don't want this," the young woman hissed as Vinni's head turned toward her.

A quick prophecy for her, composed of the darkly radiant colors of her aura. "Your current gallant will leave you within this eightday week."

She shrieked and clamped one hand over an ear, one on her mouth. Vinni sensed other people withdrawing from the wide sidewalk around them. He raised his voice and *thrust* his knowledge mentally to her. "You will meet the love of your life before Discovery Day next month."

Her whimpering sobs cut off abruptly. "What?"

But his Flair focused on the young and very interesting Cal Marigold . . . and the boy's aura seemed to expand to mix with Vinni's, a very unusual occurrence, but Cal was the only reincarnated individual Vinni knew who sometimes recalled his past life.

"Cal," he crooned.

"Yes, Vinni?" The boy's voice went high with fear. Vinni sensed both women moving close to embrace the boy.

"You can have a good and uncomplicated and successful life with a loving woman—"

"I know I have a HeartMate now. I wanted a HeartMate and the Lady and Lord promised me one while I circled the Wheel of Stars during my time between lives."

All right.

The woman on the right, Foo, separated herself from Cal, pressed against the wall of the brick building, making her silhouette as small as possible, hiding from Vinni and Cal both? Maybe.

Vinni wet his lips as the paths for Cal narrowed from a multitude to five, the future he'd just revealed remaining because Vinni had told Cal of it.

"If you hold faith," he murmured, seeing that the darkest two paths could only be negotiated if Cal believed in himself, or leaned on his personal support system to help him through.

"What!" demanded Cal.

"If you hold faith, you will be fine. But the golden future with your HeartMate"—the white path in the middle and the golden one toward the right, the last before the wide and gentle trail—"has a big dip into a dark—"

"—such as a storm-tossed sea on a shaky ship?" asked Cal in a deeper voice with a sailor's accent, like the man he'd been in his previous life.

"Yes."

"I'll take it."

But the five futures remained.

Vinni narrowed his eyes. Something else he needed to perceive, to tell the boy. Breathing in a pattern that honed his gift, his magic, his foresight, he waited. He peered into the darkness shrouding four of the five paths, couldn't see the exact dangers threatening the boy . . . "The dark portion of your path is not soon. You will reach it after you become an adult."

He felt the shock of terror from the boy. "My . . . my parents and sister?"

"Are fine," Vinni replied swiftly, irritated that he'd frightened Cal, and more than once. That was why he preferred people make appointments with him, where he could evaluate them in his specially furnished office that lessened any trauma to his clients and to himself.

Cal had recently suffered through First Passage to free his Flair, and his parents hadn't contacted Vinni to scan him.

"Vinni, the dark time?" Cal's voice remained high, but steady, in control. Good lad.

"Your parents and sister remain fine. You will endure personal trials."

A shaky sigh. "Okay, then."

And, suddenly, Vinni felt great warmth along his side, realized he'd turned cold during the vision. Chilled, sweating, he never knew how each prophetic session would affect him, had tried to keep notes . . . Yes, Avellana pressed against him. Good.

"Cal—" began Foo Diguetti.

"Not done." Vinni snapped. The other aura shrank back so he couldn't see it, and Cal's five paths became clearer; he strained to see the rise of the hill from the deep. A girl stood on a path branching off to the left, which led to a throbbing heart. The blond girl looked like Cal and his mother, but with Cratag's lavender eyes. "Lena."

"Lena?" Avellana asked in a soothing tone, close to his ear. He smelled her and the physical distress of his body decreased.

"Lena leads Cal to his HeartMate; the introduction is through her."

"*Okay.*" Cal sounded a little more chipper. Had he stepped forward?

All the paths with the shadowy dip and Lena and the branch to the left, especially the one with the brightest emerging road, came more into focus. The easy trail on the right seemed to dim—Vinni affecting Cal's decisions even now.

"But if you choose to follow your career in the arts, as an actor and dancer and singer, you will not meet your HeartMate."

"What?" That came from three throats.

"A good career, an excellent career, nice wife, couple of children, but no HeartMate."

"The Lady and Lord *promised*."

"They didn't promise to make it easy," Vinni shot back. "Gotta work for your HeartMate. Some . . . smudge there, some reason you didn't have her in your last life—" And he'd never been so blunt before about reincarnation.

Avellana slipped under his arm and wrapped her arms around him.

"Yes, some of us have to work hard for our HeartMates." Even he, Muin T'Vine, FirstFamily GreatLord who'd known of his Heart-Mate all of his life.

"Oh. Do I go back to a life on the oceans?" Again the hint of the sailor's accent.

"No." Vinni felt sure of that. Then he watched as a large bubble rose from the paths, seemed to elongate into an oval, then four bubbles converged, popped, and he stood in the middle of an empty sidewalk and saw Cal staring at him, scrutinizing him.

Vinni spoke of the last detail he'd wrung from his foresight. "Have you ever considered being an airship pilot?"

Pure joy showed on the boy's face and he went into a quick, impromptu tap dance, sliding and spinning.

Well, what boy *hadn't* dreamed of being an airship pilot?

"*Really?*" Avellana and Foo asked in unison in thrilled wonder.

All right, girls also dreamed of becoming airship pilots.

Cal twirled to face them again, tapped a rapid pattern, and gathered the gazes of his audience, people who'd drawn near to watch the performance, now that Vinni wasn't doing his own scary show. Then Cal stopped and made a flourishing bow. People laughed and clapped, including Avellana and Foo.

Foo came up and took Cal by the hand in a no-nonsense manner. Her smile pointed toward Vinni and Avellana looked strained. "Come along, Cal. I promised to take you home."

"Thank you, Foo, but I don't think I'll be needing voice lessons in the future," he replied mildly.

She tossed her long, tawny mane and met Vinni's eyes, if only fleetingly. "Thank you for your advice, GreatLord T'Vine."

Oh, yes, he made her nervous, and people once again hurried around their little group. He could always sense when people altered their course so they could avoid him.

For this very reason—most people dreaded an impromptu reading. He gave Foo a half bow. "You're welcome."

"We know the Cherrys, who own Cherry Transport," Avellana offered. "We could set up a meeting."

Both Cal and Foo gave her an odd look. "We know Raz Cherry very well," Cal said.

The son of the Cherrys who'd gone his own way. The famous actor. Cal had even had a small part in one of Raz Cherry's productions, hadn't he?

Vinni let out a discreet breath. "Merry meet."

Foo hesitated, as if it *hadn't* been, but Cal gave the next line, "And merry part."

"And merry meet again," they all finished the small ritual.

With a tug of her hand, Foo hustled Cal off to the rare public carrier that routed through Noble country and to the end of the line outside the Marigold estate. They ran with the energy and abandon of young things and made Vinni feel very, very old at thirty. He glanced at Avellana, who seemed solid and mature, though she might be only a few years older than Foo.

Responsibilities.

He let his shoulders sag. His body had warmed too quickly in the humid summer night's air and his clothes wicked sweat away, but he hadn't prepared for an intense vision and his hair felt damp with layered perspiration.

She glanced up at him. "You are tired. Where do you want to go?"

He—or she—could teleport to his suite in his tower, but that would definitely lead to lovemaking and he wasn't quite sure that either one of them could handle that. They'd both refrained from initiating the HeartBond, and part of that was their current emotional conflict, but they physically yearned for each other.

Loving should be for dream sex only.

And how he suddenly hated that.

"Let's go to the Thermarum Baths," he said. The baths and spa springs included both natural, tech, and Flaired pools.

"Yes, we will have a lovely soak, and we can drift down to that tiny nodule of the pool that we like so well," she agreed, obviously understanding the danger of being alone in either of their homes, too.

On a planet like Celta with high sterility and low birth rate, sex before marriage was expected. How unusual he and Avellana were. He began to think not only unusual but unnatural in not making love to their HeartMates.

The Noble-class baths would keep them on display so they'd keep their hands off each other, but give them a place for private conversation. Not many people would be there this Playday evening, a night with near endless entertainment possibilities.

Though the spa did have popular times for status-seekers and performance artists to see and be seen by the rest of the members and guests, most of society would be at a play or concert or club.

He could imagine the wonderful scent of the natural springs, the small curve of the tiny pool just big enough for the two of them, the blessed heat of the water and the herb-infused silkiness of the liquid against his skin.

Still, the morning had begun with an attack on her and he sensed the lingering darkness of enemies as well as the general malaise of ill-wishers from his Family who didn't know her as well as they should have.

He sighed, feeling the burden of the continuing mistakes he'd made with her.

Eighteen

She slipped an arm around his waist. *"Are you doubting your vision of Cal Marigold's future? Your Flair?"*

He blinked down at her and smiled. "Not this time. I gave him the absolute truth."

"That is good." She brushed her lips over his mouth and kissed his cheek. "You will have to call a glider or teleport us. I have not been to the baths often enough to be able to 'port us, though I can give you Flair and energy, of course."

"Yes," he murmured. He didn't tell her that sometimes in the depths of winter, when the days turned gray and snowy and he couldn't bear the loneliness as Head of the Family, he often went to the baths. Like many places, it held a standard teleportation room with unwavering light. He reached out mentally, found the teleportation pad for the baths, and took them there.

They left the public pad to exit on one side of the main, large kidney-shaped pool, separated from the water by lush hedges. Vinni scanned the area. Though the primary pool looked sparsely populated, most of the couples pools set within the curves appeared occupied.

Then the heightened buzz of conversation abruptly stopped.

"Oh," Avellana sighed. "I see Bani Horehound here. He and his lover passed us on the sidewalk. They must be talking about us."

"Me. Talking about me." Vinni's lips twisted. "I'm always fodder for a good story."

To his surprise, she elbowed him and her voice sounded snappish. "What of it?"

"I don't like it," he replied with more than a little heat.

She just shook her head. "Muin, you cannot tell me that others with Flair that involves personal human relations do not have acute and impromptu times when their Flair rises."

He coughed. Her wording provoked the image of how his body would rise at inappropriate times more than his Flair.

A dark glance from her came his way. "We have several friends who might have such a problem. Did you ever speak to anyone else about when their Flair comes unexpectedly in public?"

"No." But Avellana had a point.

"I would imagine a person would cover when that happens, as anyone would. But you do not have that luxury."

"No, everyone knows when I go into a trance," he responded with only a little bitterness. "I wonder if Saille T'Willow's Flair for match-making occurs at inopportune times to distract him."

"You can ask," Avellana whispered.

"Yes, I can. You helped put this in perspective." He squeezed her hand, scanning again for a free couples pool.

She slanted him a look. "Or they could be talking about me. I have recently returned from a long time away, I am your HeartMate, and I have announced I am moving to Multiplicity." She linked arms with him, smiling up at him. "Let them talk. And the more they talk about Multiplicity the better."

"Hmm."

"You said that earlier."

"I could ask my folk if any want to relocate to Multiplicity. Whenever someone leaves T'Vine Residence we buy property for them, if they want. Or we give them enough gilt to buy property elsewhere."

"So do the Hazels, though our Family is not as large as yours."

He nodded, then saw that people had broken into groups and though conversational-toned talk had resumed, a great many discreet glances slid their way.

Avellana sniffed. "We know most of the people here, but no one has waved to us or invited us to join them."

"Who do you want to talk to?" Vinni asked.

"Just commenting," she said.

At that moment, a rotund man in the bath uniform of light blue and gold bustled up to serve them.

"Greetyou, GreatLord T'Vine"—a bow from the man, who wore a manager glyph embroidered on his chest and cuffs, then a pivot and a bow to Avellana—"and GreatMistrys D'Hazel." The man beamed. "So *pleased* to meet you."

"Greetyou, GentleSir," Avellana murmured.

"Is the farthest-west small couples pool off the main pool available?" Vinni asked.

The man's face folded into disappointment. "I am so sorry, but no. None of the small baths outside are free now, nor will any open up for at least a septhour, GreatLord." He paused, then gestured to the east. "I *do* have a private terrace area, changing salons with waterfalls, and, of course, pool, surrounded by latticed flowering plants, very beautiful. Free for the rest of the night."

Vinni and Avellana gazed where he'd indicated and saw a portion of a tall screen of climbing flowers separating the private area from the rest of the pool.

"Very romantic," the man pressed.

Though Vinni's heart jumped at the idea of Avellana and privacy . . . he opened his mouth to refuse when Avellana answered for them. "I am sure that will be fine."

He was sure he'd lose his battle for control and they'd make love for real.

"You honor us, GreatLord and GreatMistrys." With a whisk of fingers, the attendant produced the key on his open palm and inclined his torso.

Avellana plucked the bespelled key from his fingers and sauntered in the direction of the man's pointing hand.

Vinni pulled his gaze from her swaying backside, swallowed, slipped the man a gilt note, and followed. "Thank you, Phae."

"My pleasure, GreatLord T'Vine."

He caught up with Avellana as she entered the main doors to the building. Resurgent lust dried his throat, and he'd cleared it twice by the time they reached a fancy door painted green with a large frosted oval glass insert. "This isn't wise."

Without even looking at him, she said, "I am tired of being good, Muin."

"Uh."

"And weary of operating on someone else's schedule other than mine—ours."

She pressed the key in its outline on the door; it vanished and the door swung inward. It opened into a tall-ceilinged entryway of green-veined white marble walls to their left and right that formed a short hallway to the turquoise pool. As promised, lattices covered with colorful and fragrant blooms separated the area from the rest of the baths, which lay mostly to the right. There came a low murmur of other voices to his ears.

They entered and the door shut and clicked locked behind them.

To the left elegant golden script on a polished reddwood door stated, "Lady's Boudoir and Waterfall"; to the right, "Lord's Salon and Waterfall."

"Pretty." Avellana approved.

Vinni grunted, still having trouble finding words, since he stood close enough to Avellana to catch her sweet-salt scent. Whether the remnants of the fight or the vision had tweaked his hormones—probably both—his mind fogged with desire.

Before he could grab her, she lifted to her toes and brushed a kiss on his mouth. "I will see you shortly in the pool." She traipsed to the door and through it and he lost the opportunity.

He stepped into the elegant suite furnished for a nobleman but paid little attention to the ambience, translocating his thick robe from his personal locker in the standard public area. He'd keep his waterfall short because he wanted to spend more time with Avellana and fully experience the luxuries of the baths. And maybe he lied to himself. What he really wanted to do was pounce on his HeartMate and forget everything else—the attack at dawn, her moving to Multiplicity the next day . . .

The small marble boudoir impressed Avellana as a luxurious jewel of a suite. The dressing room held bespelled racks that would keep her clothes warm in the winter as well as smoothing the wrinkles from the garments. Within a scented cedar wardrobe hung a selection of robes from thick, soft fleece to a series of short gossamer negligees, no doubt intended to engender lust in a partner. Avellana studied those, thinking that she might purchase a few of that type herself for Muin.

For now, though, she stripped and took a light robe suitable for summer.

A separate sitting room held a large couch that also looked welcoming for a pair of lovers.

Even the toilet and the bidet appeared to be the latest in luxury.

She stood under a brief waterfall to cleanse herself and noted that three of the four walls contained staggered nozzles to give the bather a sensual experience.

As she exited the large stall, she caught a movement from the corner of her eye and pivoted. This time the blow aimed at her head took her on the shoulder. Pain radiated. She ignored it.

She spun as Muin had spun during the melee and her mind sent out a wordless shout to her love. They linked once again, giving *her* a physical edge. Her vision went to multiple images and she swallowed, controlled her own surprise and fear, and tried to clamp down the panic whooshing through her from Muin.

As she fought the internal war against their emotions, she let her body automatically hit and block blows. But the man fought better, grunted and took her strikes, then found an opening. Hard hands grabbed her. She thought she heard an underbreath mutter of "One, Save the Vines—"

He planned on teleporting them away.

No!

No! Muin roared mentally.

The man flinched. Avellana kicked again and again, struggled hard, then went limp and they fell off balance in the direction she hoped . . . close to a greeniron handrail along shallow steps to another door to the pool. She wriggled, wrenching her arms free to grip the bottom of the rail set in marble.

He could not teleport with her anchored to the rail. If he was powerful enough, he might be able to yank the rail from its mooring and bring it with them, but she believed he lacked such strength. In fact, she believed *she* could teleport *him* away.

The door slammed open, hitting the wall. "Avellana!" Muin yelled.

"I will get him, Muin, and teleport him to your tower! I am the stronger Flaired!" She released the rail, curled to sit, reaching for her assailant. His arm around her waist fell away and he jerked from her.

"No!" he cried hoarsely. "Fligger." He vanished.

Muin slid to a stop, then sat down abruptly next to her as if his knees had weakened. "Lord and Lady, Avellana." He put out a hand to stroke her and she realized her skin yet held some dampness from the waterfall and she was nude. Her assailant had not cared to assault her sexually, or not here in the baths; perhaps if he had taken her somewhere else . . . but she thought he seemed *repulsed* by her.

"Avellana!"

"Not again." She stood and whispered a couplet to finish drying, then spellwords that removed the sting from the bruises sinking into her skin and muscles. "I am all right, Muin." She tried a smile and thought it worked.

"Lady and Lord." He rose in a single, smooth motion and gathered her close. She wrapped her arms around him, liking the feel of his robe.

"I am *fine*, Muin."

His breath shuddered out from his chest against her. "Yes, I can feel that. Thank the Lady and Lord."

"We can stand here as long as you want, Muin, but I suppose there will be more septhours with the guards."

"I'm afraid so," Muin said. "And this time I will call on the liaison between the FirstFamilies and the guards, too. *He* can investigate the case."

Avellana said nothing but held on to Muin until their breathing and heart rates subsided to normal.

He huffed a breath and his mouth flattened. "The more I consider it, the more I believe Phae, the manager, steered us to this place on purpose."

Avellana frowned. "I felt he *was* delighted to see me and wanted to please us."

Muin tilted his head. "I have enough of a connection with him that I can speak with him telepathically."

She allowed her surprise to show. "You do?"

His mouth turned wry. "The winters without you have been long, and I like company other than my Family . . . and I got into the habit of coming here after the melees."

"Oh." She blinked; perhaps he had been as sad as she during their time apart. Her anger at him continued to chip away.

Phae Thermarum, please respond, Muin snapped mentally, on a stream that included Avellana.

As he sent the communication, Avellana wrapped herself in a plush, nonrevealing robe.

"Let's see if we can find him in the pool, the reception area, or his office." Muin frowned. "I'm not sure we should run through the baths looking for him. We don't want to hurt the business."

"No."

"Casual but swift efficiency." Muin took her hand and they left the private pool. Though concern for the man she had met briefly and liked ladened her, a small portion of her regretted not frolicking with Muin in the pool and making love with him.

She copied her love's casual manner as they hurried through the baths, the pool area, and the building. They ran across several other attendants at work but not the manager.

When they reached the office, she and Muin insisted the second-in-command unlock the door—they found signs of a struggle and smears of blood, and no Phae Thermarum.

A whole station's worth of guards arrived, as well as the First Family liaison who had already been briefed on the previous assault and everything else. Muin seemed to know the man, and she let him handle the questioning as she translocated another outfit from home and dressed.

Muin had also immediately notified the Thermarums, and the older GraceLady herself appeared to organize the questioning of the patrons and take charge of the baths.

No reports of the missing Phae surfaced, and none of the city death groves stated they had received his body.

Unfortunately, the chief tracker in the world was pursuing another criminal out of town.

This time, Avellana took a memory sphere and essentially relived her attack as well as explaining in her own words, and that sped up the questioning process. She also allowed herself to be put into a trance to relive the assault.

Naturally her parents and sister had shown up at the baths and supported her during the minor ordeal but had fussed much less than usual.

The guards released them all before midnight, with a perfunctory query as to whether she would like to be apprised in the future about this matter. Muin asked that, too, and while she appreciated being treated as a normal adult woman, she decided to focus on the more positive aspects of her life. She did agree to appointments later that day to pick up a protective amulet, which would have teleported her to a HealingHall as soon as she had been hurt, and personal armor, which would have prevented the blows in the first place, though it might not have stopped a person from teleporting with her.

She fell wearily into bed listening to her FamCat's whining that he had missed all the fun since he had been hunting. Halfheartedly, she mumbled praise for a couple of rat corpses she saw from the corner of her eyes before she banished them, then relaxed and considered the pleasure of the next day at Multiplicity as she slid into sleep.

Nineteen

*H*e hadn't gotten his soak, though one of the bath Healers had banished the aches and pains left over from the melee, the inner tremors from his prophetic vision for Cal Marigold, and Vinni's race to Avellana.

He'd returned to the Residence and didn't feel like soaking in the large, rectangular pool in the waterfall room of his suite, so he teleported up to the new sunroom that would only fit two comfortably, him and Avellana. Always just two of them alone; any children he and his HeartMate had would stay on the nursery floor until they moved into their own suites.

Yes, he contemplated children. And the fact that he and Avellana had been prevented from perhaps making one tonight. An even more difficult loss of opportunity to accept than the bath meditation.

He walked to the southwest rim and the waist-high wall of the tower, thinning the dome to air. Though he could see the Varga Plateau, and the darker smudges of what he thought might be the section of rolling hills that would hold the town of Multiplicity, he didn't know if the village would be visible without a telescope during the day. He'd get the best on the market.

At night, he might be able to see her lights. Just as if he walked to the north side of his tower he could see the wall and the lights of Druida City but not be able to distinguish D'Hazel Residence.

Resetting the dome so the lush tropical greenery wouldn't suffer, he moved back to the lit stone-rimmed pool. He groaned as he slipped into the roiling and almost painfully hot water of the small tub—not quite the scent he liked as he hadn't been able to duplicate that from the Thermarum Baths. The Vine ladies concocted their own recipes, supposedly good for easing the aftereffects of the Vine Flair.

His predecessor, D'Vine, had had some sort of floral perfumed salts he couldn't abide.

He pressed the button for more of the tangy citrus scent, narrowed his eyes as the green-flecked liquid dumped into the tub.

He'd soak and see if the herbal waters and the minor Healing spells of his pool seemed to be as efficacious as the Thermarum Baths.

But though he sank up to his neck in water, his brain didn't turn off. Edged thoughts cut into his peace.

First, Family matters. Though the FirstLevel Healer had examined G'Aunt Bifrona and reported her in good health, Vinni didn't doubt that she would pass on soon. She wouldn't be here by the New Year in the autumn. Another ache, this one in his heart. He *would* miss her, no matter how much she meddled and irritated. But he'd have to set up a smooth transition for the next lady of the household.

He caught his breath. Avellana. Stup! That aspect hadn't struck him before.

The stringent steam rose and he went dizzy, more from the thought than the deep inhalation of potent herbs.

Surely this indicated destiny? That he should wed and HeartBond with Avellana as soon as she'd requested? The Lord and Lady, and perhaps Avellana's personal spiritual Hopeful Journey, pointed to her becoming D'Vine soon.

Finally.

They'd been proceeding too damn slowly, more at their Families' pace. And Vinni admitted he'd stretched the time out.

Had made love less than a handful of times.

Next Family problem—the faction of the Family who worked against them.

He *must* winnow out that bunch. Plot and plan and get rid of them somehow—to another estate, hell, to another continent if possible.

But not to Multiplicity.

He sensed when Avellana and Rhyz slipped into her bed in D'Hazel Residence, and he acknowledged that dream sex tonight would be most unlikely. Again.

Vinni had confirmed with Antenn Blackthorn-Moss that the architect would keep an eye out for Avellana in Multiplicity after Vinni delivered her when the builders gathered—a septhour before WorkBell.

In his head, the echoing snuffles of Rhyz reverberated, and Vinni sensed when both FamCat and Avellana slept.

With a murmur to reheat the water, and the release of additional scent and spells that brought forth, his mind finally quieted and he listened to the ripple of the liquid. He'd like birds in this tower-top paradise, too. He'd ask Avellana . . .

Come to bed, FamMan, I am lonely in this big suite, insisted Flora, and he teleported there.

*E*yes watched her. She could feel them as she stood at the designated observation spot on the hilltop. The sun, Bel, lit the valley and she used the shooting rays of dawn to scrutinize the panorama, turning slowly in place.

Her business partner, Antenn Blackthorn-Moss, and his workers and subsidiary builders walked the pretty streets below. The craftspeople wended their way through the area where the first homes would be raised, too busy to pay any attention to her, finalizing each step of the process.

Rhyz FamCat prowled near the far end of the hill, tail flicking, alert, but apparently he saw no one watching her, either.

The people who set up the long tent behind her, the chairs and twoseats, tables and food no-times, had left a half septhour ago to cater a more important event in Druida City.

Studying the slope, she decided that, unlike the outcropping across the valley where she had been attacked, if someone pushed her here, she would simply roll gently down to the plain, perhaps picking up bruises from hidden rocks, but not suffer much damage.

The back of her neck prickled. Yes, someone watched her. As she narrowed her eyes, she saw that a . . . hawkcel? . . . flew a little oddly, like one of its wings had been damaged.

Several notions tumbled in her mind to form a conclusion. She had heard that the private investigator Garrett Primross used intelligent feral animals as informants. That man now handled the investigation of the assaults on her. She thought Muin considered Primross a friend. Did Primross spy on her with the hawkcel? For his own investigation or on Muin's behalf?

Sending out a thought to the bird, she questioned, *Do you watch me for Primross?*

I look for a good place near good folk for a nest.

Oh . . . Yet before she could pursue further conversation, the bird headed back toward Druida City.

She *would* ask Muin about Primross. She supposed she should be thankful that her Family and lover had decided that Rhyz and Antenn were sufficient to watch her today instead of hiring a bodyguard. Of course she would be taking time out from the raising of Multiplicity to be fitted with the protective amulet from T'Ash *and* personal armor. She quashed the resentment that she would not be here to observe every detail of the construction of this first phase of the community.

Below, a multitude of calendar spheres popped into existence, chiming and ringing and playing cheerful melodies, signaling Work-Bell, the beginning of the business day.

Antenn, several of his staff, and a couple of subcontractors headed toward the town circle and stood near a neat tarp showing the ends of large rectangular timbers. Avellana had thought that the Community Center would be the last building erected that day, in the evening hours, but Antenn must have changed the schedule. She only hoped it wasn't because of her.

He had prepared a challenging roster for the day. Two of the model houses would be erected, to entice buyers from those who would come to gawk at the construction. Four of his designed homes would be raised, one a tiny house.

Like her, and the other people who had already bought homes, new observers would comment on the originality of each dwelling and be impressed.

People would see a planned community built before their eyes. Druida City, too, had been a planned city, built by the colonists. The Earthan folk had anticipated that their descendants would fill the city in two generations. But buildings—homes and multi-unit dwellings and business fronts and warehouses—yet stood empty in the walled city.

Since then, Gael City and the villages had grown organically, depending on their type—like fishing or mountain towns or artist colonies.

This would be the first totally designed community by native Celtans on this continent, and pride washed through Avellana that she was a vital part of the project.

Rhyz trotted back, a dead mouse in his mouth that she only had to admire for a couple of seconds before he ate it.

And in that minute that her cat distracted her, she missed the very beginning of the erection of the Community Center in the middle of the town green circle.

Since that eight-sided stone building had inspired her own octagonal house, which would be raised later today, she had wanted to see the entire process.

A line of vehicles on the road caught her eye, led by several old Family gliders that would hold fifteen people, and a couple that appeared to be rented for grovestudy groups.

She found herself smiling, no, grinning at the thought of company, at the deep pride of being an integral part of a new and wonderful project.

I am NOT in T'Vine Residence. I am OUTSIDE. I am coming to see the new place! Flora, Vinni's housefluff Fam, sent mentally to Avellana.

Rhyz gamboled around Avellana, streaming telepathically, *I will protect you when you get here! Oh, I sense Other Fams are coming! Hooray!*

He hurried to the top of the path that rose from the flat parking lot halfway up the hill. There he sat tall, nose elevated, awaiting the newcomers. Avellana returned to watching the green tiled roof of the Community Center lowered carefully onto the stone pillars. Her home would be constructed of brick with even larger windows proportionally . . . and would be three stories, each smaller, with the last big enough for a studio.

At that moment, the gliders pulled into the flat, brush-denuded space, parked, and children poured from them, followed by indulgent adults.

"We *missed the start!*" one small girl raged as soon as she reached the hilltop. She ran to the edge, her stare fastened on the circular town green, already laid with grasses and several flower beds.

Below, the builders of the Multiplicity Community Center cheered as they admired their finished work. The new arrivals joined in and the contractors looked up and waved at the observers.

Avellana reluctantly turned toward the tent to act as hostess and found several people in aprons proclaiming "Darjeeling's Teahouse" pulling food from the no-times and arranging it on the long tables, setting up urns of caff, tea, and iced beverages.

The summer's day would be warm, but not stifling, and certainly cooler than Druida City. When she sauntered to the western side of the hill, she could see the shore of the Great Platte Ocean, within the easy walking distance of two kilometers. A path had been made, but no road.

Then Muin walked toward her, looking fabulous, finished with his first consultation before anticipated.

The light limned his face, and even with all the trouble yesterday, the lines in his face seemed less deeply graven. Her heart eased. Yes, she worried about him, too.

His hand dipped into a hidden pocket of his forest-green trous, and when he withdrew it, he held a jewelry box.

As he joined her, he said, "I received word that your protective amulet had been created." With a minor spellword the box top lifted, revealing a huge, gorgeous deep-green teardrop diamond. Inside the stone floated her tiny girlhood ring.

Avellana felt her mouth drop open. "How did he get the little ring into the crystal?"

Muin smiled wryly. "I asked. 'Professional secret,' T'Ash said. But between you and me, I think he talked to the stone and requested that it accept the ring into its center."

She stared at the fabulous piece in front of her, watching the gem sparkle as it lifted from the box and the rainbow-metallic chain of glisten floated over her head, then settled just above her breasts.

"It is truly a marvelous necklace."

"Yes. And the chain is extra strength and bespelled to stay with you should it break." Muin's smile turned crooked. "And either or both the chain and the gem will transfer you to Primary HealingHall in the event of even a minor injury."

Like a cut on her hand, a bruise on her backside. She would not let the function of the piece dim her delight in the gift. Reaching up, she put her palms on each side of his face and drew his lips down to hers for a kiss.

A mind-spinning kiss as incredible as the amulet.

Someone coughed and Avellana withdrew her mouth from Muin's.

Her sister, Coll, glanced at them, then waved a piece of papyrus in her hands—the new schedule of the buildings going up. The Community Center, the tiny designed home, a model house to be sold, another bespoke house, another model, Avellana's home, and, last, as First Quarter Twinmoons were at their apex in the evening light fading to night sky, Arta Daisy's large, three-story layered circular home.

Avellana would miss that construction since she and Muin would be leading the Vines in ritual.

"An impressive project in a very nice landscape." Coll sounded surprised.

Dipping a curtsey, Avellana replied, "Thank you, that means something coming from one of the premier botanists of Celta."

"You're welcome. I like the Community Center, too. And your former governess's home."

"What?" Avellana spun and saw that the tiny house—square with an equally small one-person tower—had already been erected. She had missed that while kissing Muin. "My ex-governess served as a front for me in this matter."

Coll said, "Our parents and I, and I'm sure Vinni, realized that."

"Yes," he said. His gaze had gone to the gaggle of Fams coursing back and forth on the hillside—at least some of them. Muin's house-fluff and a couple of others sat near a food no-time.

"It says the next house to be built is a small mansion," Coll read. "A home available to purchase."

"Yes." Avellana beamed.

"What?" asked Coll.

Leaning close, Avellana murmured, "Antenn modeled that after the legendary BalmHeal Residence."

"Oh!"

"'Each home is unique but will fit in with the whole community.'" Avellana quoted the Multiplicity brochure.

"So a smaller edition of BalmHeal Residence," Muin said. "That's a good publicity angle."

"But it is not public knowledge," Avellana said. "We are spreading the word by rumor only."

Muin lifted his brows. "Very clever."

"Thank you. It will be the largest home so far, though there are two unsold properties that could hold greater houses."

"I think you and Antenn will sell that mansion today," Muin stated. "It's going up next?"

"Yes."

Papyrus rustled as Coll consulted the list again. "All the homes can become intelligent Residences?"

"Absolutely," Avellana replied. Her sister, along with others who had drifted over to listen to their conversation, would spread the word—and facts—about Multiplicity later.

"Even that one?" Coll pointed to the tiny house of Avellana's former governess.

"Yes."

"Has she commissioned a secret HouseHeart for the HeartStones that will become intelligent?" Coll pressed.

"I do not know," Avellana stated. "I did not ask her." She smiled and sent mentally to Coll and Muin, *My home will have a HouseHeart.*

Both nodded.

"I truly like the looks of this area," Coll stated. "The hills, the stream, the ocean in the distance. Very well done."

"Thank you."

Coll glanced at her wrist timer. "Now I must go. I'll see you tonight when we join you for the ritual at the Vines."

Avellana's stomach clenched with nerves, but she did not betray them. "I am glad you and our parents are coming."

"The Hazels are always welcome to celebrate with the Vines," Muin said.

With a nod, and keeping all the printed material on Multiplicity that Antenn's firm had produced, Coll teleported away.

Muin sighed, then glanced around at the people in the tent, the gliders on the road of more curiosity seekers, the organized activity of the builders on the plane. "I have appointments today and have to go, also." He cleared his throat. "You've memorized your part of the ritual?"

"I have had enough time," she confirmed.

"Good."

She reached out and took both of his hands in her own. "We will do fine. Our Families will be impressed."

"I'm sure."

"We have both taken part in many rituals during our lives and had various roles in them, even if we have not led them as a couple, and the ceremony tonight is simple and lovely."

"Right." He gave her a brief kiss, gestured to the rest of the Vines spread out on the ridge. Those included youngsters to view the historic event with an instructor, and two guards along with the Vine Chief of Guards. "They'll be staying until I return."

She would not argue. "Very well." She patted his cheek. "You are doing well in controlling your overprotective streak."

"Thank you, I've been trying." He gave a half bow, straightened, and vanished, smiling.

I am here, too, to guard you, Rhyz affirmed.

And I can listen for heavy footsteps and fast breathing and other signs of alarm, and I smell very well, Flora added, her nose wrinkling up and down.

"Thank you," Avellana said, then strolled into the tent for a cup of caff. Now plenty of gazes followed her, since others knew her home would be built today.

Twenty

The abrasion of his nerves had begun the moment he woke that morn-
ing. He'd curbed them, as always, but had to put more effort into his
slippery control.

He dropped Avellana off at the valley that would hold Multiplicity, managed breakfast with his Family, then took a nice break with
Avellana, and finally headed onto his major appointment of the day.

In return for the retrieval spell on Avellana's amulet, Vinni met
with the Alders again, for the third time that week, this appointment
with all four generations. He continued to probe his Flair to straighten
out their tangled succession. Though a long-lived Family, they produced fewer than usual children and the title had bounced around the
last couple of decades when the holder felt he or she couldn't handle
the stress of the job anymore.

And Vinni finally found the next GreatLady in the youngest, a
ten-year-old girl with a lively, charming manner and impressive sense
of self, named Incana.

Her elders had clucked around her, protective, before their Family
consultation. During their linked circle, Vinni had felt a surge of
pride in her when he'd announced she would be an exceptional Head
of the Family. That the future should be solid and bright for them all.

There'd also been a huge flow of relief from the others, especially the eldest.

Since the prospective D'Alder didn't have a HeartMate, Vinni had agreed to keep an eye out for a good husband for her from a more prolific Family, such as the Clovers—and the current T'Alder had made an appointment with a matchmaker right then and there.

Then Bifrona gave the much-more-cheerful Family caff and flat-sweets and Vinni spoke privately to the girl as one former-child-GreatLord to a prospective one. He anticipated her stepping up to her title and position as Head of the Family after two years of training.

Incana seemed levelheaded and determined enough to study for the position. As he took her hand and led her to her parents, grand-parents, and great-grand-aunts, he informed them that she shouldn't be kept at home but placed with some of the other FirstFamilies children in a grovestudy group as well as taking training at The Green Knight Fencing and Fighting Salon.

He found himself smiling as the highly pleased Family left, and let his own shoulders drop in relief. *This* situation regarding a First-Family should finally have been resolved.

After meeting with the Alders, he skipped lunch with his own Fam-ily and headed back out to Multiplicity in his new two-seated personal glider. On the way, he called up several articles that had run in the *Druida City Times* about the community. Apparently, the daughter of the newssheet publisher had purchased land along with an architec-tural design from Antenn. That canny guy had run advertisements in the paper, so, in turn, enthusiastic stories had been written.

The more Vinni read, the prouder of Avellana he became. She'd done all this without his or her Family's knowledge or approval, had judged the project and chosen well.

A splinter of hurt remained that she hadn't shared the excitement she must have felt with him, but with her business partner. Vinni'd have to get over that. His own fault. He acknowledged that he'd been blind all the while to the mistakes he'd been making with Avellana.

In the past.

He parked his glider, strode up the path, and entered the tent on the hill overlooking the site. His Fam, Flora, snoozed out of the way in a patch of sunlight. He gave her a couple of pets and she wiggled her nose in sleepy acknowledgment but didn't move. Right now about thirty people stood or sat, watching the activity below. Avellana stood outside the tent, a gentle breeze teasing stray brown hairs from her formal braids, her streak of white hair tucked away.

Moving closer to her, he noted three new houses, each unique, dotted the landscape.

A middle-aged tough-looking guy, lower Noble, Vinni guessed, and his more elegant wife circled a fanciful house. The steep shingled roof . . . waved . . . over the second-story row of odd oval windows set under the eaves. And the first-story rectangular windows outlined in golden wood contrasted with the creamy plaster. Steps led up to the round-topped double doors tucked under a conical entrance. The whole home made Vinni imagine ancient legendary little fey creatures living in it. Still, the couple radiated pleasure at their new house.

It sat near the entrance of the community in the north, facing west toward the observation hillside, and just within what appeared to be the lines of the outer wall that would go up.

Good.

Antenn must have received Vinni's gilt for that particular feature. Yesterday he'd contributed the amount anonymously to the community fund bank account. He'd gone through Avellana's former governess and friend, so it appeared that a current Multiplicity member had made the donation. He'd promised the woman that he would, indeed, buy a town plot.

He scanned the homes: the tiny square house with minuscule tower that had gone up first; the whimsical, organic home the couple had already entered; a dome of reddwood tucked between a gentle spur of hills that showed a discreet "For Sale" sign on the trimmed grassyard in front of it. Vinni narrowed his eyes. He liked that one . . . but the stream didn't wander on the property and he realized that he preferred the idea of running water near him.

T'Vine Residence commanded the top of a hill, with deep wells, but no unconfined water.

Currently Antenn supervised the building of a smallish mansion of red brick—no doubt the house based on the BalmHeal Residence—that sat at the end of the shallow valley backing against the highest ridge. For Vinni, the house seemed . . . more substantial than he'd want as his own private home, another surprise.

He said to Avellana, "I thought that structure was second to be built and would be constructed while I was gone. Shouldn't it be finished by now?"

Avellana turned to him, smiling. "Antenn changed the schedule again." She swept a hand at the tent and toward the path where more people, lower Nobles from their dress, walked over the lip of the hill, all craning in the direction of the town going up. "Antenn decided to wait until he thought there would be the most people observing, early afternoon."

Vinni nodded. "Very clever. This begins to look like a real town." A group of builders had moved to the center circular green and the main street spoking off from it. "When are the shops going up?"

"Starting tomorrow and for the next few days. We do not have as many shops as homes, and we do not wish to build business space and leave it empty."

"Also well thought out."

"As a community, we prefer to build our homes and enjoy them before public commerce comes to our town." She paused. "I believe the grand opening of the shops for outsiders will be next month, after we have more businesses committed." She gestured to the tent and a small table at the near end. "During the morning break, Antenn added a table that shows my holographic model of the full town including all the homes, model houses for sale, and the street of shops. We will have two eating places."

Vinni glanced at a smiling woman in the deep green apron of Darjeeling's Teahouse dishing out food. "Including a restaurant by Darjeeling?"

"Yes. One of the managers of the Druida City teahouses lives here with us. Her abode will be raised tomorrow, along with Vensis Betony-Blackthorn's." Avellana lifted her chin. "The other FirstFamily individual who has invested in the town. He chose a classic, elegant home of Earthan style with pillars and a lower-level courtyard and gardens."

"Each house unique and appealing to a special personality," Vinni murmured. He glanced at the table but saw no mural. It seemed as if more people wanted to see the reality built in front of them instead of a model.

His curiosity resurged as he wondered exactly what her home would look like, then he decided he'd like to be surprised, too, since she hadn't already shared her design with him. Another small stinging emotional hurt to banish.

A few builders gathered around the southwestern corner of the model of BalmHeal Residence, and viewers clumped around Vinni and Avellana. He thought they sensed her mood intensifying, and surely they must know that she belonged to the new community.

Everyone watched as a tiny, fourth white sculpture settled onto the roof corner of the small red brick mansion. As Antenn and his cohorts stepped away from the house, obviously finished, applause broke out on the hillside.

Next to him Avellana hummed with pleasure. "My home will be raised next!"

Yes! Rhyz sent mentally to Avellana and Vinni. *I now have permission to go down there. To supervise the building of Our house!* Disdaining the path, he raced down the hillside.

Avellana caught Vinni's hand. "I think I will stay up here with you, out of the way." Her lips quirked. "Rhyz will be distraction enough, especially since all three of the teams will work on my home." She straightened beside him.

"That will be something to watch," Vinni said, as every builder in the town converged on an area—Avellana's property—on the westernmost street of the town, midway between the northern and southern borders.

"You must have had your pick of properties; why that one?"

"It is the closest to the path to the ocean."

"Oh."

With all the teams working on the house, it took only minutes to excavate the basement and shore it up, then lay the foundation and raise the frame. A pile of yellow stones appeared on the property, along with a vat of perma-mortar. Though Rhyz ran around the area, hopping now and then in glee that echoed through Vinni's mind, he didn't seem to get underfoot.

"Your house has many corners!" Vinni exclaimed, surprised. Of course their forebears had instituted the circular shape as the basis of much of their culture, but most homes remained square or rectangular.

"Octagonal," Avellana confirmed. "I like corners. And it has a main front door, a lesser back door, and two of the double sliding glass windows on each side open as doors. Four entrances, like the Hopeful Cathedral. I wished to celebrate my religion."

"Glass doors," Vinni muttered under his breath.

"Armorglass. My home is strong."

Bricklike stones zinged across the sturdy composite foam metal beams, the girders produced by the starship *Nuada's Sword*. Yes, his love's house would be strong.

The wide front porch and deck made the first story of the house look larger than the second level, equally full of windows, and with a much smaller top story, consisting of windows with only an edging of brick. His heart constricted as he understood she—and Antenn—had designed a perfect art studio.

Rhyz raced up the porch stairs, then circumnavigated the structure. Apparently the deck encompassed the whole house. When he came back into view, he hopped up to the railing and called out mentally, *The outside is done. Come see!*

At the same time, Antenn called telepathically, *Come on down!* So Vinni hurried beside his love down the trail to the valley and her house. He'd find out exactly when the shieldspells would be going up, and make sure the top security expert would be making them.

Avellana flung herself into Antenn's arms burbling gratitude, and only the knowledge that the architect loved his HeartMate kept

Vinni from prying her from him. Still, Antenn smirked at Vinni over Avellana's shoulder.

Then Avellana pulled away and took the steps to the deck and walked around the front of the house. She inspected the wood of the wide porch, the stylish small pillars and railing, humming to herself— one of the simple tunes they would use in the ritual later.

Vinni moved close to Antenn and murmured, "The town wall."

Antenn jerked his head in brief agreement and grimaced. "I got the gilt, and the wall will go up tonight after Arta Daisy's home." He paused, slid his gaze to Avellana, who moved to the next octagonal side and looked in the wide windows. "Some of us didn't want a wall around the town."

"Like you," Vinni stated.

"Like me. And my partner. If the majority of the community members hadn't already voted on a wall, I would not have accepted the gilt or put one up." His lips compressed. "I'd been hoping to convince the others that a wall wouldn't be needed. Or that the new people buying into Multiplicity wouldn't want a wall."

"Plenty of reasons to have a wall," Vinni responded stiffly. "Wild animals—"

"—Bad people, tradition," Antenn ended for him, then flicked his hand as if sending those arguments away. "Not sure how many big and threatening wild animals there were here on the Varga Plateau before the fire two years ago, but that destroyed a lot of habitats. And I know you're concerned for Avellana's safety."

"You don't think the remnants of the Traditionalist Stance group would attack this?"

Antenn's face hardened. "I've fought those folks on several levels and won. Maybe they'd think of revenge, but I'm well able to defend this place."

Vinni grunted.

"Come *on*, Muin. Come see my beautiful home. My very own place," Avellana called.

All right, more than a splinter, more than a twinge of hurt. How

was he going to deal with this? Impossible and wrong to blame her,
bad to keep hanging on to negative guilt at himself, too. But he'd have
to deal with this, and before the ritual tonight, or he could ruin that.
He—*they*—dared not fail tonight. Not with such a simple ritual.

He found himself clenching his jaw, and when Avellana glanced
at him, she stilled. Tilting her head, she asked mentally, *Muin?*

So he went with the other concern that she would understand.
Clearing his throat, he nodded at her house as he joined her on the
porch. "Nice wide stories. Your home looks more horizontal than
vertical. Huge windows. They seem thinner than armorglass. What
of the stone you're using as bricks? How strong are they?" he muttered.

She tucked a hand around his arm. "All the best materials, I
promise. I know how you fret."

He gave an inarticulate grumble but couldn't deny the fact.

"And the township has scheduled the placement of the strongest
shieldspells for our homes and shops at the beginning of next week."

"Two days from now, long enough for—"

Avellana lifted her brows. "For what? For someone to set a trap in
my house? I assure you, we, the members of the community, will have
guards." She paused. "Furthermore, the houses will be occupied—"

"You aren't coming out here tonight after the ritual!" Vinni felt
blindsided with the blow, the sense of loss. Avellana in her home, a
place she hadn't invited him into even now. Abandoning him.

She wet her lips. "I have not decided." A little sigh escaped her.
"No doubt it would be more sensible to stay in Druida City." Her
gaze slid to his.

He grabbed her fingers and lifted them to his lips. "You know you
are welcome to stay with me in my suite."

Her chin dipped in a nod, but she gazed through the windows,
watched the inner wall panels being laid, smooth and tinted a creamy
color.

Letting a breath sift out, he said, "Organizing furnishings and
moving them in tonight could be . . . difficult." He wondered about
the bed. What size bed had she chosen?

She nodded, expression serious. "This is true. Better to furnish the house tomorrow. Perhaps midmorning." Not looking at him, she said mind-to-mind, *I do not trust myself with you anymore, Muin.*

Hurt stabbed through him. He had to settle into his balance to keep from rocking back as if from a blow. And he hid that from her, too.

But she continued, *I do not think we will be able to be together physically and not initiate the HeartBond.*

Relief dizzied him.

Come, FamWoman. We must explore inside! Rhyz bolted from the front porch through a newly made swinging Fam door. Avellana sent Vinni a laughing look and followed her cat, entering her house through one of the sliding glass doors.

Vinni allowed himself a shudder in delayed reaction.

Antenn glanced at him, then away as if he'd seen too much. After a moment's hesitation, he strolled up to Vinni and murmured, "I'm not going to let you hit me."

Vinni raised his brows.

"You look like you need some sort of release, but it isn't going to be hitting me." Looking at Avellana visible through the windows, he went on, "You might want to take a little sparring time at The Green Knight, or spend time in your HouseHeart or something before that ritual you two are leading for your Family tonight." He gestured widely with his arm. "I will be here most of the evening and into the night."

"Good."

Antenn rolled a shoulder. "Yeah, building your damn wall." He smiled, with teeth. "But if you have some excess energy or . . . irritation . . . I can assign you to one of my subcontractors and we'll be glad to work it out of you."

"An untrained laborer just to provide Flair," Vinni muttered. "Nice to be appreciated."

Now Antenn's smile flashed with real sincerity. "Yeah, you First-Family GreatLords are so very good at being humble." But then his brows dipped and he added quietly, "I don't understand what's bothering you, but don't spend a lot of time beating up on yourself or trying to figure stuff out. Remember what we learned at The Green Knight. Sometimes it's enough to physically act and let emotional problems unknot that way."

And Antenn knew him very well. "And sometimes you could be correct," Vinni replied. He let loose a little sigh. "You sure I can't hit you?"

"You can't even try."

"Muin!" Avellana called. "Come in and up to the third story and look out!"

Twenty-one

Vinni's heart constricted. Invited into her home now, and casually, as if Avellana had never thought of abandoning him. But this was *her* place, not in any way his or theirs. Rather reluctantly, he walked through the double doors and—the house already smelled, *felt*, like Avellana. He didn't know how that could be unless she'd been hooked into the energy of Antenn and his crew during the raising and Vinni had failed to notice.

The open interior of the first story surprised him, and he caught a flash of Avellana's swirling robe and glanced up. The center of the house featured a fancy greeniron staircase spiraling upward through the floors, surrounded by open space. The second level looked like it had rooms walled off, and a central inner balcony around the stairs.

He ran up the twisty steps to the third story, about a third of the size of the first two, again all one chamber. The floor-to-ceiling round-topped windows gave a three-hundred-sixty-degree view of . . . everything. To the west shone the rippling waters of the Great Platte Ocean; to the south, hills rising into mountains; and not too far away on the plain, the road to Gael City. Turning, he saw more of the plain and rolling hills to the east. And to the north the Hopeful Cathedral stood proudly, then in the distance, the tiny smudge of

Druida City, the bulk of which was the starship *Nuada's Sword*. He couldn't discern T'Vine Residence on his hill.

He looked away from the horizon and focused on the township itself, Multiplicity Community Center due east, the four unique homes dotting the area below.

"I want one," he said abruptly. He'd promised Avellana's governess that he'd buy a place the night before, but now he truly *wanted* something of his own. Not generational. Something new.

Blasphemy! At least his Family would say so. And if he let the tiniest whisper of that feeling out to his huge castle Residence, it would hurt the intelligent home's feelings. He'd have to be careful.

And he wanted to be part of a community, not just his Family, or the highest status of all of Celta, the FirstFamilies. New faces, new neighbors, out of the rut he just realized he'd somehow fallen into.

"Oh, Muin. I can *feel* your yearning." She glanced at his face, then the valley. She took his hands, brushed a kiss over his mouth. "But if you want, I will share this with you."

"A generous offer, but I want one of my own. Something designed for *me*."

"Good idea," a dusty and sweaty Antenn replied, boot heels clattering on the last of the stairs. He strode to the southeastern windows, set his hands on his hips, and nodded. "Exactly as planned. Damn, I'm good." Then he glanced at Vinni. "And your reaction is exactly what I hoped for. People wanting something new instead of living in old buildings constructed by our ancestors. After all, those folk came from Earth. *We* are Celtans. Native born to this planet."

Avellana nodded. "There will be lesser sons and daughters of the Nobles, even the FirstFamilies, who do not want to live with their Families, in the Family home."

"Sacrilege," Vinni murmured.

Antenn shrugged. "Maybe."

"What of you?" Vinni pressed. "You live in the Turquoise House, and if you become T'Blackthorn, you'll live in that Residence."

Antenn's face softened. "I must admit I won't be establishing a home here. I love my intelligent Residences." Then his eyelids lowered and he murmured, "But I don't think there will be a member of a FirstFamily living in Multiplicity for very long."

Vinni's political antenna quivered and his gaze sharpened. "No?" he asked casually. Taking Avellana's hand, he said, "Of course Avellana will live in T'Vine Residence when we marry and she becomes D'Vine. What of your brother, Vensis Betony-Blackthorn?"

Antenn's lips pressed together, then released. "Of all Straif Blackthorn's adopted children, I think Vensis is the one most likely to succeed him."

Huge news indeed.

"Then we will find someone . . . some*ones* else from the First-Families to buy homes here. I believe we need that cachet." Avellana gave a decided nod.

Flashing a smile, Antenn patted her on the shoulder. "You're right. Always good working with you." He looked at his timer. "Last roofing and touches here, then break time for a meal. Also a change of shift. See you two later, or, if not tonight, tomorrow." He teleported away, and a couple of minutes later Vinni saw him step out of the Community Center.

"Pretty, pretty place," Vinni murmured. His eyes focused on a small fold of land next to a hill marking the southwestern end of the township, the curves of a brook glistening in the sun curling in a wide arc around what would be a perfect place for a house.

"I like the aspect very much," Avellana said, then glanced around the room, down the staircase opening at the other floors. "After we are wed, I can use my house as my studio, and with the four doors like the Cathedral, a chapel sometimes."

Vinni tore his gaze away from . . . *his* . . . land and frowned. "Are there others of the Hopeful religion in Multiplicity?"

Avellana hesitated. "Yes, but he . . . she . . . they . . . do not . . . flaunt their beliefs."

Vinni knew that if he pressed, Avellana would tell him, but he wished to continue to build rapport with her, not make her withdraw even an iota from him. Particularly since he figured she wouldn't be happy with him as soon as she learned about the wall.

Abruptly, he stated, "I will be buying land here. This house or the one I build here can be a retreat for us, a getaway place, still close enough for me to handle any emergencies, but far away enough from the Family that they don't see and hear and sense everything we do. That's begun to wear on me lately."

She nodded. "I understand. This time apart has been hard on you, too. You did not have me here in your daily life for support."

Stepping close, he framed her face with his hands, stared at her. She looked at him with big solemn eyes. "You need an heir."

With a crack of laughter, he dropped his hands to wrap an arm around her waist and draw her to him. Felt the warm and sexy softness of breast and thigh against his side. To test himself, he kissed her nose. Yes, that sent a surge of lust through him. Lost. He was lost.

"I love you, Muin. I love touching you." She loved the feel of his skin, the slight bristle of his late-day beard under her palms. She had shaded many of her words this last week with tints of the truth, but her love declarations were complete and sincere.

"We can run away," he said.

The very concept made her gasp. *"Run away!"* Her breath expelled shakily. "You would not!" Setting her feet and sinking into her balance, she said, *"We* would not. We have responsibilities as the heads of the GreatHouse T'Vine." Her voice emerged crisp, but she did not care. "I *never* ran away. I have been sent away."

He leaned over and kissed her temple. "We've talked about that too much; let it go."

She sniffed, then replied, "I am having trouble letting my long and underlying irritation go."

"I know. It's a solid strand in our emotional bond. Just try."

"Yes, I will continue to do so. But we will *not* run away."

"No. I would never abandon my Family or the Residence, no matter how much they irritated me. But recent events in the FirstFamilies have placed that option in people's minds, including my hidebound Family."

She nodded. "Yes."

Then he narrowed his eyes, and she had not seen that calculating smile of his for a long while. "Or we could pretend to run away." His mouth curled. "And *the Family* doesn't seem to know me or us so well as to understand we would never shirk our responsibilities as others have." His expression hardened. "Those who . . . don't appreciate you . . . in the Family must be shown they could be playing a dangerous game, should I leave." He grimaced. "But one of the things that's keeping me here and in the Residence is the lack of an heir. That is a concern for all of us."

"Yes."

He made a circuit of the room, staring out all the windows except the ones to the north and Druida City. "There is no Vine who has sufficient Flair in prophecy to follow me."

Tilting her head, she said, "I did not keep track of all the Flair power in your Family members. I know you need an heir, but not for that in particular. That is one of the reasons you worry for my safety. Because we are HeartMates and though we are not HeartBonded yet, if I die you will follow and leave a FirstFamily without a head who can practice the Family Flair."

"Your safety is primary with me because I love you," he spit out, and yanked her close. He pulled her up the few centimeters between their mouths and his lips crushed hers.

Desire overwhelmed her surprise. Rarely had he been so fierce with her, so uncontrolled, but his need, his huge love swamped her own emotions.

Perhaps their conversation had opened this need in him. One she had been oblivious to. Perhaps it was the emotional changes he, and they, had been through this last week.

Perhaps it was because of this new house around them, the freedom of being alone and simply themselves.

Suddenly her own fierce need rose to meet his. The scent of him and new wood and stone and sunlight enveloped her in one of those crystalline moments that she would remember always. The moment she kissed her love in her new home. The septhour she and he made lo—

Yowl! The cat shriek echoed throughout the house. *You are not paying any attention to US!* Rhyz sounded highly offended.

A broken moment that would never come again.

FamMan? asked Flora sleepily.

We are Family, too. And we were promised a treat right now and you have not taken us, Rhyz scolded.

"What?" Muin asked. He sounded as dazed as she felt. His breath came in quick pants and, like her, he was ready to mate.

You SAID we would go to the mysterious Yew estate and visit the FamCat Baccat and See All There Is To See There! Not very many Fams are allowed in because they try to Chase the Raven. I told You We would not Chase the Raven. I promised. And You said We could come to the appointment that will give My FamWoman personal armor.

Avellana frowned. "What?"

He PROMISED Flora and Me could come if I told You last night that getting personal armor was a good idea AND I DID.

Avellana stepped away from the heat of her lover, his aura that enfolded her. "You suborned my Fam."

"That I did," Muin stated. His expression appeared impassive to most, but hurt had filtered back into his eyes.

She sighed. "I understand."

Rhyz arrived, grumbling, his mouth full of . . . Flora, whom he let go to sit on Muin's feet.

It is time to leave for Your appointment and Our treat. I 'ported with Flora so she would be with Us. Antenn called your glider to outside Our new home.

Avellana walked to the windows showing the front grassyard and the gliderway. "Oh! You brought your new twoseat glider. It looks very elegant sitting in front of our house."

Muin grunted.

"A very nice picture for those who observe," she approved. "They will visualize their own glider on the new road in front of their own custom home. We *will* make more sales by the end of the day, I am sure."

Turning back toward her love, her own heat subsiding a little, she saw him bend to pick up Flora.

I promised not to Chase the Raven, too, Flora said. *I have heard there are special munchies in a wonderful garden at Yew Residence.*

"Did you, now?" asked Muin.

So Baccat, the Yew FamCat, says, replied the housefluff. *He says Yew estate is best!*

"All Cats say that," Muin pointed out.

A loud bang reverberated throughout the valley. Avellana ran toward the noise outside the north windows and caught her breath as she saw Antenn and a team at either side of the wide gliderway leading into Multiplicity. She pointed. "Look at that! Tall pillars have been erected by the entrance to our community!"

I must go see! Rhyz said.

I want to go see, too! Flora added.

Picking up Flora in his mouth, the cat teleported away, sending back a last thought. *We will see and then wait for you in the glider.*

Avellana narrowed her eyes to study the situation better, paying little attention to the teleport-hopping of the Fams from her house to the entrance of the town.

"Rhyz is getting good at teleporting around here," Muin said.

"Hmm," Avellana replied absently. "The builders are setting a greeniron gate between the pillars!" She huffed and paced the few meters of her room, then back. And forth.

"Let's look." Muin waved a hand and the nearest window magnified the entrance so the activity jumped into view as if they were a meter away. "Nice pillars, unique. Rectangular with carved Celtic knotwork." Yet not looking at her, he murmured, "Antenn might have gotten one of the sculptors who's working on your Cathedral. Truly, the pillars and gate make a statement."

Stopping again to look out the window, frowning, Avellana muttered, "It appears as if a wall is going up. We did not have a wall in the plans."

"No?" Vinni asked.

She shrugged irritably. "Down the timeline, for next year, perhaps the one after, but not now."

"Ah."

That single word clued her in. Whirling, she stared at him. "You did this, did you not? And I can see how. You provided the gilt, funneled it through my governess's account and"—Avellana flicked a hand—"up goes the wall. Before more roads, the solid pathway to the ocean, the reinforced banks for the streams." She blew out a breath. "Muin!"

"Yes?"

"Walls, Muin? Walls to put me behind instead of the open space of freedom?" She flung out her arms, feeling overdramatic, but wanting to emphasize her point.

Anger suffused his face and he stomped over to her. "Nothing is enough! Not the protective amulet, the personal armor, others keeping an eye out for you, the gate and shieldspells around your house and your town. Nothing. I would swaddle you in cushions and set you in a corner of T'Vine HouseHeart to keep you safe, if I could."

She stared at his rant. "Muin—"

He made a cutting gesture. "But I know I can't. I know you would leave me and that is the worst thing I can imagine. You being taken from me. You leaving me. Being without you in my life."

"I am sorry, Muin. I will let you protect me as you will, but I insist on living my own life as an adult."

"I know." He grabbed her, yanked her close, nearly stifling her against his body. "You're right. You die, I die."

A great sorrow washed over her. "I am sorry that you live—have lived—with such fear."

He simply held her, and rocked. "You would have thought I would be reconciled to death by now, I've seen it in visions and portents and auras enough, but I am not. Perhaps my own, but never yours."

Her chest constricted at the thought, at the *feeling* emanating from him, at her own imagination of trying to live a life without him. No full life would be possible without him. No life at all.

"But you know we are so closely emotionally tied together that one will not survive the other's death." She paused and gave him a deep truth. "I know this and, I admit, it comforts me."

His breath shivered from him. "I must admit, I didn't think of that until lately, when you pointed it out. You're right, the notion we'd die together is some comfort. But I don't want to last even a minute without you."

"I hope that does not happen," she responded. "I would promise so, if I could."

Muin shrugged, and she felt every muscle in his body.

"I'd rather hoped we lived until a great age. My predecessor did. Not having an heir yet, I'd planned on being around for a long time. And you, too. I don't like the threats to you."

"I think you have made that clear. Let us go to D'Yew for my personal armor, then we can prepare for the ritual tonight . . . separately."

A grumble rose from his chest. "We had the MistrysSuite in T'Vine Residence redesigned and decorated for you two years ago. Since Antenn knows your taste so well, I'll contact him for an update." Muin paused, then added casually, "Tonight you could stay in that suite in my tower in T'Vine Residence." He cleared his throat. "Alone, even."

"My parents wish me to remain at D'Hazel Residence until I move into Multiplicity." Now the rumble in his chest sounded more like a growl. She ignored it. "My parents did not come today." She could not keep a mournful note from tinting her voice. "Perhaps tomorrow."

He squeezed her. "Perhaps. Your Family will take part in the ritual tonight. We will link with them and sense their emotions."

She leaned against him. "And we will prevail against those who have tried to separate us."

He kissed her briefly on her lips. "So I believe." Without releasing her from the circle of his arms, he angled his chin toward the windows facing east. "I still want a house here."

"I am sure Antenn will be pleased to create one for you."

"I'm sure about that, too."

Their calendar spheres popped into existence and pinged together. Avellana's said in her mother's voice, "You must leave now from Multiplicity to reach your appointment with D'Yew in a timely manner."

The pretty tune on Muin's sphere ended with no such warning, but they knew the final note indicated the last-minute countdown.

Vinni kept his arm around her waist as they descended the staircase, wide enough for two, which he hadn't noticed before.

He felt *freer* for those emotions he'd let out and expressed, outer layers of a hard kernel that still lurked inside him. How could he escape his rut and send his life in a different direction? Well, starting his true life with Avellana as his HeartMate would definitely help.

Near the front door, he let his arm fall but kissed her cheek. "Tonight," he said huskily. "Our first time as leaders of a ritual circle for our Family. Tonight we'll take another step as a couple together."

When she lifted her face to him, her deep blue eyes showed her usual serious expression, with a hint of melancholy added. "Yes, another important step in our relationship, in our betrothal." Her mouth thinned, then she continued. "And that portion of your Family who do not approve of me as your bride forced us into this situation."

"I'm sorry for that," he responded immediately. His lips twisted. "I'm sorry for a lot of things."

She gave a little sigh and shrug. "We brood on our failures. Both of us. Perhaps the reason that some of your Family doubts us as a good leading couple, because our humors are much the same, because we tend to the sober, and because we doubt ourselves. An unhealthy habit."

He brought her hands to his lips, one after the other, kissing her palms, flicking his tongue on her palm, tasting her and that wisp of her essence, taking it into him, letting it settle in his groin once more and give him a pain-pleasure buzz.

"From now on," he said huskily, "I will try to keep my mood light when you become sad, and you can do the same. That way, we may traverse our life path in a more cheerful frame of mind, lighten both our spirits as we progress."

Her smile bloomed. "Yes. Just as you have done right now."

"I'm no longer brooding, for sure, and you're more lighthearted," he agreed. Inhaling deeply, he opened the door so they could go out once more in public.

They'd just reached the bottom of the steps when Antenn shouted, "Hey, Avellana!" He gestured to the house behind them.

Setting his arm around his beloved's waist, Vinni walked them to his glider, then turned them both toward their friend, who grinned. Sure enough, Avellana's new home—her *studio* when she became D'Vine—stood finished and perfect. He'd been aware of the roof going on, and now a weather vane garnished the top of the house.

He narrowed his eyes. It looked as if Antenn had coated the brick with some sort of glassy spell that would shriek an alarm if anyone entered uninvited. Good.

Avellana pouted. "I missed watching *so* much today: some of the raising of the Community Center, my former governess's tiny house, now the last touches on my very own home!"

"Don't worry," Vinni soothed. "I see that Antenn has a professional viz recorder and operator down there. I'm sure he saved it all." Vinni kissed her temple. "Especially the building of the wonderful, unique home for Avellana Hazel, *the* person of highest status in Multiplicity. Excellent marketing."

"All right. But watching a viz is not the same. And tonight, I will miss Arta Daisy's multi-level circular home being constructed. She wanted a whole morning scheduled for it, and today, of course, but Antenn insisted that the Community Center go up first. So she decided to have it erected during the First Quarter Twinmoons apex." Avellana's smile showed briefly. "I like her very much. She tends to be dramatic."

Vinni grunted. "Like all the Daisys."

Avellana stared at her house. "It looks better than I had imagined." She did a few small dance steps in a most un-Avellana-like manner. He'd make sure she'd loosen up along that life path, too.

"For sure you are happier now." He grinned as he led her to the glider and handed her inside.

Twenty-two

A few minutes later, Vinni pulled up to another set of pillars. These rose a full four meters tall, rectangular and smooth with armorcrete, tinted a pale green, with an incised design of thick Yew tree trunks.

The greeniron gates here curlicued in fancy shapes that would barely let a kitten through, let alone a housefluff the size of Flora, or the medium-sized Rhyz FamCat.

A slight wavering in the air showed a field of additional shield-spells on the gate and in the walls. At one time, this estate would have been the easiest of all FirstFamily areas to break into, due to the enmity of the Yews to the best shieldspell practitioner. Not now.

Atop one pillar on a thick horizontal capstone sat a large, gray cat, appearing like a sculpture himself. *Greetyou, T'Vine and Avellana Hazel, Fams Flora and Rhyz.* He leapt down in front of the gates. *I am pleased to welcome you to my demesne. Fams, you may follow Me.* Long tail waving, he strolled along a path to the right of the gates.

Avellana touched her door and it lifted for their companions to hop out. "Dinner is in a septhour and a half," she reminded them.

She closed the door and Vinni thinned the windows of his glider. He waved a hand at the new and large opalescent scrystones set into the pillars, then addressed one. "Vinni T'Vine and Avellana Hazel to meet with D'Yew. We have an appointment."

"Please leave your glider outside the greeniron gates," Draeg Betony T'Yew's voice came.

Vinni and Avellana looked at each other.

"Draeg is being very cautious," Vinni murmured. He flicked his fingers to lift his door, went around, and took Avellana's hand as she exited the glider. "I know him from my days at The Green Knight Fencing and Fighting Salon; he was the master's favorite protégé."

She scrutinized his face. "You are not telling me something."

"You know me too well, as you've proven several times this morning." He answered lightly, squeezing her fingers. "What did you hear about the last attacks of the Traditionalist Stance extremists?"

He'd sent her away as soon as he'd figured out trouble brewed.

Frowning, Avellana said, "They targeted children. I think they tried to poison Marin Holly's and Walker Clover's children?"

"Yes." Vinni bit the word off, squelched the anger and uneasiness as he lowered the glider doors by spell—too quickly, because they slammed shut. He thickened the windows until they reached armorglass status, with the capacity to sound an alarm if someone tried to breach them. "The Traditionalist Stance fanatics don't believe children of former Commoners should be acceptable in Noble circles."

"But Walker Clover *Tested* for his GrandHouse nobility," Avellana insisted. "And he married his HeartMate, Sedwy Grove, a woman of the FirstFamilies. Walker's children have excellent pedigrees. Anyone would say."

"Anyone *should* say." Vinni nodded, then grunted as he muttered a Word to move his glider, hide and protect it. "But the Traditionalist Stance people don't want any more Nobles, especially Nobles raised from former Commoner families."

"And they fear people with different Flair," Avellana stated. He heard no quiver in her voice. "That is why you wished me to stay away earlier this year."

"There *were* 'accidents.' I worried for you."

She sighed. "I know." She walked with him the few strides to the locked gates. "Did they also threaten D'Yew?"

"I did tell you that members of the movement were found in the highest Families. Several held the Yew name."

Avellana gasped, stopped, and looked at him with wide eyes. "Truly?"

"Yes. And I don't think that we caught all the extremists, perhaps not even the current secret leader of the Traditionalist Stance."

Her frown deepening, Avellana said, "The Yews were always the most conservative Family, and the past two Heads of Households showed a nasty strain of . . . I should not speak so negatively about them. So many people hold negative views of me."

Her words flicked him on the raw. "That is not so!"

"Yes, Muin, it is. They believe I am fragile. I cannot be trusted to take care of myself. I am accident prone. I *had*—perhaps continue to have—brain damage. And people whisper about my psi power, whether I am truly a holo mural artist."

"And you're HeartMate to the equally odd Vinni T'Vine." He made a cutting gesture.

She came up and stroked his cheek. A lot of touching going on between them today, absolutely great. "You are not odd."

"I am so considered, for stopping when visions take me and spilling futures for good or ill without warning or thought before people. Makes them nervous."

"It is just your great Flair in action. People have always been wary of the FirstFamilies' great Flair."

Vinni snorted. "Maybe so, but I guarantee your sister's botanical talent is a lot less scary to people than mine."

With a nod, she said, "To others we might be alarming. Even to your Family, which is why we are leading them in the ritual tonight, to show them we are regular people. And you fear for me because of this hiding or missing leader of the Traditional Stance. You think he or she remains free and dangerous to me."

He didn't respond.

"Because my Flair is the oddest and most fearsome of them all."

"Hey, Vinni, it *is* you," said a man's voice from the pillar scrystone.

"Hello, Draeg. You couldn't tell from my expensive glider and the coat of arms on it?" Vinni replied.

"Not taking any chances, is all. Baccat has also announced that he's entertaining Flora and Rhyz. Gates are open now."

The greeniron swung with no sound along the smooth ground. Vinni strode hand in hand with Avellana up the gliderway and to D'Yew Residence.

Both Draeg Betony-Blackthorn T'Yew and the Head of the Household, Loridana D'Yew, stood in the large entryway of their Residence. A heavily muscled man six years younger than Vinni, Draeg stood easily in fighting stance but held hands with his even younger blond and willowy HeartMate, a new adult at no more than eighteen.

They bowed in greeting, and Avellana and Vinni returned the courtesy.

"Before we do this, I wish to ask the price for my personal armor," Avellana asked.

Uh-oh.

"A golden favor," Draeg said.

Avellana stilled an instant beside Vinni, withdrew her hand from his, and stepped aside. "No."

Avellana! Vinni protested mentally.

No. And they take advantage of you being a wealthy FirstFamily GreatLord. Of your FEAR. Her mental tone simmered.

Draeg's heavy brows went up. "No?" He slanted Vinni a surprised look. They'd been close enough in the social gang of The Green Knight Fencing and Fighting Salon that he might be able to catch Vinni's sheer desperation. Draeg frowned.

"I am sorry to have wasted your time," Avellana said. "But if you know much about me—"

"We do," Draeg said.

She nodded. "Everyone in FirstFamilies Noble circles seems to." She drew in a breath. "Then you will know that I had rough Passages, particularly the first when my brain synapses were faulty and unre-paired. My mother, D'Hazel, paid a golden favor for D'Marigold's help. My life has already cost one golden favor. I cannot accept that it must cost another."

Vinni met Draeg's eyes. Avellana had disclosed a Hazel Family secret. Vinni narrowed his own eyes in steely threat. Draeg rolled a shoulder as if dismissive of the information. He would keep the secret that seemed small to him.

And in the time that had happened, D'Yew rushed forward to embrace Avellana, who held rigid for only a few seconds before hug-ging back the younger woman.

The GrandLady shot a glance at Draeg and Vinni. "HeartMates have expectations, but we need to be flexible."

Avellana sniffed, relaxing a little more in the teen girl's embrace. They were much of a height. "I have had to be flexible all of my life."

"We can out-think men. Come, let's talk and walk down to the stables and I'll show you my horses and we'll figure out a good price for your personal armor."

What Vinni could see of Avellana's face appeared surprised. She hugged D'Yew back tightly, then released her. "I would like that. We can barter, a few holo paintings . . . or perhaps property."

"You can explain that to me," D'Yew said, and led the way, a bounce in her step, toward the door. She cast a glance back at Vinni. "And it won't be as much as Draeg said. T'Vine helped me earlier this year, and I don't forget."

"I did promise a token," Vinni said. "Any color."

"No," Avellana said. Her chin lifted. "This personal armor is for *me*, and *I* wish to pay for it. You know, I have a partnership in Mul-tiplicity and could pay you in land there . . ."

"You *do*?" D'Yew sounded thrilled.

"You forget," Draeg scolded Vinni mildly after the women had left. "Unlike most FirstFamilies' daughters, Loridana has lived for some time outside a Residence and a great estate. A wise move from your HeartMate, to offer Loridana more land outside this place." Draeg clapped a hand on Vinni's shoulder. "Why don't I show you my latest mosaic? Actually, I'd rather show Avellana, but you will do."

"Fine."

*T*his is the life," Draeg said as they stood just inside one of the back doors of the Residence, not quite a castle, but with a couple of towers and a crenellated top. Draeg's voice held pure satisfaction as he stared at the semicircular mosaic pavement showing a woman riding a horse. Nice work. Not at Avellana's level, but then she practiced her holo painting as if it were her main Flair. Draeg worked as a Grand-Lord and a fighter.

Now he slouched casually, smiling out at the gardens, the woods behind the estate. "Plenty of space for me to make my mosaics." He rolled his shoulders. "Last year—Cave of the Dark Goddess, the last few years were miserable, but after I met Loridana—Lord and Lady, everything changed for the better."

Vinni nodded. "You suffered through some tough times, even after meeting Loridana."

"Handled everything. All for the best," Draeg replied. He turned his head toward Vinni. "It'll work out for you, too." He paused. "Guaranteed."

"You're the prophet now?"

"Just got a good feeling."

Vinni snorted. "Got the good feeling that all guys who have HeartMates will end up happy. Not necessarily true."

At that moment the Residence said in a mellow female voice, "The ladies await you, gentle sirs, in the blue room."

Vinni and Draeg strolled back to a salon, Draeg saying, "It will be all right because we're finally going to catch the last main fligger of a Traditionalist Stance leader. Then those fliggering maniacs will be gone and their fanaticism a bad memory. Good fliggering riddance." His expression turned predatory. "And you let me know if you need any help in taking him down. Any time. I'm damn glad to offer any assistance—"

Inclining his head, Vinni said, "I'll keep that in mind."

"You do that."

A few minutes later Avellana walked with him back down the long gliderway, arm in arm.

Other than their farewells to the Yews, they hadn't spoken.

"So you negotiated with D'Yew?"

"Yes." Avellana smiled up at Vinni. "She remembers you fondly."

"Good. That's good."

"She also told me her whole story—of her wretched Family and her determination to live on her own, and how her love of animals saved her. She made me realize that my life has been privileged. I have always had people loving me. Perhaps I thought I received too much tender kindness from my Family and you, and—"

"Perhaps in the wrong ways?"

"How can there be wrong ways to love? Real love, not obsession."

"I admit that your Family and I overprotected you, and determined your life based on our fears for you."

"But Mother paid a full gold favor for help for my Passages, and that includes aid including to the death of the Head of the Household if cashed in. A huge price. Because she loves me." Avellana paused. "But she would pay that for Coll, too, if necessary, or for Father, of course. We are a loving Family."

"Yes."

"So I have been blessed. That is knowledge to cherish."

They walked a few more meters before she said, "I liked how Lori's story ended, how she triumphed and took her place and claimed her HeartMate. But it did make me realize that I have missed a lot of current events, though I *was* here on one fateful day."

Vinni grunted. "I kept you informed."

"Yes, with facts but not human stories." She made a cutting gesture. "And it is time for me to do this, before the ritual where the irritation will be noticed." Stopping him, she took both his hands, met his eyes, and matched his stare. He felt their emotional bond open wide, expand to the greatest thickness. Then, linked, he *saw* her *reach* for the thread humming with irritation, pluck it. They both gasped.

Then she yanked and it broke.

They cried out, shuddered, fell into each other's arms.

Owie! screeched Flora mentally.

What was THAT!? Rhyz demanded.

Vinni got the idea that the Fams had been dozing in a garden. Rhyz sounded particularly grumpy because he'd been roused from a catnip dream.

Between pants, Avellana stated telepathically to them all, *Years of simmering resentment, gone.*

Yay! trilled Flora in their minds, with true and simple joy.

Hrrmmph! growled Rhyz.

We are leaving in a few minutes, Vinni sent along the communication channel among them. *You may come with us now or stay in the garden.*

I can 'port to the glider! Flora sent cheerfully. *Baccat says no food for housefluffs and I can't munch from gardens.*

Rhyz chimed in, *Baccat may try to impress Me with His food. I will stay here.*

Please teleport to me when I call you after my ritual cleansing, Avellana stated. *I wish for your support during the further preparation for leading the ceremony tonight.*

I will come then. I have always supported You, as no other!

The slow burn of Vinni's irritation expanded, threatening to burst his kernel, just as he'd lost control twice earlier. Unacceptable.

I love you, Rhyz, until later, Avellana sent.

Looking up at Vinni, she frowned as if sensing his annoyance. Also unacceptable. She rubbed her hands up and down his arms, then gifted him with a small smile. "For now my long rancor has been banished. I cannot promise the feeling will not return, but it will not be tonight." She narrowed her eyes but appeared as if she looked inward. "There seem to be tiny fragments. I will deal with them before our important ritual, also."

He inclined his head. "Thank you." He hesitated. "I need to take care of an emotional problem, too, before tonight."

Now sadness washed over her eyes. "We are so much alike. But I love you, Muin."

"Love you, Avellana." Linking fingers with her again, he drew her quickly from the Yew estate. He didn't like that they'd experienced such a personal moment here. Thought negativity might linger on this estate. Hoped no other Yews lived who belonged to the Traditionalist Stance and reported on them.

No doubt Loridana had ensured that no one held those views during her Loyalty Ceremony earlier in the year. She'd do that, and Draeg would have made sure, too.

Outside the gates, Vinni called the glider, then paced away from her. "Let's see this personal armor."

Her mouth formed, *Shield,* and a sphere encased her for an instant, then contracted and he noticed a sheen on her skin, then the spell seemed to sink into her. Mentally, she said, *I have a power stone that I can use for a certain amount of time at full strength. I can also activate the spell at percentages of strengths and for various amounts of time. Very flexible. We negotiated to have a power stone for three years.*

Walking up to her, he put a hand on her shoulder. Or meant to. He couldn't touch her. Frowning, he said, "That's a drawback."

Avellana smiled, kept her reply telepathic. *Yes, a big deficiency. Good thing we didn't pay a golden favor for it—though I would have expected a lifetime quantity of stones. Instead I gave her a parcel of land in Multiplicity.*

Good job! Vinni congratulated her.

Poof, Avellana said mentally as she formed the word silently. The spell vanished and his hand curved over her shoulder. Warmth flowed between them physically as well as emotionally.

Avellana said aloud, "Both Loridana and I are very pleased she will be in Multiplicity. Her home will be small, but she will be another FirstFamily presence in the community, and she will keep some of her animals there, stridebeasts and horses and perhaps llamas."

Avellana grinned. "Another unique feature of Multiplicity that may draw residents."

"Very good," Vinni agreed. Glancing at her, he said, "Promise me you will always initiate your personal armor before you leave D'Hazel Residence."

Her brows went up. "Even if I am going in a glider to the Hopeful Cathedral or teleporting to T'Vine Residence?"

He gritted. "Always. If you join others who will defend you, you can, ah, use your judgment as to whether to banish the spell, but—"

She stopped his words by kissing his mouth. Fisting his hands, he kept them from her, still thinking Draeg or someone else might be watching. The man must have instituted and trained more Yew guards.

Avellana settled back, smiling. "I promise I will always initiate my personal armor before I leave D'Hazel Residence."

Vinni inclined his head. "Thank you." Then he handed her into the glider.

Flora appeared then. Vinni picked her up and snuggled her. She didn't give him the comfort he needed. Probably an ocean full of comfort wouldn't soothe him. His jaw clenched until his teeth hurt, so he stopped. He put Flora on Avellana's lap and they both hummed with serene pleasure.

When he entered the glider, the door slammed down.

Avellana petted Flora. *Now we must start preparations for the ritual.*

Vinni couldn't, yet. He *had* to get rid of that damned clump of inner anger and guilt.

Twenty-three

Vinni dropped Avellana off at D'Hazel Residence and 'ported Flora to her basket in his sitting room. He deliberately didn't go home—to T'Vine Residence. He couldn't follow the complete and long procedure for cleansing and meditation before a major ritual, as Avellana would—

It occurred to him that he didn't know exactly what her preparations would be, how different getting ready for a ceremony might be for those of the Hopeful Faith as opposed to those who believed in the Divine Couple. Unlike the public ritual itself, he didn't think she'd need to combine routines.

His teeth hurt again and he stopped gritting them. Before he stood with Avellana in the sacred Vine grove along the side of the Residence, he had to get his head straight, his mind working right. Rid himself of unproductive negative emotions like envy, resentment, and guilt with regard to Avellana.

He'd take Antenn's advice and work on the physical to smooth out mental and emotional knots. But somewhere other than T'Vine Residence.

If Multiplicity had been empty—or with the two Families who had moved in that day—he would have returned to the quiet and space there. He sensed through his friendship bond with Antenn that the man directed several crews building the wall and was doing his own preparations to raise Arta Daisy's large home. So Vinni sent Antenn's architectural office a formal notice that he'd like to buy land in the community, with a visualization of the property he wanted. He also requested a meeting with the man about designing Vinni's home.

No peace at T'Vine Residence, or Multiplicity. He didn't want the structure and other people training at The Green Knight Fencing and Fighting Salon. He wouldn't be returning to the baths any time soon, especially since Phae Thermarum remained missing.

That left one good place. The long teleportation to the Great Labyrinth in the north should drain him of some excess energy. A brisk walk around part of the crater's edge should finish this particular exercise off. Not as beneficial as a full, meditative walk from center of the Labyrinth out, but Vinni didn't have time for that.

Exiting his glider, he sent it home, sucked in a big breath, and teleported to the landing pad gazebo near the top of the path down into the labyrinth. The scent of the air, cooler than that of Druida City, higher in altitude, full of fragrances from all the offerings and Family shrines below in the crater, wrapped around him. Yes, here he could find his balance.

He'd covered a kilometer around the rim path when a whirl of *seeing* smashed into him. He stopped and let it spin through him in a tornado of colors but didn't grab at the vision to hold and tame and understand. He simply stood and shuddered.

When his physical sight cleared, he saw a sober-faced Abutilon Gwydion Ash walking slowly to him.

Vinni's gut clutched. The large young man who might be doomed. Vinni shot his gaze around the panorama, but this didn't . . . quite . . . match the time and place of his visions of Gwydion's demise.

Still, Vinni's Flair spiking as it had confirmed a bad future continued to lurk for the Ash second son.

Gwydion stopped walking, too. He bowed to Vinni with practiced courtesy. "Greetyou, T'Vine."

After clearing his throat, Vinni called out, "Greetyou, Gwydion."

The young man's face relaxed at the use of his middle name. He didn't like Abutilon. He sauntered up. He held a half-meter piece of wood that looked like a twisted tree root. With a frown, he asked, "Problem?"

"No."

The youngster of seventeen, a gentle giant with Ash's inches and muscle but not his dangerous edge, Gwydion smiled at Vinni but tilted his head. Then he put the piece of oddly shaped wood that looked like a natural sculpture aside on a large flat-topped boulder.

"I think you do have some problem nagging at you." He rolled his shoulders in his roomy tunic. Though not a blacksmith like his father, as an animal Healer the boy worked with large animals such as llamas, horses, and stridebeasts that took strength to hold and manage.

Sweeping a hand from Vinni toward a small, level meadow a couple of meters away from the edge of the labyrinth, Gwydion said, "Why don't we spar a little, GreatLord?"

Obviously the boy sensed more than Vinni felt comfortable with, but then he *did* Heal animals every day, and humans were animals, too.

With a shrug, Vinni said, "Sure." Then he decided to be more gracious and bowed. "Thank you for your concern and help."

"No problem," Gwydion said. He moved with natural, youthful grace to the glen and stood in an easy fighting stance.

Vinni joined him, gave him a fighter's bow, eyeing the larger young man. Probably not as easy to defeat as he might think. All to the good, he *did* need to rid himself of grumbly thoughts that stuck in his head and made him restless.

The boy returned his bow, settled into his balance . . . and watched and waited for Vinni to make the first move.

So he did. The young man had been trained by the best, of course, but so had Vinni. And Vinni had had to fight longer and harder for what he wanted, at The Green Knight, in his Family, and in his life in general, so he beat the boy, taking him down and wrestling him to surrender.

Still, he panted when he rose, offered the teen a hand, and pulled him to his feet. Yes, the youngster had muscle and strength, and would fill out more. Vinni had.

Gwydion grunted as he dusted off his clothes, shook out his shaggy-cut thick black hair, gave Vinni another sweet smile. "Dad says I don't have the killer instinct." His eyelids half lowered. "That's okay. I'm a Healer, not a fighter, but I'm thinking that I need to spend more time at the forge to develop my strength more." He paused, then added thoughtfully, "And perhaps attend fighting training more often at The Green Knight."

Vinni's words took more effort than he'd expected, but he said, "Couldn't hurt."

Gwydion nodded. "I'll do that, then." He walked back to the boulder where he'd set the tree root, picked it up, and let his fingers find folds in the wood. No doubt seeing Vinni's gaze fastened on the piece, he smiled and held it up. "An interesting find, isn't it? I discovered it lying near the center of the Labyrinth."

"The Ash, your Family shrine, the world tree," Vinni murmured.

"Just so. I believe it to be a piece of black walnut."

Vinni grunted.

"Like I said, an interesting shape, and something I can add to the altar tonight for the celebration of First Quarter Twinmoons."

More people were celebrating tonight than Vinni had anticipated, than he'd ever considered would observe such a minor ritual.

His smile broad, Gwydion said, "Like you and Avellana, it's my twin sister's and my first time leading a Family ritual." He ducked his head. "You gave Jasmine the idea and she asked the parents and so it happened." His lips firmed. "I wanted something special for the altar."

"It's big, you could almost make an altar out of the piece itself."

The youngster looked at the root again. "Maybe I could, but I like how the earth formed the wood, or how the wood formed itself when burrowing into the earth."

"Is woodworking your creative Flair?" Vinni asked reluctantly. His heart hurt talking to the boy-man. He'd tried to ignore this particular child of Ash's—one with great and shining potential to change the world . . . if he lived past the equally great darkness of a life cut short.

Big shoulders shrugged. "I suppose. I haven't done much to discover my creative Flair. I love animals and Fams. My youngest sister is the true artist in the Family. My twin also knows hers."

The twin sister with a good future and no shadow over it except a brother's death.

A scry-pebble alert sounded, and Gwydion reached into his trous pocket. "As if our talking conjured her up," he muttered. "Hey, Jasmine."

"Where are you? *At the Great Labyrinth!* Come home, now! We need to get ready!"

"We have plenty of time," Gwydion protested. "You're anal about time."

"Now!"

"All right." With another smile at Vinni, the boy vanished.

And Vinni sat on a nearby boulder, his knees slightly weak. Another thorny problem he'd been avoiding had just confronted him.

Abutilon Gwydion Ash could change the world. For the better. Vinni knew all the signs, he'd seen them enough—on the people who'd discovered the cure for the plague. On entrepreneurs who'd built a new industry that made the planet better. On the boy's father, T'Ash, who'd spearheaded the abolition and cleanup of the slum Downwind in Druida City.

His own scry pebble lilted with Avellana's tune as his co-leader called him. "Greetyou, dearest," he murmured to her, and saw her concerned expression smooth. She blinked as if recognizing the place.

"You are at the Great Labyrinth."

"Yes."

"I love that place. Did you ask your Lady and Lord to provide you with something special for the altar?"

"Something will come to hand," he said.

She nodded. "I am about to begin my meditation process. I wanted to say I love you and to ask what has been bothering you."

"I am angry at myself for my treatment of you."

"Do not be." She gifted him with a sweet smile. "I can be irritated with you for that. Tomorrow."

"That hurts, too."

"But during this ritual tonight, I will send any resurging remnants of my anger away along the four pathways of the Journey. You could give yours over to your Lady and Lord." She paused. "And we can both ask our spiritual entities for guidance."

"Good idea," Vinni said. He stood and strode toward the nearest teleportation pad. He preferred to come and go via pad. Always safer if a vision happened to take him before, during, or after the act of teleportation. "I love you, too."

"I know, Muin. I will see you later. We will be *perfect* tonight."

"Yes. Until later."

"Blessed be." She ended the call.

He arrived on his bedroom pad.

Antenn and Avellana and the Ash boy had been right. Sparring with Gwydion had done Vinni good, rid him of negative energy and doubts, and distracted his mind to another difficult problem he'd been avoiding.

But he'd struggled to find a path, any way to save young Gwydion Ash before, and failed.

*V*inni hadn't found a special item for the altar, a tradition for when a person became the leader of a ritual, priest or priestess of the Lord or Lady, for the first time.

Of course he'd led his first ritual circle the year he'd become T'Vine as a child of six.

He should have considered that this would be the first time he and Avellana would lead a circle—*ritual*—together, and that it wouldn't be exactly a circle. Their first sacramental ceremony together. And he should have looked for a proper new offering for the altar. Maybe in Multiplicity—*no, bad idea*, and he continued to have a slew of bad ideas. Multiplicity was Avellana's current-house-soon-to-be-studio,

his own retreat, perhaps. *This, T'Vine Residence*, would be her home
and best they both remember that.

A ripple of unease seemed to waver in the air around him. Frowning, he left his bedroom for his sitting room. And there, on his cache
table, from the Family, lay several objects that people had contributed for the ritual tonight, maybe something he was supposed to
choose for his own special offering.

No.

He sucked in a breath and began coughing. One item polluted the
atmosphere with more negative emotions than he'd held in his own
person for the last week. Toxic.

Damn.

He touched it and it disintegrated immediately, leaving only a
whiff of mind-scent of the guards. Didn't know.

Damn. Members of his Family continued to oppose Avellana.

Well, hopefully some of those would change their minds tonight
as they participated in the celebration of First Quarter Twinmoons.

That was the goal.

He scried Avellana back, and said quickly, "I think we should find
a special item for our first ritual altar together. When you're ready,
scry me and I will meet you at the entry gate at the bottom of the
gliderway up to the castle. We'll walk up it until an item presents itself, then 'port to the sacred grove."

She inclined her head—her head atop a pair of bare shoulders. He
wondered if she was naked. "A wonderful idea, Muin."

Clearing his throat and directing his mind *away* from sex, he
said, "Later," and signed off once again. But warning continued to
itch at him, so just before he turned his mind and body to preparing
for the ritual, and took himself in to bathe under the waterfall, he
scried T'Ash Residence and asked for Gwydion.

The young man's mild visage looked out at him from a screen.
"T'Vine?"

"I want to request that you do *not* go to the Great Labyrinth by
yourself for the rest of the summer."

Gwydion's brows dipped. "You're sure?"

"Absolutely."

"Okay."

But Vinni thought his warning hadn't sunk into the man's consciousness. Still too young.

"Can I speak with one of your elders?" he asked.

Gwydion laughed. "Only Nuin is here; the parents are in the HouseHeart." With an impish smile, he yelled, "Nuin, get off the scry with your latest girl, T'Vine wants to speak with you!"

All right, Vinni was being used for brotherly torment. Wonderful.

A scowling Nuin Ash, the oldest child of that Family, bumped Gwydion away from the scry panel. "Yeah?" He stopped, looked surprised when he actually saw Vinni, did a quick half bow. "Greetyou, T'Vine."

"Greetyou, Nuin," Vinni responded. "Please emphasize to your younger brother, and your parents, that Gwydion should not go to the Great Labyrinth alone until after . . . the first frost." That felt right.

Nuin's eyes flashed surprise, then an arrested expression. "Okay. I'll tell everyone. Thanks." He paused as if trying to think what to say next.

"Merry meet." Vinni started the standard farewell.

Nuin appeared relieved and inclined his head. "Merry part."

"And merry meet again."

"For sure!" T'Ash Residence's scry panel went dark. Vinni wondered if he should have spoken to the intelligent Residence itself, but the wall timer chimed and he had to start ritual preparations *now*. His own Residence might not report to Bifrona or the others about his timeline . . . but maybe it would. In any event, he did not want to give any member of the Family the chance to criticize his or Avellana's actions tonight.

You must begin your waterfall NOW, stated T'Vine Residence telepathically.

So Vinni stripped and began breathing in the pattern to cleanse body, mind, heart before he became a vessel for the Lord tonight . . .

if that happened. Or if he manifested one of the entities Avellana
believed in: the childlike self, the vital adult, the elder, the spiritual
guardian.

He blanked his mind.

Twenty-four

*W*hen he met Avellana at the bottom of the hill, just inside the guard gate, she wore a formal robe of dark blue overlaid with spun silver in a Celtic knot pattern. Beautiful and appropriate for a First Quarter Twinmoons ceremony.

And she shimmered with the personal armor spell. With a curve of her lips, she asked, "Will you defend me?"

If he'd been wearing weapons, he'd have clapped his hands on sword and blazer. Instead, he bowed. "To the death." Straightening, he spread his arms. "As will all the guards in T'Vine Residence."

With a nod she whispered, "Poof," and dropped the armor.

He wanted to pull her close, feel her soft body against his. Connect with her by physical touch. So he held out his hands and waited for her to clasp them, then closed his eyes when their fingers met. Skin to skin.

Not quite as good as lips to skin, or lips to lips, or anything other than hands. But she radiated serenity and settled him just at the first touch of their palms sliding together.

He had not managed to reach a deep meditative state earlier. Being with her helped that.

"Greetyou and blessings of the journey together, beloved," Avellana whispered.

"Greetyou and blessings of the Lady and Lord," he replied. He began to regulate his breathing. That would help, too, keep inhalations and exhalations in the right order and timing.

Avellana's breasts rose as she matched the rhythm of his deep breaths.

"Your robe is lovely, but not as lovely as you." He brought their linked hands to his mouth and kissed her fingers.

"The robe is new and will serve very well for tonight." Her breath sifted out. Glancing around, she smiled. "It has been a long time since we walked up the hill together. Usually I teleport to your tower or the public rooms."

"Yes."

"We can use this time as a walking meditation."

He didn't know about that, but though he sensed his Family watching—the guards below and above at the gates, others from the multitude of windows in the tall fortress walls—no one else hung around the gliderway.

"We will join our energies in meditation before we lead the ritual." She tilted her head and flashed him a genuine smile. "As we will do for the rest of our lives."

He swallowed hard. "Yes."

"And we *will* find an offering for our first altar together."

"Of course we will." He couldn't see his future, or hers or theirs in detail, but he could feel the feathery waft of destiny for minor matters, occasionally, as he did now. "The Lady and Lord will bless us in this."

"My Deities of the Journey are full of joy and laughter and will grace us."

She swung their hands and he let her cheer sweep through him, ease away snags of edgy nerves.

They proceeded in quiet companionship.

Avellana spotted the item first, since she watched where they walked and he looked at her.

"Muin, a feather!" She dropped his hand.

Feathers often fell around the castle. T'Vine Residence contained a falconry that included several varieties of birds.

But Avellana bent down and swooped up the plume, and after he watched her robe outline her pretty backside, he focused on the long thing—about a half meter of feather, with horizontal strands a good ten centimeters wide.

"Zow," he said. He didn't even know what bird this came from. "Rather like a peacock feather with a fancy eye, but not from that bird."

"Four colors!" she exulted, brushing the fat top with her fingers. "Gold, orange, red, and a deep purple *heart* in the center. Wonderful!"

"Yes."

She narrowed her eyes. "Hmm. I can use these colors and this feather in a mural, perhaps in my home and . . ." Beaming up at him, she said, "A lovely offering, and we know our divine entities bless us and our purpose tonight."

He nodded.

When she took his hand again, he held the feather with her.

"You seem easier this evening, Muin."

"So do you."

She chuckled. "The benefits of meditating in my childhood rooms, I believe. Though I *am* anticipating living in Multiplicity." She sent him a sultry look from under lowered lashes. "Until we wed and I come here."

It occurred to him that he should follow his HeartMate's previous advice and give those feelings that continued to weigh on him to the Lady and Lord before he made the first formal step of the ritual. Those lingering doubts and worries stuck inside him. He should have faith that the Lady and Lord would provide him with inspiration to find his way.

Avellana's own preparations had obviously included scattering those fragments of her negative emotions to the four directions.

Thinking of directions, feeling the gazes of his hidden Family, he wondered how many would actually show up for the ritual.

He'd hedged his bets.

That morning he'd considered his Family member by member and whom he could absolutely trust. To his surprise, he came up with about a quarter of the folk he led whom he believed were honorable, and he thought three-quarters of his Family would follow him if he didn't do anything too revolutionary . . . or stupid. That relieved him.

But right now, he understood that he couldn't expect all those who supported him to be at the ritual. Some would be working, some would have other plans. Some, like his chief guard, simply weren't spiritual and only appeared at the major holiday ceremonies when all the Family was expected.

Vinni *had* tapped four of those he most trusted, who would follow him and Avellana and work together well, to handle the directional energies so important in every ritual circle. Thankfully all four were intrigued by the small changes to the standard ceremony and could easily learn their lines.

Before he and Avellana had reached the last curving incline to the third gate of T'Vine Residence castle, they were notified that the Hazels had arrived and awaited him and Avellana with the rest of the participants in the sacred grove.

Sliding an arm around her waist, he teleported them to the altar at the center of the grove, then released her. She turned and curtseyed several times to his relatives who circled them, about twenty of them. She dipped her head and made the same observance to her mother, D'Hazel, a FirstFamily GreatLady, and grinned at her own Family. Vinni followed suit, and then he and Avellana placed the feather on the altar.

She glanced up at the castle towering above them, then shot Vinni a look as she realized the altar and the compass points had been moved slightly to accommodate the Hopeful's sacred directions. Vinni didn't know if anyone else had observed it, but he felt the oddness as tension in his shoulders. The grove lay near his personal tower and he wasn't accustomed to seeing his rooms from this angle during a ceremony.

Flexibility in his life must be key.

With a nod to his flautist, Vinni signaled the woman to begin the Gathering Song. He and Avellana awaited a few late arrivals, then closed the circle and intoned the Welcoming Blessing.

They all joined hands in the circle, as always dedicated to the Lady and Lord, Avellana had accepted that. As they summoned the guardian energies, the people Vinni had placed at the four directional points not only included the Celtic elemental names but added a line about a childlike self, and a vital adult, emphasized the guardian spirit, and spoke of the crone, the wise one nearing the end of her journey. And when they linked all energies and Flair to proceed with the ritual, those four faded back and brought others with them so the circle became more of a rounded square.

From then on Vinni took two personas in the ceremony, the mature and greatly Flaired man and the guardian spirit—as guardian of the Family. Avellana revealed the naturalness and innocent acceptance of a child, and reflected the experience and endurance of an aged person who'd seen much of life.

Then, to the surprise of most of the Family, the circle drew together, then separated into two parallel lines, with Avellana and Vinni at the top. He nodded to several Family musicians—the flute, a fiddle, and a drum—and the celebrants began a slow march that everyone recognized. The lines changed as couples opposite each other took hands. A procession for Avellana around the grove, this journey in accordance with her religion.

The rest of the ritual was gorgeous in its simplicity. They held candles and sang ancient songs almost as if they were children welcomed to take part in their first ritual.

Avellana's inherent serious manner, and her obvious spirituality, lent every gesture, all her words, grace.

Vinni had been proud of her before, and awed by her murals, but in this one event he knew that she surpassed him as a person of deep faith and sincerity. He'd kept his mind on alliances and maneuvers within and without of the Family for so long that he wondered at his character now. Certainly he didn't have the purity of purpose his lover did.

But she *shone*, as a person, as his HeartMate. Through the ripples of feeling from those of his Family who'd attended the ritual, they noticed that, too.

For First Quarter Twinmoons, linking hands in a circle once more, they accessed the energy of the Family and curved that Flair into a sphere into the air above and the earth below. They sent power and blessings into the plans and goals they'd formed for the Family during the New Twinmoons ceremony at the beginning of the month. Then, in silence, the whole of the gathering shared strength and bolstered the unspoken personal goals of the individuals taking part in the ritual.

Finally they closed the rite with a quick spiral dance and song, then thanked the entities and dismissed the circle.

Cheer pervaded the company as they trooped from the grove down to the wider paved terrace that served as an open-air dining area. Though each had partaken of a mouthful of food and drink during the ceremony, now they feasted.

Unfortunately Avellana and her Family didn't stay for the after-party. She gave him a brief hug and kiss, then teleported home with the Hazels.

And Vinni circulated among his Family, those who'd participated in the ritual, and those who moseyed in to partake of the good food from special no-times dedicated to ceremonial meals. He kept his most charming, genial, and easygoing mask on for everyone, Great-Lord T'Vine, Head of the Household.

That wasn't his true self. Not the man he wanted to be. Not the man he *would* be with Avellana. He missed her.

Definitely time to start their life together.

Though as people drifted away into their own lives, he could sit, talk, and relate more with some Family members with whom he didn't often speak.

Bifrona stayed until the last, then they cleaned the area with a housekeeping spell. She seemed smug that everything had gone off well, and reassured that Avellana would make an acceptable Great-Lady D'Vine.

Good enough, though Vinni felt tired to his marrow.

The mixture of his and Avellana's religions had worked well, a relief, and something he'd definitely tell the priestess who'd crafted the ceremony.

With the approval from Bifrona and the knowledge she'd sent that endorsement to her faction, he believed he and Avellana had won over everyone at the ritual. She'd gained additional acceptance.

Unfortunately, not even a majority of Vines had participated in the ritual. Since he guided the ceremony as the god as Lord and the avatar for two of the Hopeful religious spirits, Vinni had concentrated on manifesting those qualities and not figuring out exactly why those relatives came or stayed away. An itch on the nape of his neck seemed to warn him that his primary adversary in the Family had not been present.

Still, he would remember the faces and the voices of those who'd partaken in the wonderful rite, know they didn't oppose him.

As he lay, lonely, in his great generational bed, he analyzed each moment of the ritual because something nagged at him. And he found that there had been a tiny, slimy thread of disgust and anger. Not from one of those who participated, but one who watched, hidden by the rings of trees of the sacred grove.

An inimical observer, and one that he and Avellana failed because there was no room for charity in the soul who watched. All beliefs set in stone, rigid. All emotions roiling at some sense of injustice. He probed that, tried to get a single fact from the thread, caught only a flash of warped belief: Avellana was a mutant, and any heritage from her would be harmful to the Family.

In her own bed, Avellana, too, considered the ritual. Muin had smiled down at her when she had said the final blessing, and she had let a breath showered from the radiant stars beaming down on her shudder into her . . . then out. She had been nervous throughout the evening, from the moment she put on her formal robe.

She had covered her anxiety well, she hoped. Anxious until she walked down the path to the center of the edge-rounded square and looked into Muin's eyes to join speaking and responses with him.

Then, of course, she realized that she had felt his utter support in the back of her mind, as a bedrock of emotion flowing from him to her, and should have relied on that. She was unaccustomed to having him so near that she *could* depend on him. And wary that if she leaned on him, it might rouse his protective instincts even more.

But leading this ritual had taught her—as she hoped it had shown everyone else—that they were a couple, HeartMates, if not yet Heart-Bound.

Equal and able to provide strength to the other when she or he needed it. Her smile that had been a mask at the beginning of the ritual curved naturally at the end.

And as she drifted into sleep, she felt the tug of him, the *need* of him for coming together.

Dream sex. Her breath hitched, then let out on a sigh. All she could give him now, until he understood that the next time they truly lay together, they would HeartBond.

She yearned for that more than sex.

She came to him in his dreams and at her first mental touch his body filled with lust, even as his mind shivered with relief. It had been years since she'd initiated lovemaking . . . actually since the final occasion that they'd made physical love.

That instance had been before the last two times he'd sent her away. That particular moment, he realized with a heart-pang, when she'd thought they'd wed shortly and be together forever.

Two years ago.

Once again they stood in the T'Vine sacred grove, this time in the small, heavily wooded copse directly beneath his tower. In the way of dreams, though the time remained night, he could see her well. She wore a filmy gossamer wrap that flowed around her, hiding then revealing her body. His mouth dried.

Holding out her hands, she smiled and sent his name to his mind: *Muin.*

You are so lovely, he replied.

Brown hair free and swinging and wavy from being bound up in braids for the ritual, white streak gleaming silver, blue eyes dreamy. Lips curved in pleasure. His own eyes stung with the emotion of seeing her.

Thank you for coming, he sent from his mind to hers.

You called me.

Did I? I wasn't aware of that.

She shook her head slowly. *Perhaps it is that we always call to each other, our blood, our hearts, our spirits.*

Yes.

It would always be "yes."

Her feet did not bend the grass or brush against the wildflowers as she came to him, and he suppressed the brief pang that this remained a dream.

I love you, he said.

I love you, too, she replied, smiling, and that smile seemed to show in twinkling eyes he should not have been able to see . . . her whole being sparkled. Not just because of his own vision but the revelation of her spirit self.

Sweat beaded on his body as his sex rose, thick and hard. He felt all too physical, and he wasn't wearing a thing—neither of them seemed to be visualizing clothes for him.

Muin, she whispered telepathically, as she stopped before him, lifting her hands to toy a little with his chest hair.

Close enough that his shaft slid against the smooth skin of her stomach. Absolutely no good control of the rhythm of his breathing. Well, no good control of anything. His jaw clenched to be able to just stand there and not pounce.

Then her fingers brushed across his bare chest—avoiding his nipples, which were sensitive—to stop at his sides.

Muin, you have developed your torso more . . . I noted that earlier, at the baths. She sounded wistful. Like she might seduce if given time. Really good.

He grunted, managed to whisper back, *Been training a lot. Keeps me outta the Residence and away from Family. Miss you less.* As usual, his brain began to fog.

Her hands slid back across his torso. *So very sexy.*

Gl-lad.

Her fingernails flicked his nipples. He jerked.

She hummed in approval, and he blinked to clear his eyes and *look* at her. Hair already tumbled as if he'd grabbed her head and kissed her hard—which he did now. Least he could do, if he wanted her to take charge.

More than physical pleasure throbbed through their bond; her simple delight at being with him cleared a bit of the lust fog from his brain enough to humble him.

He'd usually rated that low—just being with her—before these last days. After all, they had a bond and communicated often, but now he thought he would crave her company for the rest of his life.

He took her hands, still smoothing his chest, and moved them down to his straining shaft. *I wish we were together in person.*

Their exchange of visualizations and physical caresses had often satisfied him, but not now.

Next time, the HeartBond, she whispered telepathically, and a golden glow enveloped them, mind, body, rolling through the bond between them. Powerful HeartMate love.

Been such a fool. More feeling than words, regret.

Her love flooded him, nothing negative in that stream. His hands went to her hips and the thin silkeen fabric melted away under his need to feel her skin. He thought she panted roughly, but he'd gone blind.

Need. No words for that, only reverberating emotion. He took what he wanted, cupping her butt with his hands, striding back a couple of steps to a wide tree he could brace against.

He lifted her, and she moved, and then she was sliding right down onto his cock, and he was thrusting into her, hips angling, pumping.

Tight, wet woman surrounding him. Her arms fiercely embracing, her fingers tangling in his hair, pulling, edge-of-pain sensation adding to the rush of spiraling passion, hot pleasure winding into spectacular orgasm.

She joined him in the rhythm of loving, legs clamping tight around him, dampness where their bodies touched and moved and strove for completion.

Loving sex. Loved, loved, loved sex.

Loved Avellana.

Muiiinnn! She cried out, head flung back, telepathically and in reality.

The contractions of her around him yanked him from man to pure savage animal, claiming his mate, plunging into her until he imprinted himself into her very cells.

He roared, let the strength of his climax blast through him, shake him. Shake them both.

She'd subsided against him.

The tree felt rough against his bare back and butt; if he'd been concentrating on it, he could've scraped the hell out of himself. Flaired dream quests could be real enough, act on the body as if he—they—were there physically.

He stepped away, still holding her backside, enjoying the feel of her body limp and satisfied against him. He managed to sink down to the smooth and grassy ground, crushing wildflowers as he did. Their scent mixed with that of his and Avellana's sweaty loving.

She arranged herself on top of him. *Nice broad chest, I need to train more so I match you . . .*

No, I like you . . . softer.

Her low murmur hummed against him as her lips kissed the hollow of his neck. *Muin, I am so glad I have returned and I am with you.*

Yes! Avellana, beloved . . .

Yes, Muin?

Please fight sleep. I want to hold you.

A slight chuckle, her warm breath moving against his skin as it cooled in the summer evening. *Yes, I want to lie on you, appreciate you.*

You always do, appreciate me.

I love you, Muin.

I love you.

He, too, fought sleep, because when either of them gave in they would slip into true rest and dreaming and away from their lover.

Inhaling deeply of the air, he tried to stay awake, wished the night a little cooler, focused on the bright swirls of the galaxies in the sky . . . thought he felt Avellana's weight fade from him, his arms settle onto his own chest, soft mattress under him, snuffles from Flora through the open door to the sitting room . . .

And fell right into nightmare visions.

Twenty-five

The vision roiled through him, dark and ominous and deadly: Avellana, a toddler, falling from a window; a young child, grabbed by those who would sacrifice her; Avellana falling into the street when seven, a glider zooming down on her. More recent images of her, morphing: Avellana, five years ago, pale and sweating and dying from the plague, finally, in a practical new tunic-and-trous set, Avellana staring openmouthed at a blazer hole in her chest, before her eyes dimmed and she crumpled to the ground.

He woke on a shout, sat straight up, shuddering, the smell of panic-sweat drying on his body bitter to his nostrils. Two of those events had actually occurred.

"Lord and Lady." His voice rasped from his throat. "Av-ellan-a." Now her name broke on his lips, but his mind sent the call of it winging toward his HeartMate.

Wha—? Her response came sleepily.

His panting gasps smoothed a little. *Avellana.*

Yes, Muin?

Scrubbing his face, he said a spellword to clean himself and his bedclothes. The linens and bedsponge rippled under him.

Muin, you are in great distress! What is wrong?

He coughed. *Vision. Of you in danger.*

Oh, Muin. Now she sounded a little wary.

Bad. Very bad. That he mumbled aloud.

Lord and Lady, he *hated* when the visions came after lovemaking, and more often than not, they did.

Because when he thought of Avellana, he let his fear rule him more than their shared love.

He *must* break that habit.

Thump! A soft, plushly rounded Flora landed beside him and snuggled under his damp palm. *Pet! FamMan pet me and feel better!*

As usual, he reached out and stroked his Fam. Her hair stuck to his fingers.

Avellana didn't say anything else, but he could feel her and she seemed to be checking out the bond between them. That had grown as large as a bridge cable with absolutely no filters. He hadn't had time to hide anything from her.

This is the first time I have been here, in Druida City, when you have been plagued with such a vision-dream about me and shared it, she stated. She sounded considering, though he wished she hadn't used the word *plagued.* He'd sent her far away and safe to a southern Hazel estate during the plague years.

Yes, he could *feel* her scrutinize their bond.

You do not wish me to stay here, in Druida City, Muin.

No.

I will not leave again. Not with just Rhyz.

The visions of you dying FEEL real. They always do. He didn't control the tone of his words, rough and unsteady.

I am sorry. Her mental voice sounded stiff and he thought she sat up in her bed as he did, but with a straight spine. No doubt her covers lay smooth and unbunched.

I am sorry you suffer so from these nightmares, she said. Her sigh whispered to him, then she continued, *I promised not to leave D'Hazel Residence by myself. I confirm that I will always at least have Rhyz with me, and when I leave, I will wear my protective amulet and initiate my personal armor.*

He forced out strangled words. "That will do, for now."

She gave a little cough and when her voice came, it was the wisp of a whisper. *I will also give away those garments I intended to wear today to move furnishings into my new house.*

Avellana! You have a tunic-and-trous set like that? Oh, yes, that shook him.

I will give them to a cuz working here in D'Hazel Residence who is my size and has similar taste. They are brand-new.

Avellana!

Muin! she shot back. *I am trying to compromise. If particular clothing or furnishings or whatever appear in your dreadful visions about me, tell me and I will dispose of the items.* He heard another sigh from her, then an inhalation. *I will not leave Multiplicity or Druida City. I will not run away. It is time we be more active about finding any enemies and dealing with them so we can proceed with our lives.*

He grunted as he rolled from bed, whisking his arm over the linens to refresh the herbs banishing perspiration. Sweat had continued to coat him during his conversation with Avellana. Flora squealed in surprise as the spell fluffed her, too. His thoughts grumbled.

And Avellana replied to his emotions. *We must also put all our irritations and doubts and fears behind us and act together.*

Clumping into the waterfall room, he stated, *We tried that yesterday.*

She replied, *And we did that well; my parents and sister and sister's fiancé complimented us on our lovely ritual. I will be giving them copies of those so they can include me—and us—in rituals in the future. We, as a couple and with Vines, will, of course, celebrate with my Family, too. Occasionally they will include aspects of my religion with theirs.* Her voice took on a mournful note. *I compromise there, too. Most of the rituals in which I participate will be dedicated to the Lady and Lord and emphasize the standard Celtic religion.*

Even as he stepped into the waterfall and let steamy water sluice over him, he felt the strain of such compromises, so many compromises in her life, and he offered, *When only we two celebrate together, we can follow Hopeful practices.*

A pause and blooming hope from her. *Truly, Muin?*

Yes. He massaged his scalp; maybe that would help his thinking. *Consult your spiritual leaders and get a primer for me of basic rituals. We will do those.*

We Hopefuls are less tied to planetary and seasonal festivals because our Journey began on the starships.

He stepped from the shower and let blasts of air dry him. *All right, then.*

Her huge sigh trembled through their bond and he sensed her mind fuzzing with incipient sleep. *Go to sleep, Avellana.*

You must rest, too, Muin, she murmured, then her thoughts faded.

Soon, he replied, and held her mind gently until it slipped away. He took the omnivator to his sunroom, then opened the dome. And he focused on the emotions flowing between them, mostly simple love.

Letting out a breath, he walked to the southeastern point, and there in the dark distance showed pinpricks of light where there had never been any before. Multiplicity.

Checking on Flora, he found her back in her basket in the corner of his sitting room. He placed his hands atop the low wall. No night chill of stone here, nor any lingering warmth from the summer day. He stared at those lights and shifted his shoulders as he became aware again of the burden of Family and Flair.

If he returned to bed, the nightmare might plague him again.

Another few lights in a line appeared—the town wall going up around Multiplicity—and a twinge of sadness flicked through him. He had insisted on that wall and now felt the loss of . . . freedom, expansion . . . that Multiplicity represented.

Yearning suffused him, the continual instinctive need to sleep with, be with, *bond* with Avellana.

Instead he turned away from the sight, his gaze sweeping the top of the tower, the walls of T'Vine fortress, the one glider way up and down the hill, and in the near distance the other walled town, Druida City.

He took the omnivator back to his rooms.

"Residence?"

"Yes, T'Vine?"

"Set a morning meeting of the Family at WorkBell in the main-space. Morning Family duties will be excused until after the gathering."

"Yes, T'Vine." The silver sphere of his calendar sphere popped into existence. "Done."

"Thank you." Yes, time to find and vanquish his enemies.

To that end, he arranged papyrus around him in his bed, then began to read reports of the recent Loyalty Ceremonies that the Yews and the Clovers had sent him, and finally fell back to sleep in his comfortchair.

This time when Avellana and Rhyz left D'Hazel Residence before dawn, they took a Family glider. Rhyz lay on the passenger seat, all four paws up. His abdomen appeared fatter than when they had stepped off the ferry from Mona Island an eightday ago.

Avellana had dressed in shabby tunic and trous good for physical work. Not so good to impress buyers, so she had left a message for Antenn that she would not be available to meet prospective community members today unless he felt she must. Then she would initiate a Whirlwind Spell. Since like most people, particularly men, he hated that spell, he would probably order their salespeople to be on site and enthusiastic.

A few notes had passed between them, left in their scry memory caches. Arta Daisy had participated in the raising of her home and been rapturous. Reporters from the *Druida City Times* had documented the process, so more observers should show up today to watch the building of Multiplicity.

Antenn had also communicated that he and a night crew had constructed a sixty-centimeter-thick wall around the community, and that Muin T'Vine had purchased a parcel, as had twelve others.

In return, Avellana had informed her business partner that she had traded one of her own estates to Loridana D'Yew and that transaction had already been legally recorded. Avellana had agreed to meet him that afternoon to discuss their partnership, Multiplicity, and their success.

The glider stopped at the tall gates now blocking off the town. She frowned at the equally tall walls and the slight shimmer indicating a midlevel shieldspell dome had been placed. No more than a couple of seconds passed before the gates opened for her, and then they passed silently through the mostly undeveloped streets of the village until the vehicle drew up in front of her brand-new home.

The community consisted of all sizes of lots, but Avellana, a child of a FirstFamily, had chosen one of the largest, in the area for bigger homes, though her house itself was a modest one, suitable for one person, or a couple.

She had lived in tiny cottages, rattled around alone except for Rhyz in huge and empty vacation houses, D'Hazel's as well as dwellings Muin had arranged.

Not anymore.

Now she had her very own home, designed according to her own needs.

Others must have felt like her, wanted houses or studios or homes that would reflect their individual selves rather than an established Family castle constructed by the colonists for an enormous Family. Or they wanted to found their own Family line, and do it here, in a new community.

Though she saw a couple of lights in occupied homes, no one stirred outside in the cool dawn.

She and Rhyz stepped from the glider as the sun came over the eastern ridge, spilling light into the valley. Shining on the large front windows of her home. Her pent breath released at the sight of her octagonal house. Angles instead of the curves.

Her suite in Muin's tower, and her very own round tower in T'Vine Residence, awaited her—very pretty places, and she would grow to love them, but this building reflected *her*. Not the colonists who became the Hazels and built their castle, nor the Vines who erected that massive Residence.

Her. Antenn Blackthorn-Moss had interviewed her, and they had looked at house shapes and structures and . . . He had designed a building that made her smile whenever she thought of it.

As she entered, the sprightly smell of newly turned earth and cut wood beams and mortared stone made her stop and grin. Her very own as no place she had lived in had been.

Perhaps others who lived in Residences or Family houses identified more with their home, but she never had. As soon as she became truly aware of herself as a person, an individual of the Hazel Family . . . Muin had informed everyone that he and she were HeartMates. She learned that she would spend most of her long Celtan life in T'Vine Residence. So she and D'Hazel Residence had not closely bonded.

Then she had been sent away to live with the catalyst, D'Marigold, during all three of her Passages to free her Flair.

And, later, whenever Muin sensed danger to her, which was far too often, she had been stashed in one town or another.

Now, and here, she had built a home of her own. For a while.

All planned out. She would leave D'Hazel Residence and move here within a couple of days, and live here until she and Muin finally wed, then she would keep this as a studio. Slowly she walked through the open first floor that contained mainspace, kitchen, playroom, dining room, and waterfall.

Rhyz tore around the level, then up the stairs, claws clicking on the greeniron.

Avellana dropped the personal armor and spread her arms, breathing deeply, all constraints on her . . . mostly . . . gone. The glint of her amulet caught her eye, but T'Ash, like Antenn, had fashioned a piece completely to her taste, so she loved the necklace and enjoyed wearing it.

So very light, this house, and she could see all around her. Just what she wanted. Now she cherished these first moments of being in her own home by herself—Rhyz had thinned one of the windows or exited through a FamDoor to check out his property. A place no other Fam had lived, or would live without his permission. They both prized that.

Pausing for a moment, she watched the sun clear the hill, again felt the emptiness; only light and her own energy filled the air. Never had she been in an unfurnished house—or cottage, or, By the Four, a Residence.

She paced through the open level, then went upstairs. The second story held her wedge-shaped bedroom-sitting-room-waterfall suite, two guest rooms with waterfalls, and a tiny teleportation closet big enough for two people, all chambers accessible from the inner balcony. The doors stood open. She did a quick check of energy in her home and found only the solid and reassuring presence of Rhyz rushing in and out. No old and lingering patterns, all bright and new and shiny.

She entered each room, visualizing the furniture and accessories she would move in today. Most would come by glider, but a few smaller items she would bring over from D'Hazel Residence. Soon enough she would learn the light in various spots of the house instead of the small, windowless closet with the same steady glow used in all the D'Hazel Residence teleportation rooms. She closed that door, then mounted the steps to her studio.

As she sat on one of the uncushioned window seats and looked west to the ocean two kilometers away in the blue-gray distance, she understood that she had modeled her house somewhat on D'Marigold Residence, where she had spent weeks before, during, and after her Passages.

The greater part of that house stood in tall circular plaster layers like a wedding cake, with huge arched windows that kept the place light.

Now, straight walls of mostly glass surrounded her, and she could see south to the foot of the hills, or look out to her neighbors in the valley, or to the northern plain that showed a good view of the Hopeful Cathedral, one of the reasons she'd wanted this particular plot.

Yes, she had followed instinct and joined with Antenn and would make a lot of gilt on this venture, but she also had her own home.

Standing, she called mentally to her FamCat, *Rhyz, I am returning to the glider for the HouseStones!*

Yesss! Me, TOO! I will 'port and meet You at the glider!

She preferred to run down the steps, then through the empty house and out the front door she had left open. Once outside she let the early-morning summer air fill her lungs, caress her nostrils with the scents of Multiplicity—plain grasses, cultivated grass and flowers planted in the spring and now thick and blooming, the hint of humans, and the freshening ozone of building Flair and new materials.

Only her home stood on the street, no one across from her or to either side. Right now she could see the town circle east of her . . . and the carillon bell tower that had also gone up last evening. To the north, at the very top of the valley, the semicircular horizontal stories of Arta Daisy's armorcrete-and-stone home rose dark against the sky, about twice the size of Avellana's own house. Arta would be moving in furniture today, too. Just beyond Arta's home loomed the new wall, and that would comfort the woman.

Turning, Avellana frowned at the wall now behind her home, at the end of the grassyard and cut into the bottom reach of the hills. Antenn *had* placed a thick, elaborately carved oak door in the wall where the stepping-stone path to the ocean lay. Avellana grumbled.

I am here! Rhyz enthused, hopping up and down. He kept his neck tilted back so the bag holding the HouseStones Avellana had gathered did not brush the ground.

She turned away from the sight of the tall wall and shrugged; the barrier marched around the valley, no going back now.

Avellana checked the glider doors; they were secure, so Rhyz had teleported in and out of the vehicle. She took the sack from him and walked back into her house, shut the door, and secured the whole building with two layers of shieldspells.

Her home contained a basement, windowless, a tiny shrine to the four guardian spirits who guided the Hopeful traveler on her journey.

And in the center of that small four-armed-cross chamber lay a trap-door that opened into a narrow chute, straight down into another room, this one small and oval, no more than three meters long.

Avellana had negotiated with the moles who had excavated other HouseHearts to make one for her own home—that would someday become a sentient House.

Now with the smell of rich earth surrounding her, she let Rhyz dig the hole where she would place the Flair-imbued stones with the tiny sparks of life and incipient intelligence. One smoothed nugget of dark amber came from the HouseStones of D'Hazel Residence. It had already been linked in a network of cognizant stones, as had the variegated agate Muin had given her from the cache of Vine Heart-Stones in that Residence.

Done! Rhyz said, and when she went to the hole and knelt with the sack, she *felt* what her Fam must have, the point of throbbing Flair that gathered all the energy lines of their home together into a node, or sent energy flowing from that place through the new build-ing. The heart of the house, the HouseHeart.

She upended the bag, let pebbles roll out . . . small rough-edged rocks, smooth stones, crystals . . . from places she and Rhyz had lived, the last being a piece of rose quartz that she had found on Mona Island. She settled back on her heels and Rhyz butted in again, stirring the new HeartStones with his paw.

Done! he announced again.

Avellana slowly ran her hand above the arrangement of the new HeartStones, reached down and ensured that they touched each other, felt the zing of Flair through her, sent an equal amount back into the stones. When she practiced rituals here in her house, she would funnel more strength to those stones so the intelligence would grow. Sometime in the future, the Flair would reach critical mass and the House would become an aware individual with a personality. Since that usually took two centuries, she would probably not be around to see it happen, but the thread stretching into the future, from her and Rhyz, satisfied a need within her. She had founded a House.

Then she stood and cleansed her hands, flicked dirt from her clothes and Rhyz's paws and fur with a spell. "We will lay the red sandstone flag floor ourselves this evening, as the twinmoons shine brightly in the sky."

Vinni and Flora will help us, Rhyz insisted.

Avellana paused, wanting to keep her house to herself, held the selfish feeling close for a moment or two, then let out her breath and the egotistical need, inhaled the acceptance that sharing would make the experience richer.

"Yes."

Twenty-six

That morning when Vinni awoke after too little sleep, he let his brain unfog naturally, lying back and considering the embroidered canopy over his bed. Another antique mural, sensing his wakefulness, activated and moved, showing a view of walking through a forest.

He should talk to Avellana about this, someday, as he preferred this particular position for thinking. Someday she'd share this ancestral bed with him. No, *don't* think of that, not right now, when he had problems to ponder.

Avellana wouldn't leave. Wait, that wasn't what she said. Avellana wouldn't leave *without him*. So he would go.

At that thought, absolute relief washed through him as if he'd averted some danger. He had to get them out of here, Druida City. And not just because of the danger that had passed by them. He needed time with her, alone, and without anyone watching and judging. Where, he didn't know. The five estates the Family owned, two here in Druida, three outside, all were occupied by Family members. Multiplicity was too close.

And the more he thought, the more he recalled the nightmare-vision last night and how it had tarnished his loving with Avellana, as well as their previous triumph of the First Quarter Twinmoons

Ritual. And the more sensitive he became to the energy flows of his relatives.

He got up and dressed for the Family meeting at WorkBell, then took the omnivator down to the bottom of his rectangular tower. There he unlocked the door to the round tower that held his public rooms, stepped through, and stopped at a whiff of treachery.

The same trace of hostile feelings he'd sensed last night. The slight current of rot that must have triggered his vision-dream.

He had to face the fact. The person who worked against him in the Family might not just be concerned about Avellana and him marrying, but might be a true and vicious enemy.

He'd refused to see that before. Hadn't wanted to believe that one of his own relatives might be a member of the Traditionalist Stance.

Might be the one threatening Avellana. One of his own Family.

Might even be the secret head of the movement whom they hadn't been able to find or catch when the also-betraying Yews and their group went down.

Furthermore, he'd have to acknowledge that he hadn't rooted out enemies years ago, when they'd harmed Avellana and he'd disinherited several, then had another Loyalty Ceremony. Somehow they'd hidden and remained in the Family, like a viper waiting to strike.

He had to *accept* that someone he knew, and might love, plotted the death of his HeartMate. A Family member he might care for, cherish, work hard to help, would betray him.

Yes, that hurt, enough so he doubled over and panted.

T'Vine? asked the Residence, telepathically.

Not able to speak, Vinni replied mentally, too. *Lock down this tower and my own.*

Done!

He couldn't leave a threat to Avellana at large. Not one embedded in the heart of his Family.

He had to consider his options, and the first was right here, talking with him. *Residence, you know of the Traditionalist Stance movement?*

I know, T'Vine. We have held meetings with our FirstFamilies allies within my walls. A pause and a slight creak. *Though there were aspects of that particular political platform that were excellent ideas.*

The shock of that last statement shouldn't have surprised Vinni. The Residences, as nonmobile sentient beings longer-lived than any human, had proven to be more entrenched in the past than interested in the future.

He cleared his throat, answered aloud, "I agree. The Traditionalist Stance may have had some valid points, but they did not propound them in an acceptable manner. From the beginning, an element of greedy self-interest tainted the first leader, then the movement rapidly deteriorated into murderous fanatics. Targeting children."

"I do not forget." T'Vine Residence's voice came aloud and stony. "Many suffered from those fanatics, including one of the oldest Residences and the youngest babe-in-arms of a FirstFamily. Taking life—any life—is *a crime. We act unto others how we wish others would act unto us, and WE HARM NONE along our journey of self-discovery and self-actualization.*"

"Right," Vinni muttered.

The Residence continued, female voice coming from speakers set in the ceiling. "This—*my* personality—has been in place for nearly a century and a half. I do not wish to lose it as has happened before to *other* Residences who have not proven flexible with their new Heads of Households."

Vinni had only heard of one Residence that had happened to, so T'Vine Residence knew more than he did. But, though immobile, the Residences and the starship *Nuada's Sword* did have a communications ring.

And new Houses were becoming aware every year. That might help keep their brains from stratifying. Maybe it was time to introduce another couple of Flaired stones into the brain-web of the Residence, one of them to take the place of the agate he'd given Avellana for her home. Think about that later.

He didn't want to have to watch his words with his home, tiptoe around notions instead of being blunt and clear. The Residence had stated bedrock beliefs, but would the House hold to those?

If Vinni *had* to change the personality of the Residence to be more in line with Vinni's own goals, follow his lead, best to handle that fight right now.

Switching back to telepathic communication, Vinni said, *I believe we harbor another traitor or traitors in our midst.*

A long groan came from beams overhead and the Residence spoke mind-to-mind, also. *Not again.*

A person who has assaulted Avellana, who fears her Flair, who would kill her to prevent her from becoming D'Vine.

Nooo!

Vinni had never felt such a cold and bitter wind blast through the Residence, and from the outcries of his Family along their bonds, neither had anyone else.

Softly, softly, with the quietest whisper of his mind, he addressed the Residence. *You did not know this.*

No! the House whispered back. *Great Flair is to be prized.* A pause. *No matter what kind of Flair that might be.* So the Residence might know Avellana's Flair for reviving the newly dead. Vinni hadn't ever told it that, either. Secrets kept on both sides.

T'Vine Residence continued, *Such psychical, magical power is what makes us, the FirstFamilies and Residences, the strongest and wealthiest Families on Celta. We must encourage that so we remain strong and wealthy and powerful.*

All right, then. Vinni swallowed. If he spoke aloud, he'd clear his throat, but this was not something he could wish to speak aloud. *I do not ask you to violate the privacy rules you have vowed to uphold.*

I would not do so, T'Vine Residence shot back. *My walls would begin to crumble, and my self disintegrate.*

Rather like humans breaking Vows of Honor.

That is so. Though humans are shortsighted enough to forget this.

Vinni coughed. *I do ask you to note the comings and goings of our Family. To be aware of angry feelings or traitorous words in other rooms than the bedrooms, which are off-limits.*

I will watch and listen for evil sentiments and behavior.

*Good. Naturally, only report what you find extremely suspicious
to me. People are allowed their irritation at others and at me and
general Family ways and you.*

*Yes, T'Vine. But I am currently a very reasonable entity. My
mental health is well.*

Vinni sensed a shade of doubt from the Residence . . . with regard
to the future? He scraped his wits to find reassuring words for the
Residence and said, "Your glory days, and ours, as a Family, are yet
to come."

The Residence seemed to sigh and settle around him. *I so believe.
Good. Back to our problem.* Instead of proceeding to the Family mainspace across the narrow courtyard, Vinni sank into one of
the chairs Bifrona had insisted on providing for this room. *Residence, you can recall when Family members are within your walls,
correct?*

Slowly the answer came. *I can. I might not pay attention to those
who are here or not moment by moment, but I can . . . remember.*

Vinni wouldn't say that the Residence *recorded* events moment by
moment, but the House wasn't human. He went on speaking mentally.
No doubt the Residence recalled telepathic conversations, too, but
maybe not as easily as actual sounds within its walls. *Residence, please
check on the presence of our Family members for the following times.*
He paused, thought back. *Two days ago, Playday, at dawn. That night
after MidEveningBell. Both these instances are when Avellana was
assaulted. You may or may not know that a man from the Thermarum Baths went missing at this time, also.*

The stones of the Baths are not sentient, the Residence replied.
*The Thermarum Residence HeartStones may be viable in the next
decade.*

I understand, Vinni replied. And now, like a human being, T'Vine
Residence might be distracting itself with minutiae instead of con-
templating a hurtful truth. *We must find any Family members who
threaten Avellana.*

T'Vine Residence agreed.

Vinni paused. *I had a nightmare last night about danger to Avellana.*

I know, I felt your primary Flair radiate to and through my walls, the Residence replied.

A grunt escaped Vinni; he didn't like talking about this, was damn tired of it. *As always I wished to immediately send her away.*

The House replied slowly, as if picking its words. *That response has not been . . . wise . . . for some time.*

I have finally understood that. I am considering my options. They may include staying at Avellana's new home in Multiplicity for a couple of nights.

A creaklike sniff from T'Vine Residence. *Brand-new houses, OUTSIDE Druida City. They won't be intelligent for a good nineteen decades. That NEW home she will reside in CANNOT protect her.*

And the House continued to drop bits of information that Vinni didn't have. As far as he knew, the absolute minimum amount of time for a house to develop intelligence consisted of two hundred years.

Obviously the network of Residences had information he didn't—and maybe not just him. He wondered who might keep up with that kind of information. Well, naturally, Antenn Blackthorn-Moss, who lived in one of the newest Residences to become sentient—the Turquoise House. But Antenn hadn't said anything to the FirstFamilies about such data. Vinni would have to prompt the man—again something that could wait.

She is as protected as she can be. Vinni sent a calming thought. *She has an amulet from T'Ash and protective armor from D'Yew.*

I know, stated the Residence, but it began creaking around him. *You should bring her here and put her in our tower and I will protect her.*

Vinni shuddered. *I like that idea, but she would leave and never come to us again.*

A pause and the creaking stopped with a house-groan of strained wood.

We will find our enemies, inside and out, Vinni stated.

Yes! the Residence agreed. Sounded more like a promise or a vow to Vinni.

Meanwhile, I will be . . . away . . . with Avellana. I thank you for not expressing disapproval for any absence.

We will find the enemies, and you and the Family and I must proceed with the wedding. I have been working on that with D'Hazel Residence, who has been dilatory.

Right.

I have noted that a good relationship for a couple includes being alone with time away from their Families.

Good, Vinni replied, and then, pulling his thoughts back to the distressing conclusion of an enemy in the Family he had to deal with, he said mentally, *I know that my schedule, meetings, and appointments are usually available to the Family. I wish to put a privacy lock on those as of now.*

Yes, T'Vine.

Also, for your—not ears—knowledge only, in the future, I will not be at every meal. I will show up as I wish on a casual basis. You may inform the cooks of that.

Done!

I will not attend every internal Family meeting I'm scheduled for. They've always seemed too many to me, and this is a good time to cut back.

He felt his mouth set into a grim line, the thought of enemies in the Family sickening, the idea that someone—or more than one—hated him so. It had to be hate, didn't it? At least disrespect, putting their notions of whom he should marry—his *HeartMate*—over Vinni's own judgment.

He *was* the Head of the Household. If someone had problems with that they should have challenged him, followed legal procedures. Instead they hid and snuck around and assaulted the woman he loved.

Because they *couldn't* prove that someone might be a better GreatLord or GreatLady than he. The whole thing made him sick.

T'Vine? prodded the Residence mentally, and Vinni understood that he'd stayed in the round tower too long.

He forced nausea back, tried to think of his own procedures.

Residence, to cover our internal investigation, I will explain my absences and varying schedule as due to the fact that my beloved HeartMate is in town. We have the wedding to prepare for.

Yes.

Another pause, as T'Vine Residence probably scrutinized Vinni's schedule and Family commitments.

This investigation will be time-consuming for me, the Residence said. *Who else can we use for help?*

Who do we really trust? Vinni replied. He thought of the guards—they'd had problems with the guards before. His Chief Guard joined the Family within the last few years, had clasped hands with Vinni and taken a Loyalty Oath, a Vow of Honor. Vinni hadn't seen any signs of physical deterioration from a broken Vow of Honor in anyone.

I don't know who else in the Family to trust. Perhaps you can consider our people, who YOU would trust, he muttered mentally.

You will be late to the meeting you called if you don't leave now, the Residence reminded him.

Being late would be a discourtesy. Fligger that. Lord and Lady knew that harboring enemies in the Family ready to harm his Heart-Mate was a fliggering discourtesy.

But he'd risen to his feet at the prod. *One moment. I must ensure my consultation chamber is free of any whiff of evil.*

I sense nothing, the Residence shot back.

With quiet steps he moved into his consultation offices, one of the most secure chambers in the castle. After all, he—and other very powerful people—went into trances here. Extending all his senses, he found no trace of negativity.

Residence, we can mark off all the people who visited this room in the last two days.

Yes, T'Vine.

That included Bifrona, and when he thought of her, a vision rolled over him—that a great upset in the Family would trigger her death. His gut clenched.

He glanced at his wrist timer. "I'm going to be a trifle late. Good for them to wait. I've been on time my entire life. Residence, we will update each other later. The Druida City guards and Garrett Primross, the private eye, are also investigating."

Yes, T'Vine.

Still inwardly grumbling, Vinni left the round tower behind him and crossed the narrow courtyard. If he called for another Loyalty Ceremony—his *third* as T'Vine—not only would it signal weakness within the Family, it would stir up his unfriends in the FirstFamilies.

Those who'd broken alliances with him a few days ago.

Doors opened in front of him and had him straightening, donning the complete manner of a GreatLord. Striding to the front of the room, he swept a scrutinizing gaze over those who'd come when he'd called. Not nearly as many as who should've. He couldn't help his nostrils widening or his lips forming a slight curl. No, not much respect for him . . . or maybe they just took him for granted, he'd been GreatLord for so long.

He stared at those of the Family who'd gathered, his Chief of Guards, who sat stolidly with no expression, though Vinni believed the man seethed with impatience at this gathering and having his work schedule screwed up. His old tutor, who looked, as usual, supercilious. Bifrona, who stood by the door, her hand at her throat, her eyes lifted in exasperation.

He saw no best friend, no confidant in those faces before him. Whether due to his taking on the title so young, or, probably, the fact that there were no people within five years of his age, his best friends and companions did not lie here within his Family.

His closest companions were men from the other FirstFamilies— those in his relative age group and with whom he'd trained at The Green Knight Fencing and Fighting Salon. Along with some once-Commoner Clover men whom he'd trust more than any of those facing him.

He would not make that same mistake with his own children. They should have siblings and close confidants within the Family. Lord and Lady knew the Clovers did, and the Hollys . . . a couple of others. Not Saille T'Willow, though. Another thing to face; despite wedding HeartMates, the FirstFamilies were thin on children.

People fidgeted, and suddenly he'd just had enough of Family.

"I'm leaving to spend time with my HeartMate in Multiplicity," he said shortly. "We may also make the rounds of the Vine estates."

A wave of surprise and irritation from the now-still group washed over him. As if he were abandoning them. He locked down his own anger from surging through Family bonds, then gave in to instinct and teleported away. In the brief instants between T'Vine Residence and Antenn's business courtyard, more than annoyance touched him. A spear of malevolence, an image of Avellana dead, from blazer shot—this someone else's visualization.

But he landed on the teleportation pad in the back of Antenn Blackthorn-Moss Architects, located on one of the main streets near CityCenter.

Vinni allowed himself a little time to consider that inimical Familial touch, settle until the red fury before his eyes faded. He wanted to beat something up. He'd have no problems with any of his mature male relatives—and that was what that trace of evil felt like, a man in his prime.

If he teleported right back . . . he still wouldn't find the sneaking, hiding villain. Leave the investigation up to the Residence and Garrett Primross.

He would continue to work on protecting Avellana—tell T'Vine Residence that the hater was on the premises now and had lately been in the round tower.

Avellana would welcome him in Multiplicity.

Twenty-seven

So he rode with one of Antenn's staff to Multiplicity.

The woman took out writestick and papyrus and began questioning Vinni on house ideas since he'd bought a lot the night before. She pointed out passing homes through the glider windows and managed to focus Vinni on something other than danger to his HeartMate.

When they stopped briefly at the entrance to Multiplicity, he approved of the wall and gates. The woman informed him that Antenn's office had received more inquiries into the town that morning, and most preferred having a wall.

They headed up to the observation hill, where Avellana awaited him. She wanted to watch more homes being raised. He found her outside the filled-to-capacity tent and close to the gentle edge of the hill, on the outskirts of the crowd.

"What's going up today?" Vinni asked.

Avellana pointed to the first lot inside the gates, the foundation of the house facing east. An elaborate belowground courtyard had already been laid out, with long sweeping stone staircases on either side up to a terrace also defined by stone balustrades.

"Nice lower level," Vinni said.

"Vensis Betony-Blackthorn's home," Avellana stated.

Of a design reminiscent of the home he lived in now. This one showed a classical Earthan style of white stone with pillars and stylish windows; Vensis's house seemed the most elegant to Vinni. He shrugged. "Very pretty. I suppose it suits him."

Avellana turned to him, brows raised. "Of course it does; Antenn's designs are masterful." She tilted her head. Her eyes narrowed and she sent him a telepathic stream. *You yet worry about me.*

Always, he returned mentally.

I and my Fam will not leave again at your command.

He took her hand and lifted it to his mouth, kissed her fingers. *Not without me.*

"What!" she exclaimed aloud.

"Let's talk about this privately," he murmured.

She slid her arm around his waist, and before he understood her action, she'd teleported them to a small closet and he knew from how instantaneous the transfer was that they'd gone to her home.

"What the fligger?" he swore, taking the two strides to the door and yanking it open to see the second level. "You can't know this place quickly enough to teleport to it!"

"Muin, of course I can."

He scowled, then looked back at the small rectangular room. If he stood in the center of it, he could touch the longer walls with his fingertips.

Then he blinked and stared into the tiny teleportation chamber filled with pale greenish-brown light that accented golden-brown walls.

"How did you make this place look exactly like a teleportation room in D'Hazel Residence?"

Her eyes held a slight disbelief. She opened her hands. "It is the light, Muin. Everyone knows that teleportation depends mainly on visualizing the light of the space where you will land. I work in light. All my holographic murals are created by tinting and bending light." She shrugged. "Of course I can use my Flair to solidify them into sculptures . . ."

"Like those sculptures of the Lady and Lord you gave me as my last Samhain—New Year's—gift, thank you, again."

"That is right." She raised her chin. "I can also draw and paint in two dimensions. I have worked hard at my craft, Muin, the same as you have done."

"Of course," he agreed.

"But it is primarily light." A line etched between her brows as she concentrated. She waved a hand and the tint of the room became blue, with the walls seeming greenish. "T'Vine Residence public teleportation rooms." Her brows dipped more and the light brightened until it became more blue-white. "Your personal teleportation chamber in your suite."

He nodded.

Then the atmosphere turned a rich golden amber as if sunlight flowed through gold-orange-paned windows.

"D'Marigold Residence, main-level teleportation chamber." The words fell from his lips without thought.

"Yes."

"Lady and Lord, you are wonderful."

She smiled.

"How many places can you remember?" he asked.

"Those four, for sure, and though I believe that Families and Residences would not often change their teleportation light if they have dedicated rooms, I do not think I would depend on that."

"Good point. I assure you, I will not have any in T'Vine changed without your input."

She shrugged. "My holos are nothing but bent and colored light." She lifted a finger and a small image of a green apple with stem and leaves appeared and rotated. "Ephemeral." She snapped her fingers. "Here and gone."

He sucked in a harsh breath. "You mean your murals could be banished with a Word?"

A roll of her shoulder. "It depends on how much Flair I, and others, invest in them. I fully believe my holo paintings in the Hopeful Cathedral will last as long as the building." Her eyes took on a distant look. "My early work . . . mural attempts . . . is mostly gone."

"What?" His chest constricted. "Never thought of that. Your cre-ative work vanishes."

"Sometimes your wind chimes break," she pointed out.

"Not if I can help it," he muttered. Not since he'd been a child. *He* still had the first wind chime he'd made of thin glass strips.

She spread her arms. "Life is like that, Muin. We journey through it. Here, then gone. Ephemeral." Again she tilted her head. "I would have expected we agreed on this. You *see* multiple futures all the time, most of which don't come true. All the other paths you see are transitory."

He grunted but didn't want to discuss that without thinking about it, so he returned to the previous topic. "The light's like D'Hazel Resi-dence, but not the scent."

She chuckled. "The fragrance of GreatMistrys Avellana Hazel's home in Multiplicity."

"Huh." He took the couple of steps to the balcony and looked down. "Your furniture is in."

"A minimal amount came a few minutes before I went up to the observation hill." She inhaled and exhaled deeply, as if taking in the scent of her new home. An aroma that would have only minuscule traces of himself and Flora, for now.

Avellana went on. "I do not think I will furnish this space more, as I will not be spending a plentiful amount of time here. Not as much as I anticipated."

"I told the Residence I'd be here with you tonight, and then I told my Family I'd be leaving."

Her eyes widened as she stared at him.

"It's been a couple of years since I visited the Vine estates outside Druida City. I don't have any upcoming vital appointments for a full three eightdays." He'd checked his calendar sphere.

"A vacation, Muin?"

He hadn't had a vacation in . . . never.

"Absolutely." He nodded, grabbed her and whirled her around, then set her down within the circle of his arm. "We can leave from here, tomorrow morning." Glancing around, he saw the open doors to a couple of sitting rooms as part of suites. "Got beds?"

"Of course," she squeaked, then wet her lips. "Not the primary bed, yet, though. That should be delivered later today by Clover Fine Furniture. I commissioned a piece."

"Good. Let's see what you have."

A faint cheer came from outside and her expression clouded. "We're missing the building of Vensis's home. I must be seen taking an interest in my fellow community members. He will notice if I am not there." She brushed her hands along her opposite sleeves. "Even though I am only in my work clothes."

Vinni grumbled, then said, "Vensis is a tracker like T'Blackthorn. *Those* work clothes are grubby."

She just sniffed, took Vinni's hand, and began walking fast. They'd circled down the stairs and gotten to the front door when she stopped and turned to him, disappointment drooping her mouth.

"We cannot leave Multiplicity or Druida City. We have the matchmaking meeting with T'Willow tomorrow morning."

Frowning, Vinni said, "I'd forgotten. Hmmm. Plans." His frown turned to a scowl. "I've heard that having a matchmaking consultation with Saille T'Willow is only slightly less exhausting than an appointment with Vinni T'Vine. We should plan on staying here tomorrow night. Go into Druida City for the consultation, return back here, leave the next morning. There are others living here now, right? And building will continue tomorrow?"

"Yes. The Parises, Arta Daisy, and my former governess have all moved into their homes. Vensis Betony-Blackthorn will begin staying here tonight."

Vinni whistled. "You all acted quickly."

"We are all the founding members of Multiplicity, and we all had homes designed that we want to live in. *Homes.*"

"I understand." Vinni reached out and opened the door. "Well, we won't be alone in the town, and that's good. I can wait two days to leave." He let out a breath. "That I keep the matchmaking appointment might reassure my Family, but right now, I am heartily

sick of them." As soon as she'd initiated the house shieldspells, he
caught her hand and kissed her fingers. "What do you think of our
new itinerary?"

"All right," she agreed, though she sounded cautious.

"Good." He went down the front steps with her, drew in a breath
of air that smelled nothing like Druida City. Nor did the view appear
like any he'd find there, not even in one of the huge parks. Country-
side with a small town being built.

With every step they walked up the hill to the observation tent,
he felt as if part of the burden of responsibilities weighing on him
cracked and fell away. His muscles became looser and he enjoyed the
warm sunlight on his body, glad he noticed such small pleasures
again.

Avellana walked with him, hand in hand, swinging their arms,
then said quietly, "I have changed my mind."

He tensed.

"You, *we*, should give our Families a little more warning." Sighing, she glanced up at him. "I had planned on staying tonight with
my Family in a private gathering. I believe you should attend dinner
with your Family."

He grimaced. "I suppose you think I should schedule a formal
dinner to include all the Family, especially since not all of them came
to our ritual last night. Some might want to talk to me before I go."

"Yes."

He made a disgusted noise but pulled out his perscry. "T'Vine
Residence."

"Here, T'Vine," the House replied.

"Please inform the Family that there will be a formal dinner with
everyone invited at the time of the usual second serving."

"Yes, T'Vine."

He ended the scry and put his pebble in his pocket. They continued up the hill road. A thought occurred that made him smile. "That
will have people scrambling to change their plans, including the
cooks. I think I've been too accommodating to my Family."

Avellana watched him with narrowed eyes.

"What?"

"I think you have been very courteous to your Family, something that many other FirstFamilies' Lords and Ladies are not. I like that quality in you."

He grinned. "Yeah, but that was then, this is now, and we are running away."

She sniffed. "Taking a break."

His Fam's mental voice came to them both. *I have just heard that we are going adventuring!* Flora sounded enthusiastic.

That's right, Vinni sent back.

I have always wanted to see other places.

He sure hadn't known that.

But we will need to take my basket bed and my pillow and my blanket and my toys. So I am comfortable.

Of course, Vinni murmured.

Rhyz's mental voice snorted. He appeared and trotted ahead of them, tail waving. *I am always ready for adventure.* His whiskers twitched. *I do not need anything special.*

"Except catnip from *Nuada's Sword,*" Avellana murmured.

Except that, Rhyz confirmed. *I have been a very good Fam, a kilo, please.*

And Vinni understood that though he'd wanted to go with impulse, when including others, adventuring took planning.

Twenty-eight

$\mathcal{A}$s he'd expected, most of the Family showed up at the formal dinner. He pretty much spent the long meal of many courses watching his relatives while appearing not to scrutinize them. He noted that the guards who'd attended the ritual the night before didn't attend; they'd be patrolling the castle. Vinni had spoken with his Chief of Guards, who'd informed him that he'd already planned a field training exercise with his core team outside the walls and asked leave to miss the dinner. Vinni had agreed and made sure that those guards would have a banquet in their mess hall when they returned.

All of the upper staff, including Bifrona and Arcto, his former tutor, both disapproving, were present.

Boring. No sparkling conversation. Not even much affection.

He felt no hate-filled spears of emotion directed at him, so he didn't think the person assaulting him and Avellana sat at the tables.

Perhaps the attacker hadn't dined with him since before the assaults. It took a sly and clever individual to be able to hide such feelings when in Vinni's presence as Head of the Household, GreatLord T'Vine.

But . . . but . . . he began to think that the person who struck at them might not be the master intelligence behind this whole matter. He didn't like that idea.

So he acted as charming as he could, blanketed the room with sincere appreciation that kept the rest smiling and relaxed while he studied them. Not hard to keep up the love of Family welling in him. He *did* love his Family. And during the whole meal, he targeted his relatives and sent them love, each by each.

Maybe if they *felt* that, they could, and would, stop this insane course before they all reached the point of doom.

Vinni sat until the slowest diner swallowed the last bite of cocoa mousse and Bifrona stood, indicating the end of dinner.

Then he gave a toast, as he had at the beginning of the banquet. This time he drew upon his Flair, and that of the Residence, to infuse the room with sparkling blessing.

On the murmur of approval, he left the room and crossed to his public tower, through that to his private space, and up to the Great-Lord suite.

There he spoke with the Residence about those of his Family who could be eliminated as the attacker, about a quarter of his relatives, far too few.

He also read the reports of his allies. As he'd requested and they'd all agreed, they'd scrutinized their Family members. None of them believed they harbored the secret leader of the Traditionalist Stance among their relatives.

Vinni wished he could be as easy in his mind with his own Family.

He paid particular attention to those allies who'd managed to retain some ties with the Families who'd repudiated the Vine contracts.

No person was suspected to be the Traditionalist Stance leader.

By the time he'd finished annotating the reports and consulting with the Residence, a septhour had passed and his spirit had worn weary.

He'd be glad to get away.

He wanted some fresh air, but not the emptiness of his personal garden or rooftop spa. So he strolled through the courtyard toward the Family garden.

A teenaged girl shuffled by a potted tree in a corner, her body in a pale tunic and trous bending and swaying as if to catch his attention.

"Hey, Vinni," called a couple of the guards as they passed, changing shifts.

He addressed them by name and returned their greeting, even as he noticed from the corner of his eye that the girl had faded more into the twilight-shadowed far corner.

A whisper that felt more like a shout on her part came to his mind. *Good dinner. Felt nice. Need to speak privately with you, T'Vine!*

He dipped his head in acknowledgment, then waited until the two guards coming off duty from the guardhouse met him in the courtyard as he casually paced its perimeter. He spoke to them for a moment, then slowed his steps until they'd exited the yard to their quarters. Since he still felt eyes on him, as he passed the corner, he murmured, "I will be walking in the outer east garden." A place often used by all Family members. He cast his gaze briefly toward the girl. "Please meet me there, Lauda. I will be glad to speak with you."

He thought he saw the dip of a quick curtsey, then he continued to the main door of his public tower and crossed through the slice of entryway, through the sitting room, then his consultation chamber, to the remaining room, a private area with several doors, all only keyed to him.

He may have not demanded another Loyalty Ceremony, but earlier he'd changed all the spells on the doors he wanted to keep personal and private to himself. *No one* could enter where he didn't want them to go. And the Residence would obey him in this, too, and would inform him of any attempt at entrance.

Well, of course Avellana could enter any and all of his private spaces, though he didn't think the other Family members realized that. He smiled.

Then he teleported to the narrow east garden between the towering walls of the castle itself and the outer rampart. Expanding his senses, he sighed with satisfaction that only he and Lauda walked in the darkening shadows as night banished day. He strode to her, noting that she stood near the bench at the portion of the wall a guard would reach last when patrolling.

Bowing, he said, "Greetyou, kinswoman Lauda."

"You know my name."

He inclined his head. "And that you live on the garden level of the west side of the main building, and you are a journeywoman cook."

She pulled a face. "A cook for the secondary Family dining room."

"Are you not happy with your work? Do you wish a change? What of your quarters, are they acceptable?"

She stared blankly at him. "That's not what I came here to talk to you about."

He gestured to the fancy marble bench. "Please sit. We can deal with other issues after you answer my questions."

After sitting down, and watching him do the same, she shrugged. "I like being a cook. I just don't like the first dining room cooks and staff acting all special."

"All right. Would you care to train to be in that kitchen? Is there, ah, some specialty you would prefer?"

"I'm fine."

"But you did notice when you sat at dinner tonight that the first dining room cooks and staff all worked. Would you like to move to dinner in the first dining room from now on?"

Her smile bloomed. "Yes, thank you, T'Vine."

"Done." He sent a telepathic note to the Residence, who approved of it. Then he asked, "And your quarters?"

"They're fine, too, thank you kindly for your offer, T'Vine."

He sensed she wouldn't accept calling him by anything but his title. He wanted to cross his ankles, but his trainers in the fighting arts would seriously disapprove, so he kept his feet flat on the ground and ready to spring. Though now he sat so close to this relative, his small bond with her fed him information. She spoke the truth about herself, but worried about another matter.

"How can I help you?" he asked.

Angling toward him, she considered him, her fingers pleating an apron over her tunic. "You know my brother, Bicknell, married our second cuz Perna, and he and she was banished from the castle for marrying too close, but they are HeartMates!"

Vinni blinked as he recalled the circumstances. "I didn't banish them."

"No, that was 'afore you were an adult."

"But they went to a small holding that the Family owned near Gael City, a summerhouse purchased for my predecessor when she was a young woman. When I became an adult, your brother and sister-in-law came and swore fealty to me, and asked that they be allowed to purchase the property."

"And you let 'em!" Lauda replied fiercely.

"Yes. They'd proven they'd prosper without Family funds, and deserved to keep the fruit of their labors themselves." He winced at his own pompous tones, but that's just what fell out of his mouth.

"That's right," Lauda said with satisfaction. Then she crumpled her apron in her hands as she lifted her gaze to his. "Finally they are having a baby."

"And you want to go there?"

"No!"

"No," he repeated.

"It's all through the castle that you said you was going to leave the castle for a bit." Her chin came up. "I'd like you to go to my brother's and be an Oracle for the babe."

"Perna's close to delivering?"

Lauda nodded.

"I am bound to act as Oracle at the birth of any Family member who asks." He paused. "Neither your brother nor your sister-in-law have requested me to determine the type and strength of the baby's Flair, or for any indications as to the child's life."

"I'm asking." She took a breath. "And it's a small property, but a pretty one." She turned her head to face the wall of the castle but watched him from the corners of her eyes. "And there's a separate cottage on it."

"Ah. A separate cottage," he repeated, smiling slowly. "I'd forgotten. An intimate retreat for *my* HeartMate and me?"

Lauda shrugged. "If you want."

"Though they own their own property, they remain part of the Family and I have connections with them." He nodded to her. "As I do to you. I also have their scry images and can request an invitation."

She hummed, then said, "Or you can, like, be in the neighborhood and drop in." She sighed. "They are very sensitive about Family judgments."

"Naturally they would be. But I am of the opinion that if they are HeartMates, the Lady and Lord blessed them that way, and they fulfilled their destiny."

"Huh," Lauda said. She stood and smoothed the wrinkles from her apron with her hands and a couplet.

Vinni rose and inclined his torso. "It's a pretty drive to Gael City and I can check on our town estate there." He frowned. "If Bicknell and Perna don't wish to house Avellana and me, there are plenty of other places we can stay. I have friends who will give us houseroom if the cottage is unavailable." He wasn't sure whether he'd like to actually sleep in the Gael City house . . . It wasn't a Residence and couldn't warn him and Avellana whether some sort of trap had been set.

This request didn't feel like a trap . . . not with a casual "drop in sometime," nothing specific enough to set up an attack . . . he didn't think.

"Good night, T'Vine." Lauda curtseyed, then walked away, spine straight, and from her flowed relieved satisfaction. A feeling that his own grin echoed.

He believed that sending out the warm feelings during dinner had encouraged Lauda to speak with him, and now he had a purpose to add to his travels. Not simply "get away," but "get away and act as Oracle to a new Vine."

His chest expanded as if he breathed in life itself. A new Vine.

He loved acting as Oracle.

As he lay in bed that night, he traced the small bond he had with Lauda to find the thread leading to her brother, Bicknell, and then the wisp to Perna. Then he concentrated on discovering how soon the babe might come. He'd had plenty of experience in determining the time of birth.

Within the week, for sure.

He fell asleep with a smile, but as bad dreams and worse visions threatened, he slept lightly.

When he awoke at TransitionBell, doom hovering black around him, he yearned for his HeartMate.

Avellana? he whispered along their bond.

I am here, Muin, she replied a little sleepily. *Rhyz left a moment ago to hunt.* She sighed.

He shouldn't ask her . . .

What, Muin?

Come to my small tower rooftop teleportation room, please?

A long pause and he sensed her checking out their bond. She sighed, then sent, *More dark dreams, Muin?*

As usual, he replied.

I will come, though if we spend much time together we may not be as physically, mentally, and emotionally prepared as we should be for a formal matchmaking consultation.

Saille T'Willow won't care, and he'll take that into account. Vinni found himself smiling. *It doesn't matter if I'm battered and exhausted, I will always love you and know you're my HeartMate.*

She paused and he thought she sniffed wetly at his declaration. *Thank you. I love you, too, Muin, my HeartMate. I will be there shortly.*

Good. He paused. *I do have SOME good news.*

But she didn't answer, and he rolled out of bed and dressed in light trous and shirt, took the stairs to the rooftop, and opened the door for her after she'd arrived.

She wore a too-thick nightrobe. Probably underwear, too.

"Your amulet and personal armor stone?" he demanded.

"I have the stone on my person and I can initiate the spell with a Word or gesture. I also have my amulet." She patted her chest and Vinni swallowed. That chain and stone would be between her breasts.

Ignoring his half arousal, he took her hand and led her past the fern-shadowed hot tub to the wall and pointed out the few bright lights of Multiplicity in the distance. She sighed, this time sounding contented, and leaned against him as he encircled her waist with his arm.

Then he told her of Bicknell and Perna Vine and acting as Oracle, and Avellana lifted her face to look at him with shining delight.

Trapped. Net. HEAD in NOOSE in net! HELP! Rhyz sounded frantic. Vinni heard the echo of choking.

Avellana gasped. *I must go!*

Vinni grabbed her, both arms around her waist. He felt her surge of power, how she visualized the teleportation closet in her new house.

"Wait a damn minute!" he shouted, aloud next to her ear and in her mind. Pulsed red danger warning from his being to hers through their link. She sagged against him at the assault on her senses.

"I must go," she whimpered.

STOP STRUGGLING! Vinni mind-shouted at Rhyz. *We are coming as fast as we can. Struggling hastens your death.* He didn't know for sure but figured a bespelled noose might constrict faster with thrashing around.

Avellana cried out.

"Your promise. Personal armor," he reminded.

With a finger flick, she snapped it around her. Gritting his teeth, he set his arm near her waist, felt the field of the spell, squeezed tighter.

"Counting down!" she cried.

"Wait! You and others have been lured before." He struggled to put his strong feelings into words, grasp the tenuous logic. "You've been moving and arranging furniture today, haven't you?" he asked her, to help calm them both down for a bit while they *thought*.

"Yes, you know that, Muin."

"You're 'porting to the teleportation closet."

"Of *course*."

"Where you know the light. Because you haven't stayed at the house through the night yet." And, Lord and Lady, he wanted to be with her the first night she did. The notion went straight to his cock and he banished the sexual tingle. Not the time for that.

But she'd relaxed in his arms. "You think someone put a piece of furniture in the teleportation room."

"Your tiny closet. Yes, I do."

"But my personal armor . . . it should bounce me away?" she insisted.

"Big furniture versus teleporting person? Who the fligger knows?" he snapped.

Rhyz wailed again, the sound holding pain and terror.

"Take us to the Cathedral," Vinni ordered. "You know teleportation rooms there."

"Yes!"

In an instant, they'd arrived. She flung open the carved wooden door and raced through the empty space toward the southeast exit. Not the one closest to the new village. He caught up with her, took her hand, sucked in a breath. "I might be able to translocate the sport vehicle . . ."

She gasped, stopped, stared at him an instant. "With my help."

He hadn't thought of that. "Yes."

"No," she said, then grabbed his hand and began to run again. "We can borrow one of the gliders outside."

"The Hopefuls have gliders?"

"Someone should be here. They are not fast." Her breath caught and he saw tears in her eyes, felt the echo of more pain from her Fam.

"I will kill whoever did this to him." The vow spouted from his lips.

She didn't stop. "Do not say this."

His mind scrambled to get to the place fast, latched on to something he should have thought of first. He yelled mind-to-mind with all his might, *Mortal emergency! Antenn to me. Cathedral plaque!*

Antenn had built the Cathedral, knew it in all its forms. The Hopefuls had erected a plaque to him that was the pride of the man's life.

"Here!" a groggy voice called. Vinni heard stumbling steps.

Avellana reversed her path and sped toward the plaque. Vinni saw the bare form of his friend, took off his jacket, and translocated it to the man's feet.

When they reached him, he still stared at the jacket. "Mortal—"

Looking into his eyes, Avellana shouted, "Rhyz is in my house, dying!"

That snapped Antenn's head up. He grabbed Vinni and Avellana, and before Vinni could draw in breath to say anything, they landed on Avellana's porch, impressing Vinni.

She hit her palm against the wooden door. "Open!" It slammed against the inner wall.

M . . . e . . . w, came to Vinni's mind, then faded.

Twenty-nine

"Rhyz," shrieked Avellana, racing up the stairs, a wordless wail streaming from her. Then her voice broke on a sob. "Rhyz."

"Lights!" Antenn ordered.

Brightness blinded Vinni as he scanned the first floor from the middle. He looked up and saw a swinging noose, then Avellana collapsed holding a limp orange cat. Vinni's heart seemed to stick in his throat, then pulsed in a pounding beat. Surely she wouldn't try to revive her Fam, use that deadly primary Flair of hers. She'd drain herself, and him, and Antenn, and all her neighbors . . .

He 'ported to her, touched the cat, felt a tiny breath expel from his lungs. "He lives."

"What?"

Bending and putting his arms under her, he teleported them to the animal Healer, Danith D'Ash, and once again mentally yelled, *Mortal emergency.*

Danith, dressed in flannel pajamas, appeared on the pad before them, stepped up, and put her hand on Rhyz.

"I'm funneling Flair from you both to Rhyz," she stated, and Vinni felt the drain.

They stood there long moments as Danith D'Ash worked on

Rhyz, the three of them linked closely enough that Vinni received impressions of her Healing . . . fixing the cat's throat and airway and the pumping of Flaired energy for him to breathe easily and deeply; the more delicate repair of the brain damage . . . Avellana began heaving with great sobs.

"I'll take him into exam room one," Danith said, deftly removing the cat from his FamWoman, and vanished.

Avellana shook against Vinni, and he pulled her close to his body so she would *feel* him, steady and supportive for her.

Waves of emotion poured through their link from her, her vague remembrance of her own brain being healed when she was a toddler, the knowledge that Rhyz had faced death before as a victim of the Black Magic Cult.

"Shh, shhh." He made more comforting sounds as he rocked her. She threw her arms around him and clamped them tight enough that he felt her terror-damp palms through the linen of his shirt. "Rhyz is safe. We're safe."

"Someone tried to kill him! That spell of the net-becoming-noose is evil!"

Vinni had to unclench his jaw so more words would emerge. "Yes, it is."

Avellana wept, right there on the teleportation pad, until they heard the chipper voice of Rhyz. *I am all better, and I got good nip, and I had an adventure.*

"Grrr," Avellana growled. She let loose of Vinni and whipped around and the examination room door opened and Rhyz swaggered out, whiskers twitching in a cat grin. "Males!"

"Hey!" Vinni said.

She took the long step down from the thick teleportation pad, then sank down onto the floor as if her knees had given way. "Oh, Rhyz!" She opened her arms.

He hopped into them and revved up his purr.

Danith D'Ash leaned on the doorjamb to the examination room. She appeared a little wan, as if the adrenaline bump, then a huge use of Flair, then the relieved crash had hit.

Taking inventory of himself, Vinni realized providing the Flair for three teleportations within a half septhour made him feel a trifle shaky, too. He walked to Avellana and drew her to her feet, then inclined his head toward Danith. "Our deepest thanks."

"You're welcome," she said simply, then added, "I never like to see Rhyz return to my Healing office."

Bad man left bad spell that GOT Me! Rhyz projected, then hissed.

Danith straightened, surprise showing in her eyes. "What!"

"Are you sure it was a man?" Vinni asked.

Rubbing her face, Danith said, "I don't think I can handle a conversation like this tonight." One hand moving so she could peek around it, she muttered, "Is this something you'll have to talk to my husband, T'Ash, about?"

He cleared his throat. "Not right now."

With a large sigh, Danith turned to the examination room and said a cleansing couplet, then came over and hugged Avellana, then him. "You can speak with him tomorrow. Now I'd like to get a little sleep until the next emergency."

"Of course," Vinni replied.

"Thank you *so* much," Avellana said. "I have authorized a transfer of funds from my bank to you."

"Fine," Danith said. She tapped Rhyz on the nose. "As for you, be more careful."

His tongue swiped her fingers. "Yesss," he enunciated.

"My glider is on the way to take us—" Vinni began.

"Me to D'Hazel Residence, and Muin home," Avellana finished. "We will leave now and walk down the gliderway to the gate to await the vehicle."

"Of course," Danith said. "Merry meet."

"And merry part," Vinni and Avellana said at the same time.

"And merry meet again." Danith smiled brilliantly. "But hopefully not in my office for Rhyz."

"Or Flora," Avellana said.

"Or Flora."

"We were at my house in Multiplicity," Avellana continued. "Have you toured the new village?"

A gleam came to Danith's eyes. "No. I understand it is a private community."

Avellana bobbed a curtsey. "I will tell the gates that you must always be admitted."

Danith raised her brows. "Thank you."

"You are welcome. We will go now. Thank you again for Healing Rhyz."

And thank you for the nip, Rhyz said, his tongue licking close whiskers.

They walked out into the night, Vinni's arm around Avellana's shoulders, and her carrying a Rhyz who would prefer to strut around himself. Now that the danger had passed, the Fam, in cat fashion, had pretty much forgotten his fear.

Vinni could still smell his own sweat and caught the fragrance of Avellana's gown as a fresh herbal spell activated, drawing away her perspiration.

I want down now, Rhyz projected.

Reluctantly, Avellana placed him on all four paws. Tail waving, he led them to the courtyard where the glider would arrive. Then he sat and began grooming himself.

Vinni cocked his head as he reported his telepathic conversation with Antenn to Avellana. "Antenn is reporting this latest incident to Garrett Primross, who is in charge of the investigation into the assaults on you."

"On us," Avellana stated.

Vinni hesitated, then agreed. "On us. Antenn, of course, is furious that his brand-new town—"

"*Our* brand-new community," Avellana continued to correct. "*I* am in partnership with him."

"Yes," Vinni replied softly. He took her hand, felt the trembling of her fingers. "I'm sorry."

"And I am ready," she stated.

"What?"

"I did not wish to leave Multiplicity and my new home so soon, but I do not want any more violence to besmirch this new place. I am ready to leave with you and travel." Her voice broke, and it sounded as if she swallowed a sob. "Again. Some more."

More adventure! Rhyz sent, then hopped to his feet and came over and stropped her ankles. *We are together, all of us.*

A tiny voice came to them. *I am not there!* Flora whined. *But I can be there, soonest. I know how to teleport to the animal Healer.*

Avellana cleared her throat but replied mentally, *That is not necessary, Flora.*

Vinni added, *We will pick you up before we leave.* He paused and rethought that. *I will send a glider for you.*

I get to ride in a glider All By Myself!

He smiled. *Yes.*

Antenn, who'd been quiet as he spoke to Primross, sent more information to Vinni, who relayed it to Avellana. "We made a fine mess of the net-noose spell and it disintegrated before Primross arrived and left no trace. As a matter of fact, there doesn't seem to be any vestige of the intruder, so the villain didn't leave much trace, was in and out."

Avellana sighed. "I *did* include blueprints of my home, and several others, in the holo promoting Multiplicity that plays in the observation tent." Her tone hardened. "I will modify that—"

Vinni put in, "Primross has confiscated that holo and Antenn will replace it with another that doesn't detail the insides of the homes."

"We prepared several promotional holo murals," Avellana stated.

"Antenn found your teleportation closet full of furniture. A wardrobe set atop the pad—"

Avellana made a choked-sob noise, but he continued. "A huge armchair up against the wardrobe, a dining table against that, and, in the room and the doorway, a stack of two chairs."

He tried to keep his voice even, but fury began to roil inside him.

"Whoever did this was determined that I be . . . hurt," Avellana said.

"That's exactly right." He sucked in a breath. "It appears that the furniture was translocated, somewhat ineptly, leaving scars on your wood floors. After Primross and the guards finish their investigation of your home, Antenn will refinish the flooring."

"I will ask that my ministers do a ritual cleansing while we are gone," Avellana said.

"Good idea. Primross told Antenn that he does not need to speak with us but would like to question Rhyz."

Rhyz hopped around. *I have not spoken with the man who can communicate with all animals and Fams.* He preened a little. *The Primross will find that I am much better than those ferals he usually talks to. I am smarter and have a better memory.*

Vinni didn't know about that. "Neither Antenn nor Primross nor Vensis Betony-Blackthorn—"

"He is there?" Avellana questioned.

"Yes. Apparently he woke during the disturbance we made, then came over. Though he isn't as good at tracking as T'Blackthorn, he *does* have a gift." Vinni didn't know the younger man very well. "Both Antenn and Primross respect his Flair and welcome his help."

Avellana's mouth compressed, then relaxed, and she nodded. "Tell Antenn that all of those men are welcome in my home at any time."

"Anyway, the men think that both traps were set by Flair, little physical moving involved."

"Someone has a good amount of Flair to do that," Avellana said.

"Yes." And Vinni had a horrible feeling that the perpetrator was a Vine.

Rhyz's purr rolled as he looked up at Avellana. *The Primross would like to speak with me NOW. Can I go? Or do you need me?*

Avellana bit her lip, glanced at Vinni.

He squeezed her hand. "Do you wish to cancel our appointment with the matchmaker and just leave Druida City within the septhour?"

Her spine straightened. "No. That would give ammunition to those of your Family who do not believe we are HeartMates and should wed. Those individuals would say we are not a good match, that we feared such a consultation. They would win." Fierceness lit her gaze. "*I* want to win. All these battles we fight."

"Yes," Vinni agreed.

Glancing down at Rhyz, she said, "You go and tell your story to GentleSir Primross. I do not think I—we—will need you during our matchmaking session—"

Bo-ring, sneered Rhyz, but that had Avellana's mouth curving slightly.

"I am sure you would think so," she replied to her Fam. "But we four *will* be leaving Druida City by MidAfternoonBell at the latest. Make sure you arc ready."

His tail thrashed. *I will be. I am always ready.* Then he disappeared, and the Vine glider stopped in front of them.

Thirty

Later, Vinni picked Avellana up at D'Hazel Residence. He'd— they'd—decided to consider the whole matchmaking deal a formal consultation. She awaited at the bottom of steps outside her squat castle, dressed in a tunic and trous that would cost a Commoner two years' worth of salary. Dark blue edged in real silver thread, with hazel leaves embroidered in silver as a border to her long rectangular sleeve pockets and around the cuffs of her bloused trous.

She stood quietly, brown hair in equally tidy and formal braids, the streak minimized, hands in those opposite-sleeve pockets. As usual, his heart constricted at the sight of her. And he disliked that the recent loosening up of her manner that being a part of the new and energetic community of Multiplicity had brought seemed to have vanished. Whether the continuing physical threats or this giving in to emotional Family blackmail had caused her to retreat into her shell, he didn't know. The sooner they got out of Druida City, the better.

Let Primross and the guards do their jobs and find and catch the villains.

He'd had a long talk with Primross as well as the Captain of the Druida City Guards, Ilex Winterberry, and given them all access to his records, as well as introducing the pair to T'Vine Residence. His home, at least, had agreed to fully cooperate with the investigation.

He thought the Residence looked forward to helping. And who knew what other houses might give advice.

As his glider door lifted, he heard the small whoosh of translocated items and noted two well-worn leather bags plopping down into the storage area of the Vine glider. His bags numbered five.

She hadn't moved, and, closer, he saw her face appeared strained. As pale as every time he'd sent her away in the last few years.

He took her hand and kissed her fingers. "I love you, Avellana, and from now on, we're together."

The skin around her eyes relaxed, the ends of her mouth curved up. "A good change, for sure."

Tucking her hand in his arm to formally escort her to his glider, he sent a wash of sweet energy to her . . . and received it back. And that gentle wave of energy sank down into the depths of his being where, once again, he realized he held a simmering anger.

Someone doubted his belief, his word, his *knowledge* that he and Avellana were HeartMates.

Avellana felt a quick flip of anger from Muin, more from the tension of his arm under her fingers than from their bond. "Be easy, Muin. We agreed to this." She paused. "And Saille T'Willow is your friend."

Muin grunted as he courteously held up the glider door and she took the few steps up to enter, then slid in and adjusted her garments. He slammed down the door and marched around the front of the glider, sat beside her, and programmed the vehicle to drive to T'Willow's estate.

Greetyou, Avellana, said Flora. She hung in a hammock attached to the bottom of the dashboard.

"Greetyou, Flora," Avellana murmured.

We are going to Willows, where there are mean cats. I will stay here. Then we are driving ALL THE WAY to Gael City. It will take days and days, but be an adventure!

"I heard that," Avellana said.

The housefluff rolled in her hammock, closed her eyes. *This is the best place in the glider. Rhyz will have to ride in back on a pillow when I swing!*

"I'm sure."

Rhyz says he is already at Willows and playing with cats.

Obviously Avellana's Fam and the trip appealed more as topics of conversation to Flora than the consultation with GreatLord T'Willow. Avellana found herself amused and the stress in her shoulders releasing.

Muin turned toward her and smiled through a sigh. "It irritates me that we're doing this to please my Family." He drummed his fingers on the seat, then raised his voice. "T'Vine Residence?"

"Yes, T'Vine?" The Residence's light voice came through the glider scry speakers.

"I don't ask you of those who gathered privately and spoke together within your walls supporting a formal matchmaking consultation with T'Willow. *And who doubted my word*, but I have changed my mind regarding the payment of his fees. I wish that each and every one of them be charged an amount of T'Willow's fee against their salaries, proportionally."

"Done. I am informing the individuals."

They heard shouts and gasps echoing.

Muin's lips curled up. "Good."

Avellana let her own sigh loose. "I think my parents and sister should also be charged."

"Really?"

"Yes."

Muin frowned. "But I got the idea they just went along with the notion. They wouldn't have thought of it in the first place, would they?"

"No."

T'Vine Residence stated, "I sent a request for reimbursement of a sixteenth of the fee to D'Hazel and have been immediately paid."

"No dispute?" Muin asked.

"No."

The glider swept through T'Willow's gates and to the front wall of the Residence. Like T'Vine fortress, the building formed around an inner courtyard and presented strong and solid walls to the visitor.

Avellana could not suppress a tremor of nerves.

"We'll be fine," Muin said in a rough tone that again spoke more of anger than nerves. Brows down, he slanted her a look. "You don't think that Saille T'Willow will deny we're HeartMates, do you?"

"Of course not," she shot back. "But I am unaccustomed to formal interviews with FirstFamilies Lords and Ladies." She sipped in and let out a breath. "The only such sessions I have attended are the mind-Healing ones with D'Sea, and she always puts me at my ease, of course."

"Yes," Muin agreed.

By then two men in the Willow red livery had lifted the doors to the glider, and one helped Avellana out of the vehicle and led her to the large door in the gold-tinted plaster wall.

It opened the moment Muin joined her and the youngish face of the housekeeper beamed at them. Avellana had rather hoped that Blush Willow Paris, who lived in Multiplicity, would be working today, to welcome them.

Avellana stopped gritting her teeth and tried a sincere smile back. Muin took her hand.

The woman led them down the hall to T'Willow's office, and another footman opened that door. A pair of huge specialized chairs that could provide comfort for hours loomed in Avellana's vision, the seats placed before an equally massive desk. Behind them, the door quietly clicked shut and she and Muin stood facing the best matchmaker on Celta, GreatLord Saille T'Willow.

A man not quite as tall as Muin, somewhat older and thicker in body with an obviously less well-defined torso, stepped forward and hugged Avellana's HeartMate, thumping him on the back. "Greetyou, Vinni."

Then T'Willow turned to her, bent, and kissed her cheek. "Greetyou,

Avellana." His blue eyes twinkled, and he strolled to the entrance to the conservatory that shared a wall with his office. "Let's have some tea."

Muin dropped her hand to slip an arm around her waist, and though his face wore a pleasant expression, she felt surprise at the greeting that echoed her own reverberate through their emotional bond.

As the matchmaker opened the door, the rich scent of verdant, blooming plants wafted into the room. Smiling, he held the door open as they walked to him—past the chairs and his desk and into the conservatory. There, in a small room defined by growing bamboo walls, stood a café table and chairs of white ironwork. Atop the graceful table were settings of floral place mats and softleaves, silver tableware for three, and a tall, curved, and gleaming silver teapot. A thin, fragrant spiral of steam rose from the spout.

T'Willow stood as Vinni seated Avellana, then took his own chair as Muin sat. The matchmaker poured a light-amber tea into delicate china cups and said, "I heard you preferred this tea, Avellana." She understood then, as she smoothed a softleaf over her formal robes, that the GreatLord honored her with this setting.

"Thank you," she said, and added a dab of honey to the cup of soothing herbal tea.

Muin cleared his throat and stared at the matchmaker. "I understood this to be a formal matchmaking consultation with you, Saille."

Avellana realized the man did *not* wear any sort of formal clothes, tunic and trous or robe.

"Did you?" asked T'Willow, pouring himself a cup of tea and bringing it to his lips.

"Yes," Avellana answered.

He sipped, let a grin spread across his face, then said gently, "There is no reason for a formal matchmaking consultation for you, Vinni and Avellana. Not when one look at you shows you to be HeartMates."

"Oh."

Muin inclined his head in respect. "Thank you, Saille."

"You're quite welcome." With a wave of his hand, he said, "I'm charging no fee for this."

"My Family members who insisted on the appointment will be glad to hear that," Muin murmured.

T'Willow laughed. "I'm sure."

The slight susurration of more than one fountain, perhaps the rippling of a human-made stream, added an element of peace to the atmosphere, and Avellana sat back as the men made small talk.

She poured a second round of tea for them all before Muin said, "Something's irritating you, Saille."

"Yes. This whole appointment. I dislike that your Families contacted me to do a full and formal consultation for you and Avellana." T'Willow's patrician jaw hardened. His blue eyes blazed as they met hers, then Muin's in turn. "I *will not allow* a man's or a woman's inner feelings of being a HeartMate to be disregarded." The Great-Lord stood and paced along the windows looking into the courtyard, though his gaze remained on the thick plant life in the small room.

Avellana breathed in deeply, savoring humid scents unencumbered by the salt and briskness of a nearby ocean. The fragrance of the living planet itself.

"What?" Muin prompted.

The matchmaker pivoted. "A tenet of our culture is that an individual can sense his or her HeartMate." He swept one hand wide. "Many people don't need me or my consultations to know when they have connected with the soul who will fulfill them. This must not be changed. People, of all social strata, *must* believe that they can discover their HeartMates, through their Passages to free their Flair, or by presenting a HeartGift, or simply by *feeling* their mate. Or meeting him or her."

"Oh," Avellana said.

He pointed at Muin. "And that's exactly what happened to you."

Muin nodded, smiled with the simple joy she had not seen in so long, and squeezed her fingers. "Yes, I knew I had a HeartMate from an early age." He paused. "I am not sure I ever thought I *did not* have a HeartMate. And when the Hazels brought their new baby to a FirstFamilies ritual in GreatCircle Temple, I understood Avellana and I belonged together."

T'Willow nodded. "Exactly right. You *knew*." He glanced at Avellana. "What of you?"

She blinked. No one had ever spoken to her about this, but then she put her free hand over her heart. "Muin has always been with me."

Another nod. "That's right, too. Every time I've ever seen you together, I could tell you were HeartMates." He flipped a hand. "Yet here you are. You let your Family denigrate your feelings—"

"I think that was because we've been HeartMates for so long."

The GreatLord snorted. "Maybe." His lip curled. "And *someone* thought your love might change or you'd *outgrow* each other or something. Just. Not. True."

"That we might not match anymore," Avellana said softly.

"You do." T'Willow took his seat again and drank down the tea. When he glanced at them again, he smiled. "One look at you and I know you match. But this must not happen again—Families insisting that they, as a whole, know better than the individuals involved."

Avellana said, "I would think that would bring you, matchmakers, more business."

He grinned. "Maybe so, but it is best that individuals believe in themselves and their natural instincts. This is not an action that must be taken from them, the right to choose their mate."

Muin cleared his throat. "Occasionally the individual is wrong."

T'Willow's brows rose. "Occasionally. I have known one instance in hundreds."

"Oh," Muin said.

"Granted," said the matchmaker, "that particular instance had long-standing, deleterious consequences, but it was one instance."

"People can deceive themselves that they love," Muin said.

Avellana stared at him. She would not have expected this line of discussion from him.

"Because they want to believe they have HeartMates? Or that they love a partner and want love from him or her? Perhaps, but I don't want Families or anyone else to put a third party in between a person and his or her discovery of his or her HeartMate. It is an individual's prerogative and responsibility to *feel* their HeartMate, and no one should take that from them."

"Huh," said Muin. He began to play with her fingers.

Avellana straightened her spine. "Muin T'Vine is my HeartMate. He has always been my HeartMate and I love him."

"Avellana Hazel is my HeartMate and I love her," Muin stated.

"Good, that's good," T'Willow said, with a lightening of his manner. He walked over to her and offered his hand. She took it and he drew her to her feet, sending a glance to Muin. "I've heard that you leave here for a trip."

"That's right," Muin agreed.

A smile hovered on the matchmaker's lips. "You can surprise everyone with your quick exit from this Residence and Druida City. My formal consultations usually last from a septhour and a half to four or five. I'll show you out through the length of the conservatory, and you can pick up Rhyz on the way."

"Thanks," Muin said.

"Thank you." Avellana smiled at the GreatLord and as he led her through the long room, she admired the plantings. "We will check on my home in Multiplicity on our way."

"Be aware that when you two *do* HeartBond, your Families will know."

That jolted Vinni and he saw Avellana's eyes go round as she gasped. "Truly?"

Saille nodded, and a smile flickered over his lips. "Yes, GreatMistrys Hazel, your father will most assuredly sense when you link so deeply to another man." Saille glanced at his own daughter, playing near a fountain. "Something I'm sure every father dreads experiencing." He returned his gaze to Vinni. "Which of your Family members will feel the linking, I don't know."

Vinni grimaced. His fingers twitched as he wanted to run them through his hair. This fashion for long hair, which he'd liked at first, wore on him. He'd cut it except Avellana liked it. "I don't know which of my relatives will realize that I've finally HeartBonded with Avellana, either."

Avellana slipped her hand in the crook of his elbow and said, "We will deal with that situation when it comes."

Saille flashed a smile. "I hope not. I hope you don't give your Families a thought."

Thirty-one

They stopped at the Cathedral first because Avellana wanted to ask the Hopeful ministers for a blessing. Muin had agreed. The four religious leaders had just returned from blessing her home in Multiplicity, and remained in the blessing-for-her-and-hers mind-set. They all gathered, including Fams. The short and moving ritual left Avellana's spirits uplifted and in more harmony with Muin and the Fams . . . and this trip.

At Multiplicity, they walked through her house, floors once again pristine, and talked to Antenn Blackthorn-Moss and Vensis Betony-Blackthorn about her house, the security of the community, and how that security had been breached. Apparently the gate scrystones—which had not previously kept records of the comings and goings of approved gliders—*had* noted one entrance and exit within a few minutes in the middle of the night before. The shieldspells of her house had fallen and no one knew why, how, or especially who had done that.

Since so few lived in the community, no one had noticed anything.

For a moment, once more, Avellana wanted to stay and defend her home, fight! But she had never been allowed to stay and fight for a home . . . hadn't become deeply attached to any with a bond like the one she shared with Muin, Rhyz, her Family. And, as always, everyone wanted her away from harm.

She did not want to be attacked again, either, especially trying to defend herself with her minor self-defense skills. She should have worked more on the physical part of her being instead of the creative and spiritual.

And she *did* look forward to time alone with Muin.

She visited the tiny HeartHouse with the barely alive HeartStones—which had not been damaged—and sent them energy and love.

Rhyz zoomed around the town, commenting on the business buildings being raised, and Antenn spoke to Muin briefly about the design of his own house—a large one-story lodge.

She joined them in the front of her home by the glider in time to hear Muin request that his place include a sunroom or conservatory.

Avellana took a few minutes to visit with her former governess and friend, and then everyone in the area circled her home and raised new shieldspells on it.

After that, Avellana and Muin and their Fams drove south on a road trip toward Gael City, finally together.

Every day they stopped their journey at a different time and stayed at the home of a friend of Muin's, usually another FirstFamily ally, in a suite or guesthouse with two bedrooms.

This was the longest period she and Muin had been together by themselves . . . ever. And though they occasionally clashed, more often than not the kilometers passed in harmony between them.

They took a side trip to the Cherry Theater and Resort in the Verde Valley. There they enjoyed a couple of plays, soaked in hot springs . . . and more of the tension of the city unwound within them. Golden moments threaded between them from simply being in love and together . . . until another early-morning wake-up call.

Muin rapped on her bedroom door before dawn and a hissing Rhyz woke her.

With a Word, she bundled herself into a thick robe appropriate for the cool mountain dawn of the Cherry Resort and opened the door.

Muin smiled at her and handed her a cup of strong and steaming caff in a travel tube. Already dressed and groomed, he said, "It's full twinmoons today and Bicknell and Perna's babe will be born tonight. If we leave now, we will get there in time."

His eyes sparkled and she felt high anticipation surging from him. She sipped the tube and considered her lover. Over the course of the week, he appeared to have become a decade younger. She hoped she looked younger, too. She *felt* younger—and more joyful—than she had in years.

And, now, she *did* deeply believe that no one would or could separate them.

Yet smiling, Muin said, "Those Vines themselves believe that they have two or three days before the baby arrives. So we will not be expected."

"You have been careful to vary the lengths of our stays."

"That's right." His expression turned serious. "I don't want anyone to anticipate where we might be at a given time."

She nodded. "I have liked the serendipity of our travels. Please give me ten minutes for a quick waterfall and I will be ready."

"Right. I'm loading our bags. Flora is already in her swing."

I have barely had time to look around the gardens this morning, Rhyz grumbled. *I wanted to lick the dew off the catnip leaves.*

"Too bad," Muin said. "We're leaving in fifteen minutes."

As Avellana swung the door shut, her Fam darted out. She grabbed the clothes she had already designated as appropriate to meet the Vines and assist Muin in his Oracle capacity, then waved her bags packed.

Pleasure bubbled through her.

*T*hey arrived a septhour after dinner bell.

The younger Vines seemed unsurprised but more belligerent than Vinni had anticipated. Standing on the threshold of the small manor house, a sturdy, dark-haired Bicknell blocked Vinni's view of Perna, but the emotions flowing to him from his relatives' bonds included deep wariness.

That irritated him, and he kept that particular feeling from reaching them.

After all, *he* hadn't disapproved of their marriage, wouldn't have, even at six, if he'd been asked. *He* hadn't banished them. In fact, he'd sold them the very nice piece of property they now stood on, including the small yellowstone manor.

He *approved* of them. He'd arrived as the result of Bicknell's sister's request, and he would provide a great service to them.

But they remained cool and close to hostile.

He'd sent Rhyz out to scout for any enemy energy that might be tainted with that of the disaffected Vines.

More concerning to him, the man and woman didn't welcome Avellana warmly, either, but stared at her as if she was weird. Or defective. Or carried a power within her that made her scary.

Only when Flora awoke and hopped out of the glider to join him and Avellana on the doorstep in the confrontation, did Perna step forward, cooing.

"I heard of Flora, but I never met her; may I hold her, please?" Perna asked, her blue-gray gaze meeting Vinni's own of the same shade, though her long, curly hair showed brown with blond streaks.

"I'll pick her up for you," Bicknell replied gruffly.

At another time, Vinni might have offered to get them Fams. Not now, with his nerves scraped and feeling fully as protective of Avellana as Bicknell with Perna.

He inclined his torso and said, "I am sorry to intrude. I am happy to provide Oracle services to you, as Lauda requested. I have acted as Oracle for many others, including Vines." Pausing, he said, "I do advise you to call your Healer or midwife. I sense the impatience of your babe and that she will be born tonight."

"Oh!" exclaimed Perna, then her tone softened. "Oh." Still holding Flora, she moved so the side of her body touched her Heart-Mate's. Watching Vinni, she wet her lips. "I feel . . . my body . . . her mind . . . is that what I feel? Her determination to be born?"

"So I believe." And now they spoke of the baby, a rush of wild, tangled, and unpleasant emotions and sensations shot to him from the three—including the in-womb child—through their Family bonds. He narrowed those links, as well as taking a couple of paces back. Since he held Avellana's hand, she came, too.

"We wish you well. Merry meet—" he began.

"Wait!" Perna's voice sharpened, then fell into quiet tones. "Bicknell, don't you think we can use all the help we can get? And T'Vine as *Oracle*."

Bicknell just scowled.

"Lauda likes him. She asked him and he came." A quick, panting pause. "And it's really happening, and right now, and I want the very best for our baby . . ."

Their forms merged together, supporting each other, cradling, loving.

Flora, caught between the two, sent humming contentment to them all.

Bicknell broke the embrace. "You go call the midwife-Healer, and rest up!" He took Flora from Perna and put the Fam on the ground, and she hopped to Vinni.

Standing squarely in the middle of the door to the manor, Bicknell met Vinni's gaze and said, "Perna wants you as Oracle. Will you stay?"

"Of course," Avellana replied for them both.

Now holding and stroking his Fam himself, Vinni said, "What was the problem here?"

"City people," Bicknell curled his lip. "And from the primary Vine bloodline." He let out a breath. "Probably got ideas and attitudes about us that just aren't right."

Vinni raised his brows. "And *you* don't have such ideas and attitudes about my HeartMate and me?"

Bicknell winced. "You gotta point." He stepped back and held the door wide. "Come on in."

Fifteen minutes later, in the room that had been designated as a birthing chamber, Vinni placed his hands on Perna's abdomen to connect with the new Vine, soothe her a little, maybe. He received another shock and jerked.

"What!" cried Perna. "What's wrong? Is something wrong with my baby?"

Avellana came over and put her hand on Vinni's shoulder. When she caught his stunned recognition, his amazement, his delight through their personal bond, she returned love and joy.

"Absolutely no problem with your child!" Vinni announced. He met Bicknell's gaze. Color had drained from the man's face. He dropped from standing next to the bedsponge to a chair.

"What?" His mouth formed the word too quiet to hear.

"How much do you want to know of your babe?"

Bicknell glared. "You already told us the gender of our child, which we asked the Healers not to reveal."

"Oops," Vinni said.

Perna patted Bicknell's biceps. "She will be born tonight, so not so much of a surprise. We have only to trigger the nursery decoration to female from neutral, and we have chosen *her* name. What else, GreatLord T'Vine?"

"She has great Flair, GentleLady." He gave Bicknell a half bow. "GentleSir."

Bicknell narrowed his eyes. "You're sure."

"Yes." More knowledge of the babe filtered through to him, mostly through his connection with her mother, but he decided to keep his conjectures to himself until the babe came.

Avellana gave a slight cough. "I would be pleased to gift you with a mural for your child if you have any free wall space in the nursery."

The couple stared at her. Bicknell's lip curled slightly. "You won't put any Hopeful religious crap mural on the walls, will you?"

Avellana's spine snapped straight and her sincere smile froze on her face. Vinni put his arm around her waist, helped her shunt aside the hurt at the insult.

"I am a professional holo painter. I accept commissions. You can tell me what you would like to have on the baby's wall. I have done murals of the Lady and Lord, or panoramas of a particular view, such as cityscapes of the starship *Nuada's Sword*, or a portion of the path up the Great Labyrinth, or a special sacred grove throughout the seasons."

Perna poked Bicknell, and Vinni got the idea the woman sent a scathing comment to her husband telepathically.

"My apologies," he muttered.

"We would love to have a mural. What of Maroon Beach? That's where Bicknell and I wed."

"I have done that often. If you have any scrys or memory vizes of the wedding ritual, I can include that. I would be glad to lightpaint such joyful moments."

"A portrait of her parents on the wall," Vinni murmured.

"Sounds great!" Bicknell said a little too heartily, then switched his attention to his lady as she grimaced with a contraction. "When will the babe come?"

"I don't know," Perna whispered, then licked her lips. "The midwife-Healer is on her way."

"Good," Vinni said. "I think . . ." He looked at Bicknell and lifted his brows.

"Please tell me your idea," the man asked.

"From my experience, in the next two septhours."

Bicknell let out a shuddering sigh, dipped his head. "Thank you," Glancing at his HeartMate, he cleared his throat. "Ah, my sister said you might be interested in staying in the cottage on the grounds tonight?"

"Thank you for your offer, GentleSir Vine," Vinni said. "We would appreciate that, and can leave in the morning. My duties for you will be done by then, and I'm sure Avellana can create an excellent mural while we all wait for the babe."

"Call me Bicknell, GreatLord." When his wife released his fingers, he stood. "I'll show you the cottage. GreatMistrys Hazel, I will get some pics and scrys of our wedding ritual for you."

"That would be wonderful," Avellana said.

*I*nspiration blessed *Avellana that evening and she finished the mural in* a septhour. Of course she had painted Maroon Beach more than a dozen times so she knew the background well, and could include the inbound flowing tide, the color of the sky, ocean, and seafoam in spring. In the wedding vizes, the couple appeared blissfully happy, and her irritation at Bicknell's comment on her religion easily faded.

Bicknell, Perna, and the midwife-Healer complimented Avellana on her work before Perna's heavy contractions brought the decorating of the nursery to an end.

Muin appeared to approve of the bustling and efficient Healer, and that pleased Avellana because she knew he would have been high-handed and dragged in a different midwife if he disliked the woman. That would have returned irritation among them all.

Now, in the last half septhour of Muin's estimate, Avellana waited outside the birthing chamber with him. He had told her that with the strength of the Flair emanating from the unborn child, he would not need to be in the room itself. Avellana thought he respected Perna's privacy. She and her husband had decided they did not want a First-Family GreatLord in the room with them.

Avellana had not contemplated the details of this particular duty of Muin's before—the Oracle, a person with foresight or prophecy, who could *see* what training might be best for a child. Or, in the case of the nobility, who should be the next heir to the woman or man who held the title.

Muin would probably not often be outside the chamber. She would have to ask him how many babies he had seen born and whether he had ever helped other than holding the baby and using his Flair.

He remained smiling and relaxed while Avellana suppressed the urge to pace, waiting for the baby to arrive. Such a tiny package of potential!

Then Muin stood, staring at the door. No more than a few seconds later a newborn's cry echoed—through the manor house *and* in Avellana's mind. *Hurt, anger, a touch of fear.*

A bond between the child and Muin snapped into place, Familial, a tiny, sparkling flow, and the cry turned into a grunt of surprise. Avellana saw the glinting silver link, felt the new energy of it added to all of the other bonds Muin held.

Then she *felt* the enveloping awe and love wrapping around the baby girl from her parents, the rush of affection from Muin, the delight and satisfaction of the midwife-Healer. Avellana blinked at the echoing vibrations of the baby's feelings to Muin and to her down their bond.

Muin strode to the door and opened it. Avellana glimpsed the baby lying on her mother's chest, already cleansed.

The door swung shut and Avellana leaned back in her chair, closing her eyes, extending her senses, so she could experience as much as possible what Muin did. A couple of minutes passed, and then she heard Muin's voice echo in her head—a strong telepathic announcement that matched words he said aloud.

I SEE that this child, Floricoma Vine, possesses great Flair and that the Flair is for prophecy. I acknowledge her now as a Vine, with the Vine Flair, and as my heir until I have a child from my own seed.

That rocked Avellana—and everyone else in the manor. She blinked at the idea. Of course Muin would have considered children as more than vague images. She felt ashamed that she hadn't. But *their* children would have Flair. Muin's, of course, but the Families that stood behind them, their parents and grandparents, might pass down their Flair. She said a tiny prayer to the Journey of the Four that her and Muin's children would not inherit *her* Flair.

And she had missed some of Muin's broadcast.

A very strongly Flaired child, a blessed child with excellent parents.

"Is she healthy?" demanded Perna.

I feel no problem with her Flair or her flow of her psi power, Muin commented telepathically, *and this very good midwife-Healer told you she is physically and mentally whole and exceptional.*

Sorrow twinged through Avellana. She had been an exceptional child physically . . . and another new thought entered her head. Perhaps she had remained so. Perhaps had she been less physically strong she would not have survived, no matter how many FirstLevel Healers had put her poor skull together after she had tried to fly.

Yes. Her spine straightened and she felt the tensile strength of that. She *was* physically strong. Though she knew her brain occasionally misfired, that she had a few blank moments, that she became obsessive about minor issues that other people would not even notice.

But she practiced all the mental and Flair exercises she had been taught.

"Will she have a long life?" Bicknell demanded.

Muin hesitated a split second, though Avellana didn't think any of the others noticed. He answered, *A long and prosperous life.*

More like he repeated than he assured. She felt the doubt . . . saw the blurred cloud over the babe in these first months.

Oh, no!

Avellana sensed Muin trying to probe the fog, and understood at the same time he did that the reason for the mistiness might be that this small Family was associated with them—Muin and herself.

She sighed.

"May I invite Avellana Hazel into the room?" Muin asked.

"Of course," Perna agreed.

So Avellana entered the room.

"Your *heir*, GreatLord T'Vine? Our Floricoma?" Bicknell demanded, his face angry.

Avellana began to close the door behind her, but the midwife-Healer picked up her bags and, with a big smile, said, "I think I'll wait outside."

"I trust in your Healer confidentiality," Muin stated, all First-Family GreatLord.

"Of course!" She slid through the door, obviously sensitive to Family dynamics.

"Yes, Bicknell, I spoke correctly. Floricoma has enough Flair for prophecy to be my heir," Muin stated. He did not look at Avellana but held out his hand. She joined him and placed her fingers into his.

"As you may or may not know, Avellana has been attacked."

Perna gasped; Bicknell stared stonily out the window at the night.

"Perhaps because she is my HeartMate and members of the Family don't like that."

"You think *relatives* might have attacked her!" Perna gasped. "*Why?*"

"Because, as we discussed when we met, some of our relatives have rigid attitudes about our Family. As you, yourselves, have experienced."

"You can't bring us into this," Bicknell said roughly. "You can't put us at risk, *Head of the Household*." He leaned over Perna and Floricoma, sheltering them.

"I will do my best to protect you," Muin stated. "As I so promised during the Loyalty Ceremony." He paused. "What you probably don't know about this situation is that should anything happen to Avellana, we are bound closely enough together that I would die, also."

"Lady and Lord," Perna sobbed. She held Floricoma close and rocked her.

Muin gestured to the baby. "I don't know whether those who oppose Avellana—or me—would prefer Floricoma as my heir or not, but the truth is that she has Flair enough to be D'Vine."

Bicknell cursed, using words that made Avellana's eyes go wide.

Pulling his perscry stone from his trous pocket, Muin said, "I will send for bodyguards tonight, *not* Vine guards, but people from the Holly fighting Family's Green Man Salon in Gael City. Two guards each for every shift, and multiple shifts. They will guard you until the villains are found."

"Wait!" Bicknell demanded. He placed his hands over Perna's and stared into her eyes. Avellana deduced they communicated mentally.

A couple of moments later, Bicknell said, "We live outside a small town where strangers would be reported. We have good neighbors who will keep an eye out." His lips firmed. "We will not invite anyone from the Family to visit." He sucked in a breath. "We would prefer to keep this whole . . . situation . . . as quiet as possible."

Avellana felt relief flow from Muin, though his expression did not show the emotion. So he wished the same.

"You've just been on a trip, right, here and there"—Bicknell waved a hand—"and not staying long, and—"

"That's right," Muin said. He shifted his weight, pulling her hand through the crook of his arm. "We've rarely stayed more than a day at a friend's house. I can let it be known, truthfully, that your sister requested I be Oracle at Floricoma's birth. I agreed out of courtesy. We stayed tonight to welcome the new Vine babe, then moved on. No one in this area except you and the midwife-Healer would know of Floricoma's Flair."

Bicknell stared at the door. "You're a FirstFamily GreatLord, you could ruin our midwife's life."

Muin shrugged.

In a small voice, Perna said, "We trust her."

"I have followed your wishes all evening, Bicknell and Perna. I won't call the Holly guards unless you approve, and I won't harm the midwife-Healer unless you inform me that *she* harmed *you* in some manner."

"Good." Bicknell's cheeks puffed out as he exhaled. "That's good."

"However," Muin continued. The others tensed. "Until a few minutes ago, no one in the Family had enough Flair for prophecy to be my heir. That makes the Family uneasy, and the FirstFamilies, too, I'm sure you understand."

"Yeah," Bicknell said at the same time Perna said, "Yes."

Thirty-two

"The babe must be officially acknowledged as my heir." Vinni took a small pad of papyrus from his jacket pocket, ripped out a sheet, and walked to the old table that held a writestick. Placing the papyrus piece down, he put his fingertips on it and enlarged and changed the consistency so it became official size. Then he picked up the write-stick and touched the point to the cream colored sheet. Concentrating, he forced ink from the pen, shaping the words into a flowing script as he imprinted them by will onto the paper, changing the color of the font as needed in three places and adding a touch of gold in the twining blackberry leaves and fruit that bordered the whole page. With a grunt, he lifted his hand and tapped his forefinger on the page to engrave his official seal on the document.

Then he moved to the scry panel and placed his hand on the frame. "Scry T'Ash."

Bicknell and Perna gasped. Avellana grinned, then let out an "Ooooh!"

"T'Ash here, who is this?" demanded a rough voice. "And why are you scrying so damn late?"

Vinni moved into the center of the screen and donned his most formal manner. "GreatLord T'Ash, it is Muin T'Vine, and I am scrying you as my ally on an extremely important matter to me."

With a grunt, the man said, "Lightspell on." The panel revealed a bare-chested T'Ash, then flickered black. When it relit, T'Ash wore a formal robe and stood in his ResidenceDen, where he kept his Flair Testing Stones.

"Yeah, Vinni—ah, Muin?" T'Ash's gaze went beyond Vinni to Avellana, and even farther, to Bicknell and Perna.

"T'Ash, please allow me to present to you my cuzes, Bicknell and Perna Vine, who are HeartBonded to each other."

"Greetyou," the GreatLord said gruffly.

"As the Prophet of Celta"—and with those words, T'Ash's expression turned serious and his body seemed to expand—"and acting as the Oracle of Celta, I hereby acknowledge that the female babe Perna delivered this evening, Floricoma Vine, has sufficient Flair in prophecy to be my heir, and I am so naming her that."

"I hear you," T'Ash said.

Vinni held up the piece of papyrus so T'Ash could see it. "I have set my intention, my hand, and my seal on this document."

"Why do you call on me as an ally?"

"You are my strongest and fiercest ally."

T'Ash looked pleased.

"I am trusting you, and only you, with this secret. So that if anything happens to me, you will acknowledge before *all* and most particularly to the FirstFamilies Council and the Clerk of the All Councils that the child is my heir, the heir to the Vines, with the Flair to be the Prophet of Celta."

"And, as your ally, you wish me to defend these parents and the babe with my body and Family if anyone challenges your will or that document."

"Correct."

Inclining his head, T'Ash said, "I understand and I accept that charge."

"I am translocating this document to your cache transnow. I will keep the scry open until I know that you have received it. I also want you to confirm the receipt of the document, date it and countersign it, and safeguard it."

"I can do that. It would be better to have additional witnesses," T'Ash said. He raised his voice. "Danith?"

The small woman immediately appeared next to her lord. Vinni blinked that she'd teleported so close to her HeartMate, knew exactly where he stood. That demonstrated a huge amount of trust on both their parts—trust only HeartMates of long standing would give each other. And Vinni believed neither of them had given such teleportation a thought, they did it so often. He wanted that trust and familiarity for himself and Avellana.

Danith D'Ash gazed at them from the scry panel. "You want us to be your Fail-Safe people, so that we know your wishes."

"That's right."

She waved a hand and the document he'd wafted to T'Ash Residence cache floated onto a desk near them. Then she placed her hand on the papyrus and said, "I hereby accept the charge for myself and my Family to protect and defend the child of Bicknell and Perna Vine, who is acknowledged by the present Muin T'Vine to be his current heir."

Grumbling that Danith had set her seal first, T'Ash followed suit.

"That's two Ash signatories," Danith said. She raised her voice. "T'Ash Residence, have you been attending to our conversations with regard to this matter of our alliance with the Vine Family?"

"I have," came a voice so resonant that it made the glass of the scry panel vibrate. "I am keeping this in my memory as a Familial charge. All of us Ashes will know of this and fulfill such a charge. If the situation deteriorates to needing to be proven before the First-Families Council, I will reveal my memories of this night to the other Residences. If we need to call upon others in our circle of alliances to keep this promise, I will confirm the events of this night."

Vinni bowed. "Thank you, all."

T'Ash grunted. "When do you think this whole situation will get done, Vinni?"

Vinni said, "I've been keeping in touch with Garrett Primross,

Captain of the Druida Guards Ilex Winterberry, and others." Vinni felt the tightness of his Flair and spoke without hesitation. "No more than two and a half weeks, by Discovery Day."

"Very well." T'Ash frowned. "Do you wish us to house the Vines? We have the house room."

Glancing at Bicknell and Perna, Vinni saw them shake their heads.

"We love where we are," Perna whispered.

"We would prefer to keep everything secret," Bicknell added.

Avellana began, "This is—"

"—a contingency scenario," Danith ended, nodding. "All is well, now let's go back to bed and get some sleep." But from her smile at T'Ash, Vinni didn't think Danith had sleep in mind. "Merry meet." She began the ending formalities.

"And merry part." Everyone in the room with Vinni said the next line.

"And merry meet again," T'Ash growled, and ended the scry.

"There, that's done. My wishes are known and the secret of them will be kept and is understood and protected by the most determined member of the FirstFamilies that I know." Satisfaction, even a slight giddiness suffused Vinni, but he didn't know why. He blinked away the emotion, the weariness, the odd feeling of lightness, and turned to Bicknell and Perna. Bicknell had risen but appeared wild-eyed, as if he'd been swept along by events that had sent an earthquake through his life, changing it. True enough. Like Vinni, he'd have to learn to master an impassive expression when that happened.

Perna breathed rhythmically, humming and soothing the babe.

Then Bicknell's jaw firmed and he matched gazes with Vinni. "T'Ash will guard our daughter?"

"And you and your wife. Absolutely feel free to contact them at any time. They have staff, guards, and adult children who have the range to teleport here and back to Druida City with you."

Bicknell sat and slumped in his chair. "That's good, then."

"All my allies will guard you if T'Ash calls them in. None of our relatives will prevail against your claim for your daughter, should you need to make it."

A disgusted noise came from both husband and wife. "That's what you think."

Vinni frowned.

Avellana straightened beside him. "We *do* have allies, and not all of those allies are as old as T'Ash. Many have more in common with us." She stared at them intensely and Vinni *felt* them snagged by that gaze, open to her words. "We know Loridana D'Yew, who recently challenged her Family and won the title and who now heads that household very well. If you need to understand your options and techniques for doing the same, you should call on her."

"Or Saille T'Willow," Vinni said with a grimace. "He knows that, too."

"Oh," Perna said in a tiny voice, then sagged against the pillows behind her.

After a quiet breath, Avellana asked, "May I hold Floricoma?"

The parents exchanged a glance.

"Not for long," Avellana assured. "A moment or two. I have not seen her."

"Yes," sighed Perna.

Avellana strode to the bed and took the sleeping baby from Perna. Vinni couldn't help it, he sauntered to Avellana's side drawn by the huge and unconditional love she felt. He made sure that all three of the other Vines received Avellana's feeling down their shared bonds. She wouldn't be formally linked to his Family until they Heart-Bonded or wed.

Vinni was pretty sure they'd HeartBond first.

After a minute of cooing into smoky blue eyes that stared up at them, Avellana sighed and held out Floricoma to her father, who took her and continued the coos in a deeper voice.

Perna said, "About Floricoma being your heir . . ."

"Yes?" Vinni asked.

"No offense," Perna said, "but as I said before, we are happy here and would not care to move to Druida City. We want to raise her here, outside the pressures of the city and those who'd watch and judge us."

Vinni suppressed a flinch. He and Avellana knew about always being watched and judged. But he'd not had the option of living anywhere but T'Vine Residence.

"I understand, but your child will be great in Flair and will need to be taught," he replied.

"By you," Bicknell said heavily.

Vinni dipped his head. "That would be best, though due to the strength and potency of our Family gift, we have many manuals and people who help train, including the HouseHeart. After all, I inherited the title at six years old."

Both husband and wife shuddered.

Drawing in a breath, he released it slowly and raised a hand, palm out. "However, since you have given me this wonderful boon, I will pledge to come here several days a month to teach your child."

"GreatLord, you will do that?" Perna's voice trembled in disbelief.

He smiled simply, sincerely. "Yes."

The ramifications of this gift pressed at his mind, but he couldn't allow them to derail his thinking right now. Later, later, later.

"You should call me Vinni."

Avellana sniffed.

He slanted a look to her. "Only my HeartMate calls me 'Muin,' and occasionally some older Family members when they are displeased with me."

The couple shared a glance. "We will."

Bicknell added gruffly, "You are welcome to stay here in the main house at any time, both of you."

"Thank you. If you will excuse us now, we will settle into the cottage. We'll leave you with your new daughter."

"Sounds great," Bicknell said, sitting on the bedsponge and holding his daughter and HeartMate.

With a full bow to them, GreatLord to those of his equal, because the babe *would be* his equal, Vinni held out his hand to Avellana and she clasped his fingers. He hoped he masked his heated and lusty reaction to her, another surge of unexpected emotion.

They left the room, then the manor, walking the short distance to the cottage. Avellana suppressed a sigh.

She would have liked to stay a day or two, to see Muin bond with the baby, and perhaps try to bond with the child herself. Instead, she said, "We will leave tomorrow as if this stop were a mere courtesy."

"Yes," Muin replied.

"We will visit the village and buy a gift for the babe to be sent here, then continue our trip to Gael City." She squeezed his hand.

He relaxed and pressed her fingers. "We won't endanger the child. I'm going to call in some of Garrett Primross's feral animals as observers, and I have a friend with a place near here who can house some guards."

She exhaled as fear twisted inside her. "We will never endanger that beautiful baby."

"No."

"And you think that by Discovery Day we will have resolved this bad situation."

He lifted her hand to his and kissed her fingers. "Absolutely." When he smiled her heart squeezed in her chest. "And we'll invite the whole small family, Bicknell, Perna, and Floricoma, to celebrate New Year's, Samhain, with us."

"I *felt* when you sensed our problems would be resolved."

Muin's smile appeared sincere. "I *can* work around my—and your—future, indirectly. If I can find people who share our futures. That's the case of baby Floricoma. She gave me a timeline for our troubles." He released a gusty breath. "Good to know."

"Our issues will be gone by Discovery Day," Avellana repeated, to get the notion set in her head. Then she let her shoulders drop in relief. She stared at him, his lips slightly curled in a smile she did not understand, though she liked the slight dampness of their clasped hands, and decided to be direct. She had learned that saved time, and if she hurt Muin emotionally, she could soothe him one way or another.

"Your emotions are—unruly. As is your Flair control." She could sense the wild firestorm within him, exultation, exhaustion. Joy, guilt at the joy, an edge of fear. She had blocked him a bit to keep her own emotions steady.

He laughed, choked it into a chuckle. "You mean you aren't used to my lack of control and unruly emotions for anything other than loving with you."

Her mouth had fallen open and she shut it. "Your . . . our emotions during loving are, ah, not standard . . ." She waved. "But they, ah, have a certain rise and fall . . . a pattern."

Picking her up, he swung her around, yet laughing, then placed her on her feet, linking fingers with her. "Yes, maybe a certain pattern to our loving. We'll change it around when we wed and love more in person than in dreams."

She swallowed. "Oh."

He turned his head so his gleaming gaze looked back to the manor. "They can see us, and they can see the gardens of the cottage and the small house itself."

"We do not care." She squeezed his hand.

"No." He glanced down at her.

"Your emotions still explode."

"Yes."

"Though your voice and expression remain . . . cool. I have been with you when you have exercised your Flair satisfactorily, and this . . . giddiness of yours is more."

"Giddiness." He snorted. They had reached the white picket fence surrounding the cottage. Instead of opening the gate, he lifted her over, then vaulted over himself.

He took her hand, held it in a dance form, and flicked as if he wanted her to turn under his arm. So she did.

"Check our bond," he said agreeably.

Focusing inward, she considered the large glowing cable, then gasped. "It has changed!"

"Yes," he said. He'd picked up on the change in their bond—after she'd pointed out how his feelings roiled. No, the result of being the Oracle for Floricoma's birth had affected him like no other.

He wanted to dance, and with his love in this small grassyard of a Vine cottage. So he moved in dance steps to music and sent the tune he heard mentally to her.

She replied telepathically, *You feel odd, inside.*

"Yes," he responded aloud, finally figuring out why. One more step and he picked her up again, spun her to the dance, put her down on the right beat.

He let the exuberance infuse them both. "Do you realize that since I became T'Vine at six, I have never had a good heir until now? A Family member I *knew* had the Flair to become the next Prophet of Celta?" His cheer caused his voice to lilt and he didn't care. He opened his arms wider than the dance decreed, though he kept to the steps. "A burden has fallen away from me. I don't have to be as careful with myself."

They came to the end of space near the front porch and turned to promenade back to the fence. "I . . . feel free." He narrowed his eyes. "So free I could *live* with you in Multiplicity."

He winked at her. She stared.

"It could be our own little love nest."

"No. It is my home and studio."

"Hmm. I could use a studio for my wind chimes workshop. I'll have to include that in my Multiplicity home. I could live there. We could live there. Unwatched by anyone, even the house." Hop. Turn. Pick her up and spin . . . and don't put her back down. Pull her close so he could *feel* her heart beat against his chest, let her sense his own racing pulse.

With every moment his sense of freedom expanded and he could hear chunks of the heavy-rock burden he'd carried and had never considered, falling away.

Avellana sniffed. "I know very well that T'Vine Residence adores you. It will always back you in any Familial discussion or dispute."

Vinni grinned. "Because I am T'Vine, the Prophet of Celta, the Oracle of Celta. And I have been an excellent GreatLord. I have fulfilled all my duties. I have been responsible. I have brought gilt to our coffers and favors and fame to our name." Now he wanted *real* music. "Calendar sphere, play a selection of dance compositions."

The orb appeared and cheerful music poured into the air. A couple of minutes later, Vinni felt eyes on them, swung Avellana around in a curve, and saw two silhouettes standing close together. Bicknell and Perna. Through his newly strong bond with them he felt a slight astonishment, but increasing trust and warmth. Excellent.

And good for them to see that he and Avellana were simple and human, just like them.

On the first note of a quiet, lilting waltz, he drew Avellana down to the ground with him to lie next to him, murmuring aloud a spell to banish lust.

They lay there quietly for three full songs, sides touching, hands clasped.

He enjoyed the feel of the thick grass, the gorgeous spirals of multicolored stars, the night sky of Celta that showed galaxies, his love beside him.

"I can't do it," he said.

"I know, Muin."

She did, but he wanted to put it in words anyway. "I can't give up my title."

"Of course not." Her hand stroked his chest.

"I like being T'Vine. Not so much being the Head of the Family, but I like using my Flair and interacting with other FirstFamilies. I love my Residence."

"Of course. You cannot give up your life. Your identity *is* as T'Vine."

He grunted. "Yes." Then he grinned. "But that doesn't mean I can't threaten the Family with it."

He heard her head shake. "Oh, Muin."

"They need shaking up."

"I am sure we are doing a good job of that now."

"Maybe. Not sure who all in the Family might have recognized my knowledge of a new Vine with excellent Family Flair, or my reaction to that notion."

"But some of your closest Family members would have felt echoes of your emotions."

"Yes." He paused. "I'm not sure whether they'll make the right and logical connections or not."

"And whether, if they make those connections, Floricoma will be in danger."

"Yes." He sighed. "We have to leave tomorrow . . . after we raise a better shieldspell around the manor."

"Yes, Muin."

"We'll continue on to check out the house in Gael City."

"All right."

A rustling noise came and Flora hopped from under a bush and onto Vinni's chest. *I felt your joy at the new young one,* she said.

Did you FEEL that she is strong in power and could be the next Head of the Household? he asked telepathically.

No, Flora said. *Just your joy.*

He petted her. *You are closer to me than anyone except Avellana.* But Flora wasn't a thinking, scheming human, not as smart as a human.

We continue our travels and to another place that smells of Family.

"Yes," Avellana said out loud. Then he heard her telepathic call to her own Fam. *Enjoy your night here, Rhyz. We will be leaving in the morning.*

A quiet mental assent and a feeling that Rhyz waited at a rat hole, hunting.

Avellana convinced Vinni to continue the no-lust spell so that they could sleep together that night. Just to *be* together, as friends, not lovers. He hadn't wanted to do it . . . but thought he might like the novelty.

He supposed he could get used to the feeling of no-lust when he was with her. Occasionally. Once a decade or so.

Thirty-three

The next morning, after a breakfast at the manor house with Bicknell and Perna—and Floricoma in a high cradle—Vinni and Avellana stood on the front porch, hands joined, bond open and flowing between them. Flora and Rhyz sat on their feet.

"Ready to raise a shieldspell?" Vinni asked.

"Yes."

He began the chant, then as she formed her part of the shield, he let his spell collapse. "Stop."

She did, staring at him.

Gritting out the words, Vinni said, "Your spell is old, not current. I did not notice that when we worked on your home."

She raised her brows. "I was one of many in Multiplicity and followed your lead. My shieldspell is the latest I have been taught." She paused. "Two years ago."

He dropped her hands, paced down the sidewalk to the gliderway, then back. "Cave of the Dark Goddess." He let out an unamused laugh. "Guess we know how your house shieldspells were breached."

"I suppose so," she said stiffly. "As far as I know, no one else reinforced my own spells on my house in Multiplicity. The very best shieldspells are slated for next week."

"Damn. I'll relay this information to Garrett Primross and Ilex Winterberry." His teeth snapped together. "Why haven't you learned—"

"Because I have been away. Usually in small towns where you introduced me to people, and they know me and watch out for me, as you asked. You have always boosted the shieldspells on my domiciles."

You always sent us away and played with such spells yourself, FamCat Rhyz said at the same time.

"All right." He flung up his hands. "All *right.*"

She removed her hands from her sleeves where they'd gone. Vinni figured she might have made fists. Or maybe she'd been tempted to use a spell against him, or punch him.

He rocked, heel-to-toe, sending his irritation into the ground. Several times. When he knew he contained the steadiness needed for a strong spell, he held out his hands and linked with Avellana, noting that she'd banished her annoyance, too. Probably quicker than he had.

"Ready?"

"Yes, beloved." She smiled.

Better than steadiness, the warmth of being loved rose in him, and when he focused on the house, he sensed the people within, and recalled the joy and gratitude he'd felt last night, and let that rise, too.

With him guiding her, teaching her the new spell, all four of them tapped into the Vine energy of the estate and fit an excellent shield around the house.

Until pain traveled through his Family bonds and bit at the back of his mind and he let Avellana finish the spell as he crumpled to the ground.

Vinni awoke on a gel couch in the mainspace of the cottage, with Avellana holding his hand, looking worried, Flora snuffling on his chest, and Bicknell and Rhyz staring down at him.

"I got you in here," the man said.

Carried, most likely, and to the cottage, not into the other Vine's home, the manor house.

"Thanks," Vinni said. Sitting up and rubbing the back of his neck, he met Bicknell's eyes. "Did you feel it?"

"Feel what?"

"Bifrona collapsed. Some major health problem, I think." Touching his temples, he checked his bond with her, dim and unresponsive. And he began to grieve. She would not recover from this physical outrage, and it had occurred sooner than he'd anticipated.

"Oh, no!" Avellana cried.

"Bifrona Vine? The head of the staff of T'Vine Residence?" Bicknell asked flatly.

"Yes," Vinni confirmed, swinging his feet down to the floor, but holding Flora close. She grieved, too.

Bicknell had stiffened. "Neither Perna nor I have close bonds to her." After a moment of stolid silence and with surprise dawning on his face, he concluded, "The closest bond we have with the Vine Family is you, GreatLord—"

"Vinni," Vinni insisted.

"Vinni."

Avellana blinked rapidly. "Do you know who will step into Bifrona's place as Head of Staff and Housekeeper?"

He cleared his throat. "No. I don't. She has deputies, secondaries—" He made a cutting gesture. "I suppose we must have contingency plans in case of such a situation—"

This time a harsh laugh came from Bicknell. "I doubt it. There are people in T'Vine Residence who definitely think they are better than others and are indispensable."

"Then, Muin, your household might be in disarray. We must leave immediately," Avellana stated.

"We'll 'port to Gael City airpark, hire a fast private airship to Druida City, rent a glider there. I think we could even get there today." He gazed at Bicknell. "I can leave my glider here for you, Perna, and the babe, or program it to go back to Druida City."

"We don't need a fancy glider." He curled his bottom lip.

"All right, then—"

"Waste, Muin," Avellana scolded. "Let us find out if anyone we know needs a glider ride to Druida City."

He didn't like the idea of some unknown in his personal glider, so just grunted in response.

Avellana rose but squeezed his hand. "Thank you for your hospitality, Bicknell." She dropped Vinni's fingers to curtsey to the man. "We will leave shortly."

"Good, that is, all right. We're glad you were here to be Oracle, T'Vine. Our gratitude."

"You're welcome." Vinni stood and inclined his torso. "Please consider being our guests at Samhain."

Bicknell jerked a nod. "Guess we might. Changes are coming to the Family, for sure."

"Absolutely," Avellana said. "Of course you will be invited to our wedding."

A smile-grimace. "Thank you."

"All will be settled by then," she reminded him quietly.

"Okay." He turned on his heel and left.

Flora whuffled, curved in on herself. *I am sad. Bifrona is good to me. She gives me treats.*

Rhyz actually jumped from the curved arm of the sofa to walk over and stretch against Vinni and lick the bulge of Flora's stomach. *I am sorry you are sad. We will go back today.*

"Yes," Avellana said. "Rhyz and I will take care of our house and each other at Multiplicity and at D'Hazel Residence, and Muin will take care of his Family at T'Vine Residence."

Vinni stepped up to her and hugged her. "And we'll see each other every day. That's a promise from me."

She met his eyes. "Yes, I promise, too."

Rhyz said, *I can spend time with Flora. Helping her.* His tail waved. *I like T'Vine Residence very much.*

All cats enjoyed status, and it looked like Rhyz would be making his move to become the primary Fam of T'Vine Residence.

On a private telepathic stream to the Fam, Vinni warned, *You must watch out for Avellana.*

Rhyz's whiskers twitched as the tip of his tail flicked. *I always do. Better than you.*

Then he teleported outside as Vinni stroked his housefluff.

Thirty-four

*T*he moment Vinni arrived at the entry gatehouse of T'Vine Residence late that afternoon, he'd been swarmed with people. Even more awaited him when he'd teleported to the public area. T'Vine Residence had already told Bifrona's deputies to continue in their areas, but Vinni figured shadowy turf wars had begun.

Looking thin and too pale, Bifrona rested comfortably in her suite, in a coma and with little brain activity. The Family had three Healers, two SecondLevel and one ThirdLevel, and they rotated staying with Bifrona and keeping her comfortable. She was expected to pass on to the Wheel of Stars and her next life within the next several days.

The Healer of Celta, FirstLevel Healer Ura Heather, had examined Bifrona shortly after she'd collapsed. And when Vinni arrived, the Healer spent a few minutes with him after he looked in on Bifrona.

Bifrona had suffered a syrthio attack, an unexpected, fatal brain blip. A Celtan phenomenon that occurred when the Earthan human reached some sort of level of disbelief about their planet or their culture.

Or their idea of Family.

Vinni could only suppose Bifrona had been forced to confront evidence of betrayal within the Family. Someone who'd broken his Loyalty Oath to Vinni, smashed a Vow of Honor.

She might have been playing games to manipulate Vinni with regard to Avellana and her status as D'Vine. His cuz would prefer to continue to hold the staff's reins, and establish that upper hand before Vinni wed. So Bifrona would be open to being maneuvered with regard to insisting that Vinni and Avellana lead a First Quarter Twinmoons Ritual and visit Saille T'Willow.

But she would never have countenanced violence to Avellana or him.

What had she learned, and how? He asked the Residence to recite her movements and found she'd collapsed in her suite after reviewing the list of people who would be having gilt deducted from their salaries for payment of T'Willow's matchmaking fee.

Had she realized, then, she'd been used? Was the betrayer's name on that list, or, more likely, *not* on the list?

So Vinni sat down and read reports. First, he compared the people on her list with ones who'd been in his tower the day he'd felt evil, and crossed some names off.

Then he matched those who'd been out of T'Vine Residence during the attack at the baths. Eleven.

That particular exercise did not help in determining who in the Family could be the villain.

Next he turned to the reports of the investigators of the assaults on Avellana and the kidnapped Phae Thermarum—who GraceLady D'Thermarum stated remained alive though missing.

Before Vinni, Avellana, and the Fams had left on the trip, he'd given Garrett Primross permission to interrogate his staff. Listening to his Family members talk of the man, and reading his report, he found that Primross had spent a couple of days in casual conversation with the Vines. Hadn't ruffled many feathers, except Duon's, the Chief of Guards.

Primross had discovered no evidence of villains but had left three of his stray FamCats slinking about as observers of the Vine Family.

The Captain of the Druida City Guards, Ilex Winterberry, had also visited, but the Family had closed ranks against him.

No help from those reports.

Vinni's allies in the FirstFamilies continued to send accounts of checking out their own Families for the secret Traditionalist Stance leader. Some of the small FirstFamilies had informal gatherings; others, apparently, instituted more formal questioning. Nobody reported any disloyalty.

His allies who'd managed to maintain ties with those who'd broken contracts with the Vines reported that those two Families no doubt contained members of the Traditionalist Stance. However, the conservative Heads of those Households didn't like violent fanatics any more than any other powerful FirstFamily Lord or Lady. They, too, scrutinized their Family members, and reported no villain.

Vinni continued to experience the awful dread that the leader was a Vine.

Of all the people on this side of Celta, Avellana could be considered the outlier in the type of her primary Flair.

Vinni knew most believed he was odd, too, since he'd demonstrated such strong Flair at an early age—and he'd never suffered through the dreamquest Passages to free that gift. His Flair had always been available to him. But his *type* of Flair, prophecy, had been known and accepted since the most ancient of days on old Earth.

Avellana, the strength and type of her Flair, scared people. In a population who continued to evolve in psi power, Avellana stood out as an evolutionary jump.

And that was the basis of this whole mess.

The Traditionalist Stance people didn't want progress, to accept that children manifested newer and stronger Flair. That, maybe, the Earthan humans had finally begun to adjust to their new home planet.

Kill the mutant, and before she breeds, and before she breeds in OUR bloodline. Yes, he could sense that sort of warped thinking smearing his relatives.

Much as he hated to think it, he thought the Vine guards might be tainted. They'd been infected by dissent, by anger, by fear of the *different* before. That group tended to be more conservative than the rest of the culture, and were trained to defend and attack.

After dinner, Vinni couldn't settle, so he walked the Residence. Only once a season did he walk through all the corridors of his home, look through every room except private bedrooms, check on everyone there, working or at leisure.

He kept his usual easy manner, greeted everyone by name, but watched their reactions to him, and if he sensed disapproval, he checked on his bond with that member. Naturally some disliked being watched, having the Head of the Household in their area. Those who would be paying a fee for the matchmaking session—going to a common Vine fund, but being charged all the same—grudged Vinni's presence.

A slight wariness at the changing status of them all with Bifrona's illness pervaded most of his Family, along with a general low-grade grief at the thought of her passing.

Lauda seemed cheerful, Arcto as smooth and welcoming as ever in grovestudy lessons, others like Nava and Lacinia respectful.

He heard no outward complaints.

At the main, upper gatehouse, he met with Duon, his Chief of Guards, to request the duty lists for the Vine guards for the current and previous month.

One thing he knew, the villain wasn't Duon. Vinni remembered the man's big hands clasping his own as they pledged their loyalty to each other, confirmed their duties and obligations, not more than four years before.

A person who'd broken such a Vow of Honor to attack Avellana would be showing significant effects of such a betrayal.

And though Duon's bond with Vinni seethed with suppressed annoyance, the man felt strong and solid.

Vinni allowed Duon to accompany him as the representative for those who served the Family as protectors as they toured the gatehouses and guards' quarters.

Of the men and women he met, only the demoted Plicat greeted him with sullenness.

The newly promoted First Lieutenant, Armen, spared Vinni a pale and sweating nod, which he shouldn't have done, as another guard took him down as they trained. Vinni recognized the winner as a brand-new guard, assigned to the force last week after he finished his Second Passage and became an adult.

He hopped around, fists waving in triumph, and Duon and Armen congratulated him. The teen hadn't been sworn in as a guard, but Vinni recalled the boy's Loyalty Oath after his First Passage at seven.

He'd been born and lived all his life here at T'Vine Residence, cherished by and cherishing the Family. The joy of the young man throbbed through Vinni's bond, easing him. He strode forward, holding out his forearm in a man's greeting.

The new guard flushed and accepted the gesture and Vinni's congratulations.

Duon and Vinni walked the castle walls. He met the new lieutenant, Fera, patrolling the west wall. Her bond with Arcto, the tutor, was stronger and more evident to Vinni. She smiled and nodded to Vinni, put on a more sober expression for Duon, but she radiated satisfaction with her job.

Down and up. Up and down, the reactions to him, particularly by the guards. He didn't mind regular Family tensions, but this wretched situation had added negativity to the whole Family, and he hated that.

He had to resolve this, soon. Or else.

After the last silent leg of the wall patrol, Duon left him with a grunt, and Vinni descended through public rooms on his way back to his own tower.

And, finally, he sensed it. Dark malevolence aimed at him. It hung in the air like evil droplets, situated in the courtyard before his round tower, as if the person had paced back and forth.

His gut clenched. Bad enough that he felt it, he thought it would sear Avellana if she'd happened to be with him and stepped into it.

He glanced around, but no one lingered in the main courtyard; most of his Family enjoyed the groves and gardens.

Raising his hands, he strode back and forth, murmuring a cleansing spell, drawing Flair from the housekeeping spells to ensure the courtyard itself became fresh and welcoming. The Family had a journeywoman priestess and an apprentice priest—both of whom respected Vinni—who could also do a spiritual cleaning of the area. He teleported to his suite, contacted them, checked on a snoozing Flora, then did what he'd really wanted to for septhours: contacted Avellana and told her he'd meet her in the D'Hazel Residence gardens.

She awaited him in her favorite herb garden, one that had been modified by her parents and sister to reflect her Hopeful faith, with a crosslike path, a sundial with globe and arrow in the center, and benches at the ends of each graveled path.

Giving him a half smile, she held out her hands. "Muin?"

He swept her close, feeling her soft curves against his body, breathing in her scent, soaking up the feel of her Flair. The expansion of their bond with physical proximity filled him with sweet relief.

"I am sure this has been an awful day for you and the Vines," she murmured. "How is Bifrona?"

"Ready to leave this life for the Wheel of Stars," he murmured into her hair.

"I am sorry."

"So are we all."

"Your message to me said she suffered a syrthio attack?"

"Yes." He loosened his clenched jaw. "I believe she figured out that a member of the Family attacked you, and it shocked her too much."

"Oh, Muin."

He grimaced. "A Vine, as you and I thought."

"That is a terrible thing, too."

"Yes." Since his sex began to harden and he didn't think he could talk Avellana into making love in person or coming to him in her dreams, he set her away from him and began to pace. "I spent most of the day reading reports and requesting more. Thinking about options." He waved a hand. "Most of the attempts against your life have involved teleportation 'accidents.' That tells us a few things."

"He or she wanted to make everyone think I perished by accident."

Inclining his head, Vinni said, "Yes, always."

"Because they are a part of the Vine Family, as they were before, and they did not wish you to discover that."

Vinni flinched and he felt as if all the fury inside him solidified until he radiated rage . . . and stone-determination that had come upon him from just seeing love emanating from her. "Yes." His lips moved enough to hiss the word out. He lifted his forearm, let it drop in a solid, cutting motion. "We are done with this."

"Oh?" she asked with a wary note in her voice.

"We have options. One we've discussed before. If we can't root them out, we leave."

Avellana's eyes widened. "If we leave we could harm your Family, perhaps the Residence, too."

"To find our enemies, I will call for another Loyalty Ceremony, for you and me."

"A *third*? During your time as Head of Household? People will object."

"Let them. Everyone in my Family must take sides in this battle we face. If they are not with us, completely, they leave." His lip curled. "I would prefer they leave. But I cannot harbor any more vipers in the nest of our Family, ready to kill us." He stalked to her, took her hands. "We cannot endanger any children. This will be a rigorous Loyalty Ceremony, the most stringent I can find that has been crafted."

"You are right," Avellana whispered. "We cannot raise children in a Family that might think they are defective or freaks or abominations. We *must* be able to trust your Family in the future."

"I think there are only one or two poisonous ones. Others might protest against me because of natural rebelliousness, or for greedy personal reasons to build influence in the Family." He managed to twitch his lips up in what might be a small smile. "But if we cannot trust *every single person* in the castle, we *will* leave." He met her gaze.

She nodded. "We leave."

"I will point out to my relatives that if we leave, our Family will not have a viable GreatLady until Floricoma is six or seven or eight. And her regents will be Bicknell and Perna. Some people in T'Vine Residence have made . . . unfriends, if not enemies, of that couple."

"It will be like when your foremother died and you inherited."

"Yes, except I grew up in a household controlled by my cuzes, who had a unified agenda and followed strict traditions." He paused. "If you and I leave, the Family will lose great influence and allies during the time it takes for Floricoma to become an adult. Other upwardly mobile Families might eclipse the Vines. We . . . they might never regain our present power."

Avellana shivered. "No one would like that."

"No. I'm a strong, young GreatLord with influential personal friends as well as good allies. My Flair, and yours, is great, and we should have powerful children. Right now the Vines are one of the premier Families of Celta. The Family would most likely lose that if we walk away."

Shifting feet, a habit she should have been broken of years ago, Avellana said, "All of Druida City has seen what happens with the lack of a good leader at the Head of a FirstFamily."

"More than once," Vinni said drily. He took in a breath, smelled the gorgeous scent of flowers, and it caused him to shudder. His decision had been made. He could speak easier. "If we leave, I will not have my NobleGilt for practicing as GreatLord, but everyone will know Vinni Vine—or whatever name we go by."

"My parents would adopt you as a Hazel."

Not his Family, not his culture, not what he wanted, but he said, "Good." He sucked in a breath, let it out. "I'll have a good business as an Oracle and seer."

"And I will continue to craft holographic murals and sell them to the Enlii Gallery and make good gilt, too."

"I like your house in Multiplicity, but it is *yours*. We will design my new home together and you can keep your place as a studio." His smile came quickly now, felt *warm* like the emotions within him. "It will do no harm to have another estate for one of our children, or grandchildren."

She flung herself into his arms, and he held her close and shut his eyes and reveled in the feeling of her. All he ever needed, really, was Avellana. Everything else—his Flair, his status, his wealth and power, the Family and the Residence—had been given to him, imposed on him with expectations.

"I love you, HeartMate," he said.

Avellana pulled back to meet his gaze. "I love you, too."

"As for my personal gilt." He grimaced. "I never considered it. There is an account, I believe."

Avellana snorted.

Shrugging his shoulders, he said, "I never paid much attention to the gilt, let the Family handle it, put most of it in the Family coffers, I think." After a long breath, he said, "I will find out when I return to the Residence and separate what I have. I have been an easy lord to work for and with. That may have to stop."

"People won't like that."

"Too bad. I *do* want to remain GreatLord T'Vine. I can affect the future of Druida City and Celta itself better."

"I agree. The last resort is walking away."

He set his forehead against hers. "We do this together."

"Yes."

"I can't and won't do anything without you anymore, Avellana."

"Good!"

So he pulled away and took her hand and they strolled to an arch of plants and into another garden.

"Back to this teleportation business," he continued slowly, piecing out his reasoning. "The villain or villains want to hide. They want to keep whatever identity they have now, the power, the status, whatever."

"They do not wish to be caught."

"No, they will try to kill us—"

"Me."

"*Us*. But if they don't succeed, they want to remain hidden."

Avellana gasped, stopped, and grabbed his forearm. "To threaten our children? We must *not* allow that, Muin."

"We won't. Tear them out of the Family, roots and all, disinherit them, repudiate them, and by the Lord and the Lady, *prosecute* them."

He slowed his strides from a near march. "So they want to remain hidden; they are cowards. They wish others to think you might have a teleportation accident. They are cowards. And they seem to prefer traps more than up-close attacks. They are cowards. I don't much like cowards in my Family."

"I think it is a quality that can be determined by certain testing? We could bring in a mind Healer—" she began.

"Maybe. If we don't smoke them out first, we will find them during the new Loyalty Ceremony. Anyone who does not wish to participate in that ceremony will be repudiated by the Family. Disowned. They will no longer be considered a Vine. That is my decision."

Wanting it *done*, he snapped his fingers, and a piece of papyrus appeared hanging before them. The very best papyrus. Marshaling his thoughts in good order, he lifted his hand and placed his palm on the document. Writing scrolled across the blank sheet. Fancy lettering at the top stated, "Mandatory Loyalty Ceremony of the First-Level." Calling his and Avellana's calendar spheres, he studied them and set a date eight days hence, the day of last quarter twinmoons in the formal T'Vine Grove.

He showed Avellana the document. "You agree?"

"Yes."

Rolling the papyrus into a scroll, he said, "We have now put a deadline on this matter. The villains will be pushed to try to harm us before the date of the Loyalty Oath, where they will be exposed." His mouth tightened. "Family Flair reveals lies in those taking the oath—the Lord or Lady, and the individual Family member."

"Which means when the person took the Loyalty Oath the last time when you were thirteen—"

"After your First Passage," Vinni added.

"Yes. She or he meant the oath."

"Yes," Vinni said. "But at some point that changed." He let out a ragged breath. "Before that ceremony at thirteen, fifteen people left the Family."

"I remember," Avellana said. She ran her fingers down his arm. "You found them all positions with other Families." She paused. "Do you think any of them—"

"No. Most of them had *not* been villains, but they resented you, or me, or that we are HeartMates. Or were negative people I didn't want to house. And most were of the oldest generation and are dead. The others are not involved."

"They must have missed their Family, perhaps did not live very long due to grief."

"Maybe." He shrugged.

"But I recall that you found them situations you believed would be better for them, and you said if they had children, they could return to the Residence, or if they, themselves, showed improvement of their attitude, they could return."

"None did."

She went on. "I am unsure when a broken oath, a Vow of Honor, might start affecting someone."

"I don't know, either. A question for a priest or priestess."

Avellana let out a little sigh. "I suppose it depends upon the circumstances."

"Yes." He made a cutting gesture. "That's something we can work out later."

"If we could sense the evil . . . and trace it back in time, we might discover the person."

"I'm pretty sure that won't happen within the time period we're working with. We're on a timeline, too."

"I understand."

"Worse for them, though. Hard to be pressured and still keep identities secret." Vengeance rose through him, lay on his tongue temptingly. He wanted to find these people who'd influenced him—

his dreams, his instincts—to send Avellana away. Whom he'd allowed to manipulate him and keep him from his HeartMate.

Who'd caused Avellana worry and fear.

Who'd attacked her.

Oh, yes, he wanted to discover his enemies and extract justice. A darker, angrier part of him wanted more than justice, wanted punishment and vengeance. He must control that part, but he could acknowledge the emotions.

Taking her hand, he held the rolled papyrus in his other hand. "I'm ready to send this ultimatum to the Family. Are you?"

"It is your decision, and I am always with you, Muin."

He snorted. "Because you agree with this action. You'll argue against anything you don't believe I—we—should do."

"Naturally." She gifted him with a sweet smile.

Taking a last minute to weigh the papyrus in his hand, he considered it. In the document, he'd set out his reasons for the ceremony. He'd inked the first line of text in red: *Anyone not wishing to take part in the ritual will be banished from the Vine Family.*

Then he flicked his fingers and duplicated the papyrus several times to be placed around the Residence, and translocated it home.

Almost immediately great shrieks echoed down his bonds with his relatives. He narrowed them to threads. Placed barriers against emotions reaching him. Blocked his scry pebble from Family calls.

"There, it's done. And I'm done being anyone other than myself, bending over to see everyone else's point of view, being flexible so as not to ruffle the Family. I am GreatLord T'Vine, and will lead as *I* think best."

Avellana brushed a kiss on his lips. "I approve. Greetyou, Great-Lord Muin T'Vine."

He circled her waist with his arm. "Greetyou, beloved."

"And you are a very good FirstFamily GreatLord and prophet," she said. "You impressed Tosa of the WhitePoplars."

He sighed. "I hoped to, and thought I sensed that, but it's good of you to tell me so."

Mouth curving, a sparkle in her eyes, Avellana continued, "She contacted me about buying property in Multiplicity. We have a meeting tomorrow."

He went on alert, sent his mind down the tiny thread of his bond to the young woman that had not quite faded since their consultation. Scouring all the information from that bond, he felt no threat to Avellana. "A simple business meeting?" he asked.

She raised her brows. "Not so simple. Another person of a First-Family who might actually live in Multiplicity."

Vinni grunted.

"And a member of one of the two FirstFamilies who is *not* our ally. We must cultivate her."

"Of course."

"Tosa is slightly older than I, so of our generation."

"Uh-huh. I'll go with you."

Avellana narrowed her eyes, then nodded. "Very well." She studied him for a moment. "What, you are not reminding me to wear my amulet and my armor?"

He chuckled. "I thought I'd refrain from irritating you."

"Good notion. We are meeting Tosa in the new, large summer pavilion in rehabilitated Downwind that will be dedicated by Grand-Lord T'WhitePoplar tomorrow, right after the ceremony, a half sept-hour before NoonBell."

Vinni sneered. "It's the first thing the WhitePoplars have done for old Downwind. Twenty-four years after the needful cleanup."

Avellana, called her mother, D'Hazel, telepathically. *Say good night to Vinni and come to bed.*

"Their Residence, their rules," Avellana said. She turned toward him but pulled her fingers from his, then placed her hands on his shoulders and gazed up at him.

Right then his stomach clenched. He wouldn't get any loving from her tonight.

She wet her lips and he hardened to semi-erectness. "Muin"—and now her voice had gone husky—"I am weary of coming together in dreams or hurried snatched time away from our Families. The next time we lie together, I want it to be in person, and I want to HeartBond."

His whole body flashed with fiery passion, love turned to violent need. His lips felt thick. "Before our wedding ritual."

"Yes. I do not wish to wait any longer. So you think on this matter. Decide whether this is what you wish, too."

After a brush of her lips against his, she vanished.

Thirty-five

He dreamed. Not of his fears or the future, but of the past.

The great hall of D'Vine Residence coalesced around him. Tall white fluted marble pillars, pale-green marble paneled walls.

Him standing on an emerald-green dais in front of a huge ancestral chair that he knew he'd be engulfed by and look stupid sitting in, and he had a six-year-old boy's dignity.

He wore a scratchy ritual robe and trous of blackberry-leaf green heavily embroidered with gold. A FirstFamily's GreatLord robe in the latest fashion.

Before him stood his Family, the Vines, ready to come to him and pledge him their faithfulness in their Vow of Honor Loyalty Oaths.

He felt too young. And pale. His mind swimming in visions, his spirit nearly drowning in the grief of his Family because old D'Vine had died. Worse, she'd passed on shockingly, murdered.

Before him, the members of the Family queued and offered their hands and he had touched them and gotten wisps of more personal visions as they recited the oath.

He'd backed up, bracing his backside against the thick chair cushion and parroted the ritual vows, but each time he felt as if a little hook had been set in him. Attached to each and every individual Vine.

Beside him and farther back, next to the sides of the deep chair, stood tall, tall guards, including the old Chief of Guards. Three men and two women, and Bifrona, the housekeeper.

When the ceremony wound down, he recalled movement on his left and right as they came around to say their vows. They looked into his eyes, and with each final Vine, the power within him from the Family multiplied. His young shoulders shifted under the new burden of responsibility as the Head of the Household. Grief laced their voices, washing to him from them . . .

His alarm pinged insistently, dragging him groggily from sleep and the dream.

The Residence said, "You are scheduled to take early breakfast with the Family this morning."

Vinni gasped a breath, struggled to order his thoughts, then sat up and rubbed his face. "How's Bifrona?" he asked, though if she'd died in the night, he'd have been informed and the Family and Residence would have gone into mourning.

"She lives." A floorboard creaked. "I have seen people stricken with syrthio before, and though no one asked me, I anticipate that she will survive to the end of the week."

"Longer than the Healer said," Vinni commented.

"Yes. This is her home, where she is honored and loved. She will linger, not wanting to pass on to her next life that might be less comfortable."

"Oh."

"I have calculated the amount of time it will take you to review the additional guard reports you requested and believe that will be a septhour and a half, which should leave you enough travel time for you and Avellana to reach the meeting place for her appointment with Tosa WhitePoplar."

Vinni grunted, rubbed his face again. The dregs of his dream lodged in the back of his mind and haunted him that he'd missed a clue.

A breeze whisked around his suite and flapped the half-drawn shades in the sitting room beyond, causing Flora to mumble in her housefluff bed. "You should prepare yourself for reactions from the Family with regard to your scheduling a new Loyalty Oath ceremony, including a full Family circle ritual and septhours of linked meditation. Both are included as part of a FirstLevel."

"Thank you for the reminder," Vinni stated politely as he left the bed and strode into the waterfall room for a shower. Instead of raising his voice, he spoke to his home telepathically. *Avellana and I have two options: remove any disloyal Vines or leave.*

The waterfall thinned, sputtered, then resumed. *I do not want that.*

None of us do. I want to lead the Vines, keep our Family strong. With a last rub of soap and a rinse, he left the enclosure. *You can tell the others that they should be careful about crossing me. I am not open to discussion about this. It IS an ultimatum.*

You usually . . . negotiate, T'Vine Residence pointed out.

Not anymore. He dressed in his most expensive tunic and trous, cuffs of both showing his rank, along with some Family jewelry, also reserved for the GreatLord or Lady—one chain and amulet made in the first decade of colonization. Along with the chain and medallion he'd commissioned for himself, for his stint as leader of the Family.

He didn't bother to don a casual, generous mask as he so often did.

Let his Family see who he was, at the skin and bone, *feel* his resolution. Not much masking of his emotions along the Family bonds, either.

He walked into the large breakfast hall that held those who preferred starting an early day, nodded to everyone, but didn't greet them by name—except the one who pulled out his chair with military precision and stood next to him, ready to serve. Who radiated staunch support.

That did have Vinni's lips easing from a hard line.

The head chef, large and radiating anger, slammed through the door from the kitchen with a raised spatula and marched to the table.

"I served this breakfast especially to speak to you, Vinni. I won't accept—" He cut himself off as he met Vinni's gaze.

"Stay or go." Vinni swept a gaze around the table; he wasn't quite sure of his feelings when some huddled in their chairs instead of meeting his eyes, but he rather liked it. Power.

Maybe liked it too much. Too bad, if this show of power would protect Avellana . . .

He glanced up at the chef. "If you wish to go, I will have a staffer pack your personal belongings and a guard escort you out." He *felt* his eyes cool to blue-gray. "You've been a good worker. I'll give you a reference."

The man's mouth opened and closed, then he backed away, pushing the swinging door open with his wide, padded butt.

Someone from the kitchen called, "He didn't make your favorite foods this morning, and his palate isn't as good as a cook's should be."

Vinni stood, "Who says this? I do not want anonymous complaints."

The chef sidled into the kitchen, and a thinner, younger man, pale enough that freckles showed against his bloodless face, slid into the room. He looked around at the quiet table of diners, then straightened skinny shoulders as he raised his gaze to Vinni's. "Ulmi Vine, my Lord."

Vinni considered the man. "What do you believe to be *your* best meal, as a cook?"

A red flush washed over his face. "Tea, m'Lord. Formal tea."

Someone suppressed a giggle.

Ulmi slumped an instant, then stood straight again. "Little sandwiches. Desserts of small cakes and candy."

"I don't believe we serve an afternoon tea."

"Not a formal one, not often." Ulmi cleared his throat.

"We probably will when I am wed." Vinni took his seat again and placed his softleaf on his lap. "If you wish to leave this kitchen at this time for a different one in the Family, let the current housekeeper know."

"Yes, my lord." He bowed, began to edge back.

"I expect scrambled clucker eggs with pale, spiced cheese and porcine strips," Vinni said. "Shortly."

So . . . he hadn't been *all* the tough GreatLord. He wasn't a T'Ash or T'Holly or even young Draeg T'Yew. But as he skimmed the expressions of the uncomfortable people around the table, he felt he'd made his point.

His ultimatum stood.

*A*fter breakfast, and running late, Vinni returned to his private office in his suite where papyrus reports lay stacked—the guards' schedule and duty list of the last month provided by Duon, and the much thicker sheaf of papyrus from T'Vine Residence. That one showed the whereabouts of every guard as sensed by the House.

Vinni began at the beginning, the morning of the dawn ferry from Mona Island to Druida City that Avellana should have taken, compared the timelines, marked down those *not* in the Residence, and went on to the next dawn encounter—and those guards who'd been solidly here at the castle.

The Residence *had* noted brief comings and goings as guards teleported around the castle, in a detailed minute-by-minute time frame.

The morning of the dawn attack at Multiplicity, some guards had gone out to a weekly breakfast at a favored restaurant in Druida City. The Residence, of course, could not tell whether they'd slipped away from that venue to attack Avellana.

His list of suspects grew longer and his jaw hurt from clenching his teeth.

He decided to concentrate on the evening he and Avellana went to the Thermarum Baths. The villain must have had a significant amount of time, perhaps a whole four-septhour shift, to arrange that, even if previously planned. After all, Vinni usually visited the baths after a bout at The Green Man Fencing and Fighting Salon.

His eyes felt raw and gritty, his teeth hurt, and his head pounded when he stopped, went back a few lines, and found the discrepancy.

Duon had the man listed as on duty. T'Vine Residence showed him gone, and when Vinni asked the Residence who had stood guard at the front gatehouse, he got a second name, not the guard Duon showed.

Carefully Vinni rose, his pulse throbbing with his headache.

"Residence, where are our two suspects?"

"One is patrolling the south wall; the other left with one of our Healers to AllClass HealingHall. He remained there, not feeling well. Our Healer has returned."

"Hmm. Please contact AllClass HealingHall and request they keep him on the premises."

"Yes, T'Vine."

"I would prefer to surprise our people with this evidence, perhaps get confessions. Can you stop the other from teleporting?"

"At your command I can drop the stone floor under him several centimeters, distracting him. At the same time, I can call guards to secure them."

"The floor drop sounds fine. I'm not sure if his friends will secure him. Best to go through Duon and proper channels on this. The guards are his responsibility. We'll see if he has any additional information that will prove us wrong."

The Residence creaked a sniff.

Vinni made copies of the relevant information of both conflicting reports, sucked down some pain relief, informed Duon that he needed to see him in the Chief Guard's office *now*, and teleported to the main guard tower.

And faced an irate Chief hulking tall behind his desk, with his own jaw muscles bunched.

"Good morning, Chief."

Stormy grayish eyes flickered with emotion, then the man went even more still. "With regard to that new Loyalty Oath ceremony, are you asking for my resignation?"

Vinni suppressed a flinch as he stepped off the small teleportation pad in the corner. "Absolutely not. I am not here for that." He blinked, thinking of the objections he'd received on his in-house scry last night . . . which had diminished to none this morning. Duon had sent no message at all with regard to a new first-level Loyalty Ritual.

But as Vinni strode to the man's desk, he stared at the papyrus sheets in Vinni's hands and focused on the one he'd written.

"You are here about my guards, thinking one of them betrayed you," Duon growled. "You continue to doubt my judgment."

"As I must admit my judgment is poor, too. I'm sorry." Coolly, Vinni added, "Are you so insulted by my appearance here to speak to you about the guards that you wish to leave this job and the Family?"

"No." The Chief sank heavily into the old chair behind his equally old desk, his hands loosely on the desktop, but not lacing his fingers. Vinni figured the man could spring up and over that desk . . . or 'port in front of it to him . . . in a split second.

Taking one of the chairs before Duon's desk, Vinni laid the two sheets on the clean and polished surface. "We have a discrepancy." He tapped the minute-by-minute report. "An inconsistency between your duty roster and who T'Vine Residence confirms took the evening shift at the first gatehouse on the seventh of Holly. The night someone attacked Avellana at the Thermarum Baths."

A low rumble still coming from him, Duon stared at the schedules, Vinni's notes, the names. Through their bond, Vinni sensed when irritation transmuted into distress.

"Residence, project audio," Duon snapped.

"Yes, Chief of Guards," the House responded smoothly.

"Plicat, to me!" Duon roared. "Fera, take over Plicat's duty trans-now."

"Yes, Chief." Fera's voice echoed tinnily through the room.

A long minute passed, two. "Plicat!" Duon demanded.

"Coming," came the resentful word. No one showed up on the teleportation pad, though Vinni knew Plicat had enough power to 'port, particularly if any strong emotion like fear spurred him.

Another minute passed before they heard scuffed steps along the hall and the door opened.

The guard, slightly flabby around his middle, looking softer than other top guards, stepped into the room. He holstered his blazer and gave a slightly sloppy salute, ignoring Vinni.

Duon stood, growling. "Salute the GreatLord!"

Squashing a sneer, the man angled to where Vinni sat—and he sprawled out his legs—and gave him an even worse salute.

"Riiight," Duon said. He tapped his duty schedule with a thick forefinger. "Explain to me why you took the first gatehouse shift on the seventh of Holly."

A shrug. "A friend asked me to switch with him."

"Uh-huh," Duon said. "Yet, pursuant to my rules, you did not report this to me, either orally or by written note."

Another shrug.

"You know," Vinni replied, "I wouldn't have known what I did on the seventh of Holly unless reminded." As it was, every day of the last couple of weeks with Avellana was etched on his memory.

He did note that Duon seemed dubious. *Maybe* good guards kept track of days, but he wouldn't call Plicat a good guard.

Slowly Vinni stood. He had height on the man, if not bulk, was in better shape. "Did you betray me?" he asked softly. "Did you know that Avellana would be attacked?"

Now a real sneer. "So concerned with your fragile lady. Put her aside, T'Vine, she won't last to be a good GreatLady."

Fury muzzed Vinni's mind, but he snapped out an order. "Did you betray me, Plicat?"

"No! I did a favor for a friend!" He marched three steps to Vinni, grabbed his hand, sent sizzling contempt along with truthful memory in vivid color. For an instant, Vinni fell, enmeshed, into the seething resentment, the basis of Plicat's character. A wavery vision began to form . . . too many futures to be very solid . . . Then the bond jerked away.

"That is enough. You are dismissed for duties for an eightday!"

Duon thundered. He stood beside them, obviously just separated them.

Vinni drew in a breath. "Be glad Duon saved you from my prophecy."

Plicat's face contorted. "I don' give a fliggerin' fligger for you, or your presentments, or your weak lady, or this Family! I 'specially won't give you any fliggerin' new Loyalty Oath!"

The Chief of Guards loomed over Plicat. "Your wishes, Great-Lord T'Vine?"

Duon's violence at the discourtesy surprised Vinni. He reacted instinctively, inclining his head in a nod, raising his hand. "I will strike you from the Family rolls. Go in peace with the Lady and Lord."

"Don' you mean some sort of 'May your journey be blessed' like that cross-folk religion woman of yours uses?"

All right. Another deep breath. "Obviously you think I am a weak FirstFamily GreatLord."

"Oh, *yeah*."

"But I have an extreme amount of power to ruin you and your life." Vinni shrugged. "Go in peace with the Lady and Lord; may your journey be blessed. You are now no longer of the Vine Family." He ruthlessly cut the bonds, severing Plicat from him, Duon, friends he had in the Family, and everyone else. Felt the echoing emptiness that now filled Plicat, watched the man gasp, double over, and fall to his knees.

Duon and Vinni stared at the sweating guy for a moment, then with a brisk gesture of Duon's hand, the Vine guard tunic fell away from Plicat and the trous green leg stripe disappeared as the whole material turned an ugly brown. "You're dismissed. Residence, pay out Plicat's final salary as of this minute. Make sure the bank knows he's no longer associated with the Family, and his account should not have any group advantages."

"Done," the Residence said.

After another couple of minutes, the now-sweat-smelly Plicat rose. His eyes held a glassy wildness.

"A Vine Family guard is on her way to escort you out," Duon

said. "Plicat No-Family-Name." The Chief of Guards returned to behind his desk, but since Vinni continued to stand, he didn't sit. "And I'm asking T'Vine not to give you a reference. I'll do it, and it's going to be mediocre."

With emotions finally catching up with him, Vinni put ice in his tone. "You can join other former guards as mercenaries along the Plano Strait. It's a hard life, but—"

"No." The man actually ground his teeth. His nostrils widened. "I'll get a job southa here, with a minor Family. A more conservative Family."

"As you wish. Residence." Vinni raised his voice.

"Yes, FirstFamily GreatLord T'Vine?" asked the House.

"Assign a staffer to pack Plicat's personal items."

Plicat sneered. "I don't need nuthin' here."

A knock on the door came, and Duon gestured it open. A guards-woman stood at the threshold, leaning back a bit as she caught the stench.

Duon said, "Escort this man from the Residence."

"I felt the sundering of the bonds between this man and the Family." She swallowed. "Come along, Plicat No-Name."

Though Plicat staggered, no one offered to help him.

The door shut behind them and Vinni's scry pebble lilted with Avellana's lushly romantic tune. Duon appeared pained. Vinni ignored him and answered.

"Muin, I am teleporting to the pad on Large Beardtongue Street now, so I can walk to old Downwind and our meeting."

"I'll be right behind you." He couldn't help himself. "You have your armor and amulet?"

Her brows raised. "Yes, Muin." She smiled and glee lit her eyes. "And I have my blazer pistol. I am tired of being *re*active in this matter."

"Av—"

But she'd signed off.

"Avellana Hazel with a blazer," Duon said hollowly. "Has she practiced any?"

Vinni was forced to say, "I don't know. I'll leave the cleanup of this mess in your hands."

"I'll confiscate Plicat's personal things, examine them," Duon said. "You want my resignation?"

"Absolutely not. Blessed be." Vinni teleported away.

Thirty-six

*V*inni *arrived on the thin and shabby pad at* Large Beardtongue Street, glanced around for Avellana, and found her talking to a young, handsome, and fashionable man.

Jealousy speared and primitive feelings resurged.

She should not even know such a guy. When had she met him? When he turned, he nodded to Vinni as if they knew each other, then hurried to the teleportation pad and away. Vinni realized the man had been waiting for him to arrive before leaving.

"He looks very well, does he not?" Avellana asked as she tucked her arm into Vinni's elbow when he came up to her. He'd planned on kissing her, but she'd turned and begun to walk so he reluctantly followed her lead.

"Who?" he asked.

Blinking up at him, she said, "Remy Gardenia, former Chief Minister Younger." Her laugh rippled. "You did not recognize him?"

"No."

"Hmmm. Well, he has not truly revealed that he belongs to the Intersection of Hope religion. He is studying with the mind Healer, FirstFamily GrandLady D'Sea."

"Oh." Minister, mind Healer, not at all like Vinni, who faced several flaws today.

He strolled by an alley and a whiff of chill air hit him. He smelled . . . something odd. Sort of attractive but with a germ of decay. Strange for an alley near a main teleportation pad. People tended to keep those clean. He stopped.

Avellana gazed up at him. "What is it, Muin?"

The touch of cold had settled in the top of his spine. He turned toward the opening. "There's something about this alley." He took a step in.

"We will be late if we detour," she said.

He looked down at her, took her hand from his arm. "You go ahead. I want to check this out."

Her mouth pursed. "We should be prompt, and be seen as a unit to all who observe. As for Tosa WhitePoplar, she knows that you are also a landowner and community member of Multiplicity."

"Go ahead." He put a little emphasis in his tone.

She huffed out a breath. "No. I will accompany you."

"You have your blazer pistol?" The words surprised him as much as her. But before he'd done more than finish the sentence, her pursenal had disappeared and she held the small pistol he'd given her by her side, in the folds of her long and fully cut tunic.

"Let us go. I will be at your back," she said so seriously that it lightened the instant.

"There is no one I'd rather have there."

She snorted. "I would like Holm Holly behind us." Her quick glance showed determination. "Do you want me to shout telepathically to my Holly trainer?"

"No, Avellana."

He stepped into the alley, found it wider and shorter than he'd thought, well lit. The beige brick walls held layered spells. He walked around a couple of crates, trying to find the smell of death and deterioration. Nothing.

"What are you looking for, Muin?" Avellana asked.

He narrowed his eyes. "Do you smell anything?"

Her head rose as she inhaled, and her nose twitched. "Automatic cleansing spells." She frowned. "I think daily, or perhaps nightly." A sniff. "Rodent and other vermin deterrent."

Casually he asked, "How does the air feel to you?" As he stood in the concrete alley, the thin soles of his summer shoes soaked up cold in the atmosphere of invisible droplets of cool mist surrounding him.

Avellana stood straight, slowly trod up to him, turned, and he sensed she tried to feel the air on her face and neck and hands, the only skin bared by her formal clothes. "The light reflecting off the spells adds heat to this passageway, and there is more humidity in the air from the ocean than usual."

"All right." With a soft-footed, fighting glide he traversed the alley. Nothing threatened. His own blazer ready, he hopped out into the cross-path at the end, swinging left, then right. No one.

His heart had thumped hard, preparing for danger, and now edginess whistled down his nerves at the aftermath of the dump of adrenaline. He swung around and saw an alert Avellana with her back to him, her pistol still at her side. Guarding him from the street.

Glancing up, he saw the building to his right rose three stories and the one to his left only two. Both roofs were peaked so snow would slide off during the winter, but both looked like they had small walkways along the edges. If worse came to worst, he—even Avellana— could 'port up to a roof. But nothing threatened from above, or from the third-story windows of the taller structure.

He sent to her mentally, *Avellana, activate your armor.*

She murmured the spellword, and he glanced back, saw the shimmer of air around her. A flash hit beside him and the odor of singed concrete rose.

"Put down your blazer," Armen said.

Vinni turned to face him. *'Port!* he ordered Avellana telepathically.

No! I am PROTECTED, you are NOT!

"She 'ports away and my cohort will kill you," Armen said conversationally. Vinni extended his senses, found Plicat behind the third-story window.

"Plicat." Armen raised his voice.

"I am here, and I have a blazer pointed at the mutant. I have nothing more to lose." Plicat's words boomed around the alley.

Vinni pulled on a mask of impassivity and sent a quick spurt of telecommunication to Avellana. *Remain expressionless. We will have to coordinate our response.*

I can do that, she said, and from the corner of his eye he saw her face set in an interested expression . . . that he recognized. How many times had she used that on him when she'd been thinking of other things?

I cannot call Rhyz, she returned to him. *He is hunting and his mind is not available to me.*

I'm yelling to Flora to wake up and get to my Chief of Guards, Vinni replied. *He should be able to trace me through our bond.*

That will take time. It is best if we handle this ourselves, Avellana replied calmly.

Armen had been a better fighter, trained longer than Vinni, worked at it every day.

Not quite as fast as Vinni was, though. Not as deceptively competent as Avellana. And not nearly as Flaired as either of them, let alone the both of them together. But though Avellana's mental speech had been fine, her body had frozen. Vinni needed to give her enough time to soak in and accept the situation.

He moved to step in front of her, locked a stare on Armen. "So. Here you are. Slinking around back alleys with a blazer, shooting at people, city guards looking to arrest you, instead of walking the halls of a FirstFamily Residence as second-in-command, admired and respected."

All the features of Armen's face twisted in evil.

"A FirstFamily Residence and a Family who will have a mutant freak and a fliggering Hopeful abomination as the GreatLady. I don't want to be part of a Family like that. Family can only go downhill."

"*She* is not the freak, the abomination, you are." Vinni coated his words with disgust.

"*Not true! I am normal!*"

"I hope not, because you are unthinking and cruel. Avellana has never assaulted anyone, has never attempted murder, has never even thought of murder. You have. You have stalked her and made her life a misery."

Armen shrugged off the words Vinni hoped would infuriate him. "Nearly got her a coupla times. She, and you, got lucky at the baths when I set up that personal pool for you."

"You killed Phae Thermarum."

"Of course I didn't. He's safe. A little battered and not liking the accommodations we gave him, but safe."

For an instant, Armen flashed on where he'd stashed Phae, distracting Vinni.

"We?" Vinni asked. Grief flooded him that another Vine had betrayed him.

Armen's teeth showed in a grimace, not a smile. "My *real* boss—"

"Duon?" Vinni questioned.

Armen snorted. "Not him, he's your man through and through."

"Good to know."

"My *leader, the leader of the whole Traditionalist Stance movement*—"

Vinni huffed. "I was afraid of that."

"Stop interrupting me!"

Inclining his torso a bit, Vinni said, "You were saying that your real leader, who, I believe, is a Vine? . . ." He kept his gaze scanning the alley, his senses focused on Avellana.

He *had* heard her say the Word to initiate her personal armor, so he tried not to let the huge inner relief that she was safe weaken him. Her armor would protect her, but he didn't know how blazer fire acted on it, how much energy the spell would absorb.

"She is unnatural and doesn't deserve to live," Armen said, as if repeating a mantra.

Vinni cleared his throat. "She is my HeartMate," he reminded gently.

"Nope. Don't think so. Nope."

"Saille T'Willow verified that."

"Now, that I know about. *He* said you'd say that, but *he* said you lied."

"And you believe whoever this *he* is more than me?"

"Acourse! He's more like me than you'll ever be."

"Don't you realize that the Loyalty Oath goes both ways? I swear to protect you."

"You ain't," Armen said decidedly. "You're too blinded by *her*."

"How have I failed to protect you?"

"You will."

"I've done nothing. You only think I *will* do something to endanger you. What?"

"Not sure, but you're under her spell, you'll do it. After she's gone, we'll find your true HeartMate for you."

"So you have no judgment of me of your own? Only what your leader said?"

"He knows you better, so he's right."

"Did this leader swear an oath to you like I did? Why do you think he has your interests at heart and isn't just using you?"

"He wouldn't do that." Armen sounded shocked.

Vinni made a point of staring around. "He's not here. You are. You're the one with the blazer in your hand ready to assassinate the Head of your Household you swore a Loyalty Oath to."

"You just got to step aside."

"So it's easier for you to believe two lies by that *he* than my truth?"

"He said it again and again, so it must be true."

A jolt of sheer uncomprehending shock came from Avellana. Then her thoughts zoomed and she sent mentally, *We cannot win this argument. We cannot break through his blind certainty about my character and yours.*

I know. Be ready to move.

I am.

"And, you know, Avellana will take a Loyalty Oath to protect you, too, when she is D'Vine."

Armen spat, "Fliggering mutant abomination . . ."

"You think so? Tell me . . ."

Vinni let the man rant while eyeing the slightly protruding windowsill to the right and one story over Armen's head. If Vinni were Holm Holly, he could do a Flaired leap to that ledge, hit it, twist in midair, and come down on Armen, engage in the fight. But he wasn't that skilled.

But he bet he *could* do something with the second-story roof, come down on Armen on his left, his bad side, even better. He'd take the chance.

Avellana sent back a wash of determination. *I can get Plicat! Jump on the sill and fire through the window!*

On my mark, Vinni said mentally.

Yes.

He fought for his life, for his HeartMate's. He fought for honor and the future. Fury surged and he controlled it, let it give him a sharp edge.

Go in three. One, Muin T'Vine. Two, HeartMate love. THREE!

With all the will and determination he had, he *wrenched* the blazer from Armen's grasp, saw a stream go wild. Thought he heard bones breaking and a gasp, but Vinni moved, leaping with another boost of Flair to the roof of the building, plummeted down onto Armen, and went hand-to-hand.

He heard glass break, a blazer zing, and a cry, not Avellana's.

The fight-vision link between the two of them snapped into being; he saw Armen reach for a knife and kicked it away. Then Vinni took him all the way down, hissing the next words. "Since yours is an offense against the Family, let the Family take care of it." Steeling himself, he snapped the bonds with Armen.

"No, no, *no!*" the man screamed, shuddering.

Hard sets of bootsteps thundered in the alley.

Another blazer appeared in Armen's hand. He put his blazer in his mouth and shot. Brains and blood splattered the pavement and the alley walls, the stench of seared flesh and pungent death.

Robin D. Owens

Avellana shrieked, fell. Vinni saw her hit the ground and *bounce*, then heard a displacement of air as her protective amulet teleported her away to Primary HealingHall.

Good. Vinni hadn't often seen violent death, and Avellana never.

Captain Winterberry and Garrett Primross rushed past Vinni to the body.

Vinni let them do their jobs.

Thirty-seven

*A*vellana arrived at the 'Druida Guard station before Vinni finished laying everything out for Captain Ilex Winterberry, Garrett Primross, and Vinni's own Chief of Guards, Duon. That man knew Plicat and Armen the best and had schedules, reviews, and reports the others could pore over. The guards and investigators bonded well since they embodied common characteristics.

Vinni was a FirstFamilies GreatLord, with other responsibilities. They dismissed him—and Avellana—and he welcomed their dismissal.

Avellana stayed only to report on the health of Phae Thermarum—good—who'd shown up at the HealingHall accompanied by the guards Winterberry had sent to rescue him.

Vinni and Avellana let the investigators work and left the guardhouse. They walked slowly along back streets and alleys, something they couldn't avoid forever so better get used to them again quickly. Vinni kept his arm around her waist, glad he could touch her again.

Avellana looked at her scry pebble playing the tune she had assigned for him—the same one he'd given her. Her brows rose. "A letter note from you, saying to meet you at the garden teleportation pad of the hotel near the Great Labyrinth."

"Interesting," Vinni gritted out. "As if we letter note between us instead of scry. I always want to see you." He hauled in a breath. "No doubt a trap by the other villain Armen spoke of, his leader." He paused. "Duon reported to his guards and the Family that I went to the Guard station and you're at the HealingHall. So Armen's master feels safe in luring you while you might be upset and confused."

"Yes." She stilled for a moment as if shuffling aside her last sight of Armen. Then she set her jaw. "Should we go see . . . ?"

"No."

Her brows dipped. "I was not lured. And I have my amulet on and my armor available at a Word. I used them before, I can use them again."

Vinni blinked as she recorded a message and sent it to him. His scry pebble did not sound. With a sigh, he said, "Someone in the Family is managing to divert your calls to me. Probably mine to you, too. I don't know how that works."

"I do not, either. I am sure others do, however. Captain of the Druida City Guards Ilex Winterberry and the private investigator, liaison to the FirstFamilies, Garrett Primross. They will inform us when we ask, later."

Vinni grunted. "So you will meet 'me' at the Great Labyrinth hotel in ten minutes, eh?"

"Yes."

"At least we know our other Vine betrayer doesn't think you as weak as Plicat and Armen did."

"I suppose not. Especially since he believes I can teleport after such a shock and to the Great Labyrinth. Though I suppose he believes I will do it in segments along the waystations instead of arriving directly at the hotel."

Vinni studied her demure expression. "Can you teleport directly to the hotel?"

She gave him a slow smile. "Yes, even farther if I wish. I may have the longest teleportation range of anyone."

He inclined his head. "I believe it." Then he scowled. "But why did you respond? I didn't want you to."

She rolled a shoulder. "Being proactive instead of reactive. I can teleport us to a pavilion on the rim of the Great Labyrinth, beyond the hotel, but not too far from it, and you can use your Flair to see who wishes to ambush us."

"That's a plan." Vinni contacted Duon mentally, surprising the man at the Guard station, and related the unusual scry to Avellana, informing him of their plans.

Duon protested, and worry zoomed to Vinni through their link, but he cut the telepathic connection. He turned his attention to the summer day, the sunshine, the great feeling of being with his love. "It's a pretty day."

Her lips trembled, and then she nodded. "The weather is beautiful and the city not too hot."

Holding out his hand, he said, "All right, we will go together; I'll give you a little boost and we can easily go the distance to the rim pavilion near the hotel."

She put her hand in his. "I love the Great Labyrinth. Every time I am in Druida, I take a quick trip to walk it."

"I know."

"The meditative path is an excellent journey. I like a walking meditation that can lead to trance and spirituality. I also like how huge the place is, and the crater . . ."

Vinni slanted her a look; she rarely babbled. Perhaps they shouldn't—

But the world around him disappeared for an instant and they alit on the teleportation pad in the corner of an open gazebo.

"I especially like that so many Noble Families have claimed spaces to show the nature of the character of their Family . . . shrines, like yours with the wine and cheese and your wind chimes . . ." She turned, angled her chin. "There is the hotel. They have added a wing since I last came—"

Vinni turned, took the couple of paces to the large opening in the pavilion where he could see the teleportation pad outside the hotel . . . set in a garden. As he raised his Flair to cast a magnifying spell, a man stepped from behind a tree trunk . . . and a door to the hotel opened and three men shot out.

Air around the first guy wavered. He vanished.

Vinni wondered if Winterberry, Primross, and Duon actually saw him before the traitor teleported away.

"Oh, dear!" Avellana hopped from the pad and took Vinni's hand.

"They screwed up," Vinni bit off, sent the same mentally to Duon to pass on to his cohorts. Asked him if they'd identified the man.

All three turned toward the pavilion and bowed in Vinni's and Avellana's direction.

We are sorry. We thought to be here before you and GreatMistrys Hazel arrived. No, we did not see the culprit.

A lower rumble came to Vinni's mind: Captain Winterberry. *My fault. I was too eager to finally finish this business and get the fanatic behind those attacks on children earlier this year.* A sigh. *I've been behind a desk too long and still didn't set a good strategy. For what it's worth, your Chief of Guards would have let you handle the matter, but—*

Another low tone: Garrett Primross. *T'Vine, you're not a guard. Not a professional fighter or investigator.*

No. Avellana's mental tone came cold and precise. *Muin is a First-Family GreatLord who knows how to organize people and delegate tasks.* She let all their minds hum in silence. *I have never seen him burst through a door with two other people.*

Screwed up, Primross acknowledged.

Avellana stepped up to Vinni and took his hand, then continued the telepathic conversation. *Muin is angry . . . and I am . . . upset. We will go to the Ash World Tree at the bottom of the labyrinth now.*

An instant later, they'd arrived, the hotel and guards far above them, out of sight from the bottom of the crater.

Vinni felt the other men teleport away.

After a long sigh, Avellana said, "What terrible events this morning." A waft of spring flowers came from her clothes, and Vinni understood the spell on the garments whisked away her perspiration. She took a couple of steps to lean back against the great Ash tree in the center of the labyrinth, pressed her hands against her eyes, and said, "I will remember that death too long. And how he hated me."

"He didn't know you."

"No," she whispered. "He did not. We met no more than three times. He listened to calumnies about me."

Removing her hands from her face, revealing a downturned mouth, she paced the grassy area to the beginning of the path up toward the rim of the Great Labyrinth bowl.

They'd have to walk out, since a natural phenomenon allowed people to teleport into the bowl, usually setting them in the middle at the bottom near the Ash World Tree, but people couldn't teleport out. You had to walk the winding labyrinth to leave.

Spending a couple of septhours along a meditative path with Avellana would be no hardship.

Avellana's emotions roiled too much for her to even breathe correctly before walking the spiraling trail out of the crater. She turned away from the start of the path, instead she paced around the Ash tree. The back of her neck warmed, spreading streamers of heat into her head, a sure sign her brain misfired. She put her hands on her head and tears flowed from her eyes and down her face, carrying away some of the wretched heat but embarrassing her, too.

Then Muin held her in his arms, making soothing noises.

She tore herself away. She had thought with all she had experienced, all the interactions with others, her meditations, her whole brain had mended.

"Only to be expected—" Muin began.

Fury spewed from her in choppy words. "I hate it! I hate not being normal. I hate that I tried to fly and fell. I hate—"

Then Muin wrapped her in his arms, but *his* warmth felt different, human and loving. Not medical and impersonal like the Healers two septhours ago.

"Don't," he said, his voice rougher than she had ever heard it. He touched her chin to urge her to look at him, puffy red teary face and all. "Don't ever say that. Your accident saved me. Saved my sanity."

"What!"

"I cannot see actions regarding myself, my future. And many, many times the future of every single individual is in flux, a river I swim in—a storm—" He cut himself off. "But you, when you took that fall of yours, it was—" In an oddly helpless gesture he lifted his hands and let them fall. "It was—is—was—a single huge beacon, a set point in all the chaos of time. At times you might have thought you were my puppet, but you're my anchor. Without you, I am adrift."

Her mouth dropped open. "I never thought."

"I never said." He smiled at her until she could smile back, until she took a softleaf from her sleeve and mopped up her face, doing a tiny cleansing and enhancement spell while the cloth hid her from Muin.

He took her softleaf, said a couplet to clean it, and dropped it back into her sleeve pocket. Then his fingers went to her head, massaged her scalp, and sent altogether different tingles circulating through her cells. His long, strong fingers trailed down to her neck and kneaded, releasing knotted muscle strands, and she whimpered in pure relief.

She wrapped her arms around him and wept, releasing more stress of the day. Threats, danger, violent death, stupid mistakes . . . and nothing totally settled.

She closed her eyes and rested against him, listening to the rapid thud of his heart, feeling the solidity of him, the controlled emotions through their bond.

After a few moments she stepped away from him. She let out one last, great sigh trapped within her, glanced around the bowl of the labyrinth. "It is quiet here, special with you. I do not see anyone near us right now."

Muin scanned the place. "Link with me and extend your senses."

She did, and they spent minutes sifting through the flourishing plant life and the various shrine offerings to pilgrims.

He said, "It's a weekday morning, people are at work, no one is updating their shrine, and no one traversing the labyrinth mindfully will reach us for at least a septhour."

So she embraced him again, felt his body against hers.

His hardening shaft.

That pleased and thrilled her. Her mouth against his wide and muscular chest, she said, "Do you wish to make love, Muin?"

Thirty-eight

Vinni stilled . . . and went stiff, including his sex. They'd only made love physically three times. Too damn few.

His heart sped up and he concentrated on evening out his ragged breathing. Then he took a pace away from her, and she let him.

They had spoken of this, their next time coming together, physically. He heard the rush of his own blood. He couldn't think—much. Scrabbled for his last few rational thoughts.

He raised his hands, palm out, and she placed hers against his. Flesh to flesh, nerve endings quivering, emotions cycling between them, soon to be overcome by the sheer physicality of sex. Palm to palm and gaze locked with hers, he whispered, "We are betrothed. If we make love and HeartBond, we will be wed."

Her steady blue stare did not waver. "I know. What do you think, Muin?"

"I think that I could never walk away from you, especially not here and now. You will be D'Vine."

"I have known that all my life. I am ready."

"Despite the dangers."

"I want you, Muin."

He could not fight her desire as well as his own.

"I love you, Muin. I will love no one else. We can take turns being strong," she said softly.

He yanked viciously at his control. Set bonds . . . not to dampen sex, just to . . . blunt his desire a little, so he would do this, this *HeartBonding* right.

"Clothes off," he murmured. Still holding her hands, he took a step back, widening their arms so he could see her. "You are more beautiful every day. I love you more every day." He saw the pulse throb in her throat, felt his own blood surge.

He wanted to pounce, closed his eyes, experienced this day, this moment. Her sweet fragrance rose around him, mixed with that of flowers, grasses, herbs. His mind spun.

He could feel sunlight as it dappled his body, heat here, cooler there.

And Lord and Lady, he thought he would break apart.

At the edge of his inner vision, he saw a golden coil of the HeartBond.

His sex thickened.

"Muin," she whispered, and he shuddered at the sound of his name on her lips, the syllable ladened with sultry anticipation—giving voice to the lusty desire throbbing between them, spiraling high.

He opened his eyes, saw her dilated blue eyes, the flush pinkening her cheeks, her tight deep-pink nipples.

And sensed her body was ready for him, wet and hot.

Control, control, control.

He freed his hands and trailed one up the smoothness of her arm, his palm tingling, until his fingers curved around her upper arm. He placed the other around her waist, began to lower them to the thick grass with muscle and Flair.

She put her arms around his neck, her glance meeting his, her plush lips slightly parted, ready for his kiss. Completely pliant in his arms.

Completely open and vulnerable.

Completely his.

And she confirmed that, saying, "I have never wanted anyone else. Never. Only you."

I have never wanted anyone else. Only you, he replied mentally. And plunged into her.

Her caught breath, the *bliss* that poured from her had him stilling to try to appreciate being with her, finally.

*A*vellana cherished the feel of Muin solidly within her, completing her. Muin pushed hair away from her face, and the tenderness of the gesture moved her, as did the softness of his blue-gray eyes that also held a dazed joy that stopped her breath.

His body had appeared so much more muscular and sexy than he had when they had met in dreams, and now he covered her, she *felt* the difference and reveled in it.

"Muin, my HeartMate."

He groaned and began to move, and though she had wanted to say more, she could not; words escaped as sensations blew through her.

At the edges of her vision she saw the glowing rope of the Heart-Bond, but Muin thrust again and again into her, caressing her sheath until all she knew was throbbing need, spiraling passion, sweaty desire to reach the ultimate climax with him. Physicality drowned other needs. The scent of him, musky with sex perspiration, overwhelmed her until she needed to taste him, and she tucked up against him, her lower body rocking, put her mouth near his shoulder, and tasted the essence of him.

Honey lemon. Lemony honey. The contradiction that was Muin. Her love. *Her HeartMate.*

And as she reached her peak, she opened her eyes, stared into his. Another shock seized her as she saw the blue, blue of his eyes, a shade she had never seen before.

So open to her, his feelings, and she felt his basic, crucial need for her, and her alone.

All that was him, his fundamental self-soul-mind-spirit, washed into her, then receded like the tide as she clutched him closer.

He kept nothing from her and even as she hit her next climax and he shuddered and their eyes met, she let her own soul-self-mind-spirit ocean stream into him, felt him cherish that feeling, let it return to her with his own.

Tears ran down her face as she threw back her head and shrieked her pleasure, experienced his as he shouted his release.

*V*inni *rolled off Avellana a long while later, feeling hulled out from* sheer passion. Too long. Too damn long since they'd made love in person.

Should have wed years ago, forget about his fears, the plague, his dread.

He stared at the Ash leaves flickering overhead from a breeze that cooled his heated skin.

She giggled. *Avellana* giggled. Vinni lifted himself to one elbow and looked down at her.

"What?"

"We are not HeartBonded," she said, amusement lilting her voice.

A frisson of shock skittered along his nerves. "What?"

She stretched her arms and her breasts moved fluidly and his mind hazed.

Caressing his face, she said, "Pay attention, Muin."

He swallowed. Now her nipples had tightened because of the cool air or something. His shaft, which had never quite gone limp, because, you know, first time in years he'd made love with Avellana in person, hardened again.

With her nails curved, she drew her fingers lightly down his cheek. He jerked at the fabulous sensation.

"Becoming HeartBonded is a conscious decision and action. I saw the golden bond but did not send it to you because I wanted you inside me so much."

"Uhn."

"So though we intended to HeartBond, we didn't."

He blinked, then dragged his mind back to the meaning of her words. Stare locked on her, he fumbled for the bond between them, huge and what he would have called golden before he'd seen the HeartBond so clearly. This link didn't appear sparkling metallic.

With effort, he averted his eyes from her nude body, focused on the labyrinth around them, still didn't sense anyone so close as to be an interruption any time soon.

Breathe better. In. Out. In, hold a little, out, hold some more.

"You're right, we didn't HeartBond."

She nodded, and the movement sent a burst of fragrance of crushed grass and ground cover with tiny flowers to his nostrils. He'd never forget this moment, would only need to recall the scent to bring it back during his entire life.

Grinning, he said, "We can proceed more slowly."

Her head tilted as if, she, too, checked on those walking the labyrinth, then she smiled and her other hand trailed down his chest and closed around him. "Yes."

And they did; he kissed her from her hairline, down her face, taking little nips along the way, on her neck, the curve of her shoulder. Using his tongue and kissing more, her nipple and breast so wondrous in his mouth, the slight curve of her belly, the rich taste between her thighs.

She returned the favor, pushing him aside, straddling him, using hands and lips on him until passion ruled all.

Then she took him inside her and rose and fell on his body, matching glance with glance, thrust with thrust.

The HeartBond. Her telepathic whisper caressed him, every cell, every droplet of blood. She closed her eyes and he did, too.

And there the HeartBond glittered. Not stationary, but rippling, swirling, dancing.

Take my HeartBond.

They'd said it together.

And the glittering gold twined them close, close, and they rose to climax together, inescapably merged forever. And shattered in exultant release.

Vinni's vision took some time to come back, all his senses. He'd exploded throughout space and time with Avellana, then they'd re-formed. Individual, but bonded.

The first thing he saw was her serious face . . . yet with a difference, a knowledge, a . . . wholeness? Like he felt whole?

"HeartMate," he said. Then acknowledged her new title and status to the world and himself. "D'Vine."

"HeartMate," she returned, leaned down and kissed him. "My HeartMate. My beloved Muin." She rolled off him. "I will let you recover. I am glad you opened yourself so to me. I treasure you." Her breasts rose and fell with a deep breath. "Now I will dress and let my mind rest."

So he subsided into the thick grass, his body loose, his HeartBond with Avellana still vibrating, his thoughts circled back to how to protect her—them—and another *past* memory coalesced from vagueness. He recalled the Loyalty Oath ceremony when he was thirteen.

This time sitting in the formal carved chair reserved for the Lord or Lady and used in the most solemn of ceremonies. Still too big for him, but not so huge that he refused to sit in it. He could perch on the edge and have his feet on the floor.

Again his Family came to him, one by one, dressed in their best clothes. Occasionally he saw a hint of amusement in his older cuzes' eyes, but when they reached him, all became as serious as he, himself.

To his left and his right stood guards, one retired now, one dead. Behind them, at the back of the deep chair, stood two others.

His Chief of Guards, Cosus, came around and took Vinni's small hands in his large, callused ones, stated that by his Vow of Honor, he swore a Loyalty Oath to the Family and Muin T'Vine personally. So did his First Lieutenant.

But the two behind Vinni?

He didn't know.

Now chill fear coated his stomach at the notion.

One or two people living in the Residence, *Vines*, who hadn't sworn loyalty to him. Who could betray him, the Family, *Avellana*, without any evil consequences to them of breaking a solemn Vow of Honor.

Focus.

He breathed deeply, evenly, in a pattern to squash the dread. Sharpen that memory. Four people beside him. Two guards who'd sworn loyalty.

Who else?

Avellana wandered into view. Her smile hurt his heart. He couldn't do without that smile.

But he wouldn't need to, ever again.

Focus!

He closed his eyes, knowing Avellana wouldn't start up the path without him. Let her drink in the plant life around them, become used to their new HeartBond.

In his mind's eye, he brought up the memory, sharpened it. Four people standing beside his chair, two in front, the best guards, two in back . . .

Not Bifrona. In his recollection, she stood, beaming, at the back of the hall, organizing the ceremony, directing others to the banquet, every inch the head of the staff. Her deputies scurried around under her eagle-eyed supervision.

Who else stood on the dais with him?

He pushed at his recollection, pulled, pummeled. The third person came around from his left, another guard, a woman who'd since moved to Gael City. Vinni would have seen her if he and Avellana had continued with their trip.

Focus!

Looking down with a sober expression, the woman clasped hands with Vinni, let her voice ring out as she enunciated the Loyalty Oath.

Then she stepped back, bowed to him, descended the dais, and raised a cheer for Vinni.

And he realized he couldn't sense the fourth person who'd stood next to the chair. Someone who'd slipped away . . . before she or he had vowed loyalty . . .

Lady and Lord, *who?*

Who would have been so personally close to him as to have stood with him on the dais?

Not the now-deceased Chief of Guards. Not Bifrona, who'd been the first to take her oath so she could run the occasion the way she wanted.

A flash of instinct hit him like lightning, and he felt as if huge blocks of understanding tumbled through his mind and smashed.

Someone had betrayed him long ago and he'd never known. Vinni *reached* for the bonds with the man, which should have been thick and strong, and found . . . nothing. Blankness.

Such terrible betrayal by a man he respected.

Had the villain nested himself in T'Vine Residence and plotted? Maybe.

Contacted other people of like mind? Probably.

Secretly joined the fanatics of the Traditionalist Stance? Taken over leadership when the first leaders had been prosecuted and convicted? Enjoyed being a behind-the-scenes power?

Oh, yes.

With Vinni coming into his Flair and the title so early, spending much time with other FirstFamily children his own age, and even with Commoner Clovers, the Vines were considered a more progressive Family.

The vicious man could certainly use that to hide his yearning for power and a hatred of change that bordered on madness.

As a mild-mannered but intelligent, well-educated, and respected *Vine*, he must have been invaluable to the upper levels of the movement.

Vinni could visualize this man, one with an evil delight in spiderweb plotting. And now Vinni could look back and match this man's demeanor, his emotions, to the rise and fall of the reactionary Traditionalist Stance movement's power.

The secret, gleeful smirk Vinni had noticed when reports of problems came from the excavation of the lost starship, *Lugh's Spear*, nearly three years ago.

Lines etched in a serious face when violence traced to the greedy directors of the Traditionalist Stance had been proven, and the men arrested and convicted as criminals.

And just earlier that year, when children had been attacked, Vinni *knew* the man used others, used younger people as fronts to direct that violence. Manipulated and betrayed a lover, to cover that he was the leader and not her.

She'd died suspiciously, hadn't she?

Could Armen have killed her? Could the main villain himself?

He must be mad, must believe as Armen had done that Avellana was a defective mutant, bad for the Family.

The revelation made Vinni sick. He sat shakily, forcing nausea down. Then he wiped his mouth, yearned for mint water to wash the bitter taste of betrayal from his mouth, settle his gut.

With a Word he drew his clothes back around himself, felt the immediate freshening spells taking care of sex perspiration and the more recent cold sweat.

Couldn't teleport out, and trying to run up the sides of the crater thick with growth and shrines took nearly as much time as walking the path. So Vinni spurted a telepathic message to Duon.

Find and restrain Arcto! He's the secret head of Traditionalist Stance! Check out his movements last spring with T'Vine Residence and the murderous attacks.

Surprise from Duon flooded Vinni; he felt the guard jump to his feet and bellow to, and through, the Residence. *T'Vine Residence, get Arcto! What? One second . . . Listen, Residence . . . I must MOVE. Later, T'Vine!* And as Duon moved, he yelled for scries to Winterberry and Primross.

"Muin?" Avellana came around the tree, frowning. "What distresses you?"

He rose in one quick move. Holding out both hands, he waited until she came and clasped them before enfolding his fingers over hers. "I know who *he* is."

"The main villain," she replied matter-of-factly.

"Yes, the main villain." He let the name out on a painful breath. "My tutor, Arcto."

Arcto, who'd come to the Family *after* the first Loyalty Oath when Vinni was six, who'd . . . been very ill the next time newcomers had been sworn in as a bunch . . . and never rescheduled the oath . . .

And been close to Vinni during Avellana's First Passage when she'd saved Flora, nearly draining the life out of everyone else.

Avellana's face crumpled. "I have known him all my life. I thought he liked me."

Vinni squeezed her hands. "Something warped in him, and I didn't see it. He covered it up and I didn't *look*. I realized he never swore a Loyalty Oath to me."

She raised her face toward him, her eyes wide. "If he never pledged Loyalty to you, then he did not swear to uphold the Vine Family, either. His bonds with you—"

"No bonds, none at all. I don't think anyone else feels them, either."

"All superficial, then, and not truly strong enough to guide him when he started going wrong."

Vinni made a disgusted noise. "We need to start back and deal with this. Arcto has disappeared, left T'Vine Residence. I feel no bonds."

"Neither do I, and I took lessons from him, too." She sniffled.

"Duon is handling the situation and Family for now. He's contacting officials in the city, probably informing our allies, too."

"No wonder Bifrona fell into syrthio shock, if she discovered this," Avellana said.

"No wonder."

Avellana sighed, then looked at the long path winding back and forth up the crater. "I had wanted to be, for us to be, more serene when we walked the labyrinth. For the path to be a celebration of our HeartBonding, a ritual journey."

Dropping her hands, he put an arm around her waist and walked with her to the beginning of the path, only wide enough for two if they brushed with every step. Lovers. HeartMates.

"HeartMate." He kissed her temple.

"We will do this together."

"Yes."

"And silently, Muin."

"Yes."

"It will be a bond." She gave him a wry smile. "The walking will force your nerves down and your mind quiet." Another sigh and she put her arm around his waist. "A bond between us, and when we reach the end of the path, we will help the Family as T'Vine and D'Vine."

"Yes."

Avellana clasped hands with her lover, her beloved, her Heart-Mate. They said a simple, nondenominational prayer asking for clarity and peace, then began the walk.

Muin's active thoughts buzzed, more like a physical sensation along her skin than not-quite-touching her mind. Truly, they had HeartBonded.

So she leaned against him. Muin's arm steadied her as they learned to walk together down the narrow path, best for one. He protected, her lover—an integral quality of him.

And as she brought up the deep well of the calm she had developed in her travels, a way of dealing with new places and new faces, and began her own pattern of breathing to drop into a meditative state, she felt Muin's breathing and heartbeat match hers.

Good, though she yet caught a whiff of dark dread.

Thirty-nine

They walked together until thorns pressed on the path so they had to go single file. Vinni led. And as they walked the labyrinth, he understood he'd made a mistake in going first. He couldn't see her. He could feel the bond between them. Also sensed her settling into a deep-blue well indicating a serene, near-trance state. He could *feel* her behind him, hear her footfalls, but that wasn't enough. Not when each step of the meditation path seemed to draw up his fears so he could deal with them before he could proceed. Damn.

But he used her strength to handle those fears.

He would *not* believe in horrible visions and dreams anymore. In fact, she'd be sleeping with him, so all he'd have to do would be to reach out.

All Vine betrayers had been unmasked. They could not hide and strike from inside the Residence. Arcto would be caught.

Inhale, exhale, calm.

Avellana wore a protective amulet *and* had personal armor.

She was safe.

She was his.

They were together.

Finally, finally, he could let the fear that crippled him go, seep away from him and into the ground with every step.

By the time they'd reached the Vine Pavilion, Vinni had managed a good trance and meditative state that helped put his problems in perspective. He'd also developed a back-of-the-mind list of action items.

At his shrine Vinni offered free wine and cheese, and, occasionally, wind chimes he made with his creative Flair.

"Let's have some blackberry wine," he said, drawing Avellana into the small room and to the long bench. Blackberry vines had given his Family their name. He always stocked at least one bottle of blackberry wine, as well as others from his vineyards, in the no-time, along with good cheeses.

She sat on the bench and stared at the large, stained-glass wind chime he'd made last year.

And his serenity faded as he opened the no-time and found only a half bottle of adequate white wine. The cheeses had been reduced to a quarter of a big, standard orange block available at any food store.

Telepathically he contacted his vintner at T'Vine Residence. *The Great Labyrinth wine and cheese no-time lacks wine and cheese. Restock them immediately.*

I . . . I'm sorry . . . T'Vine. My greatest apologies. Bifrona always handled that— she began.

Your responsibility. But his home vintner lacked several decades of Bifrona's age.

I know, my lord, but she preferred . . . And the household is in an uproar with Arcto's betrayal and his fleeing the Residence and city! Huge excitement throbbed through their link. Vinni realized that came from many of his relatives, maybe one of the reasons he hadn't settled while he walked. He'd pushed away the feelings because of his link with Avellana and her expectations that he *would* use the labyrinth as a good tool. Also, he'd been preoccupied with clearing his problems.

Vinni paused. *Arcto escap—Left?*

Yes, he spewed the most outrageous things. I swear he looked *sane, then mad in the next instant. I saw him 'port out of our castle myself, screaming he'd never go to the city, he'd establish his OWN town—Duon and others questioned me, T'Vine—*Massive respect flowed to him from her.

Vinni rubbed his forehead and replied, *Thank you for your support.*

Of course, T'Vine! Shocking events.

Yes. He cleared his throat, though she would not sense that. *About the wines.*

I will take care of that immediately. Pride lit her tones, and he felt her settle.

I want a good blackberry wine and a variety of five more of our label that you believe will appeal to pilgrims' taste. Make sure the wines are available for purchase in Druida City.

Perhaps the most popular, or those we wish to sell more of—

I'm leaving it to you. Pair the wines with appropriate cheeses and crackers. He pursed his lips. *You translocate them today, but come on up tomorrow and check on them. When did you last walk the Great Labyrinth?*

A gulp that came mentally to him. *Ah, years, my lord.*

Come up, FEEL how weary, coming and going, the pilgrims might be, or how deeply in trance. We might want some wines served at rituals, that priests and priestesses believe help the spiritual state.

Yes, T'Vine.

Stay at the inn as long as you like while you do your survey.

THANK YOU, T'Vine!

Blessed be, he ended, and gently set her thread aside, became aware of the multitude of reverberating notes from the four permanent wind chimes in his pavilion. Avellana stood, grinning and looking out at the labyrinth, head tilted as she listened.

If a wind chime hung near her, it would be sounded, by hands or spell, and joy would bubble through her at the chimes. The reason, he thought, that his creative Flair manifested into the art of making them.

He went to the back of the no-time, accessed a secret, locked compartment, and pulled out two small bottles—his personal premium blackberry liqueur and an equally exclusive Family sparkling wine.

With good eye and steady hands, he mixed them together as she watched, then poured the effervescent drink into crystal wine flutes that he'd also taken from the compartment.

He offered the glass and she took it, then waited as she sipped.

"Oh, it is wonderful!" She closed the space between them and kissed him on the lips.

Sweeping his tongue across his lips, he replied huskily, "Not as wonderful as the taste of you."

She laughed, then sobered, raising her brows. "You spoke with a member of your Family? What happened?"

"Arcto escaped, did not go into Druida City, and is in the wind and free."

"Ah."

He raised his glass. "To a long and healthy love and life with my HeartMate."

"To a long and healthy love and life with my HeartMate," she repeated.

They clinked flutes.

After they finished the drink and a few bites of cheese on the remaining fancy crackers, he cleansed the flutes and returned them and the Family's personal bottles to the compartment.

Looking ahead, he saw the path continued wide as it curved around the crater.

The time with Avellana and the wine should have removed any tension, but his brain kept busy thinking of T'Vine Residence. His nape and the top of his spine remained tight with an edge of lurking dark like a bad vision.

Avellana scrutinized him. "I think Flora would be good for you right now."

"Flora's delicate. She's never been here."

Avellana's eyes widened. "What, delicate like me?" She gave a ladylike snort. "Flora would *love* this place." Avellana's chin set. "I will teleport her."

"No, wait."

Avellana frowned.

"I'll ask her, why don't I?" Vinni said. "You prefer to be asked, right?"

"Yes. But she will want to come. She must have sensed your pre-occupation, and she would have been agitated, too."

He closed his eyes and found Flora more upset than usual. "Yes."

Raising his lashes, he looked at Avellana and let a rueful smile curve his lips. "Though I'd wanted to spend time with you alone."

"We are HeartBonded, we will always be together. And you and Flora will comfort each other . . . through the grief of being betrayed by those you loved."

"Yes." The word tore from him as she'd named his raw feeling.

"I will teleport her," Avellana said softly; she paced backward, then pointed to the ground. "There."

"I'll do it," Vinni said; he *reached* and found his Fam, asked her if she wanted to be with him and Avellana in the Great Labyrinth, and got a flow of excited agreement.

Flora hooked on to his location, siphoned some power from him . . . and Avellana . . . and Rhyz?

"There you are!" Avellana cheered when Flora materialized be-fore them on the path.

I helped 'port myself! She jumped twice.

"Good job," Avellana said.

An instant later, a pop came and Rhyz purred behind them. *I came, too. Was sleeping at T'Vine Residence, HOME, when scream-ing and yelling at the Residence woke Me up.*

Much ructions! Flora agreed, hopping into Vinni's arms. *Bad man came and made people CRY and YELL and SCREAM and SHOUT—*

"We know," Vinni said.

Then Arcto ran, ran, ran away, Rhyz ended with glee, trotting around them, nose aimed up the path.

"I thought Arcto teleported away," Avellana said.

He ran before that, legs still moving when he disappeared. Rhyz sniffed and his fur rippled over his back in disdain. *He said he and stups like him making a town like Multiplicity to live RIGHT.*

"I think that would be opposite Multiplicity and our standards," Avellana replied.

Rhyz trotted up and around them. *Catnip and catmint and other interesting plants up from here. Will see You when You get there, walking slow, slow, slow like all the peoples do.*

"Fine with me," Vinni said. He held Flora and walked hand in hand with Avellana. Perhaps none of them sank into a trance, but they stayed pleasantly calm.

Eventually Flora wanted down, and she and Rhyz made brief side trips before joining them as they spiraled up the crater.

Near the top of the labyrinth, several Families had planted overarching arborous tunnels, filled with the brightness of summer blooms and their heady fragrance. The last featured incredible roses; the Rose Family had decided to take one of the first areas of the path down for their shrine. Vinni'd doubted the choice, but GrandLady D'Rose had been cannier than he'd given her credit for.

Her floral business hadn't suffered, either.

They came out of the arbor, exchanging loving tenderness, and a movement snagged Vinni's gaze.

In the near distance, holding a bouquet of multicolored roses, stood Gwydion Ash, no protective amulet hanging from his neck, not even a weathershield wrapped around him.

"What are you doing here, Gwydion?" Vinni demanded.

The young man smiled sheepishly. "Oops. I'm only here for a minute, maybe two. To collect Mother's favorite roses from D'Rose's offering. Not far from the lip of the labyrinth, four meters, max. Not really in it." He waved the flowers, and to Vinni's horror, a flung bee landed on Gwydion's throat, buzzed.

Stung.

Gwydion slapped at it, then stared at his swelling hand, opened and closed his mouth. His throat turned puffy with a red blotch beginning to streak. He fell. And, as the allergen spread through his body, Gwydion began to die.

Vinni felt the skin over his face tighten, and all his muscles. Shock rippled through him. He'd taken care to avoid a specific event like this. Vinni had *warned* the boy! What had possessed him?

The fatal stupidity of youth.

He and Avellana rushed forward. Vinni grunted as he picked up the unconscious boy and flung him over his shoulder, ran a few meters uphill toward the crater rim. Still can't teleport out. Don't walk the spiral path. Push up the damn incline to the lip of the labyrinth, through thick and thorny brush.

Gwydion stopped breathing. The *feel* of his body changed.

Sweat ran down Vinni's face as he reached his own limits, pushed beyond them. No effort too much.

Avellana ran next to him, panting, talking high and loud. "This is my fault. I must help. I *must* save him, resurrect him. *Put him down, Muin.*"

Surprised, dizzy with the effort, and slumping, he did, just over the crater's rim. Could teleport now.

Pale skin, eyes closed, death had claimed Gwydion Ash.

Too late.

"Must save him," Avellana cried.

Vinni grabbed and held her, hoped she wouldn't persist, because if she did, he'd have to let her go.

"You're reacting. Not thinking clearly. This can't be your fault."

"It *is*! This all stems from the time I saved Flora!" Avellana wriggled.

"That can't be true." Desperation began to steal through him, shooting up his pulse rate, his breathing. Lord and Lady, why did she believe this dangerous notion? How could he dissuade her? She would give her life for Gwydion's. He knew it. Hers and his.

"When I pulled all the life force, all the energy from everyone at T'Ash Residence that day—"

"None of us died," he murmured.

"But it left weaknesses in us all. I had more brain problems, you had less control of your Flair. Rhyz has a heart murmur he did not have before. Abutilon Gwydion has this allergy to insect stings." She wrenched at him. "Let me go."

He did. "Your logic is faulty."

"You think I did not keep up with the Ash Family? That I did not research the Ashes and the Mallows? I *did*. No previous signs of such an affliction has shown before in their lines."

"The Mallows were Commoners, their line would not be well tracked—"

"We must do something *now*!" She fell to her knees, put her head on Gwydion's chest. "Not breathing. No heartbeat. My fault!" She straightened, grabbing Vinni's hand. Their energy flowed together; their Flair merged.

Avellana would save the young man.

Vinni and she would die.

The whole verdant labyrinth, too.

So mote it be.

I AM HERE! I KNOW WHAT HE SEES AND HEARS AND FEELS AND I WILL HELP KEEP HIM HERE! Flora screamed, landing on Gwydion's chest with a thump.

"I don't want to lose you, too," Vinni muttered, then heard his words. He'd pour his entire strength into Avellana, backing up her gift, drain himself. If she died, he would be so linked with her they'd circle the Wheel of Stars together until their next lives beckoned. No surviving even a year without his HeartBonded mate. No reason to. He'd put his affairs in good order.

In that first minute, he might have been able to stop her. Point out they could die, not only her, but him.

But he sensed the danger of stopping her. Her eyes had gone blank. Already she began to gather thousands of the life threads in the labyrinth. What would happen if he shocked her to the reality around them?

*A*vellana *yanked her fingers from Muin's, flung herself across Abu-*tilon Gwydion, *and placed one hand on his chest over his stopped heart, the other on the sting.*

First she *pulled* the toxin from his body, then she sensed all the plant, animal, and human life in the labyrinth.

The whole of the great crater and all the lives it held seemed to open in her brain, wove in fascinating colorful threads in a complex pattern.

She *could* set options.

No animals. No humans.

Do not link and pull their energy.

Delve deep, deep, deep into the earth, find a thread or two of each of the abundant plants carpeting the huge bowl, pull from *them* to save Abutilon Gwydion Ash.

She chanted his name in her head, *felt* his spirit, kept that confused soul hovering near.

Muin sat down behind her, embraced her. Together. Yes, they would do this together, save Abutilon Gwydion, whom she had harmed before.

Slowly, she drew energy from the thousands of threads of the plants around her. Just a little from each life. That should be sufficient, she hoped.

And as she did so, she realized the huge amount of Flair it cost her.

Draining, draining, draining her strength.

Didn't matter. So close, so very close, she drew the spirit down to the body, began tucking it in.

Knew she would need just . . . a . . . little . . . more. What else could she use?

Warmth radiated against her chest. The protective amulet! Yes! She yanked it off with her mind, translocated it to inside Abutilon Gwydion's tunic. When she brought him back, his thready heartbeat would initiate his teleportation to Primary HealingHall.

Something else, some other power source within her—the personal armor.

She initiated the armor, used the power of it, too, yes, enough. Her world began to spin and she toppled over. She did not know if she had the strength to keep breathing.

An instant of horror filled her. She was dying. Worse, *she was taking Muin with her.*

Do some— Her thoughts faded.

*W*ith *the last bit of energy* Vinni *had, he yelled telepathically to the* strongest man he'd ever known, *T'ASH, COME TO THE GREAT LABYRINTH TO SAVE YOUR SON.* Vinni got through to someone—T'Ash, D'Ash, Gwydion's siblings, maybe T'Ash Residence, "heard" mental exclamations.

Enough.

Vinni's eyes began to dim; his mind gave him a coalescing vision of a huge sparkling silver ring. The Wheel of Stars that led to rebirth calling to his spirit. Dying then. His sense of touch diminished and he only felt the fading warmth of Avellana's body near his own. With a strained murmur of his mind, he pled, *Stay with me. Don't go . . . first.*

He thought she shuddered. *Together!*

And then, on the opposite rim of the crater, stood a woman. Obviously a vision, because she towered in the sky. Slowly Vinni's eyelids lowered at the bright aura around her, but he wanted to *see*, note the blue-green ocean color of her eyes, the rich brown Celtan earth tone of her skin.

When his lashes rose, she did not stand alone, but a man, a warrior, rested one hand on the hilt of his sword and another on her shoulder.

Vinni thought he smiled. The Lord and Lady, the deities he'd prayed to and celebrated and thanked all of his life. Comforting.

He didn't know what Avellana saw, but heard her murmur, *The Spirits of the Journey.*

The Lady's aquamarine gaze seemed to spear into him.

I will do this one thing, she said, then raised her arms, swayed. Lightning and thunder and wind struck around them in a huge burst from boiling gray clouds that appeared in a summer blue sky. *I will do this for you only. Fight and survive. Or not.* She—they—raised their arms and called the furious storm.

GO! he ordered the Fams. *Teleport out of here, now! Go to the hotel!*

No! cried Flora, then, *Too late.*

Perhaps they'd live. Both Fams had lost their people before. Lord and Lady, let them be fine.

I love you, Muin. Let us go.

A tiny feathery sensation on his hand.

I love you, Avellana. Let's go, together, and be together again.

Yesss. We will always face what comes together.

He barely felt the huge droplets of rain pouring down onto his face as he closed his eyes and followed the spark who was Avellana toward the Wheel of Stars.

He let go; their sparks spiraled around each other, drew together, nearly merged, and just as they hit the outer aura of the Wheel of Stars, true blackness yanked him somewhere else, and he heard screaming.

Forty

Three days later, Vinni sat with Avellana in a private, walled court-
yard in Primary HealingHall. Today they got to wear regular clothes
and weapons.

Avellana looked too damn thin. T'Vine Residence held several
cooks, and he'd be shaking up the staff, for sure. Why not have a
competition to find the one who tempted Avellana to eat?

Easier to think on that than the fact that she'd shut him away. He
couldn't reach her. She hadn't thought the cost might be their lives.

Or their fertility.

Or that many of the plants in the Great Labyrinth would wither,
partially or wholly.

Everyone else thought he and she had been caught in a freak
storm of nature people called "The Great Labyrinth Blight."

T'Ash had found them, of course. Had dropped protective amu-
lets on each of them so they'd arrive at Primary HealingHall and be
saved. The GreatLord had teleported beyond his usual range with a
father's desperation.

He'd needed Healing, too.

As ailing HeartMates, Avellana and Vinni had shared a bedsponge, and she'd unfortunately awoken when FirstLevel Healer Ura

Heather had been informing him brusquely that, like the plants of the Great Labyrinth, their fertility had been compromised.

They couldn't have children.

Whimpering cries had come from her, then she'd silenced herself and a thick, impenetrable veil of despair had risen between them, shrouding their bond.

Worse than when they'd died, because then they had been together, now she kept herself to herself.

He'd sent loving feelings into that swallowing darkness, murmured words of support, but she hadn't responded.

Her Family had visited, of course, and, thank the Lady and Lord, had only provided love and support, too. No scolding. No smothering pampering. No major drama.

The Hazels had won weak smiles and hugs from Avellana, but she hadn't whispered one word.

She'd closed down, had refused to see any mind Healer, had even put off her Hopeful Ministers.

Her Family guessed, of course, that Avellana had practiced her primary Flair and sent three people to the HealingHall. If they talked about that among themselves, Vinni didn't know. They didn't speak of it to him, and they'd understand that he had no intention of saying anything.

T'Ash knew the secret, too. And he'd share it with his HeartMate, but Vinni believed that only the five of them—himself, Avellana, Gwydion, T'Ash, and D'Ash—would know for sure what happened.

Other people in the labyrinth had seen visions of the Lord and Lady, felt a storm rolling over them. But no one else had been harmed.

Only the plants of the Great Labyrinth.

And Vinni and Avellana.

Vinni knew damn well that Avellana would never use her primary power again.

As for the Great Labyrinth, plans for reseeding and replacing the plants had already begun, by the Families who had shrines there and by volunteers of Druida City for the general greenery. The Clovers would descend on the bowl en masse.

The FirstFamilies would meet in the Great Labyrinth the next full twinmoons, the beginning of the month of Hazel, and raise energy to Heal old growth and encourage the new plants.

That would be in a week and a half. Vinni was sure he'd have his Avellana back by then.

He hoped.

But for now they sat on a stone bench in a small and lovely garden of bright flowers and lush bushes, and Avellana didn't say anything.

Touch would be best. He'd held her, and kept her fingers clasped in his own, and, of course, wanted to love with her, but would not seduce.

There might be too much distance between them, so he lifted her onto his lap, keeping his arms loosely around her.

He paused his patter of words.

"I need you, Avellana," he whispered. "I need you to let your grief go now."

She flinched.

"We're in this together. Don't go away from me, stay away from me. In my blindness I sent you away too damn often. Now we face things together, remember?" He lifted her palm to his face, left it there with the press of his fingers.

The thick cotton fog of guilt and grief and despair seemed to part a little, just big enough for her body. A narrow glittering dark path toward one bright star showed—one meter of it, and only as wide as a tightrope. One foot in front of the other only.

She did not think she had the courage to step upon it.

But the bright and shining star of Muin beckoned, and more of his words sizzled through the numbness and hit her ears, wrenched at her. She thought he had been speaking for a while, and he had slept near, but nothing much had touched her.

Only the grayness and the guilt and the failure.

"I need you, Avellana."

Yes, those words reached her, went straight to her heart. She took a step or two along the slick-looking path.

"We face situations *together*!"

Yes, that was correct, but though she saw the path, the fog smothered the large glowing HeartBond between herself and Muin.

"Avellana!" he called. "Come back to me."

The fetid thick mist pressed around her. She had failed so spectacularly. She slipped on the path, windmilled. What would happen if she fell?

But she caught her balance. She *hated* falling. This whole Flair of hers had been due to falling at three. She had hurt her brain, and it had not Healed right.

Probably good that she could not have children. Her whole being seemed to slosh with tears as she proceeded.

"I love you, Avellana."

Yes. She had known his love forever and now that bright light showed yellow on the cloud bank of despair around her.

She loved Muin, too.

And they would face her failure, her deficiencies, together.

Hard to admit she had been so very wrong.

As he had been. In the past.

He had the courage to admit that, to mend his actions, to allow her to remain in the city against all of his instincts and fearful visions.

Muin was strong, and he could teach her to be stronger, too.

She heard the beat of his heart under her ear, found the lovely warmth cradling her was his arms. She sat on his lap.

Slowly, slowly, the thick haze diminished and she discovered herself in a beautiful garden.

The Great Labyrinth had been a beautiful garden. Once. Before she had killed it.

Her hands went to Muin's thinner face and she met his gaze with her own courage. "I . . . I," her whisper rasped, "nearly died, but worse. I nearly killed *you*!" A harsh moan rattled in her chest, a sob that couldn't quite make it out.

He rocked her, stroking her hair. "Beloved."

"I cannot stand it that I hurt so many, that you nearly died."

"I might have prevented you," he said matter-of-factly.

She stared at him sideways. "You think so?"

He shrugged. "Maybe."

A breath jerked from her in pants. "I do not know."

"I have an heir, Floricoma," he said calmly. "She will be fine, and is a prized member of the Family already. That's enough." A small pause. "You need to open our bond, Avellana."

"I cannot even *feel* it!" The words tore from her. And to her horror, painful cries followed the words. She could not feel their bond. She could not cry.

"I failed so very badly. I drained us all." Her voice broke. "Us, our Fams, up to death."

"Not quite." Instants away, a heartbeat or two.

And the worst guilt crawled up her throat and spewed out in a rasp. "I killed our fertility. Everything is my fault."

No, said Rhyz. *Your crying awakened Me from my nap.* He emerged from under a bush, stretched long in the sun, then trotted up. *We all did this together. And I did not want any kits.* He sniffed and added, *Any more kits.*

So tight, her chest, her head, wrapped in the pain of unreleased emotions. She thought she would choke, or her heart might stop. She *had* wanted children.

Flora hopped over and sat on Muin's feet. *I love you, FamWoman.*

"I love you, too, Flora," she croaked. Something should break. Soon.

No, she had already broken them all.

She could not breathe.

The flung door banged against the wall and she gasped in a breath. T'Ash stalked into the courtyard. Seeing the big, older man with rougher features than Abutilon Gwydion made shudders rack her body. More air went in and out and in, hard, hard.

She moaned, air out.

"Lady," T'Ash said softly, then came over and touched her cheek with a large, callused, *hot* finger.

Perhaps she shivered, not shuddered.

"What disturbs you?" the GreatLord asked softly.

"I killed everything!" she wailed, wrapping her arms around her abdomen and her own sterility.

"Not all of everything," the man replied.

"Not . . . not the Ash World Tree?"

His blue eyes blazed. "Do you think I would care if you had? My son or the Ash World Tree in the center of the labyrinth?" He made a cutting gesture, then dipped to one knee before her. "You saved my son, and I can never thank you enough for that." He reached inside his pocket, pulled out a gold token with an Ash tree etched on the face, put it in her palm, and curled her fingers over the piece. "It is rumored that you cost your GreatHouse a gold token." His chin jutted. "Let it also be known that you earned a gold token for your Family."

"Ah, ah, ah." More strangled breath, then the hurt shattered within her and sobs ripped from her, heavily, and tears flowed from her eyes until only the sensations of T'Ash's large, tough hand under hers, and Muin's solid presence, anchored her to reality.

The men provided silent support for the minutes it took for her body to shake out some of the grief. "I killed everything." She repeated her whisper.

"Not all of everything," T'Ash replied once more.

She felt Muin sit tall, then a softleaf scented like him dabbed her cheeks. Something dropped in her lap, and she saw a pomegranate—brown and gray, caught in her long tunic skirt. "From the Great Labyrinth." Her breath caught.

"That's right," T'Ash said, then picked the dead fruit up, wrenched it open with his hands. A multitude of dry or brown and rotting seeds fell to the ground. Avellana flinched.

"But it only takes one, D'Vine." He plucked aside a bit of thick protecting rind to reveal a tiny, perfect, glistening red seed.

He touched her abdomen. "It only takes one."

Muin's arms clamped convulsively around her. "Can you ask T'Willow to visit us?"

"Surely," the GreatLord said. "*After* I send the retired Healer, T'Heather, to check on you. I don't trust his daughter, Ura."

T'Ash drew a flat jewelry box from a tunic pocket, stepped forward, and dropped another protective amulet over her head, his face serious. "I want you to have this as you recover." Digging into his trous pocket, he handed her another stone. "This is from D'Yew, to replace your personal armor that failed during the blight. She said she wouldn't charge you for it since the storm affected it."

Avellana swallowed. Her throat felt sore . . . open but sore. "We should not tell her the truth."

"No," T'Ash agreed. He bowed to her, pivoted and bowed to Muin, then teleported away.

Avellana sighed and leaned against Muin. She looked at the dappled grass and flowers, the sunlight and shadow. She would always regret what she had done to the Great Labyrinth. She had thought to take a small amount of energy from every plant, but had caused so much more damage.

Because she could never practice her Flair without dire consequences, and she would never use that primary Flair of hers again. She would not be able to bear the consequences.

"Ah, it's back." Muin's voice lilted with satisfaction.

"What?"

"Our bond. We've Healed a bit, you and I." He tucked the golden token that T'Ash had given her into a tiny fancily embroidered pocket of her tunic, made more for show than holding any item.

She closed her eyes, the better to scrutinize their bond. Yes, a strong, thick, golden HeartBond, throbbing with emotions cycling between them.

The door creaked open and Muin stiffened.

A spell whooshed through the garden and lit upon her, paralyzing her but also dizzying her mind so that she couldn't teleport.

Muin? she asked, but his name echoed in her mind, did not reach him.

Terrible, evil spell. She couldn't even raise her lashes, and tears leaked untended from her eyes, trickling down her cheeks.

Fear flooded Muin, streamed icily to her.

Forty-one

*V*inni *stared at Arcto, and the deadly blazer in his hand pointed at* them.

"Isn't this cozy," the man sneered. He waved a hand and Vinni's numb lips warmed. "I won't let you move, but I'll let you speak."

Vinni tried out his voice. "I should have known you wouldn't have left Druida City."

"No, not before I finished this business," Arcto agreed. "You will have already noted that you cannot speak telepathically to anyone, nor can you teleport away."

"Those are old, secret, and illegal spells," Vinni said.

Arcto smirked. "We who live in ancient Residences have archives of all sorts of fascinating spells."

Vinni would have to remember that, bring it up with the First-Families.

If he got out of this.

"You're going to have to let Avellana move a little," Vinni said. He'd gotten used to sounding calm while suppressing rage.

"I don't think so."

"Her eyes are shut and she's weeping."

"Weak!" Arcto sneered. "Too weak and strange and mutant for

us. I knew that from her First Passage. We must not have her in the Family." His lip curled.

"She is in distress and is wearing a protective amulet. At a certain point, the amulet will teleport her to Intake here."

He could have kept his mouth shut, but he wanted her active and operational, not so vulnerable, huddled up on him.

He wanted her able to say the Word that would activate her personal armor.

"I know her protective amulet triggered and brought you and her here. Waste of energy saving her. And she wouldn't be fitted with a new one *here*."

"T'Ash just visited and gave Avellana a recharged amulet."

"T'Ash . . ." Arcto's upper lip lifted and his neck pulled back as if he smelled a foul odor. "T'Ash started this whole deterioration of values by marrying a *Commoner*."

"Danith D'Ash tested as a GrandLady."

"Lies!"

Vinni figured that Arcto labeled anything he didn't want to believe a lie.

Stepping around to see Avellana—who still sat sideways on Vinni's lap—Arcto still kept the blazer in line with Vinni's love.

Distract, distract, distract. Vinni scrutinized the man. At some point, Arcto had succumbed to an edge of madness that had gone unnoticed by every-damn-one.

Maybe because though Arcto hadn't sworn a Loyalty Oath to Vinni, he lived within the Vine Family, considered himself a Vine, but had to hide his true nature from most of the Family.

Lying to himself and others, believing his own lies, might be a way to cope.

Could Vinni tip him over into true madness and losing control? He didn't fliggering care about the man's health.

Vinni's mind spun with plans. He could not call telepathically. Didn't think the spell would let him even yell loudly. But he had bonds with other members of the Family . . . and Avellana sent him blessed energy and Flair through their HeartBond.

Vinni had Flair as a FirstFamily GreatLord, a man who commanded others. He began gathering that inner power, that *command presence* around him. He should be able to use that to influence Arcto.

"So." Vinni tried to look interested and not contemptuous. "You committed—that is, took over the leadership of the Traditionalist Stance movement—you *were* the leader, weren't you—"

"I *am* the leader. We will never be defeated because our cause is just."

Good thing Vinni couldn't snort or break out in derisive laughter.

"You must have more members than I think. Hard to tell when you all hide." He let his tone lower in disapproval.

"We work from within."

"You betray from within, as you have me," Vinni pointed out.

"You betrayed the Family first by choosing a mutant girl as a wife."

"My HeartMate. And we've HeartBonded."

Arcto's nostrils widened. "I know. You will perish now, when she is . . . terminated. But I can raise another child, the baby Floricoma, to be GreatLady D'Vine, as I brought you up."

"Her parents might have something to say about that, and the whole Druida City guards and Vine guards know of your villainy," Vinni said.

An icy smile. "The other Vines can be . . . handled. Have an accident, perhaps. 'Facts' can be . . . massaged."

"I always thought you were more interested in power than in the Family. Lord and Lady forfend if you had to put the Family before your own goals."

Yes, Flair built around Vinni and he pushed it out to subtly affect Arcto, whose stare fixed on Vinni. Since the man hadn't released them from the spell, Vinni knew Avellana's muscles would be trembling and cramping just like his, but her amulet would carry her away. Away from here to one of the Primary HealingHall Intake teleportation pads. Out of danger.

Rhyz stood on all paws, hair raised, mouth in a snarl and showing fangs. He'd leap and attack Arcto the second the paralysis spell released.

Flora crouched, ready to run, and she *yearned* to trip up the mean man.

Vinni didn't know the strength of the spell, but figured too many factors worked against Arcto, and Vinni'd take the man down. The sweetness of anticipation coated his tongue. He'd get justice for those Arcto had wronged.

The man blinked, rocked back to his heels.

Time to start talking again. Spear the tutor with truth.

"You. Kill." Vinni let his words hang in the air, then moved on to the terrible accusation. "You kill *Family* to accomplish your own personal goals, to gain power within and without the Family."

"No!" Immediate denial, but darkness shaded Arcto's gaze.

"You set up your lover as the Traditionalist Stance leader, then killed her."

"She didn't matter!"

Vinni opened his Familial link with Fera, the Vine guard and Arcto's latest lover. He might not be able to send telepathic thoughts, but he could sure use the Family bonds to contact Fera and let her know he and Avellana were in danger. Fera would feel his anguish, his fear, maybe even get echoes of the conversation. "None of your lovers matter?"

"No!"

"Not even the guard, Fera Vine?"

"Only as information and to mislead you. Have you focus entirely on the guards."

"Yes, the *Family* guards. You use people and Family members: Fera, Plicat, Armen. That's sure helping the Family and not your own selfish quest for power."

"No! *My* goals are the *correct* Family goals. They are the same."

"What's good for you is good for the Family?" Vinni's stationary muscles ached from the spell. He couldn't even breathe in a different rhythm than he'd been when it had taken hold. "What's good for you is good for the Family," he repeated. "That doesn't sound like logical reasoning to me. Not something my tutor would have said. But you aren't that man anymore, are you? When did you start going bad?"

A cry erupted from Arcto. "I did not *go bad*. I realized the danger of your mutant HeartMate to the Family during her First Passage quest."

Push, push, *push* against the spell with his own, stronger Flair.

"Ah. A long time for your mind to deteriorate, then. I rather thought so, since you deliberately avoided taking the Loyalty Oath at that time, when I was thirteen. After Avellana's First Passage. And you must have been deep in the fanatical movement when the lost starship *Lugh's Spear* was found."

Arcto stood taller. "Many followed my orders. *I* commanded, not you."

"Uh-huh." Vinni decided against lulling the man, liked the idea of stripping his control better. "Tell me, Arcto, what benefit would come to the Vine Family from sabotaging the *Lugh's Spear* excavation? Or worse, from murdering children? Like Marin Holly—a child of a FirstFamily? Or—"

"Keeping the high status of the Vines!"

"Oh, yes, having a murderer in our Family would impress every other Family on the planet." But his sarcasm was nearly absentminded. Anger and determination washed to him from Fera Vine. She was on the move.

Not quite under his breath, Vinni whispered, "Soon, Avellana," and he began a countdown. "Five, four, three, two . . ."

Arcto dropped his immobilization spell. Avellana croaked, "Shield." Her armor encased her. Rhyz yowled, leapt, missed. Flora hopped, tipped over.

"Coward!" Vinni yelled, lurched to his feet.

Arcto shot, but Avellana was already flinging herself in front of Vinni. The blazer stream deflected off her armor and she tumbled to the grass and *bounced*.

Arcto's gaze followed her.

Vinni shot him.

Flora screeched as the man fell near her.

Avellana yelled as she vanished.

The door burst open and several other blazer shots hit Arcto—fired by Duon, Fera, and a Holly guard.

Convulsing, Arcto died.

The Captain of the Guards, Ilex Winterberry, raced into the courtyard, followed by others. Avellana stumbled through the open door and Vinni moved to block her view of Arcto. T'Heather, the great Healer, wrapped an arm around her waist, his hand spread over her abdomen.

Even in the midst of noisy explanations, Vinni heard her mental question to T'Heather. *Can I have children?* They stopped strolling. *No more than one,* the man replied telepathically. T'Heather stared at Vinni, then sent to him and Avellana, *Vinni's sperm count is low, too, but we Healers can ensure that you can have that child.*

He dropped his arm from her waist, and the matchmaker, Saille T'Willow, took her arm and their auras impinged and Vinni saw what he'd hoped to. In T'Willow's future, his daughter still married Vinni's son.

People gathered around the body, and T'Heather stomped forward, hunkered, though Arcto had lost half his head.

A moment passed before Vinni said, "It's finally over." He cleared his throat and raised his voice, "Primary HealingHall?"

"Yes, T'Vine?" the intelligent building answered.

"Do you have audio and viz capabilities?"

"Yes, T'Vine, I have a recording of the immediately preceding events." The door creaked a little. "I am sorry, but I was not paying attention to your situation until Fera Vine and Duon Vine teleported into my walls. I do not have movement capabilities in the walls surrounding this courtyard yet, so I could not intervene physically."

By throwing a rock or stone.

Vinni shrugged, let it become a long, hard stretch. He reached out to Avellana, who did the same. His fingers slid off her armor.

She smiled and banished the spell, then took his hand.

After a sigh, Vinni said, "We'll make our final official reports in this matter, then I will take my HeartMate home."

Forty-two

$\mathcal{A}$s they returned to T'Vine Residence, pursuant to custom, the newly HeartBonded Lord and Lady walked from the bottom of the glider-way up the hill, holding hands. Avellana's FamCat, Rhyz, strutted beside them, tail waving, as if accepting accolades now that he was moving into this castle. Flora sat on an invisible Flair shelf on Muin's far shoulder, ears perked.

They checked in at all three gates before proceeding through the gardens, then stopping at the flagged main courtyard.

The whole Family had lined up in front of them.

Avellana had anticipated this, but her nerves twinged at the formal proceedings to come. Rhyz settled next to her, yet straight and proud, tail curled around his paws.

Muin, T'Vine in truth, let quiet settle over the area, until she could hear the slight scuff of a shoe as someone shifted.

Then he began, coolly, "Three members of this Family tried to kill my HeartMate, and in doing so, would have killed me."

A shuddery ripple ran through the crowd.

His next words came out gritty. "As I requested earlier this week, those of you who cannot accept Avellana or me as your Lord and Lady, your Heads of Household, can leave. Now.

"The Divine Couple, the Lord and Lady, ensured that Arcto and Armen, who lived by violence, died by violence. The consequences of breaking the Vow of Honor that is the Loyalty Oath worked on these Family members.

"Plicat has been found guilty of attempted murder; fitted with DepressFlair bracelets, which nullifies his Flair; and banished to the island for criminals."

Sobs broke out.

"As we all know, criminals with DepressFlair bracelets on that island rarely live long." Muin paused. "I am giving you three minutes to renounce this Family, your station and career in this Family, me as GreatLord and Avellana as GreatLady, and leave." His voice seemed to thunder, trapped between the high walls of the fortress towering above them.

Then quietly, too quietly, he ended, "Should T'Vine Residence, other members of the Family, or I discover that you have broken this new Loyalty Oath, you will be summarily executed and your body thrown over the castle walls and left for scavengers to eat."

Avellana wasn't the only one to gasp at this horrific threat. Her ears seemed to ring with intense and buzzing silence. Rhyz purred and that echoed, also.

Too soon, Muin gestured to the woman who had taken Bifrona's place as housekeeper. "Please come forward, place your hands within mine, and swear to me your Oath of Loyalty. I will, in turn, give you mine."

She seemed stuck in place, mouth open. Perhaps she should not be the Head of Staff.

With a cough, a man came from behind Avellana and Muin, circled them—Duon, the Chief of Guards.

"As I stated when I arrived here in Druida City four years ago, I am pleased and honored to have a home with my Vine Family and a career that serves the Family, and the GreatLord, Muin T'Vine." He offered his large hands to Muin, who set his around the man's, then glanced at Avellana. She pressed against Muin's side and touched both Muin's and Duon's hands.

Duon began, "I, Duon Dewberry Vine, promise with this Vow of Honor, that I take a Loyalty Oath to Muin, FirstFamily GreatLord T'Vine, and Avellana Hazel D'Vine, to serve them and the Family to the best of my ability . . ."

After Duon finished, Muin gave his oath, then Avellana recited hers—and swore not only by the Lady and Lord, but also by the Four Spirits of the Intersection of Hope faith.

She got a lot of odd looks at that, and Duon stared down at her with steel-gray eyes, and said lightly, letting his voice fall back into his original lilt, "Swearing by *six* deities. You'd best take care you keep your word. Wouldn't be nothin' left'a ya if you broke it."

She smiled up at him. Muin dropped his hands from the three-way clasp, and Avellana squeezed Duon's big fingers . . . with no apparent reaction except a smile lurking at the ends of his mouth.

"I *do* like you," she said. "And I repeat that I will fulfill my responsibilities to you and defend you, if need be, with my person."

He patted her on the shoulder. "You should leave the defending to me, D'Vine." Then he turned to the rest of the staff in front of them. "I am T'Vine's man. His Chief of Guards. And I agree with him. Leave now if you intend to betray him, and the Family, if you can't take this Loyalty Oath. 'Cuz if I catch you a'breakin' it, I'll kill ya myself and throw your remains over the battlements."

On shaky legs, the housekeeper came forward. "I am ready to swear my fealty to T'Vine and D'Vine."

Duon stepped to Muin's right and watched. "That's good." The guard's gaze swept the rest of the staff. "Doesn't look like no one's a'leavin', GreatLord T'Vine."

"No," Muin said, equally cool.

"Think we finally cleaned out the last of the nest of betrayers?"

"Yes, I do. I am grateful for those of you, my Family, who are staying to serve the Family, who recognize my leadership of this Family, and who welcome my wife and HeartMate, Avellana Hazel D'Vine."

A small, ragged cheer went up.

Then they proceeded with the rest of the Loyalty Ceremony, each Vine, Muin, and Avellana swearing loyalty to each other.

Finally Rhyz hopped to his feet and pranced around. Muin
bowed, Avellana curtseyed, and they were rewarded with greater ac-
clamation consisting of applause, joyful shouts, and some bows and
curtsies. She acknowledged each and every Vine, fixing names, faces,
and vocations in her mind.

The Vines split into two columns with space between them. Avellana took a breath in unison with Muin, then followed a swaggering
Rhyz and hopping Flora between the lines. They exited the courtyard
through a gate to the sacred grove, the Vines falling in behind them.

Duon raised his rough but surprisingly musical voice to sing, one
of the simple and beloved songs everyone knew.

Muin and she stopped before the altar—yet angled the way the
Hopefuls preferred. Facing her, he said, "I love you, HeartMate."

She replied, "I love you, HeartMate."

Rhyz yowled and sent mentally, *Welcome T'Vine and D'Vine,
My Family!*

Now voices roared.

Avellana turned to the Vines, who'd curved in a circle around
them. "Let us gather together in love."

And they did.

About the Author

Robin D. Owens is the RITA Award–winning author of the Celta Novels, including *Heart Legacy*, *Heart Fire*, and *Heart Fortune*. She lives in Colorado.

Ready to find
your next great read?

Let us help.

Visit prh.com/nextread

Penguin
Random
House